THE SHAKING REEDS

All the best
Jake Pedersen

JOHN PEDERSEN

THE SHAKING REEDS

MUSIC, MOTORCYCLES AND MYSTERY IN SAN FRANCISCO

ROADOILERS PRESS

THIS book is a work of fiction. The characters, incidents and dialog are of the author's imagination and should in no way be construed as real. Any resemblance to actual events or persons, living or dead, is entirely coincidental. You know who you are.

Copyright © 2016 by John Pedersen

Published by Roadoilers Press
91 Redhill Avenue
San Anselmo, Ca. 94960

www.roadoilerspress.com

ISBN: 978-0-9907540-0-8

Cover Painting: Elen Brandt
Cover and Book Design: Don McCartney

Dedication

For Judy, Keeley and Quinn
and the members of my astounding family.

Acknowledgements

I gratefully acknowledge the unstinting help of Donley Smith, Robert Hunter, Stephanie Hornish and Elen Brandt for their tough-love editing skills and advice. Also to my many friends and relatives who took the time to read and comment including, but certainly not limited to: Bud Hedrick, Judy Kaufman, The Sisters Pedersen, Michael Hardy and Ray Kennedy.

Thanks to Elen Brandt for the cover painting and Don McCartney for the design and formatting of the book. Thanks to the Roadoilers MC for inspirational insanity and to my friends for being strange and colorful enough to give me visions and ideas.

CHAPTER

THE frigid midwinter rain poured down outside the Arrow bar. Water splashed off the passing cars and soaked the pedestrians of San Francisco. The building seemed to inhale, exhale and sway along with the tunes being abused inside. The bare wooden floor had been scuffed and scarred by the brogans of countless blue collar Irishman playing and dancing the night away. Exposed timbers looked as though they had suffered so much in the Outer Richmond's perpetual fog that they were barely able to hold up the single storey roof. Strange debris was always sifting down from the cracks in the blackened and stained ceiling boards into one's pint or dinner. Occasionally the wind screeching in off the ocean and up Fulton made the complex array of cobwebs in the corners flap and the rafters pop and groan. Inside, it felt like a steam room with the jam of bodies, the dripping coats, the crush of players and the set of blazing reels that we were midway through. The dart players were completely oblivious to the music and the sound of their projectiles resounded through the bar as they thunked into the target in oddly timed intervals.

I worked my 100-year-old Paolo Soprani button accordion to its limit. Some freeform dancers were jumping around like lunatics in a drunken parody of Irish dance. My knee was wet where the spit had run out of the instrument of the flute player to my left. The bow of the fiddler to my right threatened to poke out my eye with every fevered stroke.

Eventually the set ended with a mighty finale. The players in the circle sat in stunned silence for a second before the clapping and cheers of the audience overwhelmed them. My shirt was soaked from perspiration, but as usual, the fiddlers and whistle players were cool and collected.

I stood up and motioned for the guitar player across from me to do the same. I was careful to put my box on top of my chair, as a halfhearted precaution against someone else sitting there.

We made our way over to the bar and motioned to the woman drawing the pints that we required a couple. We had been playing the Tuesday night session at the Arrow for so long that there was no need for any verbal exchange.

Sean Tierney, my oldest friend, biggest booster, most severe critic, and guitar player put his mouth to my ear and in a breath redolent of cigarette smoke, Jameson's Irish whisky and Guinness shouted, "Oh My God, what a friggin' madhouse. I think we're gonna have to kill off a few of these edjits soon. Am I just gettin' old or are we letting them kids make us play too fast? What is that mandolin player, like, ten years old? Nice look with the shirt, by the way. Lucky for you it's pissing down outside and you fit right in."

"Don't try to butter me up, soak brain. Your problem is that you get off work too early and by the time anybody else gets here you've already had six pints. It's a wonder you remember any tunes at all. Speaking of getting off early, have you seen Sloane in this mob? She said that there was some kind of deal over at the college her students had to attend so her classes for tonight were cancelled. She was going to come on over and have a few tasty beverages with us."

"More than likely she's still out driving around lookin' for a parking spot big enough for that ferryboat she calls a car."

The tank that the third member of our trinity since forever, Sloane Flynn, had hung onto, and tricked me into maintaining, was the first car her dad had ever given her. His reasoning in choosing the Buick Roadmaster station wagon was that "There's real metal in that car and it'll be fearsome in a crash." However, with more cars in San Francisco and parking more difficult every day, not to mention the price of gas going through the roof, I suspected that her fifteen-year love affair with the Buick might be nearing its close.

Sloane, Sean and I had met around grade school age on the Richmond District streets where we grew up. While Sean and I had struggled along in public school for financial reasons on his family's side, and Danish Lutheran reasons on mine, Sloane attended the prestigious Catholic school in the same neighborhood. I have come to realize after all this time that he and I had been vying for her attention for almost all of our lives. Without success, it seems, as she has been married three times and neither one of us was involved. Her latest marriage to "Gerald the Porsche owner" had come unglued in the not too distant past, and she was once again hanging with us on a frequent basis.

Having spent much of our youth at Ocean Beach in the surf, on the beach, hanging out in the back of disreputable vans, and working one menial job after another, Sean and I had to work hard just to look presentable while Sloane, the stereotypical red haired, ivory skinned Irish girl, was always turned out neat, tidy, clean and fashionable.

We scanned the crowd at the bar without seeing her and so carried our pints back to the session. As I took the box off my seat and sat down, I noticed with dread that the ancient bodhran drum player across the circle from me had relinquished his seat to an equally grey haired Uilleann piper, musically going from bad to worse. His portly self was well involved in the lengthy process of getting the pipes put together, attached to himself like some strange, many tentacled familiar, filling the bag, and God forbid, tuning up.

The hierarchy of tuning in the session goes from the most untunable instrument to the most tunable. The more easily tuned instruments always tune to the less so. While the pipes were admittedly a pain in the ass to tune and would ordinarily hold the highest position, the fact that the accordion was, for better or worse, untunable put me at the top.

After Sean and I had gone to the bar, the music had ground to a halt. The younger players were too timid to start tunes and the older players in attendance were too witless.

We regained our seats and got settled. I played a long, solid A note on the box to help the tuning process along as I glanced over at Sean and rolled my eyes a bit as if to say, "Here we go again, geezers in the house and slow tunes to follow."

Denny the piper gave a few experimental honks on his chanter trying to match up to the pitch of the accordion. Predictably, he tore the top off the thing and started unwrapping and rewrapping string from the reed to try to tune it. While carrying out this operation, he covered the fact that he was holding up the session by saying, "Eh, all this rain must have driven me a bit sharp. I'll just bring her down a bit, like so." Then he indulged in a dig that I had heard from pipers a thousand times referring to the fact that their seven reeds were made of natural cane, while the accordions hundred or so reeds were made of steel. "Must be nice to have reeds without life or soul, eh Soren? Very handy indeed on such a night."

I ignored the slur and replied, "Speaking of which, what on earth made you drive over the Golden Gate Bridge on the worst night this year? We never see you on balmy, pleasant evenings. The trip from Marin must have been epic for an old feller like you."

"Ah, wonder you might. I just happen to have played a very emotional wake not too far from this spot. I drove by on the chance that there might be an open parking place around here, and, lo and behold, there was one right out front. Tis' the hand of fate, I says. I didn't even get damp coming in."

Half of the players grunted in annoyance at the unfairness of things, and without further waiting, I launched into a set of slip jigs that I knew Denny favored, even though I suspected that we were going a bit faster than if he had started. Despite the fact that Sean and I were pretty well stomping the rhythm out on the floor, I could feel the tempo starting to slip due, no doubt, to the inexperienced bodhran player hitting farther and farther behind the beat. Soon enough Denny was enjoying the perfect lilt for his old school style piping.

The evening passed along. Jigs, reels, hornpipes, the odd slow air, and many songs thrown up by random members of both band and audience all had their go. Around the time of our second, or was it third, Guinness break, Sloane squished in, and the three S's were reunited. I noted with perverse satisfaction that Denny was also awash in perspiration owing to the physical effort required to play the pipes, and the thick Aran sweater that he affected, summer and winter.

As neither Sean nor I was officially the host of this session, entrusted to keep things moving and exciting, we could come and go as we wished so we snagged a booth and sipped our pints while Sloane drank some mixed drink or other that looked like a cross between vampire blood and pre-mix chain saw gas. She quizzed us in turn about any recent news.

"So Sean, for some reason I thought that you were being promoted to project director down at Heelan and Associates. Why did I think that? Oh, now I remember, you told me you were. And yet, during my many trips around this sodden block searching for a parking spot only partially in someone's driveway, I see your old piece of crap truck loaded with lumber and, I assume, rusting tools. Aren't you getting a bit old to be swinging a hammer? What possible transgression could you have committed to be put back on the remodel crew? And Soren, even though I know you think that Danes are water and illness proof, please, oh please, tell me that it is not your old motorbike parked up under the eaves outside. You can't have been riding that thing all the way down to North Beach every day and home in the dark at night. Utterly insane."

Sean blustered a bit at this and said, "Completely not my fault this time. Those assholes down there are gettin' to be such corporate wannabes that they had this big team work, morale building, camp out thing, where everybody had to do these bull shit games. Had I but known what was in store for me, I think I might have held off on the booze till after the rope walking stuff. They certainly had their chance to catch me when I fell and revel in my trust. Unfortunately, all that exertion and swaying around made me the tiniest bit queasy and some small amount of hurl might have found its way onto the shoes of Old Heelan, the president."

Sloane didn't even bother to bat an eye at this revelation, as if she knew that it had to be something along those lines. She did focus her gaze on me to dare me to lie about riding all over San Francisco on the old Norton during the wettest week any of us could remember.

I said, "Sweetheart, Big Red's dead. I had to take the bike, or ride the Muni, and that could take all day just to get to work, much less get home in the dark. Besides, I think the Norton likes the rain, it keeps the motor cool."

Big Red was the nickname of my 1987 Chevy Astro van that had gradually, over the years, gone from luxury conversion with deeply padded captains chairs, wood trim and shag carpeting throughout, to a rusty surfers hulk with a stripped and salt water corroded interior. Tools, motorbikes, lumber, garbage and surfboards all could be transported in comfort in Big Red. Sadly, with only 340,000 miles on the clock, the transmission had suddenly failed to transmit, and the van was forlornly passing the winter in my driveway.

The Norton she had so easily spotted up on the sidewalk trying to keep at least slightly dry was my 1969 Mercury model. The last of the old style Featherbed framed models before Norton had put all their eggs in the basket of the newer Commando. It had a long silver tank, and a seat with a sporty hump on the back, presumably to keep someone from sliding off during the rapid acceleration. I had found a rear rack at a swap meet and could bungee strap at least one accordion to it along with a bag of tools and whatever else might be needed during my business day. Easy to start, great to listen to, a thrill to drive and hard to get parts for would sum up the bike.

Sloane snorted at the lameness of my explanation and signaled to Meghan, the over-worked waitress for another round.

She said, "Soren, I know for a fact that you have never possessed rain gear for motorcycle riding. That tells me that you are getting soaked morning and night. Even the notoriously hard headed Danes and the romantic Spaniards would think this is insane."

She referred to my ethnic mix, which kids and teachers alike had always found entertaining. My mother's Mexican heritage, coupled with my dad's Scandinavian genes had left me with the look of a square headed desperado with fair skin and black hair. A lifetime of cold-water surfing had given me wide shoulders, and a fondness for shots and pints threatened to give me a middle to match.

"Listen, Slo, I'm not wet because of the dang rain, I'm soaked because before old 'Denny the Drudge' got here we were playing like lunatics. Ask Sean, go ahead. Plus, I've been cold all my life, even when it's hot, so a few degrees one way or t'other doesn't affect me much."

Sloane gave me one of her "whatever" looks and then twisted around in the booth to get a better view of the band, whose rhythm, timing, beat and tuning had deteriorated markedly since Sean and I had left off. The soggy weather apparently continued to affect Denny's reeds, as his pipes sounded like they had crept up in pitch about a quarter of a step. To make up for that he was trying to force more air through the set, and the effort of it all was definitely "taxing" his constitution. The rest of the band was either not aware of the pitch shift, or ignoring it just to be polite. With this crowd, my bet was on unawareness.

Sean and I hustled back to the session to try to bring the twin concepts of tuning and rhythm back into the mix. We forced the crowd to use their ears for a change and pay attention to one another. The tunes rolled out.

At one point in the evening, I looked up from the floor and saw, to my utter amazement, Bob Shackleford, the Marin county DA, standing

14

at the bar with an older fellow who looked very much like the famous Irish folklorist and accordion player, Tommy McCracken. I had heard McCracken was coming to town to play a concert at Zellerbach Hall but had no inkling he might attend our lowly session.

Not long after, Denny the Piper gave up his constant reed adjustments and packed away his instrument to more fully concentrate on the bar offerings. McCracken entered the fray occupying the piper's vacated seat. He extracted his much-abused looking instrument from its case and politely waited for a tune to start. His accordion had previously belonged to Joey Conroy, one of the most famous Traditional Irish players who had made his home in San Francisco for quite a few years. It may have even been played at the Arrow at some point in its past.

In his honor I started a set of reels that I had learned from a pirated tape of a concert he had given in Ireland. I had listened to the tape so many times that I knew practically every note by heart. McCracken recognized the set up and smiled. The unmistakable sound of his historic accordion made the hairs on the back of my neck stand up.

The set stretched out a bit longer than I had anticipated and by the end of it, McCracken was wincing in pain. He massaged his shoulder and twisted this way and that trying to ease his back. He stood up to visit the bar and I went along just to chat.

Bob was still at the bar and introduced us, "Tommy, this brother of the mighty squeezebox is Soren Rauhe. You know, Soren here is reputed to be pretty handy with the repairs and the tuning stuff, maybe he would be the lad to sort out the issues with Conroy's box that keep crippling you up so."

"Ah, wouldn't that be grand, to have the old fellow fixed up back here in San Francisco. I'm afraid you wouldn't be the first boyo to have a go at it, though. Perhaps you could put a bit of that mysterious and famous earthquake magic into it at the same time."

The last bit was strange but I just nodded my head and said, "Why don't you come by the shop sometime tomorrow morning and I could give it a look?"

Bob said, "I have to be in town at 8:00, how about I drop Tommy off then? You can do your dirty business while I'm over wrestling with City Hall."

"Bob, you realize we're talking about a motorcycle shop, right? I don't even think it's legal to open the doors at 8. I might be able to scratch myself in there by 9:00, though. Besides, there's a slim chance that the shitty weather might break long enough to provide some epic surfing on the dawn patrol."

"Fine, 9:00 it is."

I rejoined Sean and Sloane, deep in conversation at the booth. I gathered they were discussing the massive shortcomings of Gerald and his tendency to substitute large expensive objects and excessive gestures for intimacy. I tried to keep my mouth shut and just look sympathetic and available.

The session had floundered again shortly after we had vacated our seats.

Sean and I debated whether to step in and try to save it again, or just let nature take it course and allow the session to collapse. We voted on collapse being the more entertaining of the options.

Finally, around 11:00 I said, "I hate to leave you potential lovers alone like this, but I was talking to Bob Shackleford at the bar. That mysterious box player, Tommy McCracken, is staying at his place while in town for some recording project or other, and that famous accordion of his is in desperate need of tuning of some sort. Of course who do they wish to put it to rights? You guessed it. They wanted to bring it in really early tomorrow, but I managed to stall them till 9:00. Still, that's pretty early, so I have to piss off and catch up on my beauty sleep. Plus, sometimes the old Norton is reluctant to start when it's been soggy for so long, and I'd say that this qualifies, so I might actually have to take the Muni after all."

My day job was "Vintage Motorcycle Mechanic" but in the back of my shop, there was a bench upon which I practiced my hobby of tuning accordions. I had an air driven device called a flow bench with which I could measure exactly the amount of air passing through a motorcycle's intake and exhaust ports. I had figured out how to use it to tune accordions so that they worked well at all volume levels. Pretty well anyway. However, I shied away from complex woodworking issues because if something couldn't be welded, I would almost always hold things together with duct tape. Most of the traditional players knew of my illness, and respected the fact that I worked for the love of the instrument, rarely for profit. If an out-of-towner was in need of a tuning touch up, often I got the job just to repay some long ago favor. My shop was directly around the corner from where the old Colombo accordion factory had been located in the China Town/North Beach district, and just down the street from the fabled Guerinni factory, both long gone. I liked to think I was one of the last caretakers of an instrumental tradition that at one time had held the entire town enthralled. "The official instrument of San Francisco," it was called. In the early years of the century there were at least seven or eight actual manufacturers and scores of repair shops and dealers in the town. Now there were only one or two.

As I got up from the booth to leave, I didn't see any indication that Sloane and Sean were in any way ready to get romantic after all this time, much to my relief. I waited for a lull in what was left of the session to slide my way in and get my box, which I found lying on the floor near where my chair had been. There was much looking away and strained uh's and ah's but no one actually had seen who had grabbed the chair, and whether they had noticed the instrument sitting on it. I gave it a cursory glance and could see that at least one of the corner joints had sprung apart. Luckily I might be able to repair the damage with duct tape. I could see that everyone else thought the same, and having no one in particular to berate I had to content myself with a fierce glare at those at left in the circle.

I placed the box carefully into its wooden case and that into a custom garbage bag sealed with a twist tie against the still pouring rain. I shrugged and forced my way into my sopping wet leather jacket, grabbed my clammy helmet and forged out into the night to deal with the peculiarities of the wet Norton.

Hoping for the best, I strapped the box onto the rear rack, turned the key and heaved onto the kickstarter with naught but pure thoughts in my head. Of course, my wet foot slipped off the lever and its sudden recoil gave me a nasty chop in the shin. I knew from the feel that the Norton was the first to have drawn blood, but I couldn't admit defeat yet, so I gave another mighty kick and was rewarded with the window rattling sound of 650 cc's and a blown out muffler.

I twisted the headlight switch and was gratified to see the steady glow of the lamp just before it gave a bright blast and burnt out. I figured at this late hour, what with the streetlights and all, I could sneak the relatively few blocks home in commando mode. I bumped off the curb and down into the street and with a cautious twist of the throttle, was gone.

JOHN PEDERSEN

CHAPTER

THE rain had let up a bit outside the bar, which sat at the corner of 48th and Fulton, and the dense fog had poured in off the ocean to replace it. Combined with the fact that I had no headlight, only my defensive driving kept me from plowing into the sides of the cars that blithely pulled out in front of me.

I scooted up 48th to Balboa then over a block to 47th, doubting that anyone could identify the particular sound of my Norton so far from my house. At least, hoping not. Two blocks up 47th past Sutro Heights and finally left on Geary. I headed west a block and, after scanning the surroundings for police, turned onto 48th again which had become one way, the other way. The street went downhill at a pretty fair slant so I cut the motor, way, way up the block in deference to my neighbors.

We had worked out a system over several years where, if my home coming was late at night, I would come home from the north and coast the wrong way down the hill allowing my particularly fearsome neighbors on both sides to remain asleep. In return, my head didn't get bashed in with 2x4s, and at least several parties a year were tolerated that included all night music sessions and idiots jibber-jabbering on the porch till dawn. All I had to do was invite my neighbors knowing full well that they wouldn't attend, just to prepare them.

I coasted up into my driveway with just enough headway to come to rest against the side of Big Red, leaving the bike in gear so it wouldn't roll backwards into the street. I opened the garage door with my key. The almost-quiet electronic opener also turned on the interior lights and I heaved the Mercury up and into the only open space amid several other dead motorbikes.

I closed the door and made a half-hearted attempt to knock a bit of the water off the bike with a rag. Mostly just drying off the seat so I wouldn't have to get my butt wet in the morning. I hung my drenched jacket on a peg over a square metal drip pan and set my helmet over the hot air register. I released my accordion from its garbage bag shroud and assumed that any damage to it could be dealt with in the morning.

After filling the teakettle with water and grabbing a quick shower, as if I needed the extra moisture, I drank a glass of suspect buttermilk while the tea was steeping.

I headed to my bedroom on the west side of the second floor carrying a big mug of black tea and set my alarm clock for seven o'clock, anticipating a bit of motorcycle fiddling before I could make my way downtown. I fell asleep watching the late night TV show of a noted motorcycle collector and motorhead, idly wondering if I had a chance with Sloane this time around.

Struggling up from the murky depths in the morning, some faint breaks in the incessant gray could be seen through my window. As usual, the first order of business when arising was to go out onto my dinky and decidedly rickety balcony to stand on the wooden box that had been out there forever. This raised my vantage point just far enough so that I could kind of see the ocean and the break at Kelly's Cove in front of the Cliff House restaurant.

All indications indicated the waves were crappy, due, no doubt, to the days and days of wind and rain. Even though I couldn't go out, I felt better about the fact that nobody else would be surfing either.

I scouted the fridge and found some leftover curry I suspected would fry up nice with some scrambled eggs. The combination turned out to be peculiar, but edible. I would have made a pot of coffee, but I had been out of beans for a while and kept forgetting to pick up any. A situation I vowed to correct first thing that morning.

My leather jacket sported a nice, all-over furring of mold, and remained dank and clammy feeling. Luckily, my helmet had dried out nicely having spent the night over the furnace vent.

I had owned the Norton long enough to know the wisdom of having extra headlight bulbs sitting on the shelf, one was installed one in a few minutes. Opening the garage door and pointing the rear end of the bike outside, I gave a purely exploratory kick and was stunned when it started right up. I let it settle down to an idle, then flicked on the headlight and was further rewarded with a steady beam.

My driveway sloped away from the garage. To remove the bike and myself I had to sort of ride it in reverse, edging my way around the van and making a backwards turn at the bottom so that I could go up 48th. There were foot peg grooves dug into the tar of the driveway from all the times I had missed my footing and dumped the bike, but not this day. I glided backwards around the van, and leaned the bike against the bumper while I closed the garage and took off with a pleasant growl.

Going uphill on 48th, I took a right on Geary and followed it across the city to where it changed into Starr King Way for a block and then O'Farrell. I followed O'Farrell past Van Ness and the Mitchell Brothers porn empire till I turned up Grant and took it all the way to Broadway, right through the center of Chinatown. The early morning traffic congestion always made me glad to be on a motorcycle. Right on Broadway and a quick right on Montgomery allowed me to turn right again on Pacific and so down Jerome Alley, where my shop was located.

The streets weren't exactly dry, and the sky looked to be getting darker instead of lighter, but at least it wasn't flat out raining. With a little caution and a moderate amount of horn work, I made it in one piece.

I left the Norton idling on the sidewalk while I opened the double green doors of the bike shop, noting that my assistant, Vladimir, was not yet in attendance. The wooden doors were six feet wide apiece, and covered almost the entire front of the shop. Long and narrow was our floor plan. Hydraulic benches with restorations in progress sat on either side of the central isle, and my so-called office was hard up against the rear wall. There was a huge chalkboard over my desk and each job had it's own section. Parts on order, parts not available and needing to be specially made, pieces at subcontractors and lists of details waiting to be dealt with were all there. One whole side of what used to be my work desk was littered with accordion shreds and tools. Jammed off to the side were an old monster of a machine lathe and a Bridgeport Milling Machine, along with more pedestrian power tools.

A smallish loft held common motorbike parts and especially rare bits, as well as the corpses of a dozen or so accordions that were cool enough to someday, perhaps, warrant restoration.

Vladimir had worked for me on and off for almost five years. He had fled from pre-destabilization USSR and was a highly trained and respected engineer there. Once he had attained asylum in the US, his degrees weren't worth the paper they were printed on, and he had gotten a job at a sewer cleaning firm and worked there for quite a while before I convinced him that he could make a decent wage standing up and only getting his hands greasy. He claimed that he now made far more just fixing antique "junk" than he ever had as a Soviet rocket specialist. He had an uncanny intellect when it came to machines and could make almost anything run with whatever random parts came to hand. Once I had convinced him to actually wait for the right parts to arrive and only use new oil and unpatched tire tubes, his work was inspired. His machine work was art and often he would remake parts that we had just bought because he knew that he could make them better.

Sadly, this inspiration did not extend to arriving at work when he was supposed to. I had a pretty good idea where he could be located though, so with a good forty-five minutes before McCracken was supposed to arrive, I headed around the corner to the Uncertain Grounds coffee shop.

The place was the coffee dealing equivalent of my shop: all strange furniture, clunky cups, odd art work and "excuse me, mind your cup" as the morning devotees jammed their way down to the back where the register was situated and reversing to the front where the coffee urns were. Often, the coffee tasted like something we had perhaps drained out of a vintage Indian the night before. But then again, just as often it was stern and powerful sweet nectar.

Sure enough, Vladimir was there, bending the ear off of some unlucky bohemian about politics in some form or other. As soon as he spied me, I could see him readying his conclusive final arguments despite the fact that he was the only one talking.

I was supremely glad that today was a "Good Roast" day and filled a large to-go cup with the North Beach blend. I knew that the bearded, toque wearing coffee pusher behind the counter would add it to my running monthly total without the over dressed office worker who was ordering a very complex latte ever knowing.

As I turned around to make my way back to the shop, the flopping hem of my jacket brushed over the edge of the table nearest the door directly into the brimming cup of the person sitting there. Coffee cascaded out onto the table and over the tablet of graph paper the person had been drawing on. Completely soaked, as it were. I had an impression of brown Carhartt overalls, checkered flannel shirt, a Giants jacket, and an Oakland A's baseball hat before I spun around and grabbed a towel off the back bar. I swept what little coffee remained unoccupied with the tablet onto the floor and started trying to force some of the majority from between the pages of the book. Not too successfully, and I looked at the owner of the ruined document half expecting to get my lights punched out.

The person was standing a bit off to the side was getting a fair bit of entertainment from my futile gestures. With the bulky jacket and hat, it was kind of hard to tell who I had wronged, but I did see some blond bangs implying I might not be dealing with a typical longshoreman.

I said, "Yeah, shit, I'm really sorry about your stuff here. I feel like a jerk and not-unfortunately- for the first time in here. I think they could fill a tanker truck with the caffeine I've dumped down the drain. In fact, I think they put in the tile floors with the drain just because of me. I guess the regulars see me coming and get out of the way, or something."

The girl, for girl it turned out to be, took off her hat and allowed her long blond hair to spill out and started laughing.

"No problem there Mr. Graceful, it's not that big of a deal. I was just trying to figure out some design variations and they weren't working out anyway. You could get me another cup of coffee though, 'cause I have to get to work pretty soon and am flat cleaned out of cash."

"Absolutely my pleasure, and I'll even take you out to lunch, if you're around here at all at that time."

She mulled that over for a second before she said, "Yeah, OK, that'd be pretty good. Nothin' special, though, just lunch. I know where you work, you're the motorcycle guy, right? I'll just meet you over there around one o'clock, OK?"

I handed her a refreshed cup of Joe, "One it is, but how do you know where I..., ", and found myself talking to empty space.

Pretty embarrassed and somewhat confused, I gave Vladimir an arched eyebrow and headed back to the motorbike shop.

I reopened the front doors of the shop and figured that as long as it wasn't actually raining, it would be a good opportunity to air the place out for a little. I started sweeping the backbench of random debris in preparation for McCracken's visit.

Vladimir came in with a gigantic to-go cup of coffee and started the running commentary that he kept up virtually all day. Whatever crossed his mind or his vision was analyzed, categorized and commented on. I had learned to tune him out except in the rare event of a direct question.

After a while, I decided that we had has as much cold air as we needed. I flipped on all of the overhead lights and closed the front doors. As I did, I saw Bob Shackleford and McCracken, coming up the sidewalk. I waited for them to come in before closing the doors.

As Bob came in he was in the middle of giving McCracken a nice layer of bullshit about me, concerning my playing, and also my ability to fix any accordion reed tuning issues. I told him again that I was an admirer of his playing and also the playing of Joe Conroy.

Bob said he would return in a couple of hours to pick up Tommy.

As we made our way to the back of the shop with barely a glance from Vladimir, Tommy said, "Sure Conroy was a great player, was he not? Did you ever meet him here in 'Frisco at all? He used to give me all sorts of wild tales about the place, to be sure. Faith, I could never be sure when he was having me on or tellin' the truth. I tell you for certain, I expected to see naked hippies dancing down the street all over when I got here. But so far, nary a one."

"The naked hippies generally come out a little later in the year. It's pretty cold out for them right now, and unfortunately, I was pretty young when Joe was here in San Francisco, so I never met him."

"Oh, ah, I see. Too early in the year, is it? Ah well, isn't it always the way. Too early, too late, too this, too that."

He set down the battered accordion case on the bench and popped the latches. The box itself was hardly historic looking, all dinged and dented up, with a thick patina of nicotine from years of bar smoke. The single strap was held together with duct tape and the buttons were worn down from many years of continual playing.

I said to Tommy, "What seems to be the problem with the old guy? Other than the obvious bits of tape coming unglued."

"It's the hand strap altogether. It's too loose and quite a few lads have had their go at tightening it up, but it has never been right. More to the point, the reeds in the upper hand are flat and I'm always trying to push more air through them to get them to rise up a bit. Playing so hard is what pulls the strap screws out. My poor shoulder has been wrecked up from it for these many years, and now my back is involved. I'm likely to be crippled before long if I can't get it set right."

"The hand strap? Cripes, how complex can that be to fix, it's only screwed on to the side of the thing. The reeds might be a bit more complex, but they can't be that bad. Let's give her a look."

Tommy sat on a stool and poked his hand through the offending strap, and sure enough, it was pretty loose. Apparently he couldn't resist playing a quick tune or two as he started off on a couple of reels that I knew from the much-played tape. The particular sound of this accordion combined with Tommy's stylistic phrasing made the tunes unmistakable. When he played the high notes I could see him pushing extra hard on the bellows.

After a few trips around the musical block he stopped and said, " There's the pain coming to visit just now."

He stood up and set the box on the bench and started twisting this way and that trying to work the sudden kink out of his back.

I put on my "reading and working" glasses and had a closer look. Sure enough, the tracks of the previous attempts were not too hard to spot. There were holes all over the end of the box and the screws had pulled out of their current holes yet again. I got out a small precision screwdriver and removed the much-abused fasteners, top and bottom. Tommy pulled the stool closer to the bench to keep a close eye on the proceedings.

I decided I would need to turn some hardwood dowels to fill all of the random openings in the box and simply redrill the mounting spots, hopefully for the last time and in the correct positions. As I rummaged through the scrap woodpile, Tommy said, "So, you never met Conroy, eh? Pity, he was a great player and a great storyteller as well. Sitting here like this completely brings him to my mind. Did you know that he used to ride himself all over Ireland on an old motorbike like some of these beasts up on the stands here? He had a rack up on the petrol tank that he'd strap the box to, put a passenger on the back, and away they'd go. From all accounts it's a wonder that he lived long enough to get the cancer. Many, many days we spent together, playing the old tunes and having the odd pint as well."

Even though I was busy chucking the wood up in the lathe and getting it centered so that I could turn it down, I saw Tommy scan the shop and briefly focus on our small refrigerator, perhaps wondering if there might be a pint available just then, sort of a second breakfast. He thought better of asking, I guess, because he went on, "You know, it's funny that there was one story he told me that I never heard from anyone else, even the fellows from here that have come over and played in the pubs with us. I may have mentioned it last night. Let me think for a moment here so I get it right. Ah, just so, I remember the large lumps of it."

"Joe told me of an ancient old Dubliner he met when he was living here. He was amazed to find such an old timer still alive. This would be, I suppose, in the 60's. He said the old man came up to him after he had played an evening at one of the pubs, down in this area, I would guess. Joe said the old fellow claimed he had played the accordion as a young man and even had worked in the factories down here. According to Joe, after a few additional pints, the old man had given up his wits and started raving on a bit about having caused, and survived, the big earthquake and losing his true love due to it. He then went on and on about some Chinese mystical powers involving the reeds he had been master of when he was making and playing his box. He claimed he had given up playing as a precautionary measure after the quake. There were a few hints thrown to Joe that the actual box might somehow have survived, and could perhaps even be had. Joe thought the old duffer was completely cracked in the head, and once they parted ways, never gave another thought about it. He told me the story though, so he didn't completely forget it. And here I am telling it to you here in San Francisco. Amazing how things work out sometimes, isn't it?"

I listened to this saga while getting my huge machine lathe oiled up and ready to roll. It only took a minute to produce a tiny dowel of the correct size to plug all the holes in the patient. The size of the project was so out of scale with the size of the machine that it caused us both to laugh. I took the piece back over to the bench and Tommy swiveled on the stool to maintain his interested staring. Quick work with a drill made sure that all of the holes to be plugged were the same size. Then, using a bit of glue on each small plug, I tapped each one home with a tack hammer.

JOHN PEDERSEN

Tommy kept up a running commentary. Between himself and Vladimir, I felt like I was in quite jolly company. My mind briefly stuck on the far-fetched likelihood of an Irishman working in the Italian accordion factories at the turn of the century and having associations with Chinese mystics.

After cutting off the stubs with a fine back saw, I shaved them flush with the surface of the box with a razor sharp chisel. With that done, now all I had to do was reattach the strap in the right spot and I could move on to the real, underlying problem.

I pulled the pins that held the ends of the box on and separated the treble side from the bass. I had deduced that most of the tuning issues were in the outside row of buttons so I took that entire block of reeds out and set them on the bench. Looking at them I could see there were layers upon layers of built up pub crud obstructing the airflow to the actual reeds. I got out a long narrow scraper and went to work removing balls of what looked like cat hair mixed with roofing tar. It didn't take too long before the reeds were clean again and I fired up the flow bench and an electronic strobe tuner. Without the debris slowing down the vibration of the reeds, they weren't actually that far out but I filed wee bits here and there, just to make it look like I knew what I was doing. I checked everything once again and put the whole thing back together.

I had Tommy set the box in his lap, and I marked where one end of the strap would be, drilled the pilot holes and set the screws and strap onto the box. Then came the more critical step of determining the place to set the screws for the other end to produce just the right amount of free play in the strap. Tommy advised me one way and the other until I had what should be the exact right spots for the screws. I drilled, set the screws and handed the instrument back to Tommy for the final test drive.

He slipped his left hand into the newly positioned strap and started to play. After a few moments he closed his eyes was taken miles away by the music. I recognized several of the tunes as ones made famous by Joe Conroy. He played for about ten minutes running, and even Vladimir stopped his blabbing to listen. When he finally stopped he gave a tentative flex of his shoulder and back and declared,

"By God, I think you might have cured me. True enough, I don't have my regular cramp at all. 'Tis a miracle of modern engineering. I don't know how to thank you for doing that. I can't imagine why none of the other poor sods that sunk all them holes in there was able to get things right, but it certainly feels fine now. It's a joyous day for me, indeed. And it's so easy to make it play sweet on the upper side. What time is it getting to be? Ah, not yet even noon. Sure I'd invite you to have a celebratory drink but I'm afraid that you would think me a drunkard, or worse."

"As luck would have it, we specialize in celebratory drinking here, and we have many things to be thankful for. We wouldn't think the worse of you if perhaps we all shared a small spot of special cheer."

With this, I opened the cabinet where we generally stored our paints and flammable liquids and produced a nearly full bottle of Bushmills Black Label 21 year old malt whisky. At over a hundred bucks a bottle, we really did save this stuff for special occasions, and I certainly counted this as one.

Tommy said, "Bejaysus, will you look at that. Don't they drink like royalty here in the states altogether. Isn't it a great country?"

At the first hint of alcohol, Vladimir had ceased all work and rummaged though the bathroom shelves to find three nearly clean glasses. He came out with two coffee cups and a pint glass. Not exactly the family crystal, but I supposed it would do. Just as an extra precaution, I swabbed the insides out with a paper towel.

I poured out stern shots for the three of us and we toasted the notable occasion. A few more shots later, we were well warmed and Tommy allowed as how I might like to have a go at Conroy's old accordion, and so I did.

With the shots in me and a bit of apprehension about playing in front of the man, it took me a while to get my feet under me and find the groove. Eventually, with some purely amateur hunting and pecking, I was able to knock out a few credible double jigs from Tommy's old record, and I could see his pleasure at the homage. When I started to play Vladimir had returned to the bike he was working on.

The front door opened and admitted a slightly soggy Bob. "Howzit goin' boys? From the looks of things, the dang rain is back to stay for a while, it's black as a lawyer's heart in the west."

He eyed the sad remnants of the Bushmills and continued, "Say, did I miss something here? Is Wednesday the new "get drunk before lunch" day? If it is, I have a bunch of catching up to do."

Tommy had a good chuckle at that and came back with, "Do you know that it's not everyday that a fellow gets to have his career saved and a taste of the finest whisky on the planet at the same time."

Bob snorted and accepted my coffee cup with the remainder of the whisky in it, a couple of shots, at the most. He took a tentative sip and slurped it around in his mouth for a while before swallowing. He nodded approvingly and after finishing off the contents said, "Well, at least there is good taste somewhere in this town. This almost wipes out the bad taste of the inefficient bureaucracy of the San Francisco judicial system. Not quite, but almost. C'mon Tommy, are you about done here? We had better shake a leg or we're going to get stuck in a monsoon; and Highway 101 at Lucky Drive always floods with anything more than a sprinkle."

Tommy said, "Done we are, and I couldn't be happier. All that is left is to settle the account with Mr. Rauhe here, and we're off. Whatever the charge, it was well worth it. I'm sure that this will be an important day for myself and the accordion-playing world at large. What would be the total, sir?"

I was almost embarrassed by this not-so-subtle shit job attempt to butter me up, so I felt it was my duty to play my ordained part.

"Ah, there would be no charge at all for such a player as yourself. The honor is all mine to have performed even such a minor task for the "King of the Box Players." I only wish I might have been of more use to yourself. You don't happen to have an old motorbike in need of fixing, do you?"

Just as Tommy was about to wrap up the show, the front door gave a groan and shudder as the girl from the coffee shop opened it. She had to hold on with all her might as the now screeching wind threatened to tear it out of her grip. She just barely managed to slip into the shop and slam it behind herself.

She said, "son of a bitch, I nearly got airborne out there. What a shitty day this is turning out to be! Oh, sorry, did I interrupt a club meeting or something? It is one o'clock, isn't it?"

I said, "No, no, just finishing up a bit of business is all. This is Bob Shackleford, from San Rafael, Tommy McCracken of County Clare, and Vladmir Rostropovitch, lately of Odessa. Gentlemen, may I present, ah...ah... I have no idea."

"Jenny Farah, of the Tenderloin. Spelled Farrar with three R's, in case you were wondering."

Tommy beamed and gave an exaggerated hand kissing motion and said, "Enchanted, I'm sure. I was just about to depart with Friend Shackleford, but not before I relay how very deeply in debt to your boyfriend I am, and ever shall be. And so, without further ado, we bid you both, Cheerio!"

Jenny looked a bit nonplussed with her new status as my girlfriend. When Tommy made no actual motion to release her hand, she gave a quick tug and shoved her hands in her coat pockets.

"Yeah, me too, I think."

Tommy latched up the battered old case, and he and Bob wrestled the door open and forged out into the wind and rain with a quick parting wave. I watched them leave; then turned my attention back to Jenny, who was eyeing the empty whisky bottle and cups. Vladimir had disappeared, presumably to the bathroom to make one of his ritual pre-lunch deposits.

"Well, Jenny Farrar, is it? Sounds southern, but you don't. I'd offer you a small portion of anti-rainy weather tonic, but alas, the foreign types have exhausted the supply. Where would you care to lunch? I'm afraid my car is non-op at the moment, but I have bike here and an extra helmet if you fancy someplace out of the area."

"Hold on Bub, did you tell that guy that I was your girlfriend or something? And, if you had a part in killing this booze, do you actually think that I'd just climb on the back of a motorbike, in rain and wind like this? Are you nuts?"

I could tell that I might not be getting off on the right foot with this lady. I was pretty sure I had not offended her at any time previous to dumping her coffee on her work that morning, moderately sure, anyway.

I stammered, "Of course, of course, I was just joking a bit there. There's loads of places right here, as I'm sure you know. And no, I didn't imply anything to anybody about our relationship, the continuance of which I am in grave doubt about. I just wanted to make up for wrecking your drawings, that's all, and that tall feller there is one of the most famous accordion players of the Irish stuff in the world. I'm a bit jumpy after meeting him and working on his box. No grand plan here. We'll just walk to a place, OK?"

"What the hell's your name, anyway? I can't just call you "Motorbike

Guy."

"Oh, sorry again. Rauhe it is, Soren Rauhe."

"No kiddin', I never would have suspected you to be an O Slasher."

"Mexican mother", I explained.

"Hmmm…, well, how about Café Macaroni, over on Columbus. Kind of touristy, sometimes, but it's pretty good, and cheap, too."

"Fine with me, I don't think we'll drown between here and there. Let me get my slicker and hat."

I shouted towards the bathroom that Vladimir should lock up when he left, and got my raincoat and Sou'wester.

We fought our way out the door and walked down Pacific to the corner. When we made the turn to go down Columbus, the full effect of the driving rain and wind made itself known. We were hit square in the face, and I only retained my Sou'wester hat due to the fact it was tied on. Jenny's Oakland A's hat was not tied on, and it took flight, never to be seen again. Her blond hair streamed out behind her and water streamed down her face. I stepped in front of her to take the brunt of the gale, and we quickened the pace for the 1/2 block to the Macaroni Café.

Luckily, the severely crappy weather had decimated the ranks of the tourists, and we were able to walk right in and get a table. The wait staff acted kind of bored and listless. We pulled off our soaking jackets, and I had my first really good look at Jenny Farrar, with three R's, over our espresso coffees.

That morning I had sort of an impression that Jenny was built rather like a lumberjack, due to her flannel shirt and baseball jacket, but in fact, once she settled down at a table, she appeared small, but strong. She stood about five foot two without the hat. Her bangs accented very exotic, almond shaped eyes, faintly oriental. Combined with high cheekbones and honest-to-God freckles, I had to admit that she was quite handsome. My notoriously wild age speculation would have put her in her early thirties, slightly younger than my own almost 40ish station.

She still had a couple of shirts on, and those Carhartt overalls, but I had the distinct impression of a nice build, and a more than distinct impression of a powerful, womanly butt. No anorexic runway model pretensions. Her hands had pretty short nails, sort of on the dirty side, and the calluses looked like they came from actually working. On her feet, I could see that she wore a pair of those tan, steeltoed work boots that I always meant to get, but never did.

We sipped espresso in silence for a few minutes, savoring the relative dryness and silence of the restaurant.

Finally I said, "So, Jenny, you must work around the neighborhood somewhere if you have coffee there at Uncertain Grounds, and you knew that I worked at the bike shop, am I right?"

"Pretty shrewd, Sherlock, I do. Over on Jackson, as a matter of fact, but it might not be too wise to say exactly where. The company I work for makes reproduction antique furniture for a lot of the state parks. You know the type of place where you go in and stand behind a rope to look at the way things used to be. The government insists on pretty strict period pieces, made with the same kind of tools and finished with the same finishes as the originals. All distressed up to look like they were actually two or three hundred years old. The only creepy part is that I think we make a lot more furniture than the parks order, and the head boss might be passing off some of our stuff as authentic pieces to rich idiots at galleries. We work mostly on the second floor, so you can't really tell where we are from the street."

"Wow, that's a new one on me. But you must be pretty handy with the tools to be able to make such dead-on repros. Where did you happen to come by those skills, if you don't mind my asking?"

"That's OK. I went to technical college for it, up in Canada. Graduated at the top of my class too. That was quite a big disappointment to my family, though, 'cause they were prepared for a real legal eagle to carry on the family tradition of lawyering. Even though it hasn't always been easy being one of the only women in the field, I'm sure glad I'm doing this rather than litigating divorces like my brothers."

"Yeah, I think that we got enough lawyers in town already. How'd you know about the bike shop?"

"I see you riding that old Norton pretty often, especially now that the weather is so nice, and it's not too hard to follow. One of my old boyfriends had a BSA Victor that we used to ride all over the place. Some of the scariest walks of my life have been connected with rides on that bike. I have an eye for the old stuff, and clunky machines too, and that stuff in your shop certainly qualifies."

"Thanks, I think. Say, what number on Jackson? I don't care about the sneaky boss stuff, but I do have big chunks of an ancient accordion that was made over on Jackson. Number 478, I think. That's where the Galleazzi factory was up until the 40's. I've driven by there tons of times and you really can't tell what's going on in there now. Might be just the place, eh?"

"Well.... I'm not saying, but I will say that there are a bunch of parts in the basement that look like they might have come from accordions. Loads of other junk as well. You have to take these rickety stairs to get down there, and it's sort of creepy and dank."

"I'll be danged. Pretty strange coincidence, don't ya' think? Speaking of eerie, that Irish dude was just telling me about a story he heard about someone who worked in the accordion factories at the turn of the century who had a tale complete with true love, betrayal, mysticism, revenge, and even a magical instrument. Earthquakes included at no extra charge."

Jenny gave a snort and said, "Now there's a story I'd like to hear. 'The Saga of The Enchanted Accordion.' Sounds kind of unlikely to me."

"Yeah, me too, mostly because the poor bastard was supposed to be Irish, and working in a San Francisco accordion factory as pretty much the only non-Italian couldn't have been any picnic. Say, you know what would be cool, if I could sneak over into that basement and see what the Galleazzi boys left there. Might be pretty interesting."

"Oh, I don't know how big that would go over. Remember, you're not even supposed to know where I work, and also remember that I didn't tell you."

"I see what you mean. Let's think about this, OK? Perhaps work up a plan."

"When the hell did I become part of this conspiracy?"

Before I could get myself in deeper trouble, our food came, and while I was ready to continue to explore the possibilities of getting into the basement of her workplace, Jenny attacked her Parmigiana with such gusto, I was loathe to disturb her concentration. She cleaned out the breadbasket with no help from me.

When she finally slowed her pace she said, "Wowzer, that hit the spot. Now I'm kinda' glad you dumped that coffee on my drawings; I didn't have the cash for breakfast this morning and there isn't a scrap of food at my place. The dude I work for is sorta' spotty with the paychecks sometimes, and we're in the middle of a long stretch of nothing right now. Not to mention the rent is due right quick, as well."

"Yeah, I know what you mean. I'm really pleased that you came to lunch; I'm feeling some strange connections. You don't happen to have a glue pot, do you? With the real old time hide glue? Some jackass knocked my squeeze box off a chair last night and cracked the case, and if you believe the old timers, the hide glue sounds better than the modern stuff."

"Sure, I have a glue pot going all the time. It's the only way to make those reproductions, especially if you're gonna' beat them up a little and sell them to lazy collectors. The modern adhesives are too easy to spot."

"I could hire you to glue up my box and throw some bucks your way, and maybe have an almost plausible reason for visiting the shop. What about it?"

"I would have to mull that over. I really need to fly now, though. I'll try to give you a call before the end of the day. Give us a card, if you have any such thing."

I fished around in my wallet for one of my business cards, very stylishly designed and masterfully printed, which I never managed to have on my person. In the end I wrote both my home number and the shop number on the back of a napkin, which Jenny shoved into one of the numerous pockets of her overalls. I paid the check and we went out into a slight lull in the monsoon. Jenny said it was quicker for her to go on down Columbus to Jackson, so we split up there and I watched her double-time down the block. I admired the way she hustled along, even though I actually couldn't tell from the back if the person was male or female. I decided I might be slipping in my perceptions and so made my way back to the shop to get some real work in.

CHAPTER

S NUGLY back at Jerome Alley, I was not at all surprised to note that Vladimir had not returned from lunch. I opened up the shop and addressed the bikes that were awaiting my attention. The candidate that eventually stirred my enthusiasm was an elderly Royal Enfield.

Made in England in 1928, painted in shades of light and dark green, massively engined and quirky as the day was long. The bike was a very peculiar blend of ancient styling and strangely modern innovations.

It actually belonged to a collector from L.A. who had trucked it up in an enclosed car hauler along with one of his Ford Cobras destined for some other restoration facility. I think the Cobra was worth more than the building that housed my shop. Apparently, he couldn't find any worthy bike shops between L.A. and San Francisco who could promise a delivery date that might coincide with his lifetime. I had let optimism rule my time estimates and so got the job. Luckily, I had the Vladimir factor on my side and could get many of the unavailable parts made right in house.

Before I started working on the Enfield, I rummaged through my outdated tape collection and found the Tommy McCracken tape. I was pretty sure the album had never made the jump to CD production, as idiosyncratic as it was. The tape was in pretty bad condition, but I thought I'd give it a try in the old combo sound system that had somehow survived the incredible amount of dust and debris the shop created. First, I had to move a bunch of junk off of the flat surfaces, and then blow the skanky crud off the tape side of the machine. I put the tape inside and held my breath as I hit the power button. Incredibly, the exact same tunes I had been hearing in person earlier bounced out of the old player.

By the time Vladimir returned, obviously having continued the celebration without Tommy and myself, I was deep inside the motor of the Enfield and on the second time through the tape.

"Tovarich! Oh Yes, Oh Yes. This person is not nearly as good as player from today. Even that fellow vas not nearly as good as Soviet Union players, but still good enough for US of A, and better than this recording fellow."

"Tovarich yourself, it's the same player, in case you might be wondering. Where exactly did you go for lunch, and did you manage to eat any real food? You know that if your wife suspects you're drunk when you get home, my ass is grass. You know "my ass is grass?" It means she thinks that all we do here is drink from morning 'till night and occasionally screw around with a motorbike or two. And today, that's almost the truth."

"Yes, yes, some small amount of vodka was at lunch, but also many plemeni, vareniki, and kotley were eaten, so no worry."

"Whatever those might be, fine, but let's not use any of the big, crippling machines for a while, OK?"

"I think first I must visit toilet. Then work"

As I picked apart the corroded, gunked-up innards of the Enfield, I really felt the whole Joe Conroy--Tommy McCracken--San Francisco connection settling down over me. I also started to be very intrigued about the Irish immigrant accordion guy and all the mumbo-jumbo about his mystical instrument. I wondered if there was any way to get a bit more of the story.

I was pretty sure that given the opportunity and the right impetus, McCracken would be able to fill in all sorts of details he might have left out earlier. I wasn't sure about the opportunity, but I did know that more of the ancient Bushmills was just the lubricant needed.

McCracken was playing a concert that night at the Zellerbach Hall in Berkeley, and I suspected that if I could arrange transportation, I could talk myself in, and also corner Tommy at the inevitable after-hours session.

I thought of inviting Sloane to drive me over and accompany me to the doubtlessly locked stage door of the hall, and lend her charm and looks to the process of getting in for free, but something kept me from calling her instantly.

I tried Sean's cell phone instead. He answered on the fourth or fifth ring.

"Yellow, who might be calling a hard working fellow in the middle of his work day? Hard at work, I might add, putting fake distressing marks on a brand new solid walnut floor high atop Nob Hill. Or rather, I might further add, watching a crew of complete hoons grovel around on their knees with grinders doing the actual work."

Here Sean, perhaps for my benefit, screeched out at the top of his lungs, "Fer Chrissake, watch out for the goddamn baseboard there, the painters are due in here tomarra', and I don' wanna have to fix any fuckups!"

He returned to our conversation, "Friggin idiots, ya gotta watch 'em every minute."

I said, "Funny, I don't hear any grinding going on in the background."

"Oh yeah, well, they're actually still on lunch, but I'm sure I'll just have to repeat myself then. What's up?"

"Tommy McCracken was here this morning and after I fixed up his box, we were like long lost brothers. He's playing over at Zellerbach tonight, and I though we might take the opportunity to go give him a listen. Possibly play a bit of th' auld skidderedee afterwards. A pint or two, also perhaps. I might even kick in the bridge toll if the right transportation opportunity were to arise. Interested?"

"Tickets, tickets, did anyone mention those inconvenient things yet? Even though I doubt seriously whether a box player of any stripe could fill the Zellerbach, there could be certain pesky fees attached to such an expedition."

"If you're going to be that formal, not trusting my innate charm to slide us in past the vicious guard dogs, I'm pretty sure that I could call Tommy up at Shackleford's and have him put us on the list."

"Ah Ha, the list is it? OK, I'm in. I'll call Sloane and see if she can go as well. Hopefully we can take the monster so we don't have to all sit in the front of my truck."

"Wait a second, you didn't actually get anywhere with her last night, did you? Christ, I'd never forgive myself if I put that poor girl in harm's way by leaving her alone with you. Not to mention a missed video opportunity."

"Relax, will ya. The same old thing that always happens happened again. After listening to what an unstable asshole the recently-moved-out Gerald is for an hour, we finally get around to perhaps going somewhere and making out, but only now its too friggin' late and she has some shit to do for class tomorrow, and isn't it just grand to be such old friends and all that."

"Yeah, I think I've heard that a few million times as well. I guess if we're gonna take the Queen Mary over, I might try to get this girl I just poured coffee on this morning to go with us. If I could only find her."

Sean said that he would set it up and call me with the details. We agreed that 7:30 or 8:00 would be an appropriate time to meet, somewhere.

After returning to the large, sticky, and completely fragmented innards of the Enfield, I considered how I might go about contacting Ms. Jenny Farrar.

I also wondered more than once whether Vladimir had passed out in the head, but he finally emerged and went directly to the old Bridgeport milling machine and started doing a complex set up. Holding fixtures for previous jobs that we had been saving for ages were dug out, cleaned up, bolted down, rejected and stuck back on the shelf. Step blocks were brought out, stacked in various combinations, bolted down, unbolted, and finally put away.

I couldn't imagine what in the hell he intended to mount up, and what peculiar shape it might have to require such a complex jig, but I figured as long as he was playing with the building blocks, he wasn't turning the machine on and possibly cutting his fleshy parts off.

I scraped, unbolted and tried to do my tender best to get the Enfield apart without causing more damage than was already evident. Finally, I thought I had enough of the massive engine apart to allow me to hoist it out of the frame. I drew out the long studs that held it in the frame and let the motor settle down onto a stack of wooden blocks. I wrapped my arms around the crankcase, gave a he-manly grunt, and lifted the piece clear of the frame. I shuffled towards the engine bench with my burden as I heard the tape machine give a warning warble and groan as it started to destroy the ancient tape. I stared helplessly over at the shelf where the cassette merrily unwound and spread itself evenly over the slagheap surrounding the welder.

By the time I had manhandled the motor onto the engine stand, nothing remained of McCracken's legacy except a few random bits of tape that had not landed on or near the powerful magnets that we used to hold things in place as we welded them up.

My response was, "Oh Nuts!"

Vladimir noticed the mess and consoled me with, "This machin' is not vorking right. I have seen it do this before." I cast a severe glare in his direction, which he completely missed, having abandoned whatever project he was attempting to set up on the Milling Machine, and moved on to something completely different.

My internal clock told me that it was almost quitting time anyway and one of the meager benefits of being the boss of such a business was deciding when I had suffered enough for one day.

I dug out my much used, tattered and grease stained phone book and searched for Bob Shackleford's number. I finally found it under "A" for accordion.

Bob answered on the third ring and he allowed as how there might be a slight chance that I, plus three, could find our way onto the list. He would see what he could do. Apparently Tommy had carried our small celebration on for a while longer and was taking a nap. I asked Bob to ask Tommy if there were any other details concerning the ill-fated Irish accordion maker that Conroy had met in San Francisco.

Bob said, "Oh, Man, you fell for that old one? I've heard versions of that story a couple of times. Let's see, I think there was something about the guy being apprenticed in Dublin as a watchmaker, and some kind of mystic Chinese metal-working with the reeds connection. Um…there was supposed to be some kind of connection between a person's mental state and how the accordion worked; and get this, the capper is that the guy claimed to Conroy that he caused the 1906 earthquake. Yeah, I've heard that from a number of the old fellas."

"Okey Dokey, call me a sucker, then. Anyway, ask Tommy for me, and don't forget about putting Sean, me, Sloane, and that girl from the shop today on the list."

"Sloane, is it? I think your chances of getting on the list just went up quite a bit. By the way, there's supposed to be a session at the Widow's house after, so you might keep that in mind. Cheerio."

Bob hung up and I reflected briefly on Mrs. Carlotta Birchek, fondly referred to as "The Widow". She had a wonderful house on the flatlands of the Berkeley/Oakland border, which was opened to Irish musicians and their goings on frequently. Part of the reason was the widow's penchant for traveling musicians. As locals, Sean and I were exempt and not eligible, but had certainly seen many the easily impressed country lad swoon in her handsome presence. These affairs generally had a finite duration of the lad's stay in the bay area, but very occasionally, the widow would make sudden vacation plans to extend the bliss. Presumably the deceased Mr. Birchek had left her pretty well off, and a very long time before, as none of our crowd had ever met or heard aught of him. Sessions at her house could be lengthy, wild, and unpredictable.

She had a very large hot tub perpetually steaming away in the center of a little redwood grove on her property that invariably got a lot of usage during these events. Sitting there in the deep night, soaking away the cocktails and having the rain filter down through the trees could be a beautiful and memorable experience.

I told Vladimir that I was going over to the coffee house for a quick afternoon espresso, and that he should plan to turn out the lights and lock the door if I didn't return before 5:30.

I got a mumbled reply that I took to be assent along with an elaborate twist and stretch

Implying that his back was aching. I grabbed my rain jacket, the box and a roll of duct tape and made my way around the corner to see if I could find Jenny Farrar.

The late afternoon crowd in the Grounds was far different than the before work crowd. There were way more serious downtown types with laptops and papers spread out all over the tables. Most of the coffee cups on the tables were empty and there wasn't any socializing at all. I greeted Big Chris at the counter and exchanged pleasantries.

"Hey Sam, what it is? Kind of late in the day for you, ain't it? Don't wanna keep you up all night now, do we?"

Chris, like many of my friends and acquaintances, knew that my name is Soren. However, the closest his Northern California tongue could come to pronouncing it on an everyday basis was Sam.

"You never know, I might need some all night fortification. I'll have the single shot espresso, hold all but the most necessary sugar."

Chris's beatific expression beamed out and assured me that I had uttered the correct answer. His great height gave him an uncluttered view of the place and as he prepared my simple coffee, he asked me if I was sure I didn't need to supplement it with a 1/2 caf, 1/2 mochachino, vanilla shot, 1/2 hot no foam latte. Clearly the later patrons of the shop had pretty refined tastes and no problem asking for whatever they thought they wanted.

I replied, "No thanks, just the java. Say Chris, did you happen to see me knock a cup of coffee on a girl this morning?"

"Why should this morning be any different from most mornings? As a matter of fact, though, I did happen to see it 'cause the dude at the register was so doubled up with laughter that I almost had to take over. Pretty outstanding maneuver, even for you; is there a lawsuit brewing?"

"Not so much I just wondered if you recognized that girl that I soaked, and if she ever comes in here for an after work pick-me-up."

"Let's see, was that a girl? The overalls and Giants Jacket, baseball hat person? I do kind of recognize that get up, but I always thought it was just a smallish guy. I don't think I've ever seen her in here in the afternoon that I know of, more of an early morning type. "

"OK, never mind, I'll just settle for the coffee. I'm sure I'll see you tomorrow."

I took the tiny cup to the counter in the front window and sat at one of the tall chairs there. From this vantage, the Montgomery Street "end of the day" show was pretty entertaining. The rain continued, with plenty of blustery wind thrown in. The commuters staggered up and down the street, briefcases covering their heads, or umbrellas turned inside out. I was more or less glad to be inside.

I mulled over the problem of how to locate Jenny, and failed to come up with a brilliant solution. The only possible course of action that I could conjure was the least inspired and perfectly idiotic one. I would go and stand outside of where I thought she might work and wait for her to emerge. Or not.

At least I thought I might know where she worked. I supposed it might also be possible that she just let me think that so that I would leave her alone and quit asking questions, but what did I have to lose?

The place that I hoped we were both talking about was only a block to the east on Jackson Street. I had driven past the building for years and always admired the strangeness of it even before I had realized that it was the former site of the Galleazzi accordion factory. It was a two-storey brick building on the corner of Jackson and Balance streets. Balance was little more than an alley connecting Gold and Jackson. The bottom floor sported five black iron doors spaced evenly along the street front with arched tops. Rather like a fortress in its forbidding appearance.

I finished my tiny cup of jet fuel and slipped back into my damp slicker. I was a bit apprehensive about the garbage bag's ability to protect my accordion from the elements, but I had nothing better, so I forged out into the squall.

It only took me five minutes to take up a position on the opposite side of the street from the old building. I huddled in the very shallow vestibule of a fancy art gallery hoping for a small amount of protection. I tucked the box between my legs and hoped that the runoff from my slicker mostly missed it.

The black doors admitted nothing in the way of occupancy. No glimmer of light shone over the transoms, and the second and floor windows looked to have been plywooded-up on the inside. I thought I might have missed the mark altogether, either in the location, or the timing.

I had been there for fifteen frigid minutes before the gallery employees started cruising by the front windows and giving me the stink eye. I tried to ignore them the best I could, and adopted a look of purity and righteousness I thought might be convincing. I doubted that the inevitable police patrol would think so.

After thirty minutes, I was about to move on and find someplace drier to call Sean, when one of the iron doors opened and produced Jenny, still in the Giants jacket and another baseball hat, clutching a large leather tool roll. She stomped off down Jackson with neither a glance left or right. Before I could catch up with her, she stopped at a disreputable looking Toyota station wagon. It was white with festering rust spots only partially concealed by dirt. The back of the car appeared to have a lot of random stuff inside. She fumbled her keys and while she bent over to retrieve them out of the streaming street, I came up alongside of her.

"Hi Ya, Jenny, how's everything goin......"

As she straightened up, she swung at me with the tool roll and nearly had me in the head. I flinched back and just managed to bring my accordion case up to deflect the blow, which produced a grisly crunch. I was glad it wasn't my head. As I jumped back from her fierce glare I blurted out, "Hold it, hold it, its only Soren, from lunch, from this morning, the motorbike guy, remember?"

She peered suspiciously from under the baseball cap and wasn't in any hurry to let down her guard. Finally, she lowered the tools she had poised over her shoulder like some major league hitter.

"Holy Shit, dude, you scared the hell out of me there. Don't you know better than to surprise a girl on the streets? Man, you could get your ass kicked."

I heartily agreed, based on the sound of my accordion case, but I told her I was plenty sorry, and perhaps we could get in the car, as I wanted to ask her something.

She shook her head with disbelief and unlocked the door. She shoveled a bunch of junk off the passenger seat and opened the door for me. I climbed in and set the accordion case in my lap. The windows fogged immediately.

We sat there for a minute before she said, "So, ah, sorry for almost puttin' out your lights there, but I'm a little anxious about a few things right now. That asshole boss of mine still didn't come up with any of my back pay, and now he's even gettin' kind of hostile about it all. Jackass! I thought he might have sent one of those other jack-offs that work there out here to beat me up. Fuck that, I say. I was ready to knock that fucker out of the park. Shit, now I don't know what the hell to do. My rent is overdue by weeks and the landlord isn't exactly sympathetic about the no pay business. The one and only guy in there that was sticking up for me at all is in hot water with them now as well. Damn!"

"Sorry about all that, I'm sure, but if you don't mind my company twice in one day, I'd buy a nice dinner, well, dinner anyway, and spring for a concert by a wonderful musician, and even bring you to a posh party. How about it?"

"Dinner, concert, party? I'm hardly dressed for that kind of affair, and I'm more or less afraid to go back to what I loosely call my apartment."

"No, really, you don't have to go to any great lengths, for sure. I'll bet you have some stuff right here in the car you could change into that would be fine. C'mon, it'll be loads of fun."

"I don't know, I'm not sure I need to get involved with the dating scene right now."

"Dating scene? Jeez, ease up, will ya. It's a shitty evening, about to turn into a shitty night; what else are you gonna do? Plus, we'll have chaperones; we'll ride to the East Bay with my buddy Sean and my old pal Sloane. They're pretty much fun, and Sloane has a big-assed old Buick station wagon that has room like an ark. The concert is by that Irish guy you met in the shop this afternoon. I'm sure he'd like to have the opportunity to impress the shit out of you, in a hopefully more sober state."

"Well, as far as having nothin' else to do tonight, you got me there. I'd have to stow the car somewhere reasonably safe 'cause a lot of my tools and stuff are in here, and if some sleazeball steals 'em, Bub, I'm sunk."

"We could park it over at my house, but that's all the way over in the Richmond District by the beach, might's well be Mars. How about the parking garage, over near the Metreon down on Mission, or the Sutter Garage? Or, as long as we're sitting here on Jackson, how about the visitor spots in front of Police Central, over on Vallejo Street?"

"What are you talking about, visitor spot?"

"For my money, the safest parking spot in San Francisco is a few short blocks from here. At this time of the evening, there's always plenty of visitor spots down there in front of the Central Police Station on Vallejo between Powell and Stockton, and nobody ever gives you any shit no matter how long you park there as long as you're gone by 8:00 in the morning, or so."

"That should be no problem at all, right?"

She started up the old beast, and fished around in the back seat for a rag to wipe the windows, carried out with limited effectiveness. When at least she could see something out the windshield, we set off down Jackson to the next corner and turned left on Sansome and took another left on Pacific. A few blocks later we turned up Powell and right on Vallejo. She tucked the Toyota into the visitor spot nearest the front door, underneath the streetlight.

I dug out my cell phone, the ancient equivalent of the motorcycles that I worked on in the shop, from under my slicker and called Sean. After several tries I finally got some sort of feeble connection to go through. He picked up immediately, obviously waiting for my call.

"Hellew, where are you? Sloane and me are just about to slide up Bush at Kearney. Speaking of sliding up Bush, did you find your new girlfriend? OUCH!"

I knew that Sloane had just punched him, probably in the side of the head, that being her preferred spot for vicious retribution.

"We're at the police station on Vallejo Street, and yes, I did manage to locate the person in question."

"Oh My God, you didn't have to bail her out, did you? That makes 'em easy to find, though, don't it. Or, more likely, she bailed you out for something. I'm glad I didn't have to do it this time."

"I can barely respond to the absurdity of that statement, coming from you. But, no, we're just parking in the visitor spot for a while. So get over here and pick us up, 'cause we're hungrier than... well, hungrier than usual."

"We're just turning up Broadway now, should be there in about two minutes. Adios."

I turned to Jenny and said, "Mercifully, they're almost here. Sometimes it can take those two ages to get it together."

"Look at you, Mr. Retro motorbike, owning a cell phone, even an antique one. Well, ya' got me beat at the moment, I don't have one at all."

I struggled and thrashed out of my slicker, as possibly a bit much for the indoor activities planned, and got out of the car. Jenny dug in the back and came up with an old comforter, which she industriously spread over the contents of the back. I hated to mention that stuff under a blanket might be more interesting to potential thieves, and decided not to.

She also produced a small backpack into which she jammed a few clothing articles, presumably her evening gown and high heels.

Just as she was locking the door and checking all around the car, Sean and Sloane drove up. The back door popped open and with barely a stop, we slid in the back seat and headed for the Bay Bridge.

JOHN PEDERSEN

CHAPTER

ALWAYS the gentleman, I had let Jenny slide into the back seat first, and now she was situated behind Sloane, who was driving. I made the introductions,

"Jenny Farrar, with three "Rs", our driver tonight is Sloane Flynn and the navigator would be Sean Tierney. Jenny, Sloane and Sean. Sean and Sloane, Jenny."

Sean swiveled around in his seat to shake hands and get a first look at her. Jenny gave him a no-nonsense shake and whipped her cap off, allowing her pent up hair to spill out. I could see Sloane trying to get a look at her in the rear view mirror, but without actually reaching up and cranking it around, she couldn't.

Sean said, "So, El Dane here tells us that he dumped a scalding hot pot of coffee on you this morning. That automatically makes you one of us. Pretty shocking, ain't it? I don't know why he don't go over one more block to Starbucks where they got a lot more room. I hope he didn't wreck any of your stuff. I can't count the number of books at my house that are all deformed and stupid lookin' because somebody, wink-wink, knocked their coffee over onto them."

"Oh no, it wasn't a big deal at all. I was just drawing a Queen Anne chair leg out on graph paper trying to get the proportions correct. It didn't look right anyway, which only fits with the rest of my day."

Sloane was strangely silent up till this point, but suddenly she started in with the third degree, "So, Jenny, where are you from? Somehow you don't quite sound like a San Francisco native. Any kids that we should know of? How long have you been working as a carpenter? How very brave of you. Did you move to San Francisco for any particular reason? I suppose Soren has told you all about the three of us, going so far back and all."

Sloane was definitely acting strangely possessive, and also sounded like she stopped just short of asking Jenny if she hung out in the gay bars in the Castro.

"Well, no, we just met today and haven't really gotten into the life stories yet. But, just for information's sake, I grew up in New York; Brooklyn, to be exact. There were a lot of antique and old furniture shops in my neighborhood, and I kind of got a taste for old woodwork, so I went to college up in Canada for it. I studied furniture making, restoration and all that. As far as coming here on purpose, any job in a place where there isn't snow on the ground half the year appealed to me."

I knew Sloane enough to know that she was far from satisfied with the amount of personal information she had gotten. Before she could rephrase the questions and dig deeper I said, "So, Seanny, I don't suppose you ever heard a rumor or a story about some Irish feller around the turn of the century that came over here and worked in the accordion factories and had some claims about a magical accordion and his lost love? There was also some bit about secret metalworking and a bunch of whacky shit. Today it felt like I was the last guy to have run across this tale. How about you, got any extra details for me?"

"Ummmm, that sounds pretty familiar to me, but I can't say as I have anything for ya'. Probably one of them old guys that plays down at the Spaghetti Factory would know about any accordion related myths, but that place is so touristed up I don't know if any of the old guys are there anymore. You'd have to go down there and check it out." He continued without pause,

"So what, you fixed up McCracken's box and now you're, like family or something? That's pretty cool, eh? I hear that he doesn't like anybody that isn't a hundred years old. Even though you're gettin' there."

"As I go, so do you, Amigo. Yeah, it was fun havin' him in the shop today. He was totally into the "entertaining the help" thing, one story after another about the old guys. The repair was easy, just had to make some dowels and hammer 'em in and refit the straps along with some reed clean up and tuning. Anybody that gave a crap in the last twenty years could have done it right, but there ya go."

Sloane was not about to give up easily, "So, Jenny, where do you live? Near Soren out near the ocean? I can't stand the dampness way out there. Everything in the place always smells moldy. Oh, sorry Soren, you know what I mean. What else do you do? Play any sports? PTA? Hobbies? Brothers and sisters?"

I had to break in on this, "Christ, Sloane, give it up, already, will ya? We just met this morning, there's no big rush to get the entire file, is there. It's like the FBI in here all of a sudden."

I could tell that Sloane was sinking to a pout and as her accelerator foot slowly pushed down, I wished that we had all squashed into the front of Sean's pick up.

Mercifully, there wasn't too much traffic on the Bay Bridge, but the rain was still coming down pretty heavily and the windshield wipers were struggling to keep up with the demand. We were fairly flying along in the left lane sending out a spray like a hydroplane, when Sloane happened to look in the rear view mirror and said, "Oh Shit, the police!"

Sean, Jenny, and I twisted around to stare out the back window at the red and blue blinking lights that were coming up fast. I said, "Baby, you're screwed. Better pull over into the right hand lane pretty quick."

"Well, thank you for that succinct traffic advice. Oh, My God, I've never even had a ticket before, if this is the first one, I will be so completely annoyed."

She slowed down considerably, easing over to the right. The police cruiser kept coming full bore, and then swept by us with nary a glance, pulling off into the distance. We all relaxed and those of us not at the wheel thanked providence for sending the cops at just that moment.

The rest of the ride up to Berkeley was silent and without discussion of any kind. Sloane drove right to Everett and Jones BBQ on San Pablo, at University. The three of us had eaten there so many times that there really was no other option. Sean and I had co-hosted a regular session at a bar not too far away and invariably staggered out of the pub at closing time and into Everett and Jones for some sobering link sandwiches with hot sauce. The links were served on white bread with a scoop of potato salad, precariously lumped onto a flimsy paper plate and accompanied by an orange soda. The sauce was dumped on at the last moment, and a person had the choice of "Mild, Medium, or Hot." In order to show the rest of the terrifying late night patrons that we were no sissies, we always chose "Hot" and would sit at the counter shedding silent tears of blissful agony.

Sean's celebrated almost-wedding night feast was held there and, having brought our own libations, there is a small possibility that the bride and her family suddenly thought better of including a person among their relations who would eat at such a place. To say nothing of his friends.

Also the long and drawn out wake for Sean's mother had wound up there. We had ordered Everett and Jones take out when we had a going away party for my folks. They relinquished their house to me and relocated to southern Mexico, so as to be near my extremely aged maternal grandparents.

It was, to say the least, a tradition.

Jenny looked a bit taken aback at the "converted gas station" aspect of the place, and might have been thinking twice about my description of "a nice dinner out."

The inside of the place was, if possible, less appealing than the outside. There was a gigantic brick smoker at one end, with years of built up residue caked around its iron door. Goofy signs were stuck up all over advising customers where the complaint department was located and that they could go to "Helen Hunt" for any special treatment.

It was pretty early for the BBQ dinner crowd, so the line at the counter was short. I advised Jenny that the link sandwiches were by far the best-tasting food in the Bay Area. Sean gave us all a questioning look before ordering four plates of food and four orange sodas. As there were no late night denizens to impress with our stoic taste buds, we opted for medium sauce.

We stood back after ordering to allow the line to progress through, and watched the guy handling the orders open the iron door allowing a zephyr of the hickory smoke to escape into the waiting area. He snagged a couple of strings of links that were hanging from metal rods inside the oven, and hauled them out. My mouth was watering uncontrollably by now. He flipped the meat onto the counter and whaled away at them with a meat cleaver until he judged there to be four equal portions. A stack of almost translucent paper plates with the white bread already on them stood waiting, and after plopping the links on the bread and dumping on a modest side of potato salad, he slathered the whole mass with BBQ sauce poured from a half-gallon jar. These were delivered to the pickup counter; we grabbed them and claimed seats at the counter, staring out the big window at the drenched and deserted picnic tables.

Jenny sat to my right, Sloane to my left. Sean and Sloane tucked right into the plates without fanfare, while Jenny still looked like she had some reservations about the whole set-up.

She said, "I don't usually eat a big lunch like today and a big dinner too. Especially meat. I 'spose the plan is to just dig in, eh?"

"They don't stand on formality here, as you can tell, and obviously, neither do we. It's pretty good stuff, though. You wouldn't believe the number of times we've eaten here. We should have bought stock. Even our parents used to come with us. It's like a second home. A second home, with the walls covered in sludge, and in a converted gas station. Full of Berkeley street people, sometimes."

I decided to shut up and get down to business. Even the medium sauce made the sweat start on my neck. Jenny gave a few tentative bites and then put it away with enthusiasm equal to ours. Very soon, there were nothing but empty paper plates and mounds of napkins fouled with sauce in front of us. Also, the place was starting to fill up and the number of people standing around holding their dinners and eyeing our seats was increasing by the minute.

Sean managed to burp out, "Dudes, we'd better get going if we're gonna' get to this concert in any kind of time at all. Not to mention I think we're about to cause a riot here. Let's go!"

We shoveled our junk into the trashcan, dropped the soda bottles into the recycling bin by the door, and made a dash through the nasty weather to the car – which, predictably was locked. The four of us stood around getting soaked while Sloane fished around in her jumbo purse for the keys.

Finally we were all inside and made our way on the short hop over to Zellerbach Hall on the University campus.

Sloane managed to find an unlikely parking spot right on Bancroft almost in front of the Zellerbach. Not a particularly good sign concerning attendance, I thought. She managed to get into the generous-sized spot with only a minimum of back and forth, in and out, and over the curb maneuvering.

We made another dash across the forecourt and took shelter under the overhang of the hall. There wasn't much of a general crowd milling about inside or out. Sloane said, "Shall I come with you to make sure that we are all on the list? I know that Bob is pretty reliable, but you never know when things might slip one's mind."

Without thinking through the possible implications I said, "Nah, me and Jenny will go talk us in. Shouldn't be any problem at all, I 'spect."

We strolled through the lobby doors as if we owned the place, and after a very short wait in line arrived at the "Will Call" window. I assumed my most self important demeanor and said, "Soren Rauhe, plus three, I believe we are on the list."

The grey haired lady manning that section of the booth was visibly less than impressed.

"Well, luckily I just had that sheet out a few seconds ago. Or sheets should I say. Let me see, Rowe....I'm not seeing it."

I corrected the spelling issue, and amazingly, my name was found among the privileged not so few, and the tickets were produced. We collected Sloane and Sean from the lobby and headed directly to the bar, which was the most crowded spot in the place

White wine for Sloane, a sacrilegious lite beer for Jenny, shots of Irish whisky and sturdy Lagunitas IPA's for Sean and myself.

Jenny had her backpack with her and slipped off to the Ladies Room, presumably to change out of her overalls. She emerged a few minutes later, her hair brushed out, clean jeans, an Indian print top with a heavy white Peruvian sweater with an blue eagle on the back. The transformation was kind of startling. She stood about five two and her mid-back length hair the color we usually called "Summer Blond". Her Levis were loose around the work boots but snug from the knees on up and they showed a muscular and shapely pair of thighs and butt. Her work clothes were jammed into the backpack. I offered to run it out to the car, but she declined.

With only a few moments before the concert was due to start, we made our way straight into the auditorium; its spacious grandeur inspired me to think, "Who in the Hell booked this guy here?"

The capacity of the hall looked to be around 2,000 souls. I really couldn't think of any accordion player, from Lawrence Welk on down, who might have a chance of filling the seats on a nasty night such as this -- much less an Irish traditionalist. I sincerely hoped he had a guarantee in place.

Predictably, the seats reserved for the complimentary tickets were high up and to the side of the hall. With roughly 900 seats between the four of us and the rest of the audience we opted to move a bit closer to the action and perhaps risk sitting in someone else's seat. I doubted they would be claimed.

We settled in, the lights dimmed, the stage lights came up, there was an introduction over the house address system and Tommy McCracken strolled out to sit in the solitary chair on stage, wearing the same clothes I had seen him in that morning.

He sat down, and without speaking, started playing.

Of the four of us, I suppose I was the most affected by Tommy's presentation of the old tunes. His phrasing and dynamics were, to me, sublime. I could see Sloane scanning the crowd to see who from the social A-list was there, and who they were with. Sean had his eyes closed and looked like he was taking a nap. Jenny was enjoying the music, but not from a particularly inside view. Perhaps contemplating her recent personal issues more than becoming one with the Muse of Irish Music.

After a few sets of tunes with minimal chat in between, Tommy began a long rambling story about an adventure that he had endured in some Irish backwater, and while he was relating the entertaining details, another performer came on stage carrying a fiddle and his own chair. He sat down next to Tommy, and a soundman ran out to place another microphone in front of the fellow.

The anecdote ended with a funny twist and as usual with those types of stories in those circumstances, the last line was, "And that's how the tune got its name."

They played together like parts of a Swiss watch. Not exactly the same, note for note, but close enough to compliment each other.

A few more tunes and this episode was repeated as a tall, young, bearded tenor banjo player, with a backwards baseball cap, was added to the mix. The three of them cruised along in perfect comfort, playing reel after reel, none of which I had ever heard. The fact of which, kind of amazed and pissed me off at the same time.

By now I was certain Sean was sleeping. Sloane was astounded at how few of the old crowd was there. Jenny was, perhaps, wondering why she had come on this date, and I was anxious for the session over at the Widow's.

Intermission came and we got up and milled about. Many of the Irish session crowd were actually there, albeit spread around the cavernous auditorium so it was hard to see them all at once. I counted an alarmingly large number of them slated to attend the session, and there was the potential for another full-on night at the hot tub.

Our second round of drinks was secured and the next set began, the seats noticeably less occupied. An exceptional local piper who had come to the Bay Area from Dublin many years before now joined the trio. His present tidy, cleanshaven aspect was a startling change from when I had first met him. Longhaired, full bearded, and strumming a five string banjo was the lad I first came upon busking at Fisherman's Wharf. We had struck up a conversation and discovered a mutual admiration for traditional Irish music, not evident by his banjo picking. We had played many gigs together since. His piping, which must have been in its infancy at our first meeting, had blossomed into a great talent. Little fuss or bother with the instrument's peculiarities, just a terrific sense of timing and deep-rooted connection with the music.

The boys played on, tune after tune, until some unspoken signal told them that they were done. They were introduced once again to the audience, gave a parting wave and the stage was empty.

I said with my customary veiled sarcasm, "Nice bit of snappy patter there. And I liked all the heart wrenching songs."

Sean said, "Ah well, just another session to those guys. Let's get the hell over to the Widow's before we have to park in Oakland. We'll hit the "Pic N Pac" for a few sixers and what not on the way over. Off we go!"

I could see the wisdom of his statement. The parking situation over at the Widow's was execrable, only slightly better than the City.

We hustled outside while most of the audience was still visiting with each other and made our way to the well known liquor store.

Sloane and Sean indicated they would do the actual buying, so I dug forty dollars out of my pocket and handed it over. Jenny and I stayed in the car.

"So, are we having fun yet?

Jenny gave me a funny look and said, "At least I'm not sitting in my car out in front of my apartment wondering what to do. Those guys were pretty good players, I'd have to say, but a little light on the vocals, if you know what I mean. One tune after another might be OK if you know what you're listening to, but after a while, they all kinda' sound the same to me. The rib place was fun, though. I washed my hands twice and I still feel sticky, and when I burp if feels like there's a volcano in my guts."

"The perfect reaction to a fine meal, no? You get to relive it over and over."

Jenny came out with an unexpected laugh, pure and melodious. The pleasure it gave me instantly registered on my "Uh Oh, I like this girl" meter. I decided to throw caution to the wind, make or break, all or nothing.

I reached out and held her hand; she did not pull away immediately.

I was suddenly as giddy as a teen on his first date.

Sloane and Sean came back with much shuffling of bags and opening and slamming of the rear compartment. My hand was gently released.

The front doors were opened and our chaperones got back in the car.

Sloane said, "Oh My God, what in the name of St. Ralph do we need all the liquor for? I mean, really! It's not like we have to intoxicate this whole party, is it? I have to teach tomorrow at eight o'clock. Don't we all have jobs that need to be attended to? I wonder at you two."

Sean and I traded glances to indicate if we had heard this rant once we had heard it a hundred times. We opted to remain silent. Sloane started the old beast and we made the short distance to the Widow's neighborhood in quick time.

As hoped, our early departure from the concert had afforded us a parking space on the same block as the address. Not exactly right out front, but in the past I had been forced to park many blocks away, even after cruising the area for ages.

I grabbed one of the bags of liquid wonderment from the back in one hand and my box in the other. Sean did the same leaving only a couple of individually wrapped single bottles for Sloane and Jenny to carry. We walked up the manicured driveway and Jenny marveled at the stately grounds and the impressive architecture.

Having been there before, we knew it was useless to go in by the front door, as there was generally a pile of instrument cases, coats, and what not to forge through, so we made our way directly around to the back of the house.

The property was bounded on three sides by stately redwood trees and at the end of the driveway a two-storey coach house/garage had lights blazing inside. Often when the sessions inside became too large or numerous, one or more would start up in the garage. There was plenty of room on the ground floor as Carlotta's current Jaguar took up only one of the three flagstoned spaces. There was a stack of folding chairs against the wall, and numerous spanking clean workbenches lining the walls. Upstairs there was a cozy apartment that housed yet more sessions, and sometimes traveling musicians or bands.

The back of the house sported a wide deck and double French doors which opened into one of the living rooms and also the hallway to the laundry room. We headed straight for the laundry room, as the washing machine and utility sink were generally full of ice, all the better to cool beers. From the level of the deck, one could see the copse of redwoods where the hot tub perked invitingly; still empty this early in the evening. Inside the house, Sean and I dumped our burden of brews in the already half full Maytag. From the utility room, we made our way through the kitchen where a huge pot of some sort of soup gurgled on the stove. Sounds of a half-hearted session eased out of the living room.

Carlotta, "The Widow", intercepted us midway along the hall. Mighty hugs crushed each of us, including Jenny, to the formidable bosom.

After introductions, Carlotta said, "Thank God you lads have arrived. I thought I was going to have to send for the Music Police. Please, if you value our friendship, get some instruments out and create some actual music."

"Kinda abrupt, but I'm game. Let's go Sean."

I couldn't imagine a lack of musicians in the house, but if the hostess calls, one must answer.

Sloane snagged Jenny and said, "Let's take a tour of the chateau and get better acquainted, shall we? The boys must go play for a while."

For some reason, I wasn't sure I was particularly comfortable having Sloane chit chatting alone with Jenny. Not that I had that many skeletons in my closet, but I rather preferred getting them out in person. The die was cast, however, and off they went to explore the architecturally significant palace.

The living room boasted high open ceilings with massive exposed beams. Tasteful details abounded at beam-ends and joints. The walls were a marvel of dark virgin redwood paneling and flashing mirror bedecked sideboards sparkling with cut crystal. Elegant chairs were placed exactly in a cozy circle. There were armchairs and deep sofas situated near a chuckling fire. In general, it was the antithesis of every low dive, session spot known to man. We would have thought ourselves in heaven except for one serious detail; every musician already there but one was holding an Irish bodhran drum and gazing expectantly at the one and only melody player, a hapless and half-baked whistle player. He returned their stares with a wide-eyed, panic-stricken glare.

As we came in, he sprang from his seat and made the absolute most of our meager passing acquaintances. We could not have been more warmly welcomed.

Sean said, "Jeasus, Mary and Joseph, this might not be hell, but you can feel the heat and see the outskirts from here. I think I'm gonna' faint!

Just to stretch the anxiety to the breaking point, Sean and I sauntered over to the nearest sideboard and studied the whisky selection. Our bottles of mediocre whisky were added to the existing array on the sideboard. As we chose a single malt scotch far nicer than those we had brought and poured out a couple of tumblers the room was ghostly silent. Finally, even we couldn't take the stress and we sat down. I got out the box complete with duct tape, and Sean his old Louden guitar.

Once set, we wasted no time in powering through a series of quick reels, the inexperienced drummers banging their arrhythmic heads off.

As long as Sean and I listened to each other, the tunes went along nice and sporty. We didn't have long to wait before some other old timers drifted into the circle and filled out the melodic aspect of things. As the session filled, so did the rest of the house with folks laughing, drinking, assaulting the foods presented, and having a good time.

Half an hour or so later, the temperature was rising and I felt the need for a bit of a break, After the debacle the night before, I was wary of leaving my accordion on a chair, so I tucked it away in the case and let some other enthusiast take my spot.

I refilled my water glass of whisky, tucked a bottle of beer into my back pocket, in case I needed a chaser, and went looking for Jenny and Sloane. It didn't take me long to find them on a covered deck on the second floor. The view was over the back lot and we could see that the garage already had another session going on in there. From the sounds emanating, the session was populated mostly by pipers, who were all well below concert pitch. Possibly even as low as Bb, compared to the D of our session. Guys like that tended to group together, and if you and your instrument was not capable of tuning down two whole steps, you were excluded from participating. The garage was the perfect place for them.

"Hiya girls, what's going on up here? Have we toured the whole house and taken a good inventory? Found anything of note?"

Sloane said, "Just the usual envious array. Your music there sounded a bit heavy on the random beat side, am I mistaken?"

"Ah, no, I wouldn't say so. I think the Adult Education classes for Beginning Bodhran must have just let out near here somewhere. It's settling down now, though."

Jenny said, "In a house this size, there must be powder rooms all over the place, I just haven't seen any, care to direct me to one."

Sloane and I both pointed across the room to a closed door. Jenny headed that way. When she had closed the door behind her, Sloane said, "I don't know, Soren, there's something strange about that girl. So, I don't know, common. I hope you aren't getting serious about her. I think that you can do better."

Her remarks took me completely off guard.

"Do better? I just met her this morning and hardly know anything about her at all. And, as if you didn't know, I haven't done shit so far in life."

Sloane edged closer to me, "Well, as it turns out, I may have been a bit hasty and neglectful in my treatment of you in the past. Being now, as it were, available, I hope that this Jenny won't drag you off into some tangential relationship."

I was, frankly, almost too stunned to speak. Sloane had never indicated that she had ever seen beyond the Sean/Soren unit. As long as Sean and I had been vying for her attention, she had pretty much never indicated that she thought neither of us was suited for more than a maintenance man's job at her inevitable coronation. For her to make a blatant play for attention while I was in the company of another woman, however new and casual, was outside the realm of comprehension.

JOHN PEDERSEN

She edged even closer and draped her arms around me in a sort of a one-sided embrace. Luckily I was saved from further clumsy thought and action by Jenny's return from the bathroom and the arrival of Sean. He apparently didn't think too seriously about Sloane's languid release of my person. She slinked out like a self-satisfied cat.

Jenny said, "What's with her? Was she trying to lift your wallet or something?"

Sean gave a bark of laughter. After he had gotten that out of his system, he said, "Say, you know about that accordion player thing you were talking about? Well, Big Jim Sullivan is here, and if anybody in this town knows anything about that deal, it would probably be him."

"Yeah, you're probably right. Pretty late for an old guy to be up, though. I'd better get down there and see what I can dredge out of him before he falls asleep on the couch."

Big Jim Sullivan was by most accounts the guiding light and steady savior of traditional Irish music in San Francisco during the dark days of the forties and fifties. Days when it was not at all popular or hip to play that traditional stuff outside the home. Jim and a very few others had kept at it, playing wherever and whenever they could. He had started out as a piper, but an injury to his left hand had forced him to adopt the button accordion as his instrument. He was definitely well into his late seventies, perhaps even his eighties at the time.

Jenny and I headed downstairs, while Sean had a good scan of the potential occupants of the hot tub from the deck.

I found Jim tucked away at a corner of the kitchen table, a minute glass of whisky in front of him. His niece, Theresa, hovered nearby. In the event he should decide that more whisky was needed, she would soon overrule. Jim's speech was slightly slurred, a lasting reminder of a stroke a few years earlier. A few of the older guys that might have played music once, or were just involved with the Irish Cultural center, sat at the table with him.

Jenny and I sat down at unoccupied chairs, not quite as near as I would have liked, and I waited politely for a break in the conversation before introducing myself for the fiftieth time, and Jenny. Jim's eyes naturally and honestly settled on Jenny while I asked him about the mythical accordion player.

Eventually he had filled up his eye-holes with handsome girl and turned to look at me. He said, "Do I know you? Are you a player or what?"

I answered that I grew up in the Richmond District, what high school I went to, what sessions I had played at with him and when, and told him that I played a Paolo Soprani chromatic box from the teens, with burled walnut on the outside.

"Oh Hell, I know that box, pearl buttons on the right and silver on the left, eh? Sure and you, you're a Swede, or something like that, right."

"Yah, a Dane, actually, but yah."

Jim smiled at us, and I could almost see the gears grinding in his memory. None of his buddies had anything to add to my telling of the story, but finally Jim's eye's narrowed and he said, "Sure, I heard that story; Blarney if ever I heard any. But, I didn't hear it from Joey Conroy, I had it from the man himself, as crazy as he was. If ever a fella like you could get into the Bohemian Club, you could see his photo on the wall along with the first accordion maker in San Francisco, an Irishman!"

Even though I had only heard the story that day, and didn't have an ounce of energy invested in it, I was oddly very excited. Jenny looked thoughtful.

CHAPTER

AFTER Big Jim and his cohorts had a good long chuckle at my expense, they went back to discussing whatever it was that we had interrupted. The kitchen was becoming a focal point for the hungry mob, and the oven was doing overtime work cranking out loaves of soda bread.

Jenny and I eased our way out of there and back into the front room where at least there were some regular players among the over-represented drummers. The tunes were flying out with short pauses for breath between.

We made our way over to the sideboard and I was not at all surprised to see that both the bottles that Sean and I had put there were bone dry. Luckily, there was more on hand of adequate, if not legendary, quality.

One of the players in the circle caught my eye and gave me a twitch of the head to indicate that if I was ready to sit in, he was ready to relinquish his seat, but only to me, not some wing-nut with a fiddle and a case of the shakes. I subtly asked Jenny if she would like to, perhaps, hear a few tunes on my squeezebox, accompanied by fifteen of my dearest friends. She said it might be interesting to see someone who was having their intestines dissolved from the inside out by "Medium" BBQ sauce play tunes at the same time.

The excellent fiddler who had offered me his seat divined my intention and killed the current tune, standing as if to leave the circle. A young pup saw this as an opportunity to move from the furthest reaches of the outer circle to the coveted inner ring. His hopes were dashed by a severe application of stink-eye by my friend and he sat back down.

Jenny gave a nice snort of derisive laughter when she saw the edges of my box swaddled in duct tape. I tried to rise above it. I slid into the vacant seat and had a good look around. The players there had some competent instrumentalists among them, but hardly anybody I would have considered the spark plug of the session. Mostly they were content to let someone else start the tunes and set the pace and just play along. I figured I might as well be "the decider" for a while.

In order to show Jenny my versatility, such as it was, I started right in with a slow air and song. I played the melody on the box and then as I sang the verses, I played the chord accompaniment only. The song was a story of a young lady called Molly Ban who goes walking in the dusk and is mistakenly shot by her lover when her white apron is mistaken for a swan. A pretty emotional song, but with a tonal range as mercifully narrow as that of my singing voice. Only two other players cared to join in, Sean from the sidelines on his guitar, and a masterful flute player from San Francisco who sported a regal beard and a scruffy beret.

I thought I carried it off with marginal success, but when it had ended there were shouts of delight from listeners and players alike. The sessions tended to be a bit tune oriented at times and a nicely sung song always lent an elegant touch.

After that it was jigs, reels and hornpipes for a while. When I looked up, Jenny had wandered off, and I figured I should go locate her and keep her company. I scanned the players standing up and saw a fireman fiddler from Oakland who had taught me loads of tunes over the years, and gave him the head twitch. The passing of the seat was smooth. I squeezed my way back out of the circle, stowed the box and set out to find Jenny,

Improbably, I finally found her out in the garage listening to the flat session. There were several pipers, twice as many fiddlers and a lone bouzouki player. The clear leader of the session tensed up and narrowed his eyes at me until it was clear that I had not had the bad taste to bring an accordion in with me. After that it was all smiles and friendship.

Ms. Farrar was sitting on one of the workbenches and had a slightly perplexed look about her. She said "So, aren't these guys playing the exact same stuff that they are playing in the house?"

I answered, full well knowing how lame my answer was going to sound.

"Well, yeah, I suppose they are. But they're playing in a different key. Lower in pitch, a step and a half. Lower. You know, like, lower. In pitch."

I stopped talking, as I knew that there was no way to justify the concept to a non-piper. The Irish Uilleann pipes are made as complete and utterly complex instruments in a range of pitches. Each one plays exactly the same as the others, the music just comes out in different pitch ranges. Therefore, pipers with sets of a like pitch cluster together.

Jenny gave me a look that I interpreted to mean, "If this date gets any weirder, I'm walking home."

I thought we had better keep moving before any more questions were asked, so I bid the flat fellows good bye and steered Jenny back out the door. As we climbed the steps to the deck, we could see Sean over by the hot tub, casually stripping off his clothes. There must have been a few other occupants by then, and I could only assume that some of them were female. I glanced over at Jenny to see if there might have been a glimmer of interest along the outdoor bathing lines, but saw none, so we continued on inside the house.

We grabbed beers as we passed by the washing machine and once inside the kitchen Jenny said, "So, what was that old dude talking about, some club where you could go see photos of your mystery accordion guy?"

I was almost reluctant to begin to describe the Bohemian Club to her. But, unless we were going to talk about something really boring like myself, or something completely unknown, like her, it would have to do.

"OK, there is this notorious club in San Francisco that was started way back in the late 1800's by some artists, musicians and journalists. They have a big, block-long clubhouse down on Taylor in the city. After the founding of the club, it started to attract wealthier types that wanted to hang around with the artists and writers. Before too long, the rich guys outnumbered the real Bohemians, and so it has been since. The club is still really attached to promoting the arts, but I think a lot of back room political and business deals are made there as well. It's pretty expensive to join, and you have to have sponsors and all that shit. The only time I have ever been inside was to play in the pit for one of their shows. Even the pit guys have to dress in a tie and jacket. No women there, either. So, like Jim was saying, there is a long hallway that leads to the bar where photos of past members are displayed. I was working when I was there so I barely got a look at the upstairs at all and I didn't get to see the picture he was talking about. But, it kind of sounds like the sort of thing that might be there."

"Why don't you just go in and look for it, if you're interested at all?"

"Not so easy to do if you aren't a member. But ya' never know, I might be able to weasel my way in that far somehow."

By now we were in the thick of the living room crowd. The session players were pounding out the tunes; there was a dense mob clustered around the long tables with the food and drink.

Suddenly, it was as though the whole party was holding its breath. There was a longer than usual pause between tunes. The chatter ebbed away to a bare murmur. The front door clunked open and Tommy Mc-Cracken and his whole retinue burst in upon the scene. A dozen hands reached out to shake his in the first few moments of his attendance.

People that had attended the concert voiced their approval, old friends touched base, introduction to the players in the band were made, if at all needed. Fresh supplies of food and booze were miraculously conjured up in an eerily biblical fashion.

The tunes started fresh with a newfound vigor. Jenny watched all with an amused expression.

McCracken was smothered by The Widow's greetings on a level reserved for those more intimate than old friends. The band was escorted to the food and drink with gracious deference.

With plate and cup in hand, Tommy finally spied us and made his way over.

"Ah, just so, the lovely Jenny with three R's, and the savior of my sad shoulders and back. How are you charming young folks making out this evening? I trust Bobby arranged for you to get into the affair all right? It was a grand hall, to be sure. Wonderful sound system from the stage, anyway. We sounded like a host of angels in the monitors, I would have to say. Splendid it was, just splendid. And didn't the old box just work a treat. I can't thank you enough."

All this was delivered while facing me but looking at Jenny.

I said, "We got in no problems, thanks to Bob. Great tunes, lots of them I don't think I've ever heard before. Good fun. Sad about the rotten weather, though. I'm sure that more folks would have turned out if they weren't worried about floating away on the highways. Still, a good show."

"Thanks, thanks, I'm sure you're right about the rain, but as for me, I give it no mind at all. All the more reason to remain indoors and enjoy other pursuits, eh?"

This was delivered with a bit of a leer at Jenny and a wink at me. I expected to get some negative reaction from the leeree, but instead she gave a laugh and said, "Dear God, you guys are all the same aren't you? No surprises from any of you. Say, Soren, weren't you gonna' ask this guy about the accordion player?"

Tommy perked up a bit and waited expectantly.

'Right. I was pretty entertained with your story about the Irish fellow at the turn of the century and his real or imagined powers and difficulties. Any chance you have any more details to add to that? I might be the last person in San Francisco to have heard about this fellow. Big Jim Sullivan, in the kitchen there, claims he even met the man himself way back in the forties or so. My interest is piqued."

"Alas, all the facts available are those that I gave you. If you can imagine, I think Joey Conroy might have had a glass or two in him when he told the story to me. I'm afraid that if you need more of the tale, you'll have to hunt for it yourself. But, on a more positive note, perhaps we should step over to the sideboard and have another celebratory drink in honor of my repaired squeezebox."

"The honor would be all mine."

The crowd parted as Tommy strode over to the whisky supply, and I managed to squeeze through in his wake. After a toast or two of decent but not great whisky, I was about to suggest that he and I find one of the less riotous rooms and have a few tunes together, when the front door burst open and a pink-haired girl in her mid-twenties pretty much stopped the session cold. She had Doc Marten work boots on, and horizontally striped stockings that ended in old-fashioned garters long before the hem of her skimpy skirt, which was a shocking pink to match her hair. She had a powerful bosom, which she almost covered with a leather bustier.

Without preamble, she whipped open her small accordion case and removed her instrument, a delicate looking French Chanterelle two row box. The straps were made of chrome chains and leather and allowed the box to hang low in front of her like a rock star's electric guitar.

She started playing a French song called "La Bastringue" and stomping her boots and singing at the top of her voice. The session meekly followed her lead.

Tommy was slack jawed with astonishment. I saw the chance of a couple of choice tunes together fly out the window.

Jenny was pretty impressed with the new player as well. "Hey, I know her. I've seen her playing on the street down by the Embarcadero. Man, she really likes to put on the whole show out there. From the little I've seen, I'd say she makes a fair amount of money from tips."

"That's how she makes her living. That, and playing gigs with her band, which I'm sure will show up at any moment. They're probably still in the van drinking up all the alcohol they brought with them, just in case there might not be enough to drink in here."

"Wow, that thing sure is loud."

"All the better for the street, my dear."

At this point, we were far out on the fringes of the serious tune playing. Suddenly, Sloane flew around the corner from the kitchen and literally threw herself at me. She was laughing in a demented kind of way, and I had to step back to avoid being knocked over and flattened. It appeared as though she might have had a run-in with the cocktail table, or maybe the washing machine. For a girl that didn't generally tolerate loopy drunks, she certainly acted like she was well on the way.

She made several half-hearted attempts to give me big slobbery kisses, which I avoided easily. I said, "Say, I wonder if we might not find old Sean and perhaps set a course for the city. I think Sloane here got into the catnip, or something."

Jenny turned without a word and went to search out Sean. She didn't look particularly upset, but she didn't exactly look overjoyed, either.

It didn't take long for us to gather up our stuff, say goodbye to anyone that might notice we had gone, and depart. Sean opted to drive, and Jenny offered to sit in the back seat with Sloane in case she might need someone to hang onto her while she heaved up out the window. I took this as a rather good sign, not exhibiting a jealous nature. Of course, if she happened to let go of Sloane while she was hanging out the window, my opinion would have been totally reversed.

As it was, we made the west side of the bridge with little drama. Sean did a masterful job of piloting. Sloane managed to keep up a continual stream of mumbling all the way over, and Jenny and I held hands over the seat. Sean glided over to Vallejo and the police station. This was not exactly the place either of us wanted to linger over long, drunk or sober, so he ditched us with a minimum of fanfare and rumbled off to deposit Sloane in her cozy bed, alone, I was pretty certain. She would be in no mood for any shenanigans come the morning, and I think that neither of us wanted to be in the same part of town with her and her hangover.

This left Jenny and I standing outside her car in the frosty drizzle.

"So, I suppose I should offer to drive you over to your shop, or to your house, or wherever it is that bikers go in the dark part of the night."

"Well, I'd hate to put you out at all, but I am in a bit of a pickle here. Unfortunately, I live way the hell out there in the Richmond. But, without trying to sound creepy or anything, if you are anxious about your apartment situation and want to give it a pass tonight, you could stay at my house."

Her look of sheer disbelief was almost worth the near certain ass-chewing I was about to receive. At least I knew she couldn't straight out kill me so near the police station.

I went on, "No, really, I have this whole house with heat and a shower and at least one extra room that's not full of junk. Hot water. Clean towels. Privacy. I swear to God, I won't try to compromise your reputation. Not tonight, anyway."

I seriously doubted if my reassurances were doing anything for her, but she did say, "Shit, I'm freezing, let's get in the car, at least."

We climbed over the junk that had fallen into the front seats from the back and Jenny started the car to get what heat could be had. The windows were completely soaked on the outside and fogged up on the inside. The defroster blasted full on for a few minutes before conversation was possible.

She said, "Listen, Sam or Soren, whatever, I've had enough sudden relationship disasters to last me a lifetime. I might not be the sharpest chisel in the toolbox, but to jump into something like this when feeling needy and confused about shit is, in my experience, the worst possible thing to do. Plus, I'd say you have that Sloane girl gunning for you.

While you guys were playing and we were spying through that house, all she was on about was Soren this and Soren that. She might be a late bloomer, but I think she's not gonna' give up too easily. I don't mind driving you home to east jerkwater, but I don't think any pajama parties are happening tonight."

"Once again, take it easy. Will ya'? Just because I happen to have a few motorbikes, and I also happen to squeeze out a few tunes now and again, it doesn't mean I'm a raving sex maniac. I'm a big boy and can control myself if I have to. In any case, I had a really good time with you today at lunch, and at the concert and party, but I wouldn't attempt to predict where this might go. However, wherever it goes, I don't think it's going there tonight. I do have the house, and it is reasonably clean, for a guy living alone, and you would be welcome there. If you want, I'll even screw around in the garage until you get all nice and cozy and settled. It'll be just like a hotel that's free, and where there might be goofy stuff in strange places. You know they have those, and people pay big bucks to stay in them."

I'm not sure if it was the heat that finally seeped into the interior of the car, or my flashy wit, but Jenny started to giggle. Then she said, "Ah, fuck it, let's go. But no funny stuff, get it?"

"Fine, no funny stuff it is."

Just as we pulled out of the parking space, several cops came out of the building perhaps interested in who might be idling their car for so long in that spot, and what they might be doing inside. I waved at them as we sailed by, and interpreted the timing as another good omen.

Over the river and through the woods, or in this case, through the city and all the way up Geary Street, we went.

Jenny's driving had a decidedly New York metropolitan style to it. She accelerated hard, braked hard, changed lanes fluidly and rapidly, and anticipated holes in traffic to slip into. The old Toyota tried gamely to keep up with her demands. I wondered if there were any correlation between her driving and her sex life, and then immediately put the thought out of my head as too dangerous.

I directed her up the streets until we pulled into my driveway, quite quietly, by my standards. Jenny parked up behind Big Red and turned off the ignition. We sat there for a minute reveling in the warmth that the heater had finally grudgingly produced.

Jenny said, "So, what, you live here all alone? "

"Yeah, that's the case, alright. I lived here as a kid. A few years ago my folks decided that it was too foggy and clammy in San Francisco, so they moved down to Baja to be near my mom's folks. Instead of selling the place, I moved out of the hovel where I lived and moved back in. I took over paying the mortgage and send them some extra cash that they live off. Even with all that, it comes out pretty cheap. It's the only way a guy with a job like mine can afford to live around here. I suppose there's a chance they might someday decide to move back, but I kinda' doubt it. Sean lived here with me for a while, but he found it took him too long to get to his job in the morning. Not to mention that he's a complete slob. Good natured, but slobby. It might not be exactly the perfect time to mention this, but I was actually thinking of trying to find another room-mate so I could send the folks a little more dough each month."

"Oh fer cripes sake, let's not get ahead of ourselves, here. Remember, you're staying in the garage for a while, right?"

"Oh, yeah, the garage. No problem, let's just get in out of the cold for now. "

I grabbed my box, and stood there with open arms while Jenny hand-ed me her tool roll, backpack, another unidentified bag of stuff, and a sleeping bag.

"You know, you might not actually need the bag, I have sheets and blankets, just like regular people do."

"Oh really, I've seen enough single guy places that claimed to have that stuff to know that there's a wide credibility gap there. Unless your parents left that stuff here, did they?"

"Well, actually, they might have."

"I'll just bring in the bag for insurance, OK?"

She locked up the Toyota and we went up the stairs to the front door. I unlocked it and stepped aside so she could enter first.

Once inside, I looked over the living room with a stranger's eye, and it didn't look too bad. Perhaps a little over cluttered with accordion bits and goofy motorbike pieces, but at least most of the stuff was on shelves.

Jenny surveyed the room while I turned the heat on high. She walked over to a shelf where I had placed a number of over polished pieces of a Brough Superior SS100 motorcycle.

She said, "What's up here? This looks like a kind of altar or something. Are you really that freaky about motorcycles?"

"Oh, well, yeah, sort of. Most guys that are into the old bikes have an unattainable Holy Grail, and mine happens to be the 1932 Brough Superior, to be exact. Over the years I've come across small bits at swap meets and places like that, and just collected 'em. I doubt I'll ever have enough to even start putting one together, but I guess you never know. Hope springs eternal. One time I actually ran into a guy that had the exact bike, all disassembled, and was ready to get rid of it. I gave him this number to call, and when he did, he got my mom on the phone. She was taking down the details of the bike, and when he got to the price part, she had a hemorrhage. The guy was asking $5,000 for the basket case, and my mom said that I never would or could pay $5,000 for anything, much less a basket case. She told him to piss off and never call here again, and sister, that was that. Of course, she was totally right, I've never had that much money all at once, especially way back then. But right after that, the same bikes went through the roof, up to about 100,000 English pounds. Which reduced my chances of getting one, somewhat."

"Tough luck, there, I like the sound of your Mom though."

I laughed and went into the kitchen to put on the teakettle, while Jenny further investigated my collections of crap. Every once in a while I could hear her laugh or give a "Yuck" over some aspect of the décor.

When the kettle had boiled, and the tea was made, I called her into the kitchen to sit at the old Formica table and pour while I canvassed the fridge and cupboards for snacks.

The fridge yielded little in the way of late night snacks. Some strange dried meat products, some Basque cheese, some small hot peppers stuffed with anchovies and a selection of left over Chinese and Indian dinner boxes. I settled with only removing the milk.

The cupboards held more in the way of cookie and shortbread remnants. I arranged what there was artistically on a plate, and then scored the fantastic find of an unopened bag of Milky Way bite sized candy bars, left over from Halloween.

The cookie bits and shreds didn't excite Jenny too much, but her eyes lit up when she saw the Milky Ways.

"Hey, you read my mind! So, quit doing that right away, or else!"

"All part of my plan. Of which the next part is to check the spare room to make sure I didn't leave any incriminating evidence lying around, and to get down the big blanket. Fluff up the pillows, and like that."

I went up the stairs to the next level and snagged a clean towel out of the hall closet on the way. I put the towel in the bathroom and checked the sink and shower drain for clogs of hairs, and even dug out a fresh toothbrush out of the drawer where my mom had stockpiled them a few years before.

The spare room was relatively tidy, I only had to shovel a ton of books and papers off the bed, and kick them into the closet to make it presentable. I pulled a large comforter off the top shelf and folded it at the foot of the bed. An all out welcoming effort on my part, I thought.

I returned to the kitchen to find my tea lukewarm and the bag of Milky Ways half gone. I thought best not to make any sarcastic remarks at that point.

"So, the room is first on the left, up the stairs, the bathroom connects. As per our deal, I'm gonna' check the garage and see if there's any exceptionally interesting things I can do out there. Seeing as how there's no heat out there, I might not be interested too long. Do you have everything that you need to feel cozy, warm and secure?"

Jenny gave me an appraising look and said, "I'm not feeling too threatened right now, so I think I'm cool. I have to get into the shop right around nine o'clock or the head jerk down there starts squeaking. I assume you have about the same schedule, 'cause I've seen you in the neighborhood around then. Shall we adjourn this 'till the morning?"

"Consider it done."

Jenny gathered up her belongings and headed up the stairs. I admired the last view. I went into the chilly garage and looked over the sad motorcycle cases that lived there. With the Norton still downtown, there was a bit of extra room, and I tried to figure out which of the old beasts I would try to work up next. I had a couple of AJS 500c.c. single-cylinder bikes from the early 50's, a newer Norton Commando with the motor completely blown up, a BMW from the 80's with strange elusive issues, and an older BMW that had almost circumnavigated the globe before succumbing to rust, oxidation, and mechanics in India. All worthy cases guaranteed to not make any money.

I touched them all to let them know I was still thinking of them, rearranged a few odd boxes of parts, and let my body temperature dip alarmingly before deciding that Jenny had had plenty of time to get wet, dry and safely into bed.

I killed the lights in the garage, turned off the heat and left a single light on in the kitchen before heading up the stairs to my room.

I enjoyed a shower in the "cleaner than before" bathroom and hit the sack.

All was completely quiet. No TV, no radio, no calls for emergency foot massages. I thought to myself, "just as well", and dropped off to sleep mulling over the strange information and circumstances of the day.

CHAPTER

MY internal "get up and go surf-ing" clock went off at six a.m. as usual. I stood on the box on the balcony and looked through the crack between the trees across the street to scout the waves. The fog was far too thick to allow me to see even a bit of the break, and the instant blue tinge on my boxer-clad body was enough to drive me back indoors pretty quick. I crawled back in bed to warm up for just a second.

The next thing that I knew, Jenny was banging on my door and saying something loud like, " Hey Bubba, if you want a ride downtown, you gotta' get up – like, now. It's 7:30 and I have to eat soon or my blood sugar is gonna' hit zero."

It took me a second to figure out who that could possibly be, and then reorganize the chain of last night's events. While doing that, I jumped up and threw on some warm duds. She was still banging on the door when I emerged fully garbed and ready for action.

She gave me the look reserved for the last one out of their bunk at summer camp.

"What? I was up ages ago, I was just tidying up some paper work, or something."

"Really, well in any case, I already checked out your fridge and the cupboards, and pal, you got nothin' for breakfast. Let's go out."

I heartily agreed, and as I forgot to buy the coffee I so desperately needed the day before, I said that we might hit a local café, just to get started down the road.

Jenny had reverted to the heavy overalls and Giants jacket of the day before. I noticed that her new cap bore the logo of Colt Firearms. I wondered if there was something about her I had misjudged.

Having a plan, I grabbed my box, and Jenny her tools, assorted belongings, and sleeping bag, and we jammed back into the old Toyota.

The starter barely had the energy or will to turn the feeble engine over. I thought that there was no way we were going anywhere, but Jenny had infinite trust in the ability of the act of turning the key harder to help the starter. Sure enough, eventually the beast grumbled to life.

I thought I might take the necessary warming-up period as an opportunity to scrape some of the more visually challenging patches of crusty gunk off the windows. I got out my already useless Mastercard and went to work on the outside. My fingers were a dead, frozen white when I returned to the passenger seat. Jenny commented that they looked like a corpse's hands. I said I thought the phenomena might be related to immersion in cold salt water for long periods of time over many years. She shook her head and said that was doubtless the case.

We skipped over to Balboa and east a bit and stopped at an older, tie-dye, dreadlocks café called Simple Pleasures. I had eaten breakfast there before and thought it was just too damn healthy feeling. Not enough salt, grease, fat and cholesterol. But their coffee had a kind of slap in the face quality about it that often was just enough to propel me over the hill and downtown.

Jenny stayed in the idling car while I ran in for the java. The guy at the counter looked like he was trying to see inside my aura or something as he took my money for a couple of larges to go. He made a hand sign that looked like a guard against the evil eye, which gave me the creeps. I hoped that he didn't know something that he wasn't sharing with me.

Back in the car, which was starting to warm up a bit, Jenny said, "Based on your previous performance, and the recommendations of your friends, I should be prepared for you to pour coffee all over me, or drown my stuff in it. Any chance we could use both hands and take little sips?"

"Oh come on, I hardly ever spill stuff."

Having said that, I secretly tested the lid of the cup, and held on with both hands. Just to get them warm, I told myself.

As we headed back over to Geary, the fog-bound leaden sky opened up and allowed a ton of water or so to pour down on us.

The leprous wiper blades did little to clear the window, and I suspected that Jenny was driving more by intuition and impression than actual observation.

We flew across town sending up sheets of spray. I tried to think of the perfect breakfast joint, but was having a hard time concentrating on anything except hanging on to my coffee cup during anxious hydroplaning episodes.

In the end, I guess Jenny had already made up her mind in that respect, as she drove straight to Mel's, on Lombard, and parked in the lot.

"I hope this place meets with your approval. I've always had good breakfasts here, and it sure is easier to park here than a lot of other places down in North Beach. Whadda ya say?"

"Sure, totally good with me. As long as they have decent beers on tap."

Jenny gave me a horrified look, which was worth the price of having to say, "Just joking, just joking, relax, I'm not even half that far gone. Let's get inside, we're getting soaked."

The morning crush was well underway, but we managed to get a two-person booth far enough from the front door not to freeze every time somebody came or went.

Further cups of coffee and bacon and eggs over easy with sourdough were ordered all around. While we waited I said, "So, Jenny, back to that stuff in the basement of your building, any chance of a guy getting in there to give it a look? I'm getting more and more curious about this mythical Irish accordion guy. Not that there's any connection, that would be too much to ask, but anything down there that has to do with the old box makers would be pretty interesting."

"Yeah, well, we'll see how things go in there today. If I kill somebody, I'll have to leave town very suddenly. And I just might have to do that. I don't have anything against looking down there, but I'm sure if those A-holes thought anybody was interested in that stuff, it would become gold in their eyes. Give me your work number again and I'll try to call you later. You never know, it might be worth a dinner or something to the right person."

I certainly liked the direction she was taking, but the arrival of our food stopped our conversation for a while. It was getting close to work time when we were done, so I paid the bill and we headed out.

It didn't take too long to shoot down Lombard to Van Ness and zip through the Broadway Tunnel. We turned down Montgomery and Jenny pulled to the curb to let me out at Pacific. I ducked my head back into the car to tell her that we would be in touch, but nearly lost it as she suddenly spied a break in the traffic and took off. I jumped back onto the curb and marveled at the way the old Toyota responded to her flogging.

By the time I reached the coffee shop, my regular jacket was sopping wet. I couldn't explain why I didn't wear a raincoat, or at least a wind-breaker, but I didn't.

Big Chris was there as usual and said, "Sam, you look like a drowned cat. You didn't have to sleep out in the rain, did you? I think you need a free pass today. No charge. Say, did you ever find the guy you were asking about last night? I been keeping my eye out, but haven't seen him yet today."

"Girl, actually, and yes, I did find her. She's pretty well put together underneath all that working clothes stuff. Quite nice looking, I'd have to say."

"Guy, girl, whatever, here start with this."

He handed me a large to-go cup with a double shot of savage looking espresso in the bottom of it.

I filled the remainder of the cup from the urn and dumped in some 1/2 and 1/2, which did little or nothing to change the color of the brew. I thanked Chris for his thoughtful gesture and headed for the front door. Chris yelled after me, "Hey, Sam, did you get lucky last night with that person? Hey, Sam."

I pretended not to hear or see that the rest of the patrons had turned to stare at me. I fled out the front door.

As I walked down the alley, I noticed a young, dark-haired fellow, heavily swathed in rain resistant gear, taking pictures of the front of my building with an expensive-looking digital camera. The alley was pretty narrow and closed off at the other end, so I was kind of surprised when the guy tucked his camera away and hurried off down the alley when he caught sight of me. I didn't really think anything of it at the time, though.

I unlocked one side of the doors and slipped inside to minimize the amount of rain that accompanied me. With the lights off, it was really dark in there, only a couple of skylights with a century of crud built up on the outside to illuminate the interior. I didn't need lights to find my way around, so I strode boldly in the direction of the master switch box. I discovered with my shins the large chunks of what I assumed to be the engine block of an Italian sports car that Vladimir had thoughtfully left in the aisle.

A few years earlier, during a slow streak in the motorcycle restoration business, I had allowed some of my regular customers with deeper pockets than most to bring in parts of the engines of their collectable cars to be resurrected. One thing led to another and soon there were entire motors waiting to be stripped and rebuilt. I cursed the space they took up and the focus they diverted from bikes, but "business is business".

I may have said "Oh My" or something like that, but I hobbled forward until I was able to hit the switch. The light revealed the motor of a low level Ferrari on the dolly we used to wheel those things around the shop. Why Vladimir would have left it precisely there was anybody's guess. It looked none the worse for wear, unlike my shins. I knew that they were already bruised and bloodied by the Norton, so I didn't bother to look.

I opened the accordion case and took out my box to sit on the bench, just in case some stray rainwater might have found its way inside. I didn't want the already fragile and stressed hide glue joints to be subjected to the excess damp. I regarded the hasty duct tape repair and thought again of getting Jenny to take the box apart and repair it properly as a way to acceptably slip her some cash.

I sipped away at the coffee, only my third dose of the day, and surveyed the board trying to decide on the jobs of the day. After a short while, I rummaged through my desk to find the mangled address book again. I casually started flipping through the pages starting with the A's. Many names were considered and rejected before I finally found, "Joe Leary, that's our man."

My goal had been to find someone who might have been a member of the Bohemian Club, and might also be amenable to getting me inside to look at the photo that Big Jim had alluded to. I thought Joe might have been, or was still, in the club. He was a writer by trade, and having grown up in the Richmond district, he was also a surfer and motorcyclist. His brother Tim was closer in age to myself, but I had run into Joe many times. I recalled that he had written a play or something that the Bohemians had performed at their conclave on the Russian River, and he was mightily proud of the fact. According to Joe, they only performed their shows once, and it sounded like a lot of work for one shot to me, but who was I to judge.

I dialed Joe's number and was surprised when he answered the phone.

"Joe, Soren Rauhe here. Tim's buddy."

We chatted for a short while about surfing and bikes and the old neighborhood before I got to the point.

"So, Joe, are you still a member of that club, the Bohemians? I kind of remember that you were."

"Sure I am. Once you're in there, it's worth it to keep it up if you can. I haven't been working for a while, so I don't go down there for dinner too much, but I have drinks there pretty often. Why, are you going to chew my ass out for being a Republican or something?"

"As far as your politics, that's up to you, but a guy I know said he saw a photo on the wall there that I'm really interested in looking at. It's a turn of the century thing with a couple of accordion players in it. Ring any bells?"

"Accordion players? Not really, but I've walked past them pictures so many times I don't even see them any more. Do you want me to take a look next time I'm in there?"

" Better yet, how about you get me in there and I'll look at it myself."

"I suppose that would work, if you could come up with a jacket and tie. Not exactly lofty goals, but if I remember correctly, you don't really have to dress up for work, do you?"

"No I don't dress up for work Mr. Wage Slave, but I have a jacket. At least I can get one, so there. When would be good for you?"

"Let's see, today's Thursday, so tonight would be just right. They always have a band or a show on Tuesdays and Thursdays. We could meet down there at 7:00 or so. No dungarees, either, if you look like a slob, out you go!"

"Jeez, Joe, give me at least a little credit, will ya? How much money should I bring, I don't want to run out of funds in the middle of a cocktail."

"No cash transactions there, it's all on a numbered slip. I'll treat you to dinner, for the sake of the neighborhood, and because my Honda Pacific Coast motorbike needs some work. I'm sure you can handle that, right?"

Inwardly I groaned; working on a modern bike that had body work completely covering the motor and running gear was a real pain in the butt for me. It took half the day to get to the real problem, but I said, "It would be my pleasure to assist you in that regard. See you at seven."

The only detail I had to deal with was where to actually get a jacket and tie that more or less fit me.

Sean was totally out due to his scrawny build, even if he did have a jacket, which I seriously doubted. I couldn't think of any other guys my size that had to dress up on a regular basis. For some reason, most of the guys I knew that had the thick shoulders and lumpy upper arms weren't too deep in dress-up clothes.

I figured my best bet was to fly over to the Salvation Army Chinatown Corps thrift shop on Powell and see what was available. I grabbed a messenger style backpack, rolled the Norton out onto the sidewalk and locked up the shop. The rain had eased up a bit and I thought sarcastically a few blocks worth of moisture might be good for me.

Good or not, I was certainly moist by the time I wheeled the bike up onto the sidewalk in front of the thrift shop. There was a small marquee that I managed to get the bike mostly under without completely obstructing the door.

Predictably, the place was hopping with elderly, and not so elderly, Asian customers poring over the piles of freshly delivered clothing.

The men's suit rack had scores of possibilities. I spotted a nice Harris Tweed jacket and tried it on. With only one arm in, I was stuck and had to flail around to "de-jacket" myself. I vowed to be more selective.

Half an hour into the search, I happened onto a Ralph Lauren western-cut suit in stark black. Jacket, pants, vest, and even a black tie on the hanger left only a dressy shirt to round out the disguise. I tried on the jacket and it slipped on with nary a bind. I could button it! Still a little tight through the shoulders, but I didn't think that I'd have to do any strenuous work while wearing it.

I found a white work shirt more or less my size, which still had some sort of insignia patch sewn on the sleeve. I figured nobody would ever see that, so I gathered it up and headed for the checkout.

There was a spate of furious Asian bargaining going on in front of me. From the sound of the negotiations neither party was going to back down or alter their respective offers. I had almost decided to hide the suit in some out of the way spot in the store and try to come back for it later, when a sympathetic employee opened a second checkout line.

The elderly African-American clerk beckoned me to another register and started adding up the total. He observed, "Say, man, it looks like you made a good score here. Gonna' go out and charm them ladies, eh? I ain't sure about that shirt, though. Gotta' get them patches off it, get a good pressin', might do in a pinch."

"You're right about the shirt, pal, but I figure I can wear it to work if the high finance world don't work out for me. I think I'd need more than a suit to charm the females. There's always a chance, though. It's what keeps us going, eh?"

He chuckled and we shared a good laugh. He rummaged around underneath the counter and came up with a large, plastic shopping bag to keep the newfound suit of success partially dry. I paid and crammed the bag into my backpack where it was sure to remain wrinkle free.

The high stakes wheeling and dealing was still in full swing as I exited the store to see a parking meter cop just pulling up and eying my bike with a determined look. She hit the parking brake of her three-wheeled scooter and put her official uniform wet weather cap on. She was at least my height and probably out weighed me by 30 pounds. Curly black hair poked out from underneath her dripping brim. It may have been the first time I had seen a rain poncho look a bit snug.

I pretended not to see her as she got her ticket book out and ambled towards the bike. I hurriedly crammed the helmet down onto my head, turned on the gas and commenced kicking. The bike, naturally, refused to even poop. Frantic kicks with the throttle wide open, closed, choke on and off had absolutely no result. Finally, worn out and clammy, I had to rest. The cop circled the bike with me astride it. She said, "Norton, is it? What year is that, '67, '68? Atlas, I guess."

I pulled off the helmet and said between gasps, "It's a Mercury, 650, '69. The last of the Featherbeds, and almost the very last one made. It ran fine when I came here, I don't know what's wrong."

She twiddled her pen and said her dad had ridden a Norton in the 60's, and how much she had loved going on rides in the country. After a bit more chat about bikes in general she casually inquired whether or not I was acquainted with the fact that parking on the sidewalk was generally frowned upon.

I agreed that most of the populace should keep off the sidewalk and how unfortunate that she had spied me just as I had rolled the bike under the marquis from its previous perfectly legal parking spot. Just to get it started out of the rain, it was understood.

She gave me a hard, forbidding stare then cracked up laughing. She said she hoped that once I turned on the ignition switch, the bike would come to life so that I wouldn't be a bad example to the parkers of San Francisco for too much longer.

I glanced down to the frame-mounted switch and, sure enough, it remained in the "Off" position. I cursed myself for being an idiot and thought I probably deserved to get a ticket. I thought this to myself, of course.

The parking queen moved off, apparently done with me, and motored up the block in search of scofflaws with less interesting vehicles.

The incessant rain had slackened for a moment, so I pushed the bike off its stand and bumped it over the curb into the street. I knew the futility of kicking it further in its massively flooded state, so I just waited for a break in traffic and pushed off down the gently sloping hill. Making sure the ignition was switched on, I dropped the clutch in second gear and after a few skids and slides, the rear wheel began to turn and the motor fired soon after. I reversed direction uphill and made a beeline back to the shop before the weather had a chance to change its mind and drench me again.

As I arrived back in Jerome Alley, I saw Vladimir strolling up Pacific, giant coffee cup in hand, talking to every chance stranger on the street. It was only ten o'clock, so I really couldn't fault him too much for tardiness as I was just getting in myself. I did have time to get the door open, the Norton inside out of the weather, and the new outfit hung up to shake out the wrinkles before he finally walked in the shop.

"Tovarich! Is lovely day, yes? Many fresh opportunities."

"And the same to you, comrade. Would there be any chance you could wheel the stray motors out of the middle of the path so I don't kill myself in the dark? My shins are all crusted with blood what with the Norton kicker and that Ferrari unit there."

"Is best way to remember to finish the job, no? Leaving motors for first thing in morning."

"If you consider ten o'clock 'first thing in the morning', then perhaps. Better would be to leave yourself a note, or something."

"Da, maybe."

I tried to concentrate on the ancient Royal Enfield's motor, but my mind kept wandering back to the evening spent with Jenny and the Irish accordion mystery. I was intrigued by Big Jim's statement that the first accordion maker in San Francisco had been an Irishman. That was news to me, as I had assumed that all the makers, first, last, and in-between had been Italian. I rummaged through my addled memory banks for any accordion history lore. I came up blank and resigned myself to actually having to do some research if I was going to find out anything about the historical aspects of the squeezebox business.

The whole question faded from my mind as I got more and more of the motorbike apart and onto the workbench. I had a running list of problems that I discovered and after a while it probably would have been easier just to make a whole new bike from scratch.

There were a few phone calls but none were from Jenny. Vladimir went out on an errand and came back with more coffee and even one for me. The day passed full of actual working and even marginal progress in certain quarters, without drama.

It must have been around five o'clock when Jenny called. Vladimir answered the phone and handed it to me saying, "Is girlfriend."

I snatched the receiver out of his hand and in my most businesslike manner said, "Good afternoon, Ms. Farrar. How are things in the phony antique business today? Looking up, I hope."

"Not exactly, the boss here is getting really squirrelly about where the stuff is going, and I might have grossly underestimated the amount of this stuff he's sold. There's only one other guy here that's almost human, and from what he hinted to me, this guy could have made millions from this scam, several millions in fact. This guy acts like he's getting ready to blow the whistle somehow. Listen, we have to talk. Can I pick you up after work?"

"Alas, I have to go meet a guy who agreed to get me into the Bohemian club tonight. I think there is going to be dinner around seven, so we could meet after I get done there. Say, around ten thirty or so? I could wait at the clubhouse up on Taylor and you could pick me up there, if that's OK."

"Yeah, I guess so. I suppose I can find someplace to hang out till then. The whole apartment situation isn't much better than the work situation. We'll chat about all that later. I'll see you at ten thirty in front of that place. They do let women drive on the street in front of there, don't they?"

"I think there was an amendment to their charter to allow that. I'll be the guy in the swank Ralph Lauren suit."

We hung up. I felt good just having talked to Jenny, even though whatever was on her mind didn't exactly fill me with optimistic joy. Vladimir smirked at me as he tidied up his bench and made a big show of shoving any possible shin buster out of the middle of the aisle.

As six o'clock rolled around, I thought I might start getting my costume on. I scrubbed the eternal grease as far out of my pores as I could stand, and traded my flannel shirt and jeans for the black suit and white shirt. The pants fit well enough, slightly snug around the equator, but the shirt might have been made for me, by virtue of actually being a work shirt, I surmised. The vest actually buttoned up the front after I had released the adjusting straps in the back to their ultimate degree, and the coat didn't hinder my movements nearly as much as I had anticipated. As I tried to button the top of the shirt, I nearly passed out from lack of oxygen. Clearly a casual fit affair. I tied the tie with a four-in-hand knot just the way my dad showed me in the misty, distant past. With the knot shoved up high, no one could tell that my top button was hanging loose, I thought.

I sashayed out of the back room and Vladimir gave me an appraising look.

"Is good. Not like suits in Soviet Union, but for big guy, not too bad."

I considered this high praise indeed, and as I locked the doors, Vladimir fetched his eight-year-old Lexus from its super secret parking spot, and we headed down Montgomery to Pine and over to Taylor.

I jumped out of the car at Pine and Taylor just as the misty afternoon turned into a rainy night, so I slinked down the hill under cover of awnings as much as I could. As I climbed the steps to the massive front doors, I was overtaken by a group of seven or eight men on their way in as well. I was slightly apprehensive having to check into the club carrying a bag with all of my regular clothes in it and the accordion case, but need not have been. We entered together and deposited our raincoats and, in my case, slicker, in a cloakroom. I set the accordion case on a shelf over the coats and after briefly worrying about the security of the club, I turned and reentered the entry area. All of the men that I had come in with had blithely strolled down the foyer and I was tempted to do the same, but instead, I told my name to the fellow sitting behind the desk and he certified that an actual member was expecting me. A short phone conversation and Joe was waltzing down the hall to greet me.

I was beside myself with anticipation to get a look at the source of all the recent fables and myths. And to get a drink at what was reputed to be the longest bar in San Francisco.

CHAPTER

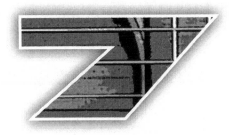

JOE hadn't changed too much since I had last seen him around the neighborhood. Thinner on top, perhaps, and a bit thicker in the middle like most of us. His complexion went quite a ways towards substantiating the 'more drinks than dinners at the club' line he had given me. He waltzed down the hall greeting everyone with his hand out and a big smile on his face. I theorized he might have been at the bar a bit before my arrival. Everybody seemed glad to see him, shake his hand, or pat him on the back.

I remembered how Joe had been a few years older than our gang and whatever he did we were bound to do as well. By watching him, we had found the best spots to paddle out at Ocean Beach and perhaps not get pounded by the waves, and the best spots to line up for great rides. Whatever mischief and trouble he got into, Tim would report to us and we would have to try it ourselves. Luckily he never got thrown into jail for too long or I'm sure we would have done time as well.

Joe was several inches shorter than myself, but his expansive attitude made him appear much taller. He finally made his way to the end of the hall and turned to the guy at the reception table, "Say, I thought you said a guy named Soren was here for me. I don't see him at all."

The gray-haired door-keeper slowly looked up from whatever paperwork he was involved with, gave Joe a bit of a look, and then pointed wordlessly at me with his pen.

Joe whipped around dramatically and stared at me. After scrutinizing my outfit with care, he said, "Sam, is that you? I know it's been a while, but Jeez, what happened? You used to be such a snot-nosed punk, how'd you get so old? A little overdressed, aren't you? All I said you needed was a jacket, a tie, and a clean pair of pants. You look like you just robbed a gigolo from the eighties of his clothes. Not bad, though, in fact; it's great to see you."

He reached out and pumped my hand for an overlong time. I had pretty much expected some sort of slagging greeting, and the one I got was pretty mild by Richmond District surf gang standards.

"Joe, thanks for getting me in here, I can see already that you are the most popular guy in the place. Not to mention, older than most of these guys, sort of a father figure, right?"

Joe grinned and chuckled, "Nah, they're mostly way older dudes in here. Some younger guys, but they generally show up at the campouts, not so much here. They just look younger 'cause that's what too much cash on hand does to you."

He glanced at the hand he was still shaking, and grimaced at the remaining grime. He looked up and grinned.

"But, enough chit chat, lets get a drink!"

He spun on his heel and led the way down a hallway of dark wood paneling that was covered almost completely over with stylishly framed photos of historic, picturesque, comic, and otherwise notable members.

Halfway down the length of the hall his arm flashed out and pointed to a wide photo. Without breaking stride, he said, "I looked earlier, you can come back and check it out after, eh?"

I caught a fleeting glimpse of a two-part photo containing mostly a grove of trees and a couple of guys sitting on stumps.

"Once you're in, you're in. You can go anywhere in the place. I'll show you around once we get the important business out of the way."

We turned left at the end of the hall and entered a large, high ceilinged room that was absolutely covered with very large, framed posters. As far as I could make out at our rapid pace, they were all advertising shows that had been performed at the club or the Grove. The dates of the performances were prominent, and some of them went back to the early 1900's.

The wide mahogany bar did indeed run the length of the entire room;

I guessed it to be about eighty feet. Very impressive, and there weren't any empty spots on the backboard, either.

The bartender had seen Joe coming and had a largish vodka and tonic waiting for him by the time he hit the bar. Joe made introductions, "Paulino, this is Sam. He's drinking on my number tonight, please take care of him and don't let him drink any of the crap that I'm sure he usually drinks. My thanks are with you."

Paulino gave me a look and we shook hands to cement our relationship. While Joe went out to work the room, I looked over the bar, nodding sagely as I spotted each of the generally forbidden exotic whiskies. I figured to test Joe's status right away, assuming I would be given a limit over which I couldn't order. I spotted a bottle of the Bushmills Black Label 21 year old like the one Tommy McCracken had demolished at my shop. I decided I might as well start at the top of the heap. I said to the waiting Paulino, "I'll have a double shot of the Bushmills 21, if you don't mind."

His shocked reaction told me I had guessed right about the booze limit for guests.

"That's amazing. I don't think I've ever had someone order a double shot in here before."

As I pondered the meaning of this statement, he grabbed the bottle of Bush and a large Old Fashioned glass and filled it right up to the brim. A good six or seven shots of booze, I calculated. My glass contained a king's ransom in liquid form if ordered at a regular bar.

"Because that's our single shot!"

I was more or less convinced he was making fun of me, but never the less, I was extremely careful to sip off the overflow before walking back out to the hallway to see what I had come to see.

The hall was deserted, and the few members who passed by on their way to the restroom didn't give me a second glance.

I found the photo Joe had pointed out and sure enough, it was a black and white photo of two fellows sitting on mighty redwood stumps playing button accordions. They wore funny, pointed jester hats. One looked to be quite a bit older than the other and had his legs crossed at the knee. He was playing what looked like a pretty normal looking button accordion except it had a silver plate covering the action where most boxes had wood, and there were a few accidental buttons instead of a complete second row. The other lad had a slightly bigger, more elaborate box with mother of pearl inlayed in the top to spell out his name which was unfortunately obscured by the other man's ill placed foot. On the other surface it looked like there were inlays of naked mermaids blowing conch shell horns. The wood of the box looked like exotic burl and there was a very fancy looking grill over the mechanical part of the action. There were three rows of buttons like my Soprani, hinting they could have been a similar fingering system. The plaque under the photo said, "C.C. Keene and C.L. Miller, 1895." Behind them were a massive downed redwood tree and several smaller ones still growing.

The other side of the split-framed photo was a reproduction of the first with the same two men, however, the saplings were much larger and the men were noticeably older. No hats this time. C.C. Keene had white hair and grizzled sideburns. He looked to be in his 70's, while C.L. Miller had developed a serious drinker's nose and an expansive waistline to back it up. He looked to be not yet middle-aged, perhaps in his early 30's. They each played the accordions of the previous photo. The legend on that side of the frame said, "C.C. Keene and C.L. Miller, 1905".

So, there it was. Big Jim had said that Keene was the first accordion maker in San Francisco, although, I couldn't imagine how he might have known. Using my keen sense of deduction, I guessed that the lad whom Conroy had met must have been C.L. Miller. I had never heard of either of them. I'm not sure what I had imagined finding out, just by looking at a photo, but I was a little disappointed to only have learned their names.

In the relatively short time I had been in the hallway, I had made serious inroads on the large glass of whisky in my hand. I figured I had nearly reached my limit of free alcohol and friendly old neighborhood generosity. I made my slightly unsteady way over to where Joe sat at the bar chatting with some other members. As I fished out a stool trying to look casual, Joe introduced me to his mates.

"Soren, meet Moe, Robert, and Cyril. Moe here owns that chain of auto parts stores you and my brother used to steal spark plugs from."

I grimaced and the men all laughed out loud. I couldn't imagine meeting one of the founders of the store whose ads had been shouting his name at me for my entire life. We shook hands and he said that Joe was just being an asshole and no hard feelings were held.

Robert turned out to be a recognizable big wheel actor and Cyril happened to be an Episcopalian Bishop, or something like that. Joe didn't exactly come out and say I was a motorbike grease monkey who hammered out Irish tunes on the accordion, but I could see that none of the three were racking their memories trying to remember where they had last seen me.

While we were having the introductions, Paulino had come up the bar with another glass absolutely full of the precious whisky. I did a double take. "There's the other half of your double, sir."

My eyes bugged out to the entertainment of the immediate crowd.

Joe finally hustled me over to a large round table and more introductions followed. Menus were handed around and a waiter took the orders. I opted for a conservative-sounding chicken club sandwich. Wine was ordered, opened, and poured all around. Several members had an animated discussion concerning better or worse vintages of this particular varietal, and several more bottles were ordered to test the theory.

Finally, Joe got around to asking me if I had found what I had been seeking. I replied I had names, a couple of dates, and not much else. He asked how much I wanted to know. I really didn't know how to answer that. To spill the entire story would sound absurd, even to me. I decided to focus on the "First Accordion Maker in San Francisco" angle.

Joe allowed as how the club actually maintained its own library, and that perhaps there might be something in there concerning those members in question. He claimed that every member, high or low, had something in the library.

A six-piece swing band had set up on the bandstand. As we made our tipsy way through the crowd, they commenced playing fantastic sounding swing standards. Almost every person on the route got a back slap or hand shake and some comment or other. Moving through a crowd with Joe was like having your feet stuck in cement – but eventually we made our way back to the hallway and then to the library.

Joe introduced me to the librarian, whose name I was far past remembering, and stated our mission. The librarian must have had a few moments to waste as he took over the search for us. He consulted a large, red leather bound volume and immediately found the name of member C.C. Keene. Miller's name was absent at this stage.

Next to Keene's name were listed several notations the librarian said were magazine articles he had written. There was also a note that claimed he had written a memoir.

The librarian looked up in triumph. I returned what must have been a very familiar glassy stare, "Well, that's charming. If you could write down the names of the magazines and the dates, I suppose there's some chance that I could hunt them down, somehow. I don't suppose that you have those articles here in the library, do you?"

"Alas, we do not catalog single magazine articles here."

He allowed that to sink in for a moment and then added, "But we do generally have the original copies from the author. The memoir, as well, if you would like to see it."

Joe laughed again at my slow double take. The librarian was already gone in search of Keene's legacy. We sat in leather armchairs in front of a nicely drawing fireplace. I briefly wondered what peculiar zoning allowed a wood fire in downtown San Francisco. Good indirect light played on the myriad trophies, medals, paintings, and decorations that festooned the walls. I recognized the artist of a series of framed cartoons. The subject matter in this series was wildly different than that of the comics in the Sunday paper. I had always wondered what the bumbling cartoon character's hot wife might look like naked, and now I needed to wonder no more.

The librarian returned with a leather folder and a slim volume. Presumably the folder held the original transcripts of the magazine pieces and the book was Keene's memoir. He wrote down Joe's number to indicate who had called for the material, and left us alone. The time was pushing 9:45 so I figured I'd better get cracking; if only I could get my eyes to focus for more than a few seconds at a time.

Spreading the material out on the low table in front the chairs, I gathered that the magazine articles were written for a periodical that was concerned with circus life. The connection eluded me, even though accordion players had been called many animal names in the past, I didn't think that it actually qualified one to write as a circus member.

I skimmed through the hand-written letters. Clearly, they were originally intended to be private, as there were many personal asides and questions about individuals. Ten wordy letters from islands in the South Pacific had been distilled into four short articles published in an early circus trade letter.

The connection became obvious when I read that Keene had toured with a minstrel show called The Golden Gate Serenaders. They had set out from San Francisco in the fall of 1858 for a tour of the Sandwich Islands and New Zealand. The weather had conspired against them and the pain and anguish reported by Keene almost made me seasick.

Typhoons had disastrously dogged the tour at every turn. Ships were wrecked, opera houses were leveled, and long-standing engagements were cancelled. Performers died on the road. The writing became cramped and shaky. Illness was sweeping through the company. The letters were sometimes stained and runny, perhaps with tears. Keene made many disparaging and negative comments about the quality and durability of the instruments he and other performers were playing.

The company had finally returned to San Francisco, barely, and was virtually bankrupt. The letters and the articles ended there.

I looked up; Joe had a copy of the Wall Street Journal spread over his chest and appeared to be resting his eyes for a moment. The time was 10:10.

I didn't think there was any way I could safely borrow the book without creating an incident so I redoubled my efforts to skim like the wind.

I found that Keene had grown up in New York and had apprenticed with the Dobson banjo manufacturers. He had become enamored with the, then novel, accordion. Having joined the hordes traveling west to find gold, he found instead an audience for his banjo and accordion playing, joining several troupes that worked the breadth of the Barbary Coast.

I skipped over many chapters that recorded again the travails suffered by the Serenaders in the South Seas. When Keene had returned to San Francisco, he had somehow arranged to inhabit a workshop with a living space attached. He started making banjos that even he stated were similar to the Dobsons he had worked on in New York. Eventually, he began making a selection of musical instruments and kitchen gadgets, accordions included. The workshop was down around 3rd street, south of Market.

My time was running out and I still had quite a bit of the memoir to look at. I flashed forward year after year to the described shows he performed, trips and tours, medals earned at World Fairs, and such.

Finally, I came to a part that described his newly hired apprentice, C.L. Miller. Miller had recently emigrated from Ireland and had some training in the watch-making field. He was a natural craftsman and musician. He was especially adept at the construction of the accordions, and focused most of his energy there. Keene felt that success might be within his reach, but after a few years together certain elements began to change. He wrote that Miller had started frequenting places in Chinatown for various reasons. Keene reported that Miller had visited an ancient maker of Chinese swords and was trying to learn the secrets of the mystic metallurgy involved in order to incorporate them into his accordion reed making. Soon, involvement with a Chinese girl had further strained their working relationship. There were hints perhaps that opium use was involved. Keene complained that although Miller was a fantastic craftsman, his ideas and secretive nature were becoming a problem.

The chapter, and Keene's business association with Miller, ended around the time of the photo in1905. Flipping through the pages in my blurred state failed to produce any further mention of him.

The time was now 10:40 and I jumped to my feet. I shook Joe awake and stammered out, "Hey up, there, Sleepy Head. I'm runnin' a bit tardy here, so I'm gonna have to bolt. Thanks a million for the dinner, which I'm sure I'll remember later, and the drinks. No doubt I'll pay you back someday. Just bring that old motorized monster you have down to the shop and we'll look into it. There was very interesting stuff in the folder, so thanks for getting me into it. All the best, see ya."

Joe was a little unfocused as he shook my hand. I hurried down the hall to retrieve my slicker and the box, both resting comfortably where I had left them.

The door monitor merely nodded as I went out the polished brass doors. Once out into the renewed downpour, I saw Jenny's Toyota double-parked a ways up on the opposite side of the street. Traffic was very light at that hour, and I headed across the street. Water cascaded down the steep hill and despite my most agile jump, my foot landed square in the middle of the torrent. I gained the far sidewalk and trekked up the hill.

When I reached the car, the passenger door was still locked and I had to knock on the window to get Jenny to let me in. I dumped the box into a small void in the back seat clutter and slithered in. The heat was on full blast and my twelve shot double made an immediate, but fortunately unsuccessful, attempt to gain its freedom. It settled for a massive belch.

JOHN PEDERSEN

Jenny grimaced and rolled her window down, raining or not.

"Thanks for sharing that, mister suave. Yuck."

"Sorry about that, but believe me, that was the best option. Sorry about the lateness as well, I got a little involved."

"It's OK, I only got hassled by the cops a few times. They love to have old cars filled with shit double-parked in their neighborhood."

She looked long and hard at my sodden and unsteady self and observed, "Hey, are you shit-faced or what? Man, we are in serious trouble here, you've got to get with it."

I assumed she was referring to her parking issues, which, frankly, didn't seem that difficult to resolve.

She continued, "I had kind of a row with the boss there today and threatened to quit if he didn't pay up. Names were called. I might have mentioned whistle blowing and the fake antique market in some negative way, and I could see that he was impressed. He got really worked up and started yelling and stuff and threatened to kill me. One of the other mokes that works there tried to grab me, and I clunked him on the head with a two by four to discourage him. I had to get the hell out of there fast, and I'm pretty sure that if that guy or one of his toads find me, I'm screwed."

She released the hand brake and gunned the motor forcing the car up Taylor. The Toyota bucked the water sluicing down the hill like a Golden Gate ferry boat going out against the tide.

I struggled to process this news, along with my wealth of historic booze, and was a little concerned when Jenny said with some force, "You'd better snap out of it, Ace, we got work to do."

JOHN PEDERSEN

CHAPTER

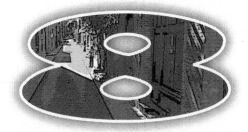

AS we struggled to pick up speed, Jenny's wipers did less and less to clear the view. I would have closed my eyes, but I thought the black swirlies might envelop me. I tried to imagine what sort of critical work I would be capable of at that moment, and failed to come up with anything meaningful.

We crested the hill and Jenny took a fierce right on Clay. I could faintly see the lights of the Transamerica Pyramid through the streaming rain and murk. We careened down the hill and sloshed over the cross streets, past the long closed shops of Chinatown. We whipped through the high rise, skyscraper canyons until at last we wailed around the corner onto Sansome Street. I gathered that we were headed back to my shop, my current stylish outfit not deemed fit for whatever coming adventure Jenny had included me in.

Finally, the old Toyota shuddered to a stop at the end of Jerome Alley. Jenny turned to me, "Listen, Soren, when I ran out of my shop, I had to leave all my tools. I'm completely sunk without them. We have to break in there and get my stuff. Plus, I suppose that if you are in a sweat to see what's in the basement, now might be your last chance, for good. Even though those guys were pretty pissed off before, I doubt they will be expecting me to sneak back in there so soon, especially with a biker-type hulk with me, no offense."

"None taken, I think. I sort of wish I had a little more warning as I may have avoided about a dozen shots of Bohemian whisky, but no sense in crying over spilt brain cells, right?" I started laughing but noticed that I laughed alone. Jenny stared at me with an unnerving intensity.

"Right, I'll wait here in the car while you get changed. And while you're in there, bring along any tools you think we might need to get in the back door. It's a big metal deal, but I think there is only a big-assed padlock on it. No alarm that I know of, why would there be? Let's see if we can get going on this, okay, I don't want to lose my nerve. Go!"

I fought my way out of the cramped front seat and grabbed my accordion out of the back. Jenny stared straight ahead. I staggered down the alley and fumbled my keys out of my pocket, from underneath the slicker. At least Vladimir had remembered to close and lock the doors, I thought.

I let myself in and stood for a moment in the pitch black, wondering if I should risk my shins on a chance walk to the back. Suddenly, I was blinded by all of the lights in the shop coming on at once.

Vladimir stood with one hand on the light switches and the other grasping an impossibly large open-ended wrench originally intended for working on steam ship engines.

"Holy O Baldheaded Jesus, what in the hell are you doing here? Are you drunk? Is your wife going to kill me? Argh, my friggin' eyes, I think I'll take the crippled shins next time."

Vladimir lowered the wrench fractionally.

"Vas strange person hanging around shop. Vas hiding something under coat. Vhen I go out to see what the hell he's up to, he runs away fast. Something not right there. Plus, accidentally drank small bottle of Slivovitz. Maybe the wife won't notice, Da?"

I had more or less figured out there was over-consumption of alcohol involved, but the late night skulker had my attention. I tried to remove my slicker and became hopelessly tangled. Vladimir lent his dubious assistance by grabbing the collar and pulling with all his might. The coat failed to come off and my arms were pinioned behind me. A perfect set up for a good solid beating, I thought.

Finally, Vlad noticed my plight and fished around in the folds of cloth until he came up with what he thought was a cuff and gave that a mighty tug, ripping the sleeve completely off my new white work shirt. Easy come, easy go, I reasoned.

Free of the slicker, I quickly went about digging out my regular work duds from earlier, and exchanged them for the suit. I idly wondered how Jenny came to view me as a biker-type hulk. Searching my memory for my last real look in a mirror, I couldn't recall anything that would portray me as anything other than a dedicated waterman and a respected and responsible tradesman. I thought I might have to take a closer look in the near future.

Vladimir was weaving around clanking the huge wrench into various machines and repair projects until I convinced him to find a seat and call his wife. I vowed to back him up on the story that there might be security issues at the shop, and that I needed him to hang out for the night and keep an eye on everything. Paid, of course. He looked relieved and probably had a backup bottle of Slivovitz hidden somewhere.

Once restored to my usual plebian glory, I cast about the shop for likely breaking-and-entering devices. I had a medium-sized pair of bolt cutters I threw into a canvas tool bag, along with a three-foot long screwdriver and a crowbar. Various small poking tools joined the team as well as a rattle can of compressed liquid nitrogen, which figured in TV breakins often.

Vladimir watched my drunken flailing about with rapt attention. He opened his mouth several times to pose questions, but refrained. Finally, unable to contain his curiosity any longer, "You have cash somewhere for bail?"

"Good point, but, no, I don't. If I get caught at what I'm about to do, bail might not even come into it; funeral arrangements, maybe. And, no, I don't have any cash for those either."

Vladimir shook his head and said he would guard our livelihood with vigor. I doubted whether he would be awake for ten minutes after I re-locked the door.

Relieved of the accordion but armed with the tool bag, I relocked the deadbolt on the green door and slipped back up the alley. Jenny waited in the Toyota, drumming on the steering wheel in apparent anxiety and frustration. I wrestled my tool bag into the back seat and barely got settled into the passenger spot before we were rocketing down Pacific. Instead of turning right on Montgomery to get down to Jackson, she screeched around the corner where Kearney and Columbus meet Pacific. Sort of headed the wrong way, I was relieved to note. But soon enough she turned right on Broadway and a block later headed down Montgomery. I was starting to get a bad feeling, and I couldn't really tell if it was the booze coursing through my system or an internal danger alarm.

Jenny unexpectedly whipped the car into an alley just short of Montgomery whose name I vaguely recalled being Gold Street. I hoped we would strike some there. We cruised slowly by what she said was the back of her building. There wasn't any available parking, so no cars were evident. There were no lights in any of the windows facing the alley, and Jenny said the windows were boarded-up anyway. I spotted the back door and confirmed that there was a monster padlock holding the metal-sheathed unit secure.

Jenny exited the alley once again in full race mode, and turned left on Sansome Street. We circled the block again, this time turning onto Jackson. As the car was the only thing moving in sight, there wasn't any problem with slowing right on down to survey the front of the building. We poked along and noted the deserted façade: no lights over the iron doors, and no lights showing on the second floor either.

Jenny spotted a parking spot a block later in front of an Oriental rug gallery. She clunked the Toyota up over the sidewalk and brought it back into the street with a wrenching grind. She looked at me and said, "What, we're in a legal spot, right?"

"Yeah, I guess. What's your plan here? Is there a plan?"

"Here's what I think. I think we should go and check out that back door. I've had to bring shit out to the dumpster back there and even though it looks impressive, I'm not sure it's bolted down that tight. Don't forget to lock that door. Let's go!"

I levered myself out of the car into the night. The rain had quit for the time being and the infamous fog was swirling up from the Bay. I dragged out my tool bag and carefully locked the door, just in case anybody might find any of the apparent refuse in the car worth stealing.

We stood around in front of the Art Gallery on the opposite side of the street for a few minutes, without seeing anything at all. No cars, pedestrians, or action of any kind. Finally Jenny whispered, "OK, I think we should give it a shot. We can go up Balance and slip right up to the back door."

We crossed the street trying hard not to look like the thieves that we were trying hard to become. There was no one to not take notice of us.

A few yards up Balance we crossed Gold and located the rear door.

I put my shoulder to a handy dumpster to shove it over a bit and obscure our activities, should any curious tourist stray down the alley in the middle of the foggy night.

Jenny held my small but powerful halogen light while I rummaged around in my bag for some long, skinny pokers I thought I might be able to jimmy the lock with. Pokers in hand, and the light playing fitfully in the general area of the lock, I inserted the devices I imagined might be able to release the tumblers.

I must have jacked the tools in and out, around, up, backwards and forwards for ten minutes or so before the light source vanished completely.

"Here, you hold the light for a sec and let me try."

I figured she might have some arcane knowledge of lock picking that I might not have been privy to and was just too polite to mention it till then.

I took the light and aimed it at the lock area with as steady a grip as I could manage in my condition.

The tool Jenny had selected turned out to be the gigantic screwdriver. Before I could advise her on the correct usage of such a tool, she had inserted it between the hasp and the door frame and heaved with all of her five foot two might, which turned out to be just enough to pop the screws out of the punky wood frame with a rending screech. I plucked the screws out of the dangling hasp and put them into my pocket for safe keeping. The echoes of the bust in had barely faded from the alley before we were inside. It was pretty dark, but Jenny said there were some lights around on the other side of the stairwell.

Playing the tiny light across the floor and keeping an eye out for noise-making floor junk, we eased out of the back room and into what had to be the office. Jenny said her stuff was up on the second floor and that we had to get to the stairs in the front of the building. We threaded our way through the desks and filing cabinets, trying to avoid bumping anything or tripping over the cables sloppily strewn across the floors in every direction.

I was almost successful, but I managed to stumble over a trash bucket with a shredder attached to the top. It kissed the floor with a metallic clang and Jenny and I froze. After several seconds of no reaction, she continued to lead the way.

"Nice move there, Grace. Is there any chance that we could keep this between ourselves?"

"Ahem, sorry about that; I think it was about to fall over anyway. Maybe I should have brought a bigger light, eh?"

"Yeah, I'm sure the light is the problem. More likely is that you're lit, but what can ya do? I have to work with the tools I have, right?"

I wasn't too sure how to take that statement, so I concentrated on easing my way up the stairwell behind Jenny and not stumbling or knocking over any of the numerous piles of lumber cut-offs stacked on the steps. There was a feeble ceiling light at the landing and we stood in its meager illumination for a moment to listen for movement other than ours. A hot rod went by on the street with an exhaust note that was deafening, even inside the building. It was followed a few seconds later by the wail of a police siren.

"That's one less pair of cops to catch us," Jenny said.

We made it to the top of the stairs without more clumsiness on my part, and Jenny set about collecting her belongings. She hoisted a large wooden toolbox up onto one of the benches, popped the lid open, and released some hidden internal catches. The front of the box fell away and revealed several drawers and cavities, all empty.

Jenny scooted around the shop grabbing chisels, planes, scrapers and tools of all sorts, and making a pile on the bench next to the box. After just a few minutes, there looked to be far too much gear to ever fit into the available space. She went to a locker on the wall and removed a bunch of clothing and her tool rolls.

Spreading the empty rolls out on the bench, she selected tools from among those spread out and carefully inserted each one into its assigned space. I fidgeted quietly until I could stand the tension no longer.

" I don't suppose that we could sort these out later, at home, perhaps. I'm all for being tidy, but wouldn't it be sort of a bad thing to be discovered jerking around in here?"

"I'm not doing it for fun, soak brain, I have to put everything in its place just to make sure that I'm not missing anything. Otherwise, how would I know?"

"OK, OK, take it easy. Is there anything that I can do here?"

"No, just chill out for a second, I'm almost done. Oh, shit, my #7 sweep gouge and my 3/4 inch straight chisel are missing. Damn, where could they be? I'll bet one of them assholes was using them somewhere. Man, if I catch them using my stuff, there'll be hell to pay."

"I'm not so sure that qualifies as the major transgression happening at the moment."

"Hmmm, you might be right. Hang on just a second while I check out this...Ah, success."

She had rooted around in a scabby looking metal toolbox of the sort sold at toy stores for kids. She brandished the shiny bladed gouge and stuffed it into its slot in the tool roll with a flourish. She rolled at least one of the sets of tools up. Only one slot remained unfilled. She cast around here and there without locating the missing prize.

"Listen, Jenny, I'll buy you a nice shiny new chisel if we can just wrap this up, OK?"

"I can't stand the thought of these assholes using my tools forever, but you might be right this time." She gathered up all of the tools and slotted them carefully into the toolbox packing it solid with hardware.

"I hate to be the wimp here, but doesn't that thing weigh a thousand pounds with all the stuff in there?"

"The box is made of willow, not as heavy as it looks. I'm sure a guy of your qualifications can handle it. I carried it up the stairs the first time."

I was far from reassured.

With a last glance around Jenny said, "Screw it, they can have anything left over. Let's get out of here."

There was a big metal handle attached to the top of the toolbox and I grabbed onto that and attempted to slide it off the bench top. I thought I heard my shoulder joints pop out as I did.

"Be careful with that, I made it in school and so far have resisted giving it to anybody."

I staggered towards the stairwell maneuvering the toolbox through the shop as well as I was able. Jenny had grabbed the pile of clothes and followed me closely. I didn't have very high hopes of making it to the ground floor without knocking over any of the scrap piles on the stairs, but I vowed to give it my best shot. Of course, I managed to almost make it to the second step before brushing up against a stack of useless crap, sending it cascading down the stairwell.

"Ah, Nuts,"

"Oh, for cryin' out loud."

Jenny pushed past me and started kicking the chunks off the steps with apparent disregard for the din she was creating.

"We have to get moving, Soren, I don't trust these wankers not to come back for God knows what."

I agreed completely in my mind, and set about easing the box, myself, a chicken club sandwich, a linear tasting of Napa County Pinot Noirs, and about a pint of Black Label Bushmills down the stairs.

I followed Jenny down and reached the ground floor with minimal incident, only gasping in pain once, having trod upon the corner of a cutoff and twisted my ankle slightly.

I wondered if a nice set of wheels under the toolbox might not help. I fetched a roller chair from the office and set the box on the seat. With this rig, I managed to navigate through the desks and various obstacles, till arriving at the back door.

I could see that Jenny was ready to bolt, but somewhere in my mind I had decided that if I was ever to get a look at the remainders of the Galleazzi Brothers operation, now was the time.

"Before we jet outta here, I'd really like to get a look at that stuff in the basement. Wouldn't take but a second. What do you think about that?"

"What I think is that if these goons come back here and find me inside, I'm dead; and if you're with me, you're probably dead too. And I'm not talking figuratively, either. Although, I'll tell you what: you go down there and see what you can find that excites you, and I'll poke around up here in the office for a minute just to see if old Jarno left anything incriminating lying around.

"Jarno...?"

"Jarno Viljanen, the guy that owns this place, the Finn, my boss, get it?"

"Oh, right, the Finn," I tried to sound like I knew even remotely what she was talking about.

Jenny offhandedly pointed at a doorway that I assumed led to the basement, and then disappeared back into the office.

I opened the door and noticed with dismay the lack of handy light switch. I wondered what the hell was up with these people that they didn't invest in a few light fixtures. I theorized that perhaps they were vampires or zombies or something like that.

I aimed my light that had blasted out so powerfully before down the rickety stairs and realized I couldn't see a thing. I ventured downward a couple of steps. When I failed to fall into an abyss, I ventured a few steps more. Eventually I reached the bottom step and played the light over the disarray that was there. Still, no handy light switch. I made my way across the small amount of floor that was free of clutter and examined the first pile I came to. Cast off office furniture, random looking pieces of old mechanical fixtures, and plumbing artifacts were all that was stacked there. I skirted that mess and tried to find the oldest and crustiest looking stacks I could locate. There was a set of shelves against the wall that looked like they might have been there for a thousand years, and I reasoned that if there was a dirtier place available, I hadn't seen it. Scanning the contents of the shelves I failed to see anything that even looked "accordion-like". There were some empty spots on the shelves and it looked like things might have been recently rearranged, but checking out the rest of the cellars contents, I didn't see where those bits might have wound up.

After a fruitless ten minutes or so, my flashlight started to waver and I thought it best to abandon any hope of finding the mother lode. I managed to work myself back to the foot of the stairs before the light quit completely, and I hugged the wall as I went up.

As I neared what I thought should be the top of the stairs, I failed to see any light from the first floor. I thought perhaps Jenny had closed the cellar door and had some negative thoughts about that. However, when I got to the top step, I realized the door was still open, but the form of a massive person was blocking the light. I just assumed that it was a person, as it had been years since a Yeti had been sighted in North Beach. Downtown, maybe, but not North Beach.

No words were exchanged, no excuses were tendered, no explanations offered. The first interaction I had with the behemoth was to have a ham-sized fist punch me in the guts, hard.

I found this preemptive type of action sadly lacking in social skill and might have mentioned it, had I not doubled over and puked the entire chicken club sandwich, linear tasting of Napa County Pinot Noirs, and the pint of Black Label Bushmills onto the brute's shoes. Remarkably, I felt better almost at once, although I didn't think that situation would last for long.

The monster acted somewhat enraged by my reaction to his punch. But while rearing back to really give me one to remember he paused at an odd point in his punch delivery. He looked disbelievingly down at his right shoulder. I followed his gaze and noticed a bloom of red spreading on the front of his dirty white T-shirt. Barely discernable, in the center of the stain, I could make out what looked like the tip of a slotted head screwdriver. This didn't really make too much sense to me until the fellow turned around forcing Jenny to jerk the weapon free. She was wielding the long screwdriver she had handled so astutely during our stealthy break-in, like a Musketeer would his rapier. A scream of rage and agony was starting in the brute's chest, when Jenny cut it short with a snappy whack on the side of his head. I stepped aside as the man toppled backwards down the cellar stairs. Satisfying thumps and clunks came up from down below.

Even in the dim light I could see her grimace.

"Ugh, what's that smell?"

"No time to investigate that, let's get moving, OK?"

In response to this, she wheeled around and headed out the door. She was holding a folder of what looked like invoices and such. I carefully stepped over the puddle of barf, grabbed her toolbox and my tool bag, ignoring the protests of my stomach and shoulder muscles, and followed her out. As I wrestled the door closed and fished the old screws out of my pocket, she said, "I think I got the goods on old Jarno. It's hard to tell, but all this stuff looks like complete fakery to me. Where's the accordion stuff? Didn't you see the boxes down there? I saw them myself about two weeks ago."

"Nah, there wasn't anything down there that I could find. Bunches of old crap, but nothing that resembled accordion stuff. Dead end, I suppose. Look, why don't you go get the car and pull it up here so that we don't have to go strolling down the street like a couple of idiots. Just in case your buddy comes storming out, I'm gonna try to get this hasp to hold some weight. Maybe I'll slide the old dumpster over against the door."

" Good idea, I'm on my way. Don't go anywhere, right?"

"I'll be here, believe me."

Jenny loped off, clasping the incriminating documents to her chest.

I kept one ear tuned to any sounds that might start up inside the building to let me know hell was going to break loose. I pounded the screws back into the holes they had been ripped out of, and thought that they looked almost normal to a casual looker. I put my shoulder against the dumpster and tried to roll it as quietly as I could. I got it as snug against the back door as I was able and had a few moments to reflect on my disappointment at not finding any of the Galleazzi bits in the basement.

Jenny had sounded pretty convinced they had been there until recently, and I wondered what sort of event would have caused them to get shifted around or even shit-canned.

Just as I had completed this last thought, I saw the lights of the Toyota turn onto the far end of Gold Street. I must say that even without the actual whisky on board, it still took me a few seconds to make the connection between that which I was leaning against and the possibility that the bits had been thrown away recently.

Jenny wailed down the street as I lifted the lid and peeked inside.

Among the random junk inside, I could just make out four or five wooden boxes without lids that looked like they might hold what I was seeking. I stood on tiptoe, extended my arm to its fullest and levered out one of the crates. There were pieces of wood and leather covered with filthy grime, but also unmistakable chunks of accordion fabrications.

I could only reach three of the five boxes that I could identify, and these I stacked next to the dumpster. As Jenny screeched to halt beside me; I directed her to get closer to the bin, and by standing on the hood of her car I was able to reach the remaining two and retrieve them. She jumped out of the car and popped the rear door open and gave a mighty shove to the junk that already resided there. I was able to get her tool box inside, and my tool bag, but looked like all the dumpster diving was going to be in vain as there wasn't a spare inch to be had. Jenny rooted feverishly around and came up with a thin length of twine and pointed to the cheesy looking roof rack. I didn't have time to argue or justify, I just heaved the boxes up there and wrapped the string around and over to the extent of its length. I had almost decided to unwrap it and do a better job when the door started rattling. As I jumped into the revving car, the hasp popped off its mounting for the second time that night and the dumpster toppled over. Peering over the junk in the back of the car I caught a glimpse of our friend shaking at least one fist in the air and scream-ing that he would kill us as we squealed around the corner and out of sight.

JOHN PEDERSEN

CHAPTER

JENNY must have had a destination in mind, as we headed directly for the Tenderloin district. I gathered that she was about to head home and briefly wondered how I was going to make it all the way out to the Richmond at 2 AM. After a few minutes of whipping around corners she looked over at me, "I think I ought to see if I can get into my apartment, if you could call it that. There's some stuff in there that I could really use. I hope the landlord hasn't padlocked the door or anything like that. That would suck."

'Well, at least we have the tools on hand to get in if we want to, eh?"

Jenny gave me a dirty look and said, "You realize that I owe them rent, right? They haven't done anything wrong, unlike that other asshole. I'd prefer to just come up with the cash and look for a better place. Not too likely now, though."

I was about to mention the extra room in my house, but thought that I might better let that lie for the moment.

"Your buddy there didn't act too happy about the way we left things. Nice work with the screwdriver, by the way."

"Well, he's the biggest asshole of the bunch. I could never understand why Jarno had that dolt around. He was hopeless with the woodwork, always busting stuff and ruining tools. Maybe they were related or something; I never could get half of what they said straight. Plus, he was always squeezing up against me and pinching my ass and stuff. I should have shoved that screwdriver right through his head, it would have served him right."

The fierceness of this made me shudder and wonder at the female capacity for sudden violence. I didn't have long to ponder though, as we slowed quite a bit as we turned the corner of Ellis and Jones.

"Ah shit, there's Jarno's van. Dang, I'll bet he and his creeps are all over the place waiting for me. How did I think they didn't know where I lived? I'll bet one of the sleazeballs actually followed me home at some point. Ick!"

She turned down a side street before we passed the large, scrappy looking white van. Not exactly a millionaire's limo, if you asked me. Without discussion, Jenny accelerated up Turk and looked to be heading westward. I sincerely hoped it was toward my house as I was quickly starting to lose my grip on reality, and consciousness as well.

"OK, how about if we head over to your place and figure all this out?"

I couldn't imagine what there was to figure out, or how I could possibly do it at the moment, but said, "Fine", anyway.

The almost deserted streets put us in my driveway in a very few minutes, and I was pretty sure I had passed out at least a couple of times by then. I hoped Jenny hadn't noticed.

She shut the car off and all I really wanted to do was to sit in the silence and fall asleep for good, but instead I forced my way out of the car with the accordion case and unlocked the garage door.

Inside the garage, I shoved motorbikes around and shifted boxes of parts till there was an almost clear spot where we could stow Jenny's toolbox and the rest of her stuff. She had the back of the Toyota open and was attempting to latch onto the handle of the toolbox to bring it inside. I briefly wondered if she could actually do it, but let chauvinism overcome me.

"Here, I'll get that, I don't want you to strain nothin'."
"Whatever."

Instead of hauling the massively heavy box, she started untying the knots I had so hastily whipped around the roof rack.

I had almost forgotten about the boxes of junk I had fished out of the dumpster. The question of storage popped into my head, but I figured whatever didn't interest me I could just pitch into another dumpster.

I used the last of my remaining strength getting the toolbox, more or less cleanly, into the garage. The boxes off the roof I just balanced on top of some motorbikes, not even bothering to glance at their contents.

Jenny grabbed her backpack and some clothes out of the car, but left the sleeping bag. We threaded our way through the garage and I shut and locked the door behind us.

In my half conscious state I asked Jenny if she was hungry or wanted a drink or anything. She allowed as how she was fine, all things considered, and would just as soon clean up and go to bed. I agreed that that was a most appealing proposition.

I turned off the kitchen lights and we went up, Jenny not needing any direction to find her own way.

After the running water ceased, I waited a decent interval before I went to the bathroom and had a quick shower, which did absolutely nothing to revive me. I tried to scrub the remains of the Bohemian Club adventure out of my mouth and figured that was probably a lost cause.

My room was dark when I returned, but I didn't have the energy or spare wits to wonder why. I flopped down onto the bed, more grateful that I could imagine.

Too late I felt Jenny's presence, and the last words I heard before I fell asleep were, "Buddy, you still smell like booze."

I suppose that I slept, dreamt, tossed and turned as a person usually does when they go to bed, but when I painfully fought my way out of the fog, it felt as though I was in exactly the same position I had dropped down in. I casually explored the far side of the bed to find that Jenny was gone if indeed she had ever been there. I wasn't completely sure it hadn't been a figment of my exhausted and alcohol-addled mind. Actually, the whole adventure might not have been real, except for my painful ankle, and head, of course.

The clock told me that it was far too late to think of surfing, so I didn't even bother to look, but I did manage to get my ass out of bed and dressed in more or less clean clothes. I made my way down stairs to find Jenny sitting at the kitchen table reading the paper and sipping a cup of tea. She casually looked up, "I found some ancient tea bags, I gather left over from your folks, the pot's on the stove. Damn little to eat, though, so let's get squared away and make a shopping list. It looks like I might be forced to impose on you for a while, and I have to have at least a few things to get by. OK?"

I was a little stunned by the sudden change in my living status, but as usual in similar situations I said, "Fine."

Jenny had on her work clothes: heavy Carhartt overalls, steel-toed work boots and a flannel shirt over a T-shirt. I wondered if she was contemplating going back to the furniture shop for some reason.

Before I could formulate a casual way to ask about her plans she said, "Seeing as how I don't have a job anymore, paying or not, and also seeing as how I've had pretty much fun hanging around with you for the last couple of days, how about if I just tag along to that motorbike shop today? I don't think old Jarno will be out searching the neighborhood for me, and even though I should be out looking for some paying work, I think I'll skip that for today. That is, if that's OK with you."

To be sure, I was thrilled at the prospect of spending the day with her, although I would rather have spent it at the beach. I didn't want to sound too excited though, so I responded with a casual nod. I briefly wondered at my sudden attachment to her, but thought it best not to dwell on it. In fact I said, "Well, I'm sure that there's something you could do down there. We'll look around."

She took that as a matter of course.

"Not that you are ruled by machines or anything, but I notice there is a blinking message machine in the other room with a pretty large number on the front of it. I certainly hope people are calling all at once, and they haven't been sitting there for ages. Right?"

I gave the phone stand in the living room a guilty look.

"It's not exactly the first place I check, but I suppose I'd better see what gives. Generally there aren't any real messages from real people, just crap."

She shrugged and went back to the paper.

I poured a cup of the strange tea that my mother favored and took it into the living room. The blinking number stood at 5. I couldn't imagine.

Message number one was from a person from some far away land offering a drastically reduced mortgage rate for a few selected customers. My response was to hit the Delete button.

Number two, however, was someone hollering over a complete din. With a replay, I could make out the actual message, which was, "You asshole, I'll kill you!" What a familiar sounding phrase that was beginning to be. The message went on, "I'm over at the Orion. You remember the Orion where we have played every Thursday night for years? I'm here playing, but I'm all alone, except for some fool from Egypt or somewhere scratching away on a fiddle like thing. If you were here now I'd punch you in the face, but if you were here, I wouldn't have to leave this message, would I? Wait, Sloane's here. Go to hell."

I had another guilty pang realizing that while I had been at the Bohemian Club, swilling whisky and wine, Sean had been saddled with some inexpert players at the session we usually played up on Diamond Heights. Once again, it wasn't as if we actually got paid to be there, but we had been doing it pretty regularly for so long that the management sort of expected us. And clearly, Sean expected me.

I moved on, number three was even stranger. "Hello? Is this the accordion guy? The accordion detective guy? Jim Sullivan told me you were finding old accordions and that you might be able to find one for me. I sold a Colombo Grand Vox back in the seventies, and I'd really like to get it back. So call me if you come across it, OK? It was black and had an anchor in rhinestones on the front. My number is...."

I recognized the name Sullivan, and the name of the accordion maker, but the rest of the message was baffling.

Again, I moved on.

Number four was incomprehensively along the same lines as number three. "Hello, I got your number from Jim Sullivan and he said I should tell you that I had a really nice Castiglione button box, B/C tuning, stolen from out of my car back in 1986, and never got it back. He said you might be able to find it, although I don't know how. But anyway, if you do, here's my number...."

Now, completely mystified, I pushed number five, just for the hell of it. It ran, "Hello, I understand that you are searching for a C.L. Miller accordion. I have one, and if you want to look at it, you can. He was a friend of a great aunt or something and the accordion was passed down through the family. My number is...."

Now I was really stunned. I thought I'd better get in touch with Jim Sullivan and find out what the hell he was telling people about me. Accordion Detective? What could that possibly mean?

The best I could come up with was that without food in me, I was missing something important. Breakfast, now there was a subject that I could understand.

I returned to the kitchen where Jenny was washing up her cup.

"Not to be too nosy or anything, but what the heck was that? Are there facets of you that we know nothing about, Accordion Hunter perhaps?"

"I haven't the foggiest idea. For a change, the only call that I did understand was the guy from India offering the reduced mortgage rate. I'll have to call Sullivan to find out what he's been telling them guys. For now though, how's about we hit a scenic diner somewhere and get some food in us."

"Yay, my thoughts exactly. I might be a little short in the cash department, 'cause I never did get the first nickel out of Jarno. Can you afford to front me for a little while? It won't be long, I promise, I pay my own way."

"No problem, I'll let you know when we get near the bottom of the barrel. Speaking of nosy, I don't mean to say that it wasn't memorable, but last night did we …?"

"Are you kidding? All that bumping and grinding, sweating and screaming. You said you'd love me forever and begged me to marry you. You don't remember any of that? I'm completely offended!"

I think the lack of fuel was dulling my never too keen mental activity. I stammered out, "Really, Oh, Jeez, I kind of don't remember that part. I mean, sure, I suppose that I might have meant…."

Jenny laughed in my face, "Oh come on, dopey, you barely hit the bed before you were asleep. Might have missed the big chance there, we'll have to see. I tell you one thing though, if you snore like that every night, buddy, this deal is over already."

I got the picture.

"Snoring is it? I suppose that would explain the sore throat and the pillows piled over my face this morning. It must have been the liquor. You didn't attempt to make me a pillow victim, did you?"

She laughed again. "I only briefly considered suffocating you; after that I just moved into the other room and the noise was almost bearable."

"Thank God I'll have another day to live and prove my manly worth to you. Let's get going before I pass out from lack of carbohydrates and grease."

Leaving the house was much easier with Jenny abandoning much of her stuff there.

Relieved of some of it's load, the Toyota felt much larger inside.

There was plenty of room for my accordion case and unnecessary rain gear.

The day was the complete opposite of the preceding ones. The sun shone with crystalline clarity and there wasn't a cloud in the sky. A slight breeze wafted in from the ocean, which, combined with the storms of the last week, probably meant that the surfing conditions were shite anyway. I felt relieved to know that nobody was out without me.

After the usual ritual of almost not starting, the car was purring like an asthmatic cat.

"Where to? It's your turn to pick, seeing as how I guess it's your treat."

"I'm thinkin' perhaps the Fog City Diner. It's still pretty early and probably won't be crowded yet."

"Off we go, then."

We cruised down Geary and Jenny decided that Park Presidio was the scenic route of the day. She drove all the way down to the Marina District before heading east. After the crappy weather, the runners were out in force, stretching muscles and pumping the old blood around. The grass was blindingly green and the bay sparkled with white caps and sunlight.

We followed the bay around to the Embarcadero and finally found an easy parking spot right next to the diner on Battery.

As I had predicted, the diner was only half full. We got seated and ordered right away. Jenny may have gone a little light due to her having to eat on my dime. I hoped not. While we were at it, she said, "So, are you going to call that old guy and find out what he's been telling people about you. No clues, no ideas, no postulations?"

"Obviously, I'd have to conclude that it has to do with me asking him about that mysterious, turn-of-the-century accordion guy. Whose picture I did get to see last night at the Bohemian Club, by the way. It turns out that his name was C.L. Miller, if I'm right. He was sitting there neat as you please on top of a big redwood log alongside another accordion player identified as C.C. Keene. Keene was a member of the Bohemian Club, and all the information I did find was mostly about him. He was a member of a minstrel troupe in the mid-eighteen hundreds and played the accordion with them. They had a disastrous tour and he wound up in San Fran broke."

I had Jenny's attention by now, "I know the feeling. But, how on earth did you find all this shit out? Not just by looking at a picture."

"Keene wrote a memoir and a series of articles for a circus magazine, and being a member of the Bohemians, they just happened to have the original right there in their library. I read as fast as I could while my buddy Joe had a little nap. So this guy, Keene, winds up here and starts making musical instruments in order to survive. Banjos, accordions and stuff like that. After a while, things are going good and he hires an assistant. Enter C.L. Miller. Miller was a natural at the trade and they get along famously till Miller got involved with what sounded like opium, politely worded. At the very least, some sort of Chinese culture that Keene didn't approve of. So, he moves on. He kind of fades from the memoir at this point, and I had to bolt out of there to meet you, so that's all I got. I toyed with the idea of boosting the book, but knowing the guys that hang out there at the club, it's probably a hanging offense. I'm pretty sure from all of this that Miller is the guy that I'm looking for.

"Whatever that has to do with what Sullivan has been telling folks, I don't know, but I hope to find out after we get to the shop. However, strangely enough, one of the messages I just got was from somebody who said he knew what and who Miller was and had one of his accordions. Wouldn't that be weird?"

Jenny had stopped eating momentarily and said, "Wow, that's amazing, lucky, lucky, lucky. And I thought you were just in there boozing it up with a bunch of Republicans and plotting to enslave the world. Shocking."

"The boozing it up part is right, but I didn't have to talk politics with anybody I met. No matter that I was dressed for success, I'm pretty much sure they could spot a working stiff from a mile away."

Jenny laughed, which made my heart flutter alarmingly.

I paid the bill and we headed over to my shop. I allowed as how Jenny's previous boss might know what her car looked like, and that we should find an out of the way spot to stash it. There were a couple of strange, semilegal, tucked away spots at the end of Jerome Alley that were often open and we tried for one of those.

With the car jammed into an almost parking spot we headed up the alley. I had a momentary flash of unease concerning Vladimir's skulking apparition of the previous evening, but I couldn't imagine whoever it might be, could be connected with Jarno and his gang. At least, I hoped not.

The deadbolt wasn't locked on the front so I didn't have to use my key to open the door. I assumed that Vladimir was still inside. Despite the bright day, it was still pretty gloomy inside the shop with the lights off, and as I made my way to the back towards the switches, I felt something slimy on the floor. I assumed that Vladimir had spilled a bit of oil, as he was known to do.

Once I hit the lights Jenny's sudden shriek nearly scared me to death. I turned around to see Vladimir rolled almost under one of the motorcycle benches and the source of a pool of blood, with footprints leading to where I stood.

JOHN PEDERSEN

THE shock of seeing Vladimir mo-
tionless under the bench had me,
in my slightly rattled state, stunned for a moment, but not so for Jenny.
She rushed to his side and checked his neck for a pulse. My thought was
that the scene was just like on TV. I was pretty sure I couldn't find my
own pulse, much less that of another person.

She yelled at me, "Hey, wake up! He's still among the living, call
911, quick!"

I was spurred into action. As I made the first 911 call of my life, I
could hear Vladimir come to some sort of consciousness, rattling off a
long string of Russian, which was only slightly more unintelligible than
his usual rants. Jenny sounded like she was offering words of comfort,
but then in a sharper tone, told him to lay the fuck down.

He might have recognized the authority, if not the person, and sub-
sided into a garbled mumbling. Jenny whipped a long string of paper
towels off a nearby roll and was holding that wad against Vladimir's
head, I supposed at the source of the leakage.

While waiting for the paramedics, I looked closely around the shop
to see if I could garner any clues about who might have clouted the poor
bastard on the floor. I failed to see anything out of the ordinary, except
the expected Slivovitz bottles, drained bone dry. Those were out of the
ordinary only because Vladimir generally kept them more hidden.

I gave up my random sleuthing and went to see if there was any aid I could offer Jenny in her treatment of the casualty.

She squinted up at me and said, "What's the deal here, Soren? Do you think this is in any way connected with Jarno and his crowd of goons? I can't imagine those guys could have made any sort of link between us, not to mention track down the location of your shop and then come in and assault poor old 'what's his name'. Oh crap, I'm getting his gore all over me. Yuck! I tell ya, when we first walked in here, I thought for sure he was a goner, but I guess Russians have more head blood to spare 'cause he didn't sound all that bad when he was yammering a while ago. Seems to have slipped down a ways now, though."

I didn't have an opinion on the plasma issue, so I went to the door to see if I could spot the Medics. I could hear the scream of a siren, which seemed to approach, and then fade to almost nothing while I listened. In a sudden burst of sound, an ambulance wheeled straight down Jerome alley, the siren absolutely deafening in the narrow confines of the space. Finally, the driver took pity on everyone in the neighborhood and killed the wail.

Three guys in firefighter garb jumped out of the back and swarmed into the shop. I needlessly pointed at the pool of blood, and incidentally, Vladimir.

One guy took over Jenny's duties with the paper towels while another was busy hauling out boxes with all sorts of supplies and medical instruments in them. Blood pressure was checked, eyes were inspected with a flashlight, and fingers and toes were tested for feeling. Vladimir was groggily reacting to bits and pieces of their instructions and conversation. The third man cornered Jenny and myself with a clipboard full of red tape. I supplied all I knew of Vladimir's particulars, including his home number and address. Eventually I suppose he decided he had enough lines filled out for some action to be taken. As the medics loaded Vladimir onto a gurney, I hoped he might be present enough for a casual question or two. I sidled up close to him, on the verge of being completely in the way,

"Vlad, brother, can you hear me? What happened in here? Who did this to you? Anybody familiar?"

Vlad waved his hand feebly and said in a hoarse whisper, "Was big man, very big, and terrible fast. Black beard, very black hair, blue coat vis gold buttons. Boots, had black boots, very large. Very angry."

JOHN PEDERSEN

He swooned and his head slumped off to the far side. The medics extended the legs off the gurney and wheeled him away from the site of the attack.

Jenny and I held hands while we watched them load the poor bastard into the ambulance and back out of the alley. I guessed that his life wasn't judged to be too much in the balance, as they neglected to turn on the siren. I wondered if there was to be any police investigation and if I would be destroying evidence if I cleaned up the mess. In the end, I suspected that assaulting a drunken Russian was so far down on the crime list that if there were an investigation, it wouldn't take place for another month or so. Jenny and I filled buckets with hot water and granulated soap powder and, using the shop brooms, swilled the essence of Vladimir straight out the door and into the storm drain.

As I slopped yet another splash of liquid down on the still sticky spot, Jenny said, from the far side of the bench, "I guess we can stop looking for the assault weapon, if we were looking for one."

She held up a foot and a half long spanner wrench, used especially for tightening the exhaust nuts on Norton motorcycles. There was definitely a small patch of fuzz that looked like it might have recently belonged on Vladimir's scalp. Accompanying the fuzz was a generous blob of sticky red stuff.

"I'd say that stands a pretty fair chance of being it all right, although, technically, I suppose the police might have preferred if you hadn't picked it up just now. Funny I didn't see it when I was doing my best investigator act."

Jenny dropped it back to the bench with a clang.

"Oh Shit! My mistake. I'm not used to this stuff, I guess."

I told her I doubted we would see any officials for a long while, if ever, and not to worry.

After I had swept the majority of the water out the door, I remembered the Jim Sullivan call that had to be made. I flipped the soiled pages of the address book till I had his number up in Sonoma.

A few rings later Jim's daughter Riley answered the phone. Despite Jim's feigned or real confusion about who I was, Riley knew me immediately. She was the youngest of Jim's several daughters and was quite a few years younger than myself.

She opened with, "Sam, oh my Sam. Say, has that Sloane Flynn landed you yet? Dad said she was all over you like a cheap suit at that party at the Widow's. He thought she had a pretty good shot at it, too, even though you showed up with some new girl. Pretty, short, blonde, not skinny, is what he told me. Funny about what sticks in his mind, isn't it. I suppose I shouldn't even talk about this on the phone, but you know that dad always sort of thought you and I would make a good couple, don't you? That is until you started in with all the Harley Davidson, Hell's Angel stuff. I thought so too, in fact, I might even still think so. But I guess it's too late, eh?"

"I'm sorry, this is Soren Rauhe. Are you sure you're thinking of the same person? I'm afraid that I don't know any Hell's Angels, nor do I exclusively work on or own Harleys. I'm just a dedicated preservationist of unique motor history."

I stalled while my brain tried unsuccessfully to come to terms with this flirty twist.

"Cut it out, Soren, I know who you are. Was there something you called about, or did you just want to chat me up with your famous sly humor?"

"Jesus, Riley, You've got me all a flutter. I hardly know what to say about all that except, can I talk to Jim?"

"Hang on, snake, you just wait till I see you again. I've been going vegan and working out. You'll be falling all over yourself. I'll get dad, he's around here someplace."

I could barely imagine Riley feeling the need to limit her diet or work on her already supremely athletic figure.

I felt a pang of guilt as I came back from imagining Riley to seeing Jenny staring at me. I harrumphed and vowed to get down to some kind of business.

As a parting shot Riley said, "Ha! I was just foolin' with ya. You still don't have a chance, here's dad."

Jim finally came on the line, "Hello, who is it speaking at all. Sure, talk up, I can hardly hear you."

"Jim, it's Soren Rauhe, I saw you at the Widow's the other night and you told me about the pictures of the accordion players at the Bohemian Club. Remember? I play that old wooden Soprani with the pearl buttons."

"Oh, just so, it vaguely sounds familiar. What would you be needing at the moment, sonny?"

After the brief conversation I had just had with Riley, I somehow had the feeling that Jim's not remembering me was some kind of an act. I had no idea why.

"Jim, I got some phone calls last night and this morning from various people who acted like I was some kind of accordion missing persons file, and they all sounded like they got that idea from you. What can you tell me about this?"

"Ah, so that's it, is it? Well, you needn't play games with me, young man, I know all about it."

"Do you, indeed? Know all about it, that is. I don't suppose you might share what 'IT' is with me, would you? I'm more or less in the dark."

"As you always were, lad, as you always were. But, as far as I know, the only reason to ask about C.L. Miller is to try to find his box. We all had a go of it back in the day, but nobody ever found it."

"Wait, you mean his accordion? Why on earth would anybody be searching for that, even if it still existed?"

"Sure, lad, I don't know where you got wind of Miller; that story hasn't been around in years, but unless you had heard about the box and it being full of precious metal and having the power, why would you even ask?"

I tried to actually think of some kind of justification for my interest, but couldn't even come up with anything that sounded convincing to myself.

"I have no idea why I care, it's just some funny story Tommy Mc-Cracken told me the other day. He thought it was appropriate because Conroy told it to him and it was about San Francisco."

"Jayses, you are in the clouds, aren't ya. All I know is that by all accounts of the day, Miller's box was special all right, and after the earthquake, somethin' happened that made him kinda crazy and give it up. The rumor was that he hid the box somewhere, and a good few fellows have looked and never found it."

"Well, an owner of one of Miller's accordions called me this morning as well, I guess he got my number from you, right?"

"As to that, I didn't even know there were any of them left except that I got the tip from old Rosalinni, the accordion repairman, that there were some folks with a Miller box in the City, and them with some sort of family connection, to boot. He said they must be on the Chinese side of the family. I've got to go now, Riley is taking me downtown to get some of that MacDonald's. I love that stuff. She's already honking at me from the car. Cheerio, lad, good luck."

And just like that he hung up and was gone.

Jenny stared at me, "I guess I'm, or, excuse me, we're supposed to be looking for C.L. Miller's accordion. Something is supposed to make it special and worth looking for. We have no idea what. Big Jim just assumed that's what I was after when I was quizzing him the other night. Oh My God, I completely forgot about calling Vladimir's wife, she must be frantic by now. Nuts!"

I came up with the number. As I dialed I dreaded the conversation that was sure to follow.

A few rings later the phone was answered by one of Vladimir's two sons, by Vlad's reports either the greatest piano player in the world, or the greatest guitar player in history. I asked to talk to their mother, and the phone was dropped with a clunk and I could hear shouting. Finally Ulyana came on and I said,

"Um….Good morning, Soren Rauhe here. I'm afraid I have a bit of serious news concerning Vladimir. Someone broke into the shop here last night while he was watching it, and bashed him pretty hard on the head. He is at St. Francis Memorial hospital now and we should be able to check on him very soon. I'm very sorry."

With what I considered terrific restraint and control she said, "Hospital? Da, I just talk to police and they tell me this as well. Police say he vas werry full of the alcohol, no? They say perhaps he do this thing to his own self. Could be, no?"

"Well, actually, if the police ever bother to talk to us here at the shop, I think they might change their opinion, us having found the tool that he was bashed with. But, I suppose they might never. I guess that's all I have to report just now. I'll call you if I find out anything, OK?"

"Da, is fine. Good bye."

I said to Jenny, "Well, she took that a lot better than I thought she might. Pretty friggin' stoic, if you ask me. I guess those Russian women are tougher that I thought." Jenny was lost in thought.

"I guess I could check in with the hospital to see if Old Vladimir is surviving alright."

"It sounded like his wife thought perhaps a nice head bash might even improve him a bit. Maybe while I'm doing that, you could dig my accordion out and give me some woodworking advice. There are some tricky joints and angles on the case there, and an expert woodworker person like yourself might be able to help me get rid of all the duct tape holding the thing together. The poor old thing is looking pretty shabby and I feel it might be negatively affecting my image as a serious musician."

While Jenny dug the old Soprani out of its case, I called St. Francis hospital and inquired about the fate of poor Vlad. The official report was that they couldn't tell me anything over the phone. And even if they could say anything, it would be only to family members. I took this to mean that at least he was still alive.

By that time, I really had expected some sort of communication from San Francisco's finest, but not a thing.

Jenny had worried the straps off the box and figured out how to get the ends off the bellows. I decided I might as well let her discover how the mechanism worked without any of my half-witted explanations. I got the piece of paper out with the phone numbers of the accordion seekers on it and found the number of the alleged relative of C.L. Miller.

I dialed the number while keeping a furtive eye on Jenny's progress with my accordion. She appeared plenty at home browsing the interior, so I concentrated on the call as the line was picked up. A woman with a very heavy Asian accent answered the phone and talked for a while, none of which I was able to understand.

After she stopped talking, I said, "Good morning, this is Soren Rauhe, somebody there left a message for me last night about being a relative of an old accordion maker named C.L. Miller. I guess Jim Sullivan up in Sonoma gave that person my number and said I was searching for his accordion. At the time, I wasn't but I guess I am now. So, that person didn't leave their name, only a number, and now I'm calling back. Would there be someone there I could speak to?

After numerous clunks and clanks and a bit of loud hollering, things quieted down and I was left to wait for a few minutes. Finally someone picked up the phone and said, "Hello, hello, is anybody still there? Speak up if you are."

I jumped once again into my explanation of who I was and how I had gotten the number. The person on the other end of the line came up with, "Oh, right, the accordion guy. Well, I don't have any idea how the dude in Sonoma got my number or why he called me, but we do have an old beat-up accordion made by somebody named Miller, and supposedly, he had some connection to our family, although unless he was Chinese he certainly wasn't related by blood. I just threw that in there, my grandma has some stories, but I haven't really paid too much attention to them. My name is Leon Zhou, by the way. You're welcome to come by and see the thing. We live over on Pelton Place, just off Pacific. It's half a block west of Grant, if you know where that is."

"Cripes, I'm only about four blocks away at this very moment. Maybe I could swing by around noon, if anybody will be around. "

"Yeah, well, I go to City College, but pretty often I come home for lunch with my grandma. Sure come on over, I'll dig out the accordion. If you want the details, I'm afraid you'll have to go through me to talk to grandma, she doesn't have much of the English even after all these years."

We made a date and I got the exact address before I hung up. Jenny was already neck deep into the accordion and was busy sketching out diagrams, making notes and labeling the guts of it. I relayed the conversation to her and she was suitably amazed.

I had only taken two steps in the direction of my bench when the phone rang again. I answered it and Sean started in on me.

"Hey, jerkbag, what's with leaving me stranded last night? You aren't completely shacked up already, are you? Oh my God, talk about led around by a ring in the nose, Dude, doesn't your new girlfriend like the old skidereedee?"

"Oh ease up, it's not like you haven't missed a million gigs. Don't worry, I'll be at The Flower tonight. Money is money after all. Instead of getting a couple of free pints last night at the bar, I was at the Bohemian Club partaking of fine wines, free whisky, and sumptuous delicacies."

"Ah, the Bohemian Club was it. I suppose you're all ready to join up, and all. Leave the old neighborhood once and for all. Did the new girl's daddy get you in there? Oh wait, she's from back east somewhere, that couldn't have been it. Never mind. So, what did you call about?"

"What? You called me, nut case. Anyway, I've got piles of funny stuff to tell you tonight about that story McCracken told me, and Jim Sullivan and stuff like that."

"Right enough, so. Get there early if you can, I think I'll need extra liquid enthusiasm after the terrible experience of last night. Plus, Sloane showed up and proceeded to drink the place dry, which I thought was my job. I got her, and the Beastwagon, all the way home again for the usual three minutes of heavy making out before it was 'Goodnight All'. I've gotta' go, Cheerio."

Sean hung up and I finally got free of the phone. Jenny was still busily stripping my box, so I randomly picked a project to work on. That day's lucky winner was a 1940 Crocker. The bike was one of about 100 total bikes produced by the company. To a casual looker, the bike strongly resembled a Harley Davidson, but to an informed biker, it was so much more sophisticated as to be unmistakable. The example in my shop looked like a complete heap of shit; however, a very similar one that had been restored nicely had sold at auction for almost $250,000. When the owner of this bike had found out about that sale, he had taken out a second mortgage on his house to be able to get his restored. For-tunately, there were plenty of manuals and enthusiasts to contact when things got confusing.

The bike had only been in the shop a couple of weeks, so I had only done a very superficial survey of its myriad problems. I got out a fresh clipboard, a new yellow legal pad, and started writing. I was still writing a couple of hours later,

"Hey, you, didn't you make an appointment with somebody to see that accordion at noon? It's almost 11:50, shouldn't you get going?"

I glanced at my watch, which was almost unreadable due to its crys-tal having been clipped with tools thousands of times and then having been soaked in salt water. I was slightly appalled at how fast Jenny had slipped into the position of social director, not to mention my own lame-ness at having almost missed the appointment I made only hours earlier.

"Yeah, I guess I'd better. Do you want to go along? We can get lunch on the way back?"

"No thanks, I think the less I'm out in the neighborhood, the better, but you can pick me up something."

I grabbed a jacket and helmet and wheeled the Norton out into the alley, so as to not stink up the shop. I assumed Jenny would be able to answer the phone if she wanted and deal with any casual drop-in's.

The Norton started fairly easily and I was hardly sweating at all as I drove up the alley and out onto Pacific. Half way to Pelton Place, that is to say, about twenty seconds into my journey, I felt a bit lazy having taken the bike and not hiked over. Ah well, any excuse to take a ride on a nice day was the foundation of my transportation philosophy.

I crossed Grant and instantly turned right onto Pelton Place. It was a long alley between two tall buildings and the noise of the Norton even hurt my ears, in a good way.

At the end of the alley, it opened up into a large parking lot that I recognized as belonging to the Royal Pacific Motel, whose entrance was on Broadway. I briefly wondered if the Zhou family lived in the motel, but then caught sight of what I assumed was their actual address.

The building was blue with painted decorations all over. There was an immense mural with Chinese lanterns, festoons of flowers and crowd scenes, as well as piano players and all sorts of things. I had seen the building almost every day but never stopped to look closely.

The apartment was on the third floor, and the stairway, while not exactly dangerous looking, was a trifle under-lit and cramped. I had a good sweat going under my riding jacket by the time I reached the door. Before I knocked, I stripped down a bit and allowed my breathing to return to normal.

There was movement inside, and I could hear Leon shouting, "It's OK Grandma, I got it."

The door opened and I was astounded at my first glance of Leon Zhou.

In my mind, I had pictured a book-toting, glasses-wearing Asian kid, dressed by his mom and grandma, fawned over by the whole family as the great hope. I figured that he would have been studying mathematics or business at college. In reality, Leon was at least my height, and I'm giving myself the benefit of the doubt, and built like a football star. He had his long jet black hair pulled back into a ponytail and sported a droopy moustache. His forearms and biceps bulged alarmingly when we shook hands. His palms were calloused and hard, indicating some very serious work somewhere down the line. He invited me in.

The apartment was not as small and cluttered as I had been prepared for. In the foyer, examples of generic 50's style furniture were mixed in with elaborately carved Chinese pieces. Leon and I headed straight for the kitchen, bypassing the living room where a TV spilled Soap Opera type dialog in Chinese.

On the Formica kitchen table sat a small accordion that I assumed was C.L. Miller's work. Leon put a kettle of water on the stove while I sat down and examined the box. It was tidy, but not heavily ornamented. The fingerboard face was made of silver, instead of wood, and there was a single row of large pearl buttons with only three extras in a second row providing accidental notes. It didn't look particularly beat-up to me, but perhaps that had more to do with my own level of tolerance than anything else.

There were silver catches on the front and back holding on the end pieces instead of the usual pins. I asked Leon if it was all right for me to look inside. He said that it was all the same to him.

I slipped the catches and the bellows came away easily and cleanly. I suspected there had been some work done on the instrument in the not-too-remote past. Inside, the reeds and blocks all looked neat and tidy. The leather valves were in pretty good shape, at least as good as the ones in my box, and the wax holding the reeds in place was not cracked. I held the box up to get a bit of extra light from the window, and could make out the tiny pencil signature of Rosalinni and the date 1965. I also saw the bold signature of C.L. Miller dated 1904. Perhaps not too strangely, the reed blocks were stamped C.C. Keene, S.F. I gathered that Miller had either used Keene's parts, or made the accordion while he still worked there. Other than these things, I didn't see anything of particular note.

Leon took a seat at the table along with the teapot, cups and a plate of cheeses and flatbreads. I reassembled the accordion, set it on my knee, and took a tentative note or two. The sound was about what I expected from a box of that age. In tune, but not super powerful. Without thinking, I expanded the first two notes into an old reel called "The Earl's Chair." It flowed out of the instrument like it had been waiting in there for a long time. After that tune had been released, another called "The Morning Dew" slipped out before I could stop it.

Leon looked on with interest as I managed to end the short set, "Jeez, I don't think I've ever heard a note come out of that thing. I thought it was dead. I sort of remember my dad saying he might take it to some guy downtown years ago to get it repaired, but I had no idea he had actually done it."

"Well, the repairman left his mark inside from 1965, so that would have been it. It feels pretty good, considering, but I don't see where it might lead me. I saw a couple of photos of the maker, Miller, from around the turn of the century, playing what I assume was his personal accordion, and this doesn't look like it. It's very nice, though."

"I don't think we have anything else of his, and I can't really even remember why we have this. We'll have to ask Grandma."

He had set out three cups and now poured tea for us, and I assumed, the watcher of TV in the other room. While he brought tea to Grandma, I saw the cheese-cutting knife resting on the plate.

I picked it up and felt the thrill of a beautiful handmade piece of art. The blade was clearly laminated and polished to a super high sheen. Examining it closely, I could see minute traces of the forging process. The handle was ebony with delicate silver and gold inlayed tracery. Testing the edge with my thumb I could tell that it was razor sharp.

Leon returned and I said, "Pretty stylish cheese cutter here. If there was to be a list of my weaknesses, besides old accordions and old motorbikes, I'd say that great blades would have to be right up there."

"Oh yeah, I made that last year in Asian Studies class. Sort of the family business, you know. Got an "A" and everything. My family still has the forge that my great great grandfather started down at the end of First right near the Bay. He knew how to make more than friggin' horseshoes, I can tell you that. C'mon in my room, I'll show you something."

I followed him down a narrow hallway lined with photos and Chinese calligraphy. He opened the door to his room and stood aside as I entered. I was shocked to see all the available wall space and level surfaces with a sword or knife of some type on them. Leon took one elaborately decorated sword off the wall and whipped it out of it's scabbard, giving me a little bit of concern for my personal safety in the confined space of the room. He showed off the blade, "According to my dad, this was made by an ancestor of mine during the Ming Dynasty – maybe even as early as the 1500's. Our family has been sword smiths for hundreds and hundreds of years, even before that. My dad, grandfather, and even my great-grandfather made some of these blades. A couple of them I made, not the greatest examples, on my part, but I'm getting better. That's why I'm taking metallurgy, along with Asian Studies. I'm trying to get all scientific and shit about the way they made their blades."

JOHN PEDERSEN

He resheathed the blade and continued, "Of course, nobody gave a damn about swords in San Francisco in the 1800's, so my great-grandpa and my grandpa were blacksmiths by trade. They just made swords and knives in secret, almost. My dad trained as a machinist but carries on in the forge as well. It's a pretty cool place, you should come down there with me sometime."

"I can't think of anything I'd like better. Perhaps we could have a few words with your grandma before I go back to work, she might be able to give me some kind of clue as to why the accordion came to rest in your family."

"OK, but if she completely talks your ear off, it's your fault, not mine. Once she gets started, sometimes it's hard to get her to stop. I have to go back to school pretty soon anyway, so she can't go on too long. Believe it or not, she was born here but was sent to China when she was just a little kid to learn the culture. When she got back, she never bothered to learn English, but I suspect that she understands perfectly well when she wants to."

We went back down the hall to the living room where grandma merely held up her hand to indicate silence, lest she should miss a single word of the drama playing out on the TV. Leon obediently held up until a commercial came on and then introduced us. I shook her hand and bowed as I thought might be appropriate. After Leon explained what I was doing there and what I might be seeking, Grandma's face grew serious and she started narrating dialog and shaking her finger at me for emphasis.

JOHN PEDERSEN

GRANDMA started speaking fast and furious. Leon shook his head and started translating. "She says that her grandfather was not the eldest son in his family. Even though he had trained many years at the forge, he was destined to be a farmer instead of a sword-smith. That's why he left China and came to San Francisco, to work metal. He started the forge down at the end of First and made shovels, picks, barrel hoops and all sorts of things people needed. He said no one here knew about swords or fighting with honor, so these things remained secret with him. Luckily, he had a son to pass his heritage; her father. She is very proud of her father's accomplishments and says she can go around San Francisco and point out many, many iron things he made that still stand and are in use."

"She says when her father was a young man, and his father was still alive, a white man – this Miller guy I assume – started to come into the forge. Miller wanted her grandfather to share the ancient secrets of the steel. Of course he refused and sent the man away. The man searched out her father when her grandfather was not there and made friends with him. She says after much talking and explaining, her father agreed to make a set of reeds for this fellow's accordion out of the same steel as the swords and knives. She says to make sure you know that the accordion was originally an ancient Chinese instrument thousands of years old called the Sheng."

"She says that while her father was working on the steel for the reeds the man happened to meet her father's younger sister, her aunt, at the place of business. She says it was very inappropriate for an unmarried Chinese girl to be talking to a man in those days. Even though her father was always there watching over them when they were together, she says it was still very inappropriate.

However, soon enough they were meeting in secret, and as work progressed on making the steel for the accordion reeds, they fell in love. Because of society, and her family's objections in general, it appeared as though it would never work out.

She says it wasn't too long before her father figured out there was something going on between them and he was angry that his little sister was flaunting all the rules of the young Chinese lady. Also, he was very jealous that she had found a lover and he still had not. She says the accordion you played in the kitchen was a present to her aunt from the man.

According to her, when one is preparing the steel of the sword, anger and jealousy are not feelings that should be in your soul, the smith must remain completely pure and neutral if the steel is to have an even personality.

But he went ahead anyway, and eventually, the metal was ready.

She says to pay attention now, because this is the serious part.

After Miller had taken the material for the reeds, and her aunt's heart as well, her grandfather found out what was going on, and her father was punished for making the steel, and her aunt was punished for associating with the instrument maker.

After a while, she says Miller returned to the forge with what he said was his most perfect instrument and wanted to play for the grandfather to prove to him that his skill was great and that he was worthy of his daughter.

Even though Miller was not invited into the shop, he entered and sat at the workbench and started playing. Grandfather cared little for what he considered a toy and less for the fellow playing it. She says her grandfather stood near the player with his forging hammer in his hand in a threatening manner trying to get him to stop playing and leave. The man did not stop, but became afraid and angry as well that the grandfather would not give him his blessing. As he played, she says, the steel in the reeds spoke to their mothers and fathers, which were the coals and the

JOHN PEDERSEN

red hot metal in the forge, and made them rise up and attack their master.

He was blinded and burned. It was a great tragedy, and her father had to assume all the work at the shop and the responsibility of providing for the family. Very sad.

She says that even after this, her aunt and the man continued to see each other in secret because they were very much in love. The man played his fabulous instrument at very fancy hotels and restaurants downtown sometimes all night, and was becoming quite famous.

As he became more famous, her father became more enraged and jealous. One time he followed his sister from their home very, very late at night to where she was meeting the man. She says it was just before dawn.

He found her sitting in the lounge of one fine hotel. For some reason the man was at the other end of the room still playing with much intensity. Her father said he was blinded by rage at this and went up to his sister and seized her arm to force her to leave. She refused and there was a commotion and struggle. The player continued to play but was watching very close, the music building in intensity. Heated words were exchanged, and then her father slapped her aunt. The accordion player produced an overwhelming final chord on the instrument and at that very moment, the walls, floor and ceiling began to shake.

She says the people at the hotel ran from their rooms to gain safety outside but her aunt, unfortunately, ran the wrong way to escape the wrath of her brother and be at the side of the accordion player. The roof fell in and as he escaped out a window with his instrument, she was crushed.

That date was April 18th, 1906. The family was very upset and the aunt was buried with much ceremony at the Chinese cemetery in Colma. However, because she was disgraced having been with a white man, her bones were not returned to China for re-burial, as was normal then.

She says the man returned to the forge to explain to her father and to apologize for causing the events that led to the death of his sister. Her father said he refused to talk to the man, but the man spoke anyway. He believed his playing had caused the great earthquake and his anger at seeing his love mistreated had manifested itself through the reeds."

Leon checked his watch, "Listen man, I have to get going or I'm gonna miss class. I'm sure that if you had days to sit here and listen,

Grandma would fill in the time completely. I think that's the gist of it, though."

I was overwhelmed by the story and my mind refused to come up with any coherent questions. As Leon cleaned the table and prepared to leave I finally blurted out,

"Could you get your grandmother to write down her aunt's name in Chinese characters?"

He asked her and said to me, "OK, she says that she will do it, but it'll take a while because she has to get the right calligraphy brush, the right paper, and the right ink. Not to mention be in a reverent frame of mind. So, if you don't mind, I'll push off here and you can just let yourself out when she finally gets done." I agreed and he was gone.

Grandma took quite a while to search through bundles of brushes that all looked exactly the same to me, and bottle after bottle of inks had to be inspected and smelled as well. Various rolls of paper had to be unrolled and rejected before the right one came to light. Finally, with all the components of a first class name-writing job at hand, she allowed herself to sit quietly with eyes closed for a minute or two before taking up the brush and dipping it into the ink.

Her aunt's name had five characters in it and each one required several lines, painstakingly performed.

Finally the task was complete; the name of the aunt was a work of art in itself. The large characters took up the entire page. Grandma waved it in the air and sprinkled the ink with what looked like fine sand until it had dried enough to hand over. She beamed a wide smile as she did.

Ordinarily I wouldn't say that I was a bowing kind of guy, but I bowed low as I thanked her for her time and her story.

Just then I believe another one of her dramas came on the TV and I was left to see myself to the door. I tucked the rolled paper inside of my jacket and clomped down the stairs.

It certainly had the feel of my lucky day, as the Norton was still where I had left it and it started without ceremony or complaint. I barely had time to mull over the tangled story during the four-block journey back to the shop.

When I turned into the alley there were eight or ten old motorbikes parked haphazardly where the sidewalk would be if there were one, and just as many scruffy-looking guys milling around while one of them banged on the shop door. They all wore various types of protective riding jackets of either leather or Kevlar, or old-fashioned waxed cotton that exuded the smell of rain-proofing. Some of them had their club emblem sewn on the back or over the pocket. The "Roadoilers" had come to visit.

Heads turned in unison as the Norton filled the alley with its racket. I managed to get the bike parked and the kickstand down before one of the louts, Kevin, ambled over.

"Hey, Sam, what's the deal here? It looks like old "Vlad the Impaler" has lost his marbles in there. Perry's been bangin' on the door and tryin' to negotiate with him for five minutes and ain't getting any closer to gettin' let in."

I allowed myself a good laugh over that. I tried to sum up the situation as I made my way through the crowd.

"As it turns out lads, poor old Vladimir is resting in hospital at the moment, having gotten his head bashed last night by person or persons unknown. Early reports are positive that he will recover whatever wits he possessed, perhaps more. The creepy blood and gore spread round the shop has all been scientifically analyzed and removed so you won't have to look for it. Motives are still unclear."

"The gatekeeper of the moment is one Jenny Farrar, with three R's, who is apparently made of sterner stuff than either Vlad or any of your lot. More of a force of nature I'd say, and not to be trifled with."

There was a certain amount of backslapping and mockery aimed in my direction after this.

The tallest of the lunks, Blake, said, "Looks like Sammy's in love, Ooo La La. Has she moved in, or are you waiting a couple of days for that?"

I sniffed and put my nose up in the air, rising above their jibes.

"Where Ms. Farrar does or does not live is none of your business clown, and if you will all quiet down I'll see if I can get her to let us in."

There was much hilarity over the prospect of myself not being allowed entrance to my own business, but finally I was able to make myself heard over the din.

"Ho, Jenny, this is Soren out here. It's OK to unlock the door now. I think I have this crowd under control."

There was a faint response from inside.

"Say again."

"I said, it's Soren, I'm back, these guys are almost like friends so let us in."

"Prove it! What did you bring to eat?"

"Ah shit, I forgot."

The door lock clicked and as it swung open Jenny stood there with a very large one-inch-drive socket wrench clutched in her hand.

"That's all the proof required, you forgot."

More laughter and rib poking greeted this.

I unclasped and pulled open the big doors and said,

"Roadoilers, meet Jenny; Jenny, The Roadoilers. Grease monkeys supreme. They have come all the way into the big city from rural Marin and other parts unknown to share their modest lunches with us. Hope against hope that it is not a purely liquid lunch as it has been many a time in the past."

Some of the smoother members of the gang sidled into the shop to give Jenny a good looking over and introduced themselves, warily keeping an eye on the 20-pound socket wrench.

I continued, "Perfectly good judgment on your part not having let them in as shiny things attract them and sometimes are too much temptation for them to resist."

I referred to several occasions when the boys had come to visit and afterwards, bits that had gone missing from bikes in my shop had shown up on similar bikes of theirs.

There was blustering and posturing but no outright denials and several six packs of beer and 1/2 pints of spirits were flashed out into the open as if to make up for the momentary lapses of some of the stickier fingered members.

Various backpacks and saddlebags were lugged inside and unloaded to reveal an assortment of snacks and deli items. Areas were swept clear of actual work in progress to make room for the feast.

Jenny surveyed the scene, "OK, if I weren't so hungry I'd still have reservations about the likes of you guys, but as it is, welcome to town!"

Beers were opened and plastic cups were handed out. Drinks were served up all around. Jenny cornered me near the 3 bean salad, "How in the heck did you get hooked up with this lot? I mean, I know they have those old leaky bikes and all, but how did they decide to make this their lunch stop?"

"Strangely enough, I have the honor to be among the founding members of the club. There used to be T-shirts, hats, oil rags and all sorts of junk you could get with the logo on them. There was even an old time string band that had the same name. A couple of these guys were in it." I pointed out three scruffy characters to her: John, Perry and Kevin." Defunct I think, or perhaps just temporarily between gigs. I think their CD is over there in the pile. They used to have this terribly funky old clubhouse up in San Rafael where they had a big BBQ every Thursday till finally they got displaced by CalTrans. Anyway, this is their big ride of the month. Most of them have to work on their bikes all month to get here and then home. I'm pretty sure one of their wives is sitting at home right now with the pick up truck keys in her hand waiting for a call. Once the food is gone and they've fingered and knocked over everything that is remotely interesting, they'll pack up and be gone."

Jenny grabbed a paper plate and a plastic fork, "Well, let's help them along."

We helped ourselves to the strange mix of foods that had been set out underneath the motorbikes on the lifts. I sincerely hoped that none of the sauces on the food had been augmented by ancient oil dripping from above.

There was much laughter, dropping of plates and half-hearted attempts to clean up. It wasn't long before the entire supply of beers and flask contents were exhausted. Steve, a large ex-fireman who had come all the way from Inverness with his rickety sidecar rig said, "Hey, Sam, doesn't Vladimir usually have some sort of nasty Russian rocket juice hidden in here somewhere? We could use some topping off right about now."

"I think he might have gotten a little too far into that himself last night. The only concrete evidence we found this morning to explain his battered noodle was empty bottles and a crusty exhaust wrench. If I could figure out how it could have possibly happened, I'd say it might have been a self-inflicted wound. Not to mention that I would not be doing my civic duty if I let you wing-nuts drink any of that stuff and then try to get back over the bridge. Better leave well enough alone."

As the gang of geezers prepared to leave I fished a spark plug wrench out of my toolbox and pulled out a drawer that held many different kinds of new plugs. After packing their saddlebags and tank bags, there was much huffing and puffing trying to re-start the old bikes. A few of them started and filled the alley with smoke and noise while the others continued kicking at their mounts with failing strength. Finally, I brought the supply of new sparkers out and quickly re-plugged one bike after another, and in severe cases of Sportster-Knee, kicked the bikes to life myself.

Eventually, everyone had a version of a running motorbike and the whole crowd set off with a thunderous roar. Predictably, as they turned onto Pacific at the end of the alley, there were horn honks and screeching brakes.

In their absence, the silence was deafening.

I set about filling a garbage bag with their refuse and added their recyclables to a 55-gallon drum.

Jenny said, "That sure took a bite out of the work day, didn't it?"

"They only come down once a month and often enough, one or more of their bikes won't run at all for the return trip, and they pay me to fix them. Putting up with them is like a business expense."

By now the time was almost 4:30, so I proposed we abandon any pretense of work and slip over to the coffee shop for an afternoon caffeine hit. Jenny said she had almost stopped up the majority of case cracks in my accordion, so we might as well.

I locked the doors and we strolled out into the fading light.

The late-in-the-day coffee crowd was out in force. Not a table or counter stool was available, so after we had ordered and paid for our coffees we had to just stand around getting in the way of the other folks coming and going.

Big Chris was manning the espresso machine and the scream of the milk steamer sounded like we were at the airport. After a while he looked up and spied us. He said something that was lost in the screech of the steamer. I edged closer and he repeated,

"I said some foreign guy was in here looking for your short friend there and – I think – you as well. He didn't know your name but he did know hers. His right arm was kind of useless and I couldn't hardly make out what in the hell he was talking about for quite a while. He acted real annoyed and when I said I hadn't seen either of you today, he wanted to know where you worked. I told him to piss off 'cause I didn't know or care, and he stormed out. I hope he's not her boyfriend, or nothin' like that 'cause you could be in trouble if he is."

"No, no, it's nothing like that, but I'd rather he didn't come calling over at the shop. I know that even if you did know where my place was, you wouldn't tell him, right?"

"Yeah, no worries there. But I hope he doesn't come back with more dudes his size 'cause you ain't really that hard to find, bro."

"Thanks Chris. Say, listen, I think we'll abandon the fancy drinks and get a couple to go. Put the balance in the tip jar."

We grabbed large paper cups and lids, filled them and slipped out of the place with furtive glances up and down the street.

We walked quickly back to my shop and went in, closing the doors behind us.

Jenny said "Shit, that didn't take long. I can't imagine how Jarno would know to send that clod over to the coffee shop to look for me. I thought that he never knew where I was before I showed up at work. Maybe he was spying on me. Ick!"

"Well, he's not too far off in any case. But in the meantime, perhaps we could get the old box together because if we want to get our free dinner at the pub, we have to get over there early."

"The what? Oh, right, the gigs must go on. It'll only be a few minutes."

She set to work reassembling my box, and I tried to make a mental plan for my next day's work, assuming that I survived the night.

JOHN PEDERSEN

CHAPTER

IT wasn't long at all before the box was back in one piece and a quick exploratory test drive showed definite improvements in airtightness. I turned off the machines and most of the lights. I figured a few lights left on would make it much harder to get ambushed inside my own shop. We locked up, and after giving the area a good scan for trouble, scooted down the back alleys to retrieve Jenny's car.

The car sat where we had left it and failed to sport any damage or parking tickets. During the starting ritual, I thought the battery had finally reached its last spark, but the engine caught at the very last moment. Jenny acted unimpressed.

We threaded our way out of North Beach and headed up Market Street, getting lost in the throngs of cars trying to fight their way out of the city at the end of the day. I gave Jenny instructions to the Flower, which was situated on upper Noe. Parking was generally the main issue in the area and I was banking on timing to work in our favor. Workers having left and the residents not having gotten home yet meant, hopefully, there would be a few spots in the same area code.

We slowly cruised by the bar but there were no chances there. I thought I recognized the same few cars sitting in the same spots from every previous visit. I wondered if there were legal rights to parking spot possession that could be willed to further generations.

A ways down the block and across the street an opening beckoned.

Before I could toss out handy suggestions about turning here and there, Jenny suddenly cranked the wheel and whipped across traffic – allowing me to visualize myself adorning the massive bumper of the truck she had cut off.

Once we were safely parked I managed to release my death grip on the door handle and grab my box. Jenny scanned the car for visible objects that might cause a thief to break in and plunder it. Satisfied there was nothing that would cause a cretin to attack this old heap instead of one of the hundreds of much nicer vehicles parked nearby, she locked up.

We strolled past quaint and bizarre shops lining the street. Jenny showed some interest in the punk clothing and the imported jewelry shops. There were no hardware, motorcycle, surf shops or music stores directly on the way, so I was immune.

We arrived at the Flower and Jenny surveyed the exposed timbers and faux English style exterior. She commented that wasn't it a slightly improbable place for an Irish session based on what she knew of Irish-English relations in general. I replied where moneymaking was concerned, politics established half way around the globe faded quite a bit.

We pushed through the heavy black door into the gloom of imported booths, dart boards, big screen TVs tuned to soccer and rugby channels and old geezers nursing pints of stout. As we passed the bar to the area reserved for serious diners and the session, I was gratified to see the barmaid start to draw a fresh pint of Guinness and pour a sturdy shot of Black Bush. I suspected these were for my personal consumption.

Sean and a companion I didn't recognize were already seated at a table for four. Jenny and I settled into the vacant spots.

Sean's friend was quite the beautiful example of the Black Irish. Long, curly black hair and creamy white skin. She had green eyes and sported bright red lipstick, which jumped out of the gloom like a beacon. She was wearing a black pullover sweater and, from what I could see, tight designer jeans. However, it looked as though she had come out on the losing end of some sort of dispute in the recent past, as her arm was cast up and in a sling and she had some puffy black and blue spots on her cheeks.

Sean was involved with his fish and chips, side order of bangers and mash, but managed to mumble out some words around his food.

I responded, "Come again Miss Manners, I don't think I quite got the drift of that."

He took a mighty swallow and a gulp of stout and tried again, "I said, this lass is a friend of mine from Dublin. Soren Rauhe, Jenny Farrar, with three R's, meet Edain O'Connell. She's just in from the east coast, but don't ask about the sling and stuff or she'll bite your friggin' head off."

Edain gave Sean a slug with her good hand that looked like it rattled him seriously.

"Don't mind your man here, he's just spoutin' off about things not at all his business like most drunkards I know do."

Sean laughed at this, Jenny didn't.

The athletic looking waitress arrived bearing my pint and shot. Jenny studied the menu while I ordered from memory. Most of the kitchen offerings of the Flower were of the deep fried or heavily breaded variety, which I have less and less tolerance for. I opted for a salad, which I knew would exceed the weekly leafy greens intake of many Irish towns. Sean had seen me order greens so many times before that he didn't even bother to smirk. Jenny looked on approvingly and ordered the same. The salads tended to be large and I doubted her ability to finish one.

Sean finished one plate of food and slid the other in its place. Before starting on his bangers and mash he said, "So, what's all this startling information you have been keeping secret? Somethin' about McCracken and Jim Sullivan and your accordion?"

"Not my accordion, dopey, some mysterious box from the turn of the century. Don't you remember me telling you the story about the guy that caused the earthquake with his accordion playing? Cripes, it was just the other day."

"Vaguely, but tell it again for Edain's sake; she likes a good display of bullshittery. In fact, she's an expert."

This earned him another bone-crunching punch from her good hand.

"OK, here it is in a nutshell. McCracken told me he had heard of a guy Conroy met who claimed to have caused the earthquake with his playing. Fine, just a story, right? But then on a whim I asked Jim Sullivan about it, and he said he had heard the same story and had even seen the guy's photo hanging at the Bohemian Club. So I got Joey Leary to get me in there and I saw the guys picture along with another player hangin' on the wall, big as life. Then I got into the library and checked out the guy's info. Turns out he was an instrument maker and also played in minstrel shows all over the South Seas and stuff like that. The other guy in the picture was his apprentice for a while. I gathered from the guy's writing the apprentice was the fellow who caused the earthquake. I left Joe asleep in the library and managed to get out of there."

"And got completely shit faced as well", Jenny threw in.

"Well, yeah, that too. Anyway, we finally got home and on the machine there was a message from somebody who owned an accordion made by the apprentice guy, C.L. Miller by name. So this afternoon I went over to that guy's house, and it turns out his family is Chinese and they have been here way longer than any of us. The guy who called me is a blacksmith, like all the men in his family have been. He showed me some knives and swords he made that were pretty impressive. Then his grandmother told me all about how this Miller guy had tried to get her grandfather to make accordion reeds out of the steel he used for swords, and he had refused. Eventually, her father agreed to make the reeds. The accordion guy and her aunt met at the forge and fell in love, and she was going to run away with him but got killed during the earthquake. And get this, the guy was playing the accordion at the same time. Bizarre, eh?"

Sean said, "When 'WE' finally got home? Do 'WE' share a home now?"

"What? Are you kidding me? I tell you all this and you want to know who lives where? You jerk!"

Edain wound up to deliver yet another shot to the arm and this time Sean flinched away.

"Jus' jokin', jus' jokin'. Yeah, that's a pretty wild story all right. I'm not exactly sure where you could go from there, though. It was an awful long time ago."

"Who knows, but the aunt is supposed to be buried in Colma somewhere, and the accordion guy spent all of his cash on a memorial for her, so I might try to go find that just for the hell of it. Not to mention, on an unrelated note, I found a whole bunch of stuff from the end of the Galleazzi accordion factory over where Jenny works. Worked. I haven't looked at it yet but there could be cool stuff in there."

Sean showed a distinct lack of interest, "Oh, I'm sure."

Our salads arrived and we dedicated ourselves to them while Sean plowed through his glutinous second dinner. Between mouthfuls I said to Edain, "Are you a player at all, would you be sitting in? I hope so 'cause it looks like we might have pretty light attendance tonight and some new blood would be welcome."

"Jaysus, even if I were, how the hell could I do anythin' with the arm done up like this. I can tell you share the same reasoning powers as Auld Sean here. Edjits. I might sing the odd song, though. If the mood happens to strike me, that is."

Sean said, "She's a great singer, which would be nice to hear for a change, eh."

"For sure. Are you going to bother to tune up tonight, having guests and all, or are you going to just start pounding it out as usual?"

"We'll see who shows up and whether they're worth the effort."

I finished up my salad and the shot and carried my pint and accordion box over to an area that was slightly raised and had been cleared of tables and chairs. They liked their sessions tidy at the Flower, no spreading out all over the entire goddamn place.

I sat in my usual chair in the corner, which ensured no random drunks could stumble over me, and got the box out. The TVs and jukebox were still on and the volume still turned up. I hoped the bar ladies might notice we had started to play and at least lower the volume and turn off the speakers in our part of the room.

I pushed a few notes out of the box and could notice the improvement in air delivery right away. Funny that I would work on other people's accordions all the time and yet neglect mine so.

Just to get my fingers under me, I played a few tunes that nobody else at this session liked to play. "The Next Market Day", "O'Dwyers Hornpipe", "The Home Ruler": all are slightly slower hornpipes and have a nice lope to them.

Before long, Sean joined me with his guitar and his battered old bouzouki. I could see a few of the more timid players milling around near the bar, waiting for us to get rolling so they could slip in unnoticed. Not likely I thought, with only two of us playing.

We played some of the most common jigs and kept the tempo down to encourage the rabble to come up and sit down, which they eventually did, one by one.

Fiddles, whistles, flutes and even a set of pipes came out. Pretty soon we were making enough noise to drown out the TVs and the temperature in the corner was rising. I was choosing and starting most of the tunes because if left to their own devices this unfocused and timid crowd would just sit there noodling around for ages and not play any actual tunes. At that moment Sean and I were the seasoned veterans, and Sean generally just didn't care what he was playing.

After forty-five minutes or so the session was going pretty well and I was soaked with sweat, so I stood up to take a break. A pair of extremely lovely flute players had arrived, the blond Rita and her raven-haired student Joelle. Singly they were great players but when they double-teamed the session magical things happened. Rita's husband, Dan, knocked out credible tunes on a fancy banjo-mandolin. Sean kept going, pushing the tempos to keep the newbies from grinding to a halt.

Jenny and Edain had taken seats closer to the band and I sat with them. The bar mistress noticed the change in the music, and seeing I had taken a break started pulling a beer for me. In mid-session I preferred one of the local brews, in this case Lagunitas IPA.

I said to Edain loudly, "Have you known Sean for long?"

"The Tierneys are neighbors down in Wicklow. Sean was there with the folks when he was just a wee lad, and even now whenever they come over we get together and terrorize the local pubs. I'm up in Dub now but the rest of the crowd still is on the land. I just thought I'd swing on over, as I was in the states and all."

"I see. But you had a bit of an accident....?"

"Don't even bother."

"Not bothering, that's me."

Sean stood up, presumably to go outside for a smoke, so I thought I had better get back in the saddle to keep things going. Jenny and Edain resumed their conversation.

The music was randomly limping along without much focus by the time I had retaken my seat. I started clumping my feet to try to get both sides of the circle playing at once, and then jumped in with the box, hitting the downbeats hard and gradually pushing the tempo up. After a few times through the crowd that had been largely ignoring the music suddenly took notice and a few enthusiastic types started banging on tables and clapping along. Not very accurately, but at least they finally realized we were there.

After another tune or two, Sean returned and said, "I just saw Sloane drive by. She didn't look in a good mood. I hope she doesn't freak out when she sees Edain here. She's kind of needy lately, don't ya think?"

"She does act kind of unsettled since shit-canning the last loser. She'd have to be to consider going home with you."

"Oh yeah, well I'm gettin' her this time, and no doubt about it!"

"Good luck there. Say, maybe you could get Edain up here to sing something. I'm kind of sick of hearing your same old songs."

We were in the delicate position of picking a song that would be easy enough for the rest of the session to be able to pick up on the fly, and yet cool enough and unfamiliar enough to make Edain want to get up and sing. After a short conference we decided perhaps an old version of "The Greenfields of Canada" might do the trick.

I started the slow air myself and got the expected perplexed looks from most of the players. Before Sean joined in, he passed the single microphone around the circle indicating that it should wind up at the end closest to Edain and Jenny. Most of the players handled it as though it were a poisonous viper while a few paused briefly thinking they might have been the intended target; not likely since none of them were worth a shit as singers and clearly didn't know this song. Finally Sean was able to catch Edain's eye and he made facial expressions indicating she should get busy.

She thought it over for a moment and then stood up and walked over to the edge of the railing separating the audience and diners from the players. She took the mic from the last guy in the circle and gently laid it on the railing. I thought that might be the end of the matter, but then she turned and faced the audience and when the top of the song came around, she started to sing.

Her voice had a startlingly pure tone and a fierce power. The first few words were lost in the general hubbub but it didn't take long till people noticed that something special was going on. As her singing built intensity, Sean and I backed off on our volume til we were cruising along in respectful accompaniment. All chitchat and dinnerware shuffling and clanking died down to nothing.

She stood ramrod straight with her eyes almost closed and the song erupted out of her. Every couple of verses she would wait while I took a break and then resume.

It is not a particularly long song, but very sad, and refers, of course, to the mass exodus from Ireland during the famine. Terribly simple and old fashioned.

At the close of the song Edain quietly spoke the last few words of the song instead of singing them. Nobody in the entire bar missed them. You could hear the ice machine rattle and a car pass on the street in the silence.

She opened her eyes and the entire place erupted in applause and cheers. She nodded respectfully and sat down. Sean and I looked at each other and took advantage of the enthusiasm to launch ourselves into a blazing fast reel, which whipped the still wild crowd into an even higher state of insanity. Pints were knocked over in the rush of half drunk ya-hoos clambering onto the non-existent dance floor to kick their legs sky-ward in bizarre imitation of Irish step dancing. With our faithful crew trailing in our wake we flogged one reel after another for all they were worth, sensing this was undoubtedly the high point of the evening.

The time was approaching 11:00, which was our cut off time due to a new upstairs neighbor with a small child who objected to the noise. What kind of feeble planning would allow a person in such a situation to move in over a raucous bar we could never imagine, but they had, and we had to respect the landlord's regulations.

We started tapering off the intensity of the tunes, choosing more re-laxing tempos and easier pieces. Finally we wrapped up the session with the last tunes that we often played called "Rolling in the Ryegrass" and "The Bucks of Orranmore". I started putting the box away and Sean retrieved his guitar case and the sack he carted the bouzouki around in.

As we approached the bar to get a farewell shot or two, Sloane stormed in the door and headed straight for us. Sean said, "Ah, shit."

She looked to be a bit off of her usual stylish and tidy self. Her de-signer jeans lacked a crease and might have been actually worked in. Her cable knit Aran sweater looked slightly too working class and her red hair was unstylishly pulled back into a simple ponytail

"Soren, Sean, are you done already? I thought this session went till at least midnight. You're not running right out, are you?"

"Sloane darling, if anyone had bet me whether you did or did not know where this bar was, I would have said you had no idea. And lost that bet, I guess. I've never seen you in here before, have I? Even though it's Friday night and all, you generally have better things to do."

"What could be more important than being with my two favorite men?"

It was at this point I suspected she had been drinking or had just gone completely nuts.

Jenny and Edain arrived at the bar having fought their way through the players, diners and just plain drunks littering the place. Sloane acted a bit put off when she saw Jenny, but the storm clouds really gathered when she saw Edain engage Sean in conversation. I reflected on the number of times the situation had been the reverse: Sean and I watching like whipped dogs as Sloane snagged one high rolling yuppie after another.

I didn't think Edain was about to take any crap from Sloane concerning who she could pal around with, and I didn't especially want to have Sloane start on me again, so I suggested to Jenny we might want to get rolling. I collected my meager cash stipend from Tony, the bar owner, and left Sean staggering between the two women competing for his attention.

We made our way down the street in the cold but fresh air. The moon was peeking over the roofs of the buildings across the street and shed a mystic, silvery light on everything.

The Toyota was unmolested and Jenny twisted the key this way and that trying to unlock the door, the recent weather having invaded the lock and made it seize up. She was about to get really indignant and start banging on the window when I tried the wing window on the passenger side and it gracefully flipped open. I reached in and unlocked my side and slid into the seat. I leaned over and popped the lock on the driver side door and opened it a bit by way of invitation.

Eventually Jenny noticed the open door and jerked it wide.

"How the hell did you get in there?"

"The wing window doesn't have a latch on it at all. The car can't be locked up very well without that, and good thing too."

"Crap!"

Jenny climbed in and performed the starting ritual, which was closer than ever to not working. Begrudgingly the car coughed to life.

"You know, if you brought the car down the alley tomorrow, I might be able to give it a tune up or charge the battery, or something."

"Let me consider it, I'm sure Jarno would appreciate the help in locating both of us."

"Well, at the moment I think we're in the clear. He can't know where you are or who I am, so screw him!"

Jenny didn't choose to comment on that.

The car finally warmed sufficiently and we headed for the Richmond. Over the moan of the engine and the growling of the bad bearings Jenny said,

"That Edain girl is pretty interesting. She doesn't give out much about the recent past though. From chatting with her I found she has kind of a grudge against fiddlers for some reason. And that Sloane, she looked kind of frayed around the edges, didn't she? Kind of losing her grip. She sure wants attention from you and Sean."

"Pretty ironic, actually. Sloane was definitely the queen of our neighborhood when we were growing up. Whatever she said, eventually that's what would happen. The boys in the neighborhood were all after her, but most of them didn't even have a chance. Sean and I were the only old friends that hung in there after she started marrying jackasses. I guess she figured if she ever got desperate enough she could have either or both of us. Although I can't really see her being satisfied with what either of us has to offer."

"Tough shit for her, eh Mr. Positive Self Image? Hey, what's with all the flashing lights and stuff?"

We had turned onto 48th and there were several fire trucks and police cars uphill from us in the middle of the road.

"Looks like some poor bastard had a fire. I hope it didn't spread to my house."

That turned out to be a far closer call than I could have guessed. As we got closer, we could see a knot of neighbors in the street being held back by a few police officers. They were looking straight at my house. My heart sunk and I wondered if something had exploded in the garage like my mother had always warned me would happen.

Seeing as how the road was blocked anyway, we parked right in the middle and got out to see what the damage might be. I smelled burning rubber and plastic.

I finally was able to see through the crowd and it looked as though the house was still standing and was mercifully intact. Not so with Big Red. The poor old van was a smoldering wreck and had been pulled halfway

JOHN PEDERSEN

into the street presumably by the fire department, to keep the house safe.

The tires were burned off and the interior was completely gone. The paint was blistered all over and smoking piles of half burned junk littered the driveway, the remains of several wetsuits and surfboards among them. I gaped slack jawed as the fireman joked around and stowed their hoses and gear. I finally got up enough courage to speak to a policeman.

"So, lucky the house didn't go up, eh?"

"Yeah, the neighbors called it in pretty fast, and we're only a couple of blocks from the fire house. That van's toast, though. Harhar."

"Alas, unluckily that would be my van, and luckily, my house. Any idea what caused the blaze?"

"Not exactly, but I'd say the oil soaked rags and newspapers in the back might have had something to do with it."

I doubted it was that simple, but I signed a police report anyway. One of the last onlookers to depart was my downhill neighbor, Walt. Even though I had spent my entire life in the house, and was only ten years or so younger than him, I doubted he would even know who I was. He and his wife Ana, and their kids kept pretty much to themselves and were traveling much of the time. He came over to borrow tools from time to time, but always in the middle of some sort of crisis so we hadn't chatted too much.

He greeted me with, "Sauron, we need to talk. Catch me tomorrow before I take off for work. Say, eight thirty or so. OK?"

I was a little confused when he invoked the villain in "The Lord of the Rings", but I finally realized that it was his attempt to pronounce my name.

"Sure Walt, I'll catch up with you then, sorry about the mess and the smell and all."

"Hmmmm…."

He left for next door and Jenny pulled her car closer to the house and parked in the street. She started cleaning everything of even marginal value out of her car and transferring it to the floor of my living room. For such a small vehicle it sure held an awful lot of debris. Finally she must have thought her worldly possessions were safe enough. I locked the front door, put on the kettle, and while Jenny went to shower I settled down to ponder the possibilities.

JOHN PEDERSEN

THE kettle boiled and I made tea. I thought of a midnight snack but having failed once again to visit a grocery store, I knew that to search for real food would be futile. I settled for merely pouring tea into two of my cleanest big mugs and sweetening it with honey.

I wasn't certain what to expect next so I carried them into the spare room in order to deliver one to Jenny. She wasn't there. I carried on into my room and found her, wet haired and fragrant between the sheets. I said, "I think I'll just jump in the shower as well, but here's a little warmer upper for you in the meantime."

"Thanks, it smells good. I wouldn't be too long in the bathroom though 'cause I'm pooped. Get going!"

I set my mug on the nightstand and fairly ran to the shower shedding clothes as I went. The bathroom was still steamy and warm as I started the water. Not used to being second in, I forgot about hot water already being in the pipes and nearly scalded myself. I spotted several unfamiliar shampoos and conditioners in the stall but stuck with regular soap and was soon drying vigorously. I brushed my teeth just in case and took off for the bedroom.

The overhead light was off and there was a soft glow coming from the bedside lamp. Jenny lay on her side facing away and as I climbed in bed I could hear her soft snores. My thoughts ran in the "Son of a Bitch" category.

As soon as I was cozy under the comforter and resigned to more waiting, Jenny rolled over and draped her arm over my chest.

"Sucker!"

"Ah, you certainly had me there."

In general, I don't think I've often had first kisses with a girl when she was naked in my bed. Usually there was a lot more anxiety and drama leading up to it. Jenny and I exchanged tentative smooches for only a few seconds before it became clear we were on the same page. Our lovemaking didn't have the usual elements of awkwardness and missed cues. We started out with a fierce, almost desperate abandon.

Sometime later while we were hunting for the sheets, blankets and pillows Jenny said, "Well OK then, that was something. If I didn't have a bunch of psycho Finns hunting me, and apparently finding me at my hideout, I'd almost be relaxed and blissed out."

"The murder of Big Red is troubling all right. I'd even say I'm pissed off about it. Not to mention that Walter is probably going to give me some sort of neighborhood watch kind of shit tomorrow. Despite all that, I'm pretty contented, thanks to yourself."

I admired Jenny's naked form as she scurried here and there. I had inklings earlier but that kind of judgment was pretty hard to make under work clothes. She was compactly built, with womanly proportions in the breast, butt and thighs. I doubted whether she would ever be mistaken for a super model. She had a waist that narrowed nicely and the muscles in her arms and legs looked defined and powerful.

She threw herself back on the bed and climbed on top of me. She said, "Yeah, me too, Buster. How about round two now that we're all warmed up and all."

I didn't have to respond verbally.

Eventually we both fell asleep and woke up in the morning in almost exactly the same positions. I disentangled myself and snuck off to the shower. As I left the room I glanced at Jenny peacefully sleeping and realized with a start that I was in serious trouble. I had rarely, if ever, felt quite so taken.

By the time I returned, she was awake and fooling with the TV remote. She said, "Where the hell is the news on this thing? I'm kind of a newshound, in case you hadn't noticed. I don't suppose you'd mind if I signed up for a real newspaper, would you? How about we do a bit of shopping today, actually make the place liveable."

"Paper, shopping, check. We'll get to that on the way to the shop, OK? Now however, I have to get dressed and go get a good neighbor ass whipping from Walter. If I'm not back in half an hour, the house and all the motorbikes are yours until my folks ask why the mortgage hasn't been paid. Just tell them you are their new daughter and send up some cash. It might work."

"Their new daughter, eh, aren't you cute. There might be a few things you need to know before I get dragged into the family."

"I doubt it. My folks probably like you better than me already, and they don't even know you."

"We'll see about that."

For the first time in my memory, I didn't bother to go out on the balcony to check the waves before getting dressed.

I stepped around Jenny's pile of auto belongings and out the front door. I walked down hill to Walter and Ana's house and knocked on the door.

Walter answered the door in a sweatshirt and candy-stripe pajama pants. He said, "Is it 8:30 already? C'mon in here, I don't think we need to be on the street."

I followed him to the kitchen where Ana was bustling around in her robe. She said, "Soren, good morning. How about some breakfast, eggs, toast, bacon? Walt, get him some coffee!"

Ana was a petite woman who showed her Basque heritage clearly. Wavy black hair, piercing dark eyes and quick hands were combined with a rapier like wit and a quick laugh. I could tell Walter liked to think he was the captain of the ship, but suspected Ana might be the admiral.

Walter is taller than me and brushed his thick hair straight back. His hairstyle distinctly reminded me of JFK and I suspected that wasn't accidental. He fussed with a complex looking espresso machine til at last it gave up a miniature cup of black mud. He set it before me with a pitcher of cream.

"Listen, Sauron…"

Ana said, "Oh for crying out loud, Walter."

"Ok, Ok…Soren."

I could see the unfamiliar sounds struggling to escape his mouth.

"Walt, just call me Sam, that's what everybody else does."

"Sam? OK great, that's great."

I could see relief flooding his face.

"So anyway, Sam, to get to the point, I'm thinking of running for school board and then maybe supervisor. When a guy does that he comes under a certain amount of scrutiny; financial, family, work history, the neighborhood where he lives. Get my drift?"

"Jeez Walt, you kind of hit me at a funny time, but I'll donate whatever I can. I'm all for you. Play at fundraisers and like that, I'm in."

"What, fundraisers and what? No, no, you're missing the point."

Ana said, "Walt, if you'd get to it."

"OK, back to the point. Sam, having that old rusted out hulk sitting in your driveway full of crap looked bad enough, but now it's beyond belief. It stinks too. So here's the deal I have for you. I'll call a wrecker and get the thing towed away, and I'll sell you the Ford for way cheaper than I have it priced. How's that?"

"I appreciate the van might not be the flashiest ride on the block, and I guess it's dead now, so getting rid of it is fine. But I'm confused about the Ford business. I didn't even know you had a Ford."

That's because it's invisible. Come with me, I'll show you."

We walked to the front window and he parted the drapes.

"There it is, across the street."

He pointed. I saw a white Ford Ranger with a matching white camper shell. Not too old, perhaps five or six years. There was a lumber rack on the roof of the shell and a small yellow bubble light in the middle of the roof. There was a round insignia of some kind on the door. No dents or caved in fenders that I could see.

"That's yours? I thought they were working on the street or something. How long have you had it? I don't think I've ever seen it before."

"Like I said, it's invisible. You can park virtually anywhere and not get a ticket. You can go as fast as it's capable of and not get a ticket. Half of the time you can drive right through the front gates of wherever you want. I've had it for a couple of years and you never even noticed it right there. So what do you say, deal?"

"I'm not sure I can afford it, Walt. What are you asking for it?"

"I have it up for eighty-five hundred. You can have it for six, or fifty five…"

Ana said, "Walter quit screwing around."

"OK, if I can use it sometimes to go to the dump or whatever, I'll sell it to you for three grand. You can pay me whenever."

He laid the keys, pink slip and registration on the table. I was stunned.

"So, there ya go, simple solutions to problems. Wait, I could use that as a slogan. Ana, write that down."

"Hell Walt, I'm flipped. It might take me a little while to come up with the cash, but I don't think it'll be any problem. I certainly think the price is beyond fair. Sure, I'm in!"

I choked down the thick coffee to be nice. I shook Walter's hand and gave Ana a hug.

"I feel pretty lucky right now to have you guys as neighbors. Thanks. Maybe we should have a BBQ or something and have some fun."

Walter showed me the door said, "Sure, that would be great. We'll abuse the wine collection."

I walked across the street to check out the newest member of the family. It was completely straight without dents or scratches. Up close the insignia on the door was a complex mix of images that could have easily have been mistaken for a town logo or college seal or perhaps that of some public works department.

I unlocked the door and released the hood latch. The engine was clean with no traces of massive oil leaks or past explosions. The four-cylinder motor was just barely bigger than that of a modern touring motorcycle: 2.2 liters of mild motivation that made me suddenly understand Walter's comment about "as fast as it's capable of."

It had a 5 speed manual gearbox and I figured it would go along at a decent speed, at least on the level. It was the extended cab version with a couple of tiny jump seats behind the front seats, but more importantly, room for instruments and whatnot.

I headed back into the house to relay all this news to Jenny.

She was up, dressed and had a cup of hot tea. She was ready to go and said, "So, was that as painful as it looks?"

"Not at all, as it turns out. They were pretty nice, in fact. He offered to get Big Red towed away and gave me a cool newer truck for almost nothing. I'm in shock."

I displayed the keys and paperwork. Jenny said, "What are we waiting for, let's give it a test drive."

Jenny didn't need any special tools to hang around the motorcycle shop, so I grabbed my box and locked up. I gave Big Red a fond farewell petting and said, "So long, pal. I'm sure you'll come back as a Maseratti or a Ferrari. You've been a good truck. Good bye."

Jenny looked on with barely disguised contempt.

We crossed the street and climbed into the new vehicle. We looked into the door pockets and flipped the ashtray open and closed a couple of times. Tried out the radio and shoved the seats back and forth. Looked in the glove box and opened up the compartment in the center armrest. Jenny held up a handful of quarters,

"Score, you're making money already!"

I inserted the key and said to Jenny, "Here goes, the ultimate test."

I gave it a twist and the engine fired up in a split second. I noticed the odometer only had sixty thousand miles on it. I hoped it was on the first time around and not the second or third. The motor settled down to a subdued burble that was just loud enough to let a person know that the engine was running. I slipped her into gear and headed uphill to Geary. There was enough power to get going up the incline, but little danger of spinning the wheels or snapping our necks.

It was still pretty early, so I suggested we head over the bridge to Mill Valley for breakfast and watch the guys on the Saturday Morning Ride. Jenny said she didn't have other plans. The trip over the Golden Gate Bridge was magnificent. It was one of those beautifully clear winter days when everything practically radiates light. The bay was already alive with sailboats, and Alcatraz sat in the middle of the water like a jewel. The water between the north and east bay sparkled like it was encrusted with diamonds.

We exited the freeway to take Highway 1 north and found the café right at the junction of Highway 1 and Miller. I tried not to make connections with the accordion maker Miller. There were tables outside on a patio and we sat at one of these, basking in the sunshine.

Directly across the street was a gas station with a huge parking lot adjacent to it. There were already about fifty motorcycles parked there, and their owners milled about in various degrees of pseudo-racer outfits. More bikes were arriving every moment and by the time we had gotten coffees and ordered, there must have been a hundred bikes of all kinds. Jenny was astounded at the variety. There were some bikes that looked like they were right off the racetrack alongside full dress Harleys. Choppers and vintage English bikes were clumped up in their own groups with their riders wearing much the same dress.

Suddenly, acting upon some unseen signal, one of the most racy looking individuals climbed aboard his bike, fired it up, and whipped out onto Highway 1 headed north. We could hear the scream of his motor as he negotiated the twisty corners that wind through the Eucalyptus trees and climb up the steep hill. Within seconds, the rest of the bikes were started and had exited the parking lot according to some ancient and mysterious natural order. Fastest guys first, slowest guys last, and non-running bikes left in the parking lot with their owners fussing over them.

By the time our breakfasts came, all was relatively silent again.

Jenny said, "Holy Crap, that was amazing. Do they do that every Saturday? Some of those first guys looked pretty serious; don't they ever get speeding tickets? Don't they ever crash and get hurt?"

"This ride has been happening every Saturday, essentially like what we just saw since around 1960. The Highway Patrol has tried a million ways to disrupt it but they only manage to change it. They've handed out hundreds of tickets and set up roadblocks and even arrested slews of guys, but it just goes on the next week. There have been plenty of crashes, deaths and accidents, but far fewer than you might expect, given how some of them drive. I only go once in a while because Sean and I surf pretty often on Saturdays. Even when I do go, I'm riding with the geezers at the back of the pack. Plenty of the bikes fall apart on the ride though, and I get to see them later in the week.

"I'm beginning to see a pattern to your business plan."

As I paid the bill Jenny scrounged around in the abandoned stack of that day's newspapers next to the cash register. We headed back into the city, only separated from it by the $6 toll of the bridge.

While negotiating Doyle Drive and Lombard Street, Jenny said, "So, do you think it was Jarno who burned up your van? It doesn't sound to me like something he would think of. Break in and beat the piss out of us maybe, but burn up a car? That would take too much planning for him or any of his clods. Like bringing a lighter or a match."

"I'm sure I don't know. Neither do I know of anyone with a particular grudge against Big Red, no angry mobs of van haters or anything. I can't think of anyone who has it in for me either; who wouldn't just walk up and beat the shit out of me if that's what they wanted. Generally I don't hang with a very devious crowd."

Jenny mulled that over while she started rummaging through the papers she had borrowed from the café. She found the front section and casually started checking out the top stories. The mayor did this, the governor did that, the president wanted to do this, but the opposition party stymied him, and all the rest.

We had just made the heroic turn across the two lanes of Van Ness onto Broadway when she gave a shriek. I was so startled I instinctively swerved the car and went over the sidewalk corner as I headed up Larkin.

"Jesus, what the hell!" She studied the paper closely and kept muttering "Oh my God".

I pulled over into a loading zone and repeated, "What gives?"

"It says here the only guy that I even gave half a shit about and the one guy that was ever nice to me at Jarno's was found stabbed to death last night."

"Wait, two guys were stabbed?"

"Same guy. Oh man, what if he was trying to protect me against Jarno's goons and they killed him for it. Ohhhh Noooo, I'm getting a really, really bad feeling about this."

"Me too, but we can't sit here. If I didn't have so much friggin' work to do, we could skip town and hide out somewhere, but I think I'd rather face the Finnish Mob than grumpy bikers with no motors in their bikes."

Jenny said, "I need to think, think, think."

"Good luck there, it doesn't usually help me that much."

She gave me a look that showed she was in total agreement with my last statement. She said," The guy that got killed was named Niklas Laukkanan or something sounding like that. I don't even know why he was there at Jarno's because he was pretty hopeless with the tools. There was something about him though, like he always had his eyes open and never missed anything. He acted like he was way too smart to be working there, but like he had to. Maybe he was an undercover cop or something from Finland. I can't imagine why anybody except the burned dealers would care about furniture fakery, no matter how crooked Jarno is. There must be something we're missing."

In my case I was missing everything from start to finish.

I was pretty sure no one knew I had a new vehicle unless they had

ESP or something, so I assumed it was safe to park near the shop if possible. I found a spot not too far from the end of Jerome Alley and Jenny and I hunkered down in the seats to keep watch for a while.

Aside from some coming and going at the architect's office there wasn't anybody around. We were about to get out of the truck and slip over to the shop when the Asian guy who had been lurking around, possibly Vladimir's attacker, walked quickly out of the alley and headed up Pacific.

Jenny said, "Haven't we seen that guy before? Who the hell is he?"

"I don't know but I think he was around the night Vlad got bashed on the head. He doesn't look too dangerous, but I guess there could be an Uzi or something in that briefcase. Maybe Jarno hired a contract hit man to take care of his dirty work. Didn't take him long to clip that other guy."

"Oh, Jesus, don't talk like that. I think Jarno is too cheap to do something like that. I gather from the movies those guys don't work for free."

"I 'spose. C'mon, let's take our chances."

We locked up the truck and scooted across the street and down the alley. The front door to the shop looked unmolested. My heart was fairly pounding as I unlocked and swung open the door.

The lights were not on any longer and my anxiety ratcheted up another notch. I supposed there was a possibility the bulbs had merely burned out, but after the most recent events, I didn't think so. I told Jenny to back up and wait in the alley.

I peeked inside but couldn't see anything amiss. I slipped in without opening the door further and shut it behind me. The shop was quite dark, barely any light coming in through the skylights. I strained my ears for movement at the back of the shop but didn't hear anything. I started slowly creeping along the wall, trying not to knock any tools off the benches or trip over any carelessly stored items.

Even though it probably only took a minute to get halfway to the back of the shop it felt like hours. I was just easing my way around the rolling bench where the old Enfield waited when I had the wits scared out of me by the ringing telephone. I jumped and series of tools clanged to the floor. The phone shrilled again and just as I hit the nearest light switch the ring was cut off and an unseen person answered.

"Da, is motorbike shop. No, is not here. Wait, maybe is here."

As the overhead lights warmed up and got brighter, I could see Vladimir lying on the back-bench, eyes closed, nonchalantly holding the phone receiver out to me. He sported an enormous turban of gauze on his head and hospital slippers on his feet. It was all a little too much to take in.

As I made my way to the back of the shop to get the phone, Jenny pushed open the door a crack and poked her head in.

"Hey, I'm getting' cold out here, is it safe or not?"

"I think it's only a ghost, so probably safe enough."

I took the receiver from Vlad without a word being exchanged. I raised it to my ear and tentatively said, "Hello?"

"Hey Bozo, it's me, where you been, I've been calling for ages. Never mind, I know the answer to that. Say, listen, I forgot to remind your lust-clouded mind last night that we have that gig today in San Anselmo. Do you remember anything about that at all? Like, five till eight, you, Mike, and me, fiftieth birthday for some loon at The Log Cabin. Does this ring any bells for ya?"

"Hmm…faintly. Mike the fiddler from Santa Rosa, right? I thought he wasn't going to play with accordion players anymore after our last debacle. Thanks again, by the way."

"Nah, nah, I guess he got over it. And who knew that the Silverado Country Club was really that serious about the band drinking on stage."

"And stealing everything that wasn't nailed down."

"Oh yeah, that. Well, Mike got over it anyway. And there's plenty of other country clubs in the sea."

"Anyway, this gig is sort of coming back to me. So, we should leave around four or so? If you pick me up here, I'll let Jenny take the truck."

"The truck? When did you get a truck? I assume that you aren't talking about Big Red."

"I'll tell you all about it later. See you at 4:00." Sean rang off.

I hung up and stared at Vladimir who hadn't moved a muscle since handing me the phone. Jenny came up and stood by my side while we waited for some kind of rational explanation to form. Finally, I couldn't take the suspense any longer.

"Good morning comrade. Is there anything you would like to share with us, like what are you doing here instead of in the hospital?"

"Da, da, is long story but mostly wife told me to get back to work, we are needing the money."

Once again, the attitude of Vladimir's wife struck me as somewhat harsh.

"And you are OK with that, I suppose. You don't look so hot."

"Is OK, just need sleep. Damn torturers at hospital waking a person up every hour for crazy things. Is like trying to get confessions at camp in Gulag. Need coffee perhaps."

Jenny and I looked at each other hoping that we weren't alone in thinking that this was totally bizarre. Comforted that we both thought Vlad and his wife were crazy, I went around the shop turning on lights and firing up the compressor. I assessed the job board and picked a couple of jobs I thought I might be able to wrap up that day. I hoped they might even get picked up and paid for as well.

One of the repairs was a mere valve job, which only required reassembly to be complete. The new valves and seats had been installed, their mating surfaces had been carefully ground to match exactly, and the ports had been tested on the flow bench to ensure maximum smooth air-flow. The combustion chambers had been cleaned of carbon and bits of previous wreckage. All that was left to do was install the 16 springs, stem seals, keepers, and the cam. I figured that I might be able to get it done in an hour and a half, so I budgeted three hours for it.

The other job I wanted to erase from the board was the rebuild of an engine belonging to an Alfa Romeo race car. The owner of the car liked to compete in vintage racing events and generally heeded the finite connection between over-revving the engine and expensive repairs. Unfortunately for him, in the heat of a closely matched championship race he had ignored the dollar signs he had stuck on the face of his tachometer at the red line. When we had received the motor it was as blown as it could be. After the teardown and assessment we found that many of the parts were absolutely not obtainable and would have to be made from scratch. Lucky for us, this was the department where Vladimir excelled. I was secretly a bit relieved he was out of the hospital as I hadn't had a big hand in the rebuild of the motor and didn't have a clue where most of the remaining parts were stored. From the looks of the motor and the progress reported on the board, I thought it might be possible Vlad and I working together could button it up in a couple of hours. The motor itself was a pure work of art with many specially cast and hand machined pieces in evidence. The brand new pieces Vladimir had made blended in exactly with the originals – except for having been a little more carefully made and perhaps a little more finely finished.

There were numerous coffee places in the area where I could get something to stir Vladimir up off the bench, but I sort of wanted to check in with Big Chris to make sure that he was still alive and the Uncertain Grounds was still in one piece.

I controlled my urge to go there and called on the phone instead.

After numerous rings, the phone was picked up.

"Coffee Shop what can we do for you?"

"Hi, is Chris there today?"

The voice assumed a singsong lilt,

"Sorrrreeee, Chris is not here today, can I help you?"

"Do you know if he's OK or when he's working again?"

Sorrreeee, I don't know his status and I'd have to check the schedule in the office, which I don't have time to do, so thanks for calling, bye-bye."

The line was disconnected.

Not exactly the benign report I had been hoping for, but at least the place was still standing; that was something to hold onto.

I called out to Jenny, "I'm slipping out for coffees, one for you?"

"Yeah, I suppose. I might just as well get all jacked up to do nothing."

"We'll see what we can do about that when I get back."

There were plenty of coffee shops in San Francisco, and many of them were in the direction away from Jackson and the furious Finns. I chose one of them and scooted over to it, staying close to the walls and peeking around corners for any sign of pursuit. I managed to get there, get coffees and return without any major mishaps other than scalded hands from walking strangely and spilling.

Vlad had moved into a chair and even though his eyes weren't open yet, he was slowly nodding his head as though to some internal rhythm. I set the gigantic cup of coffee down before him and the aroma eased his lids open a crack and shaky hands reached out as though he were taking communion.

Jenny was scratching around on the bench and making piles of similar looking items.

Organization was coming hard to Jerome Alley. I found some fold-up cardboard bins and allowed as how she could use them to stow that stuff on a shelf, if she could find a shelf with a few inches of space.

I started on the clean bench where the valve job was waiting. I had neatly laid all the components out and all the valves were just sitting in their spots in the upturned head. I had written numbers on each valve head to identify them after a curious visitor had turned over just such a setup to see the other side and all of the carefully matched pieces had cascaded together onto the floor. His "Whoops, sorry," had hardly been sufficient payment for the amount of work it took to reassemble all the bits.

Starting with the #1 cylinder I systematically tested the valves and assembled the springs and seals. I checked the lift of each valve and the possibility of the springs binding and then when all of the valves in each chamber were installed, I checked the whole setup with thin fluid to make sure there were no sneaky leaks.

The cam went on and I checked the rotation and valve operation again. As far as I could see, that sucker was ready to bolt back onto the motor.

I checked the time, just over two hours, not bad!

I called the owner and left a message to come and get it.

Jenny had completed the urban revitalization of the backbench and was getting machine lathe pointers from Vladimir. He was explaining about the slow speeds, the low speeds, the super low speeds and the back gears with the seriously slow speeds. Jenny was taking it all in and asking intelligent questions trying to connect wood lathe skills with machine lathe operation.

I dug out some large aluminum round stock and told her to play with it while Vlad and I tried to finish the Alfa. Vlad was rather reluctant to abandon his teaching monologue, but after I had been standing vacantly staring at the motor for a short while he joined me.

He dug out the box of parts and bits he had stashed in the loft and I was supremely glad I hadn't had to find that lot myself. We laid all the pieces out on the freshly vacant bench and decided who should do what.

With wrenches flying, we added pieces, torqued to perfection, tested for perfect operation, sealed, safety wired, and buttoned it up.

I stood back as Vladimir checked and re-checked the valve clearances and turned the motor over and over, marveling at the absolutely perfect and mesmerizing interplay of its parts.

Jenny had reduced the large rod of aluminum to a series of different diameter sections with a mixture of smooth and not-so-smooth transitions and finishes. I had an inspiration and said, "Say, I have to go to a gig in San Anselmo pretty soon. Perhaps you might want to take the truck and see if you can get some of the stuff from your apartment. I could call a couple of big lunks who owe me to go with you and help carry stuff and look protective and scary."

"Yeah, well, most of my clutch and shifter experience is theoretical, and San Francisco might be the hardest place on the planet to hone those skills, but what the hell, I'll give it a try. It would be good to get my stuff out of there. There really isn't any heavy stuff, though."

"Heavy, light, whatever. You can make them carry your toothbrush if you want, as long as they look deranged and ominous."

She agreed and I looked through the invoices on the board to see who owed me money and was freakishly large and tattooed enough for the job. I easily settled on a couple of lads and arranged for them to get their butts over to the shop and start acting the rogue biker part. I think they were secretly thrilled for the chance to act insane for a real reason.

Just before four o'clock Vlad called it a day and drifted off to make his way home. Sean arrived and parked his truck right in the middle of the alley and left the motor running.

At the same time Steve, who had been known to operate the kickstarters of motorcycles so hard that he actually broke the engines, arrived along with an equally fierce looking Tragedy. Trag, who was tattooed from the top of his Mohawked skull to the bottom of his feet, was the sweetest and gentlest guy I knew. He was a barber who could perform the most delicate shave and yet, from the look of him, a person would think that such an animal belonged in a special cage. Amid much eye rolling on Sean's part I gave Jenny a long, wet kiss along with the keys to the truck and we went our separate ways.

CHAPTER

I CHUNKED my box into the back of Sean's truck with the rest of the tools and his instruments. He backed out of the alley with an off-hand flair and out onto Pacific with the briefest of backward glances. In short order we were careening past Fisherman's Wharf and I feared for unwary tourists. We followed the bay and gawked momentarily at the weekend runners and hangouts on the Marina Green.

The late winter sun beat down and caused steam to rise up from the soggy fields. The old truck rattled up onto Doyle Drive and we hugged the curb as we rounded the big corner and entered the Golden Gate Bridge traffic.

For the second time that day, the beauty of the vista astounded me. Late afternoon sun was slanting in under the bridge and bathed the far reaches of Oakland and Berkeley in a golden glow.

Sean was busy trying to keep the truck more or less in the center of the right lane, not easily done given the notoriously willful steering of the vehicle. I tried to let my mind float free above care and thoughts of mortality.

We arrived at the end of the bridge and began the grind uphill through the rainbow tunnel and over Waldo Grade. We finally made it over the top in third gear with the engine groaning in protest. Sean gave the truck its head as we careened down miles of the far side of the grade. My Zen powers of detachment were tested to the breaking point. After fifteen minutes of navigating the Marin flatlands we exited the freeway at San Rafael and turned up Third Street. As we passed the San Anselmo town limit I checked the time.

"Say, we're a few minutes early, let's stop in at Amazing Grace and see what's laying around."

"Fine, I need to release a few beers anyway."

I was supremely glad I hadn't thought to ask Sean if he had been drinking at all before we went over the bridge. I knew he would have said it was no big deal but still....

In parts of the country I've visited I've seen few places like Amazing Grace: all are the existing remnants of somebody's enthusiastic, youthful vision. Started in the '60's and surviving on naiveté and charm rather than business planning, such places are becoming increasingly rare. They represent service, customer knowledge and anti-corporate ideology instead of deep discounts and cut rate everything. Christmas parties open to everyone rather than training seminars. Unlike the chain stores at the mall, their stock is so unpredictable you never know what you might find in there. The place might be full of cool, rare instruments or completely empty, according to the whim of the economy.

The place was situated between north and southbound lanes of traffic where an old train right-of-way had been. We got honked at as we pulled into the parking lot for having impeded a Mercedes cutting through it to avoid waiting at a red light. We ignored the fuming yuppie as we hit the brake and went inside. Sean had a rare burst of forethought, "We'd better keep an eye on the stuff in the back, I don't trust these rich types. You first though, I've got to hit the head."

We entered the long and narrow building and Sean went directly to the bathroom in the back. The owner came out of the shop wearing a leather apron and wiping his hands on a filthy scrap of towel. He tracked Sean's hurried steps with a smirk.

"Are the Skitheredee brothers in town for a reason or is this merely a piss stop for you?"

"We just stopped in to see you and find out if you had any old accordions or guitars hanging around that we didn't even know we needed."

"I might just, when he gets out of the can, have Sean check out this old Gibson tenor guitar; like a guitar and bouzouki rolled into one. Accordions, I doubt I have anything you'd be interested in, being a button box man."

"That's OK, we don't have long anyway. We're headed over to the Log Cabin to play at a party, but as long as we're talking about accordions...."

The repairman's wife and co-owner came out of the office and listened as I relayed the gist of the unfolding accordion story.

She had a good laugh and said it all sounded mysterious and romantic. The repairman said it sounded improbable. On mulling the whole saga over for a few moments he suddenly said, "You know what, you ought to call Pietro Guerinni; Pete. It was his grandfather who practically started the accordion business in San Francisco, right down near where your shop is. He retired years ago but he just lives in the next town. I've got his card right here on the wall, let me see...."

He went over and scrutinized a bulletin board with hundreds of cards randomly pinned to it. He peered under layer after layer in different quadrants of the board until he finally pulled out a tack with perhaps six cards attached to it. The bottom most card had a simple name and number on it. He transferred the information to a scrap of paper and handed it to me while he plunged the tack and cards back into the chaos.

Without discussing anything at all, the owner picked up the phone and dialed. When the line was answered he said, "Pete, John here at Amazing Grace, yeah, same here. I got a guy here who has a funny story about the accordion business in the old days, I'll put him on."

John covered the mouthpiece and said Pete was getting on and was slightly hard of hearing and cranky. He might not prove too helpful. He handed over the phone.

"Hello, this is Soren Rauhe from out in the Richmond District. I play an old Soprani 3 row chromatic and I heard this story about a guy named C.L. Miller who worked for an early maker named C.C. Keene."

I gave Mr. Guerinni a condensed version of the story. There was silence on the other end of the line. I thought perhaps I had made the story overly long and put the old feller to sleep but finally he cleared his throat.

"Yeah, that's a new one on me. We didn't have much time for fairy tales back in the day, we was workin' double shifts getting' the things built. I will tell ya' this though, when the Galleazzi boys gave up their shop, late 40's it must have been, we hired the whole bunch of them to work for us. There was an Irish guy working there at that time who was supposed to come over, but he never showed up for work, just disappeared. The boys said he was kind of crazy anyway and had all kinds of whacky stories. They said he never even came back for the stuff he left at their old place up on Jackson. That's the only crazy Irishman I can think of besides all the rest of them."

I glanced at my watch and wrapped up my conversation as fast as I politely could. I thanked the storeowner for his far-reaching customer service and promised to invite him to the next big vintage motorcycle ride and BBQ planned.

Sean had completed his business and gone straight to the Gibson Tenor guitar. He appeared as though he might be settling in for a long test-driving session so I reminded him that we had to be on stage and playing in less than fifteen minutes. The owner left us to our own devices and went back to work in the medieval gloom of the repair shop.

We fingered and twanged nearly all of the instruments hanging on the walls without finding anything that absolutely couldn't be lived without. We shouted goodbyes to the husband and wife and headed over to the Log Cabin. It was situated in Memorial Park and was exactly what the name implied, a large log cabin. A cannon from the First World War guarded the front door. It was a long room with a nice stage at one end and a large cobblestone fireplace halfway down. There was a side room set up with tables for food, and a bar. As our start time was fast approaching we went straight to the stage and snagged a couple of comfortable-looking chairs on the way. Mike was already there testing one of the three microphones and sipping on a pre-gig beer. We exchanged greetings and I was relieved to note that there didn't appear to be any residual awkwardness concerning our last gig together. We all agreed to run the other way if any of us said, "Want to see something funny?"

Sean and I skipped into the side room and forced our way into the throng surrounding the keg and drew ourselves pints. The birthday boy greeted us warmly and looked like he might have been half in the bag already. I could identify quite a few members of the local Irish-American families and thought we might be in for a wild evening.

We started playing and the place erupted in cheers and spontaneous dancing. I remember thinking, "This is what it's all about!"

We played for our required three hours with many breaks for speeches, drinks, cooling off and to allow enthusiastic partygoers to play a few tunes of their own. We were prevailed upon to play and additional hour. Finally it was clear that the party was winding down fast. The birthday host found us and drunkenly thrust a wad of cash at us. A quick count revealed there was far more than the agreed upon price. He hugged us all and said that we should consider the rest a tip. We split the cash three ways and then headed for home after critically checking each other for sobriety. Sean drove, having passed the test of at least counting accurately the beers he had consumed.

Once we were motoring sedately down Second and headed for the anonymity of the freeway, Sean asked, "So, what's this about a new truck?"

I thought it best to keep talking and stretch the story out as long as possible. I told him of the wretched wreckage of Big Red, the throng of gawkers in the street, the outraged attitude of Walter, and then the payoff as I was offered the new truck for cheap.

He was astounded, "Jesus, the Finn guys sound serious, and they know where you live, too. Do you want me to come out there and stay over in case they come back? We could kick their asses for them"

"I hate to disappoint you, but I don't think that will be necessary. Jenny and me are going to have to deal with the whole situation somehow. We'll have to make a plan tonight, I guess."

"Fine by me, I'm just saying you might need the Fightin' Irish there with ya."

"I think I'll take my chances without them for now. I got you on speed dial, though."

We crossed the Golden Gate and angled down 19th then west out Geary. Sean continued, "I can't believe Big Red has finally expired, although it does sort of sound like a Viking funeral, doesn't it? Cremation at sea, too bad we couldn't have pushed it off the dock at Fisherman's Wharf."

"How very ecological it would be of you, to dump a festering lump of burning Chevy into the sensitive bay. It would have made a good show though. A white trash Blue Angels."

Sean got a kick out of that and was still laughing as we pulled up in front of my house. Jenny's old Toyota was still there and where Big Red had spent the last many months, the new truck sat.

"Looks like they're doing some road work or something. Where's the new ride?"

I gestured to the Ford, "That's the point! That's it. Practically invisible."

He looked skeptical but impressed at the same time. "You should get some orange cones; that would totally do it."

"Genius. Care to come in and forage for anything that might have escaped previous drinking?"

"Nah, I have to roll on back to Geary, up near 25th. I told Sloane that I'd meet her at that bar in the Mexican restaurant at 9:30. I gotta' get goin'."

"Okey Dokey, thanks for the ride and not getting us arrested. We'll talk."

"My pleasure, altogether. A good gig, too. That Mike is quite a fiddler, if only he'd loosen up a bit and quit being so normal."

I scoffed and got out of the truck. Sean labored up the hill and disappeared. I did have to admit that my driveway, and thus Walter and Ana's driveway, along with the rest of the immediate neighborhood looked a lot tidier with Big Red on permanent vacation.

As I entered the house I was overwhelmed by the unfamiliar smell of actual cooking. Jenny sat in the living room and had a pile of papers in front of her on what passed for a coffee table. She looked up, "Holy Christ, from what I'm getting' here, I think Jarno sold way more stuff as fake antiques than as reproductions. Not to the state, either. It looks like a whole lot of it went to Europe passed off as Early California originals. That bastard made a mint and sure didn't waste any of it paying the help. Thanks for the loan of the brutes; we managed to totally clean out the place and only saw the manager once. He had one look at them two and hightailed it. Not that I had that much there, it only took us two trips apiece. I also got the mail and found a letter from back east with, ta-aadaaa, money in it. I utilized the boys to help with the shopping and fed them dinner already. Ours is simmering on the stove and it won't take a minute to finish it up. Stuffed peppers with Spanish rice, I always like to make that my first meal when I move into a new place, I don't know why. Perhaps you could open some of that wine?"

I was flabbergasted, not only had one of my generally ill conceived plans actually worked out, but shopping had happened without my participation and there was even cooked food available. All I could think was "Keeper".

I uncorked a stylish bottle of Napa Valley Chardonnay while Jenny rattled pots in the kitchen. Seeing the pile of papers she had purloined from the Finn reminded me I should assess the contents of the dumpster boxes. I went through the hall to the garage door. From the doorway I couldn't actually see a path to where the boxes sat. I thought "One step at a time" and moved in.

It didn't actually take me too long to shove aside, pile higher, rearrange and just step over whatever was in the way. I reached the first of the boxes and couldn't actually make out much of the contents in the dismal gloom of the garage. I latched on and carried it back into the living room where it looked at home amid the contents of Jenny's apartment and car.

I fetched a wastebasket just in case everything inside was not of the highest desirability and quality. The wooden box looked like the standard older-style produce crate. Deeper than the modern ones are. There was a square of thin wood on top protecting the contents. A nice layer of dust and crud coated the wood of the lid.

I eased the top off and dumped the debris directly into the wastebasket. Underneath there was a selection of oblong wooden chunks. Long and short, wide and narrow. Some were darker wood than the others, possibly walnut at first glance. I searched all the way to the bottom without finding anything else. "How very revealing," I thought.

I lugged the box back to the garage and managed to stow it in an even more inaccessible spot than it had been. I grabbed the next load. These boxes were shorter so I piled two together.

Back in the living room I could see the top box held various short runs of marquetry carefully wrapped by style in newsprint and tied with string. I reflected that each of the pieces was too short to span the entire length or width of even a small accordion and so must be a cut off. Perhaps waiting for some repair job that never came. I rewrapped them and replaced them as neatly as I could.

The next box held the first real accordion bits. There were quite a few reed blocks there – the wooden holders that arranged the reed plates in rows and allowed the air to get to them. They were far longer than those of a button accordion so I assumed they were intended for a large piano style instrument. No further information could be gotten from the pieces.

I piled the boxes back together and brought them to join their friend. The next box was noticeably heavier than the first few and also sealed with a wooden top. After I got it in the living room next to the wastebasket, just in case it was completely junk filled, I pried the top off. Inside the box were sets of reeds mounted in the Galleazzi Brothers signature brass plates. They were much heavier than the normal zinc reed plates and gave the Galleazzi accordions a completely different tone. The reeds were arranged by note; all the 'C's were lumped together regardless what size, and so on for the rest of the scale. There were twelve packets with all the reeds for a full size accordion. I was supremely glad I didn't have to sort them all out, at least at the moment. I forced the wooden cover back into the opening of the box and carried it back to the garage. I jammed it alongside the others creating a very dangerous looking pile.

The last box weighed plenty and was the largest of the five by far. From what I could see it was filled with paperwork, and I didn't have very high hopes of finding anything exciting within. From what Pietro had told me, the Galleazzis were in business from the late 1800's until the boys closed up shop and went to work for the Guerinni concern in the late 40's. There might have been a lot of paperwork in the box, but I didn't think there could be sixty years worth.

Delving in, I removed a multitude of old manila folders. Inside I found the expected business paper trail. There were invoices for materials in one folder, requests and filled orders in another. One folder held nothing but testimonials for their astounding and excellent instruments. The dates ranged from around 1910 up to the late 40's when they packed it in. There must have been an earlier box that had gotten lost or tossed.

At the very bottom of the box was a leather folio. Removing this made me speculate it might contain something different than the run-of-the-mill stuff I had seen so far. The leather was stiff and crackled as I opened the cover. The writing on the first page was longhand in a very old-fashioned copperplate style.

It quickly became clear the journal had belonged to C.L. Miller and had been left behind when they closed up and went to work for Guerinni.

There were several pages of rambling monologue about various topics, none of them related to accordions, the Galleazzis, earthquakes or secret metallurgy. Next there were several pages of drawings of angels in various attitudes standing on various styles of pedestals. After the angels, there was page after page of complicated mechanical drawings depicting what appeared to be some sort of locking mechanism.

There were several invoices tucked into the pages of the folio that were from the makers of memorial monuments and mechanical engineers. The name on the invoices was Mr. C.L. Miller and the date was September of 1906.

I deduced, with my almost completely lucid mind, these must be the drawings of the grave marker Miller had spent his money on for his beloved girlfriend. There were parts I didn't understand, but at that moment Jenny hollered from the kitchen dinner was served and if I didn't get in there quick it was going to feed the hogs.

I packed the majority of the papers back into the box but kept the folio out for further investigation.

JOHN PEDERSEN

CHAPTER

S TUFFED Peppers with Spanish rice, garlic bread, tossed salad, Napa Valley Chardonnay, what could possibly have been better? I was so thrilled with the prospect of eating at home I completely forgot about Miller's journal.

Jenny and I ate, chatted, flirted and generally had a wonderful time. She told me how white knuckled her two helpers had become as she tried to figure out how to deal with the clutch and stick shift. She had rejected repeated offers from each of them to drive in favor of toughing it out. Part of her reason had just been to see their reactions. She said she felt pretty confident now, as long as she didn't have to stop in the middle of a hill. Tongue in cheek, I said how rarely that would ever happen in San Francisco. She laughed.

It wasn't late but the lure of the bedroom couldn't be resisted. We piled the dishes in the sink for later attention and showered together. We giggled like a couple of kids as we soaped each other up and shared many long kisses and slippery gropes as we exhausted the hot water.

Where our previous lovemaking had been almost demented in its intensity, this night we were taking our time, exploring each other and finding where those elusive "Ohh-Ohh" buttons were. No surface that would support us was spared. All outside anxiety and concern was forgotten. Pulled hair, pinched limbs, charley horses and strange cramps were all laughed off as we spun out of control.

We finally slid into exhausted and dizzy sleep. When I started awake, Jenny was gone and I had a moment of panic, but she returned almost instantly with a plate of tomato and Havarti cheese sandwiches on toast. I practically sobbed with joy.

To say I previously hadn't had the best luck with women is an understatement. I generally have a tendency to become attached to a certain type of self-centered, tattooed, and punk biker woman. Being ignored and outright taken advantage of was almost the central theme in those relationships. I still sported scars where one particularly demented lover had tried to knife me after what I thought was an especially tender sexual moment.

The other extreme of my past attractions had been with girls from the beach. I'm sure among women who surf there are many who are deep thinkers and serious philosophers, but I never met any of them. The women I have known invariably were on their way to Hawaii or LA. Without exception, their parting lines to me had been "Dude, you work too much and it's too cold here!"

The fact that I had never even dated a red-haired, ivory-skinned Irish girl was ironic, even to me. Perhaps I had been waiting for Sloane all along and didn't want to settle for second best. I had noticed a similar pattern with Sean and his female friends. Whenever Sloane would have needs, we would jump and scramble, but it was never enough.

A tomato and cheese sandwich on toast was the most serious and touching offering I had ever received. Once again, "Keeper."

We gleefully spread crumbs around the bedding and watched some lame late night TV. Soon we were spooned up and sliding off into blissful oblivion.

Having gone to sleep reasonably sober, my get up clock started annoying me at 6:00 a.m. I wondered if disappearing for a couple of hours would startle Jenny too much. I postponed the decision until after I checked the break. Standing precariously on the "looking box", I was torn to see another day of mixed-up crappy surf. It was barely light enough to see the white water of the waves. What I could see of the western horizon was almost black and I could feel the moisture in the onshore wind. I nearly lost my footing and plunged over the railing into the defunct garden when a blanket wrapped Jenny came up behind me.

"What's up? Are you spying on the neighbors or what?"

I managed to get my feet back onto the deck and inside the blanket with her before answering.

"Even though a couple of surfboards and wetsuits burned up with Big Red, I have more. If you stand up here on this box you can just barely see the break down at Kelly's Cove. You never know if it's worth going out unless you look."

"Let me see."

Jenny climbed onto the box but was still too short to see over the neighbors. I grabbed her around the hips and hoisted. With my face pressed to her ass, her arms waving and giggling she managed to spot the beach.

"I can see the waves, but they're breaking all over the place, how do you surf in that?"

"That, my dear, is the point: you don't. You go back to bed with your sweetie and decide what to bring her for breakfast in bed."

"Oh you smoothie, you. I have half a mind to let you do just that. In fact, just wake me up when you get back, I'm freezing."

She scooted off with the blanket and left me shivering on the balcony.

I slid the door closed and quickly pulled on a sweatshirt, a pair of tattered old sweat pants and my ancient slippers. Jenny's eyes peeked out of a pile of blankets. I didn't doubt she would be asleep by the time I returned.

I was astounded at how much better the kitchen looked with actual food available. I took a couple of the left-over bell peppers and diced them up with some onions and mushrooms. While they were frying, I made coffee, toast and bacon. A beautifully picturesque veggie omelet finally emerged. I made up a plate and a cup of coffee and tried my hardest not to spill as I brought it to her.

I set the coffee on the nightstand and with one hand shook her awake.

"Get serious, you actually did it. Isn't this just the thing, breakfast in bed!"

She sat up and I mentally commented how much the look of the breakfast was improved by the addition of naked girl parts. I hustled back to the kitchen to finish my own omelet. By the time I returned, the TV was on and Jenny was struggling to finish half of her meal. The weather guy told us we should batten down the hatches and stay inside because there was an alarming low coming onshore soon. I remarked this was old news to us having looked out the window.

During a commercial I said, " So, do we feel like braving the elements today and taking a drive down to Colma? I'd sorta like to see where this accordion guy's girlfriend wound up. Probably won't take too long."

"Whatever you say as long as it doesn't take us up to Jackson Street. I have a sneaking feeling once Jarno discovers I pillaged his files he's gonna' go crazy. Maybe we could hit a Kinkos or someplace like that and make some copies for insurance. Put them in a safe place with instructions and all."

"Based on performance so far I'd think the subtlety might be lost on the Finn, but I guess it wouldn't hurt to try. I agree with keeping away from Jackson Street, though."

We finished what could be eaten of the meal and very soon after knocked the dishes to the floor as our morning lust ran its course. Eventually we were dressed and gathering up the debris. We piled the dishes in the sink along with those of supper. I was pleased to note Jenny wasn't a woman obsessed with washing up instantly.

I scrounged around in various closets until I turned up another slicker and umbrella. Jenny grabbed a stack of Jarno's papers and I grabbed Miller's journal.

The Ford started right up and pumped out heat quickly as we made our way down Geary to the beach, the Cliff House, and the Great Highway; always choose the scenic route being my motto. The blackness lurking offshore had nearly arrived and the wind screeched over the sand dunes making the drivers around me veer and weave alarmingly. The sand hissed against the passenger's side of the truck. The waves rose up and pounded the beach with twenty-foot hammers. The rain came on suddenly in a nearly continuous sheet causing even the most hardened idiot drivers to slow way down. I was relieved to note the previously untested windshield wipers were not too bad and missed the glass only at the very ends.

Most of the weather drama was lost on Jenny who was poring through Jarno's incriminating evidence.

"So, even though it looks like Jarno was screwing antique suckers left and right and hosing down the State at the same time, what am I supposed to do with all this? If the cops don't have time to investigate an apparent murder attempt with a blunt object, they're not going to give one little shit about some fake furniture. Say, what about your lawyer buddy, what do you suppose he'd make of this?"

"Shackleford, do you mean? Seeing as how he's the DA in Marin and not here, I can't imagine what he could do, but I guess it wouldn't hurt to call him. He might have some ideas at least."

We had reached the end of the Great Highway and continued on Skyline and around Lake Merced. The water flooded the street so heavily it was difficult to tell the lake from the road. Some of the more timorous drivers had even pulled over to wait out the onslaught. We gained the bluffs outside of Daly City and the wind drove the rain solidly sideways and tried to push us off the road.

Jenny stared out the window towards the west. "Say, listen Soren, I realize we've gotten pretty close in a couple of days and gone through a lot of drama, but there might be things about me you should know. I mean, I have a past and I accept it, but it's not all sunshine and Little Women, if you know what I mean."

I wondered what might be coming next. Death, destruction, voodoo, sex change, Republican tendencies, something strange and weird, I was sure.

I was saved further speculation as a couple of drivers who should have joined those at the side of the road managed to pile into each other and create a whirling ballet of destruction. Other dancers joined the production as Volvos, BMWs, Mercedes' and SUVs touched bumpers and spun gracefully off into the median or the shoulder. We were all going so mercifully slow there didn't look like any major wreckage or injuries happening. Threading my way between the moving, spinning contestants was relatively easy given my practice at surfing over and around rocks and kooks and dodging oblivious drivers on the motorcycle.

Jenny was white-faced and grabbing the door handle. "Oh," was her only exclamation.

Instead of joining the Pacific Coast Highway and heading south, we continued along Skyline until I turned off at Hickey and then onto Callan. Shortly after, elegant gates reminiscent of a pagoda loomed on the right. A chain link fence surrounded the cemetery but there weren't any gates barring the entrance. A slight rise obscured the cemetery proper. On a Sunday morning with the rain lashing down, there wasn't anybody around. We turned in and as we topped the hill Colma, San Bruno and the Bay were laid out before us. Serramonte shopping center was just off to the left and I thought how handy it must be for the departed Chinese elders to have a Target store right there.

A central road led straight down the hill with a cul-de-sac at the end. It looked like a quarter of a mile to the end and about the same expanse spreading out on both sides. We rolled slowly down the hill scanning the scenery on both sides. There was what might have been an office about half way down on the right, but if there was anybody in there, they stayed there. Every short while paved paths led off to either side. There were several roads creating a grid, which covered most of the cemetery.

The right hand side all the way back down to Hickey was dominated by row after row of simple markers. We didn't see much in the way of elaborate monuments over there but we explored the avenues from the warmth and dryness of the truck anyway. We didn't see any thing that looked like the drawings in Miller's journal at all. I zigzagged back to the main drag.

The uphill side of the cemetery offered much less in the way of automobile exploration possibilities. There were a couple of streets but mostly pathways, which led to a series of shrine monuments. Some of these were almost directly next to the road while others were far off in the murky distance. Water ran down the inclines and pooled up at every flat spot.

Jenny gave a shudder, " Jeez, this place gives me the creeps. What exactly are we looking for here? I'm a little hazy on that."

I stopped the truck in the middle of the deserted avenue and got Miller's journal out. I flipped through the pages of writing and stopped at the various angel depictions. Jenny scanned through them, flipping back and forth.

"I don't see anything particularly Chinese looking here; you'd think something like this would stand out around here."

"You would think so. Maybe up on the other side; there might be some more elaborate things going on up there."

We both tried unsuccessfully to squint through the flooding windshield and pouring rain at whatever might have been uphill to the right. I drove to where the first road diverged in that direction. We could only see more of the simple slab markers, but we went anyway. Looping around this way and that failed to reveal anything but more of the paths leading to the shrines. It seemed like all of the paved roads came nowhere near the larger monuments that could be glimpsed through the murk. Finally I parked, "I guess this is where I get out, if there's anything here I don't guess we're going to see if from the road. You can stay here if you want, it might get damp out there."

"Oh, right, like I'm going to fall for that old trick. I've seen horror movies too, you know. Things always go wrong when the couple splits up at the graveyard. No thanks."

I nodded at the truth of the statement and we both struggled into the unyielding slickers in the cab of the truck. Mine was a little bit too small and Jenny's was way too big. We looked quite the pair. I fished the umbrella out from behind the seat and during a momentary lull, we got out into the weather.

Without the windows for the water to run down the rain wasn't all that heavy, until it started pouring in earnest again. Jenny and I linked arms and huddled under the umbrella for a few moments before it was ripped from my grasp by a nasty gust of wind. It careened off down the hill as the same wind drove the rain straight into our faces and made our hoods useless. Jenny squealed," Oh my God, this is insane!"

I had to agree. Gentleman that I am, I tried to shield her from the worst of the onslaught by standing upwind. We set off down one of the paved paths in tandem. At the end of the path was a shrine I'm sure would have been beautiful on a nice spring day. On this day it lacked appeal. It was cut into the side of the gentle hill and there were steps leading to the top on either side. Hunkered up next to the wall we were protected from at least some of the elements. I got close to Jenny's hood and said, "This is exactly like the ones we saw from the car. I don't think these guys go for the lambs and Madonna type of monuments. We might be drowned before we find anything here."

I thought I saw Jenny's hood nod in agreement. We turned to leave and were confronted by a specter in a wildly flapping black cloak brandishing a sword at us.

My heart leapt in my chest and "Shit!" escaped my lips.

The apparition moved closer and we recoiled as far as we could against the stone face of the shrine. The shroud's hood eased back a mite to reveal a middle-aged Chinese fellow who yelled, "Is this yours?" His sword of fate turned out to be my furled umbrella. "I found it way down by the bottom fence. Not much good in this wind, eh?"

I ventured a step forward and retrieved the trashed item. "Thanks" I hollered.

He peered at us through the veil of rain and said, "Are you looking for somebody, or something? Maybe you want to come to the office and have a nice cup of tea? Too wet here for people, only good for ducks!" He cackled and turned without waiting for an answer. We followed him back down the path and across the main street to the entrance of the office. Under a bit of an overhang the three of us shook off the worst of the water before removing our rain gear and quickly moving inside. There was a reception area with informational fliers for different burial societies. Behind a desk a teakettle simmered merrily on a hot plate. Our host pulled a pot and a tin of tea out of a drawer and assembled the elements to his satisfaction. He poured the hot water into the pot and while waiting for the tea to steep he looked us over.

Without his grim reaper poncho he was a much smaller fellow. He was wearing dark slacks and a long sleeved shirt with a buttoned up cardigan. A festively striped bow tie gave the impression he was above grounds keeper or gravedigger level. He sported a large and clunky college ring.

"So, just sightseeing today, maybe taking rubbings from old markers? Not likely. Looking for a relative to talk to and make peace with? Don't think so, no. Looking over the grounds for plot for future, not so much chance. What then, if I might inquire?"

I debated how much of the elaborate story was needed at this juncture; I doubted if our host cared much about accordions and their mysteries. I settled on, "We are looking for the resting place of an aunt of a friend. She would have been here a long time because she died in the 1906 earthquake. Her name was Zhou, but I don't know her first name. I think she had a pretty fancy monument; I have some drawings in the truck. They are of angels, but we haven't seen any around here. I guess they aren't particularly common as decoration."

"An angel a hundred years old? Most of the old graves here don't have large markers because many of the bodies have been returned to China. Many of the oldest graves were moved down here from San Francisco when it was decided they didn't want any more burials within the

JOHN PEDERSEN

city limits. This search could be very complicated; there could be many, many possibilities. Could be, but isn't. I know exactly where the angel is, but you can't see her from way down here. You have to climb to the very top of the hill where the trees are; that is where she is. Perhaps she was hidden from view up there, or perhaps the trees grew up around her, I don't know. I'll draw a map for you, easy to find, but still very wet."

He cackled at his wit and poured out the tea. The warmth of the cups was welcome. He rummaged in a different drawer and came up with a map of the cemetery. He used a black marker to outline where the angel was situated and how best to get there on the paths. As he handed this to Jenny he eyed us again, "So, your friends must be very close for you to pay respects to their aunt on such a day. And quite advanced in age as well. Very interesting."

"Actually, we're just checking on the condition of the monument for them, they value it very highly and want to make sure it's doing justice to the memory of the aunt. Just taking notes for them and we don't get much time off, so it's today or never."

Jenny did a slight eye roll for me to see while the manager didn't even bother to cover his skepticism.

"Really, well what a nice thing to do, eh? Have a nice time up there, don't get wet or lose your umbrella again, might go over the fence next time, like Mary Poppins, haha."

Jenny and I collected our clammy slickers from the front of the office and slipped them on. The manager held the door for us as we ventured out once again into the deluge.

His map indicated Auntie's resting place was almost up against the fence line on the Northwest side, secluded within a copse of trees. As we walked by the truck I could feel a strong urge to climb in, turn on the heat and get the hell out of there. Instead I just ducked in and got Miller's journal, which I tucked under my slicker. We chose the path that looked like it might get us closest to the trees and set off down it.

There was another shrine at the end of the path strongly resembling the first. I peeked behind myself to make sure we were not being stalked again. We went around the side of the shrine and climbed the steps to the top, which put us on almost the same level as the trees. We had to make our way across a wide section of grass and were immediately soaked from the knees down. The knot of trees was pretty thick and we couldn't make out any details of the ground underneath until were quite close. There were no other marked graves anywhere near the edge of the trees. We followed our map as best we could, considering that every time we consulted it, the ink of the black marker ran and spread out in widening circles.

As we entered the realm of the conifers the intensity of the rain lessened but the gloom closed in on us. After casting around for a few minutes and finding nothing, we finally located Auntie's angel neatly camouflaged by many years of green moss. She blended in well with the ivy-covered fence marking the border of the cemetery. Clearly, at one time there was a view from this spot, but trees had grown and, intentionally or not, never been pruned so they completely obscured the area. It didn't appear as though the Zhou family put a lot of effort into maintaining the dignity of the monument. Perhaps, like myself, they preferred the naturally-aged look to the stark white of the marble.

Jenny and I circled the angel and studied her from every angle. She stood on a three-foot-square block of marble with inset panels on all four sides. Standing around four feet high she held her arms out in front of herself as if beseeching us to deliver something to her, a pint maybe. She had beautiful features and, even though it might have been my imagination, she looked a bit Chinese. There was a very strong resemblance to one of Miller's illustrations.

We huddled up next to the largest of the local trees and Jenny opened up the umbrella while I got the journal out and tried to shield it from the elements. I found the drawing that was similar and we compared the two. There was no doubt this was the right angel and the right benefactor, but in the drawing there were more complexities, especially in the base. In the dim light it was hard to make out exactly what was going on but the presence of the mechanical apparatus hinted to me there might be more here than met the eye. Jenny came up with the same conclusion.

"It looks like there's a secret compartment here somewhere. Look at this spring deal here and that switch. Not very clear where it is or how to trip it, though."

"Not very clear at all, I'd say."

I tucked the journal away and we got as close as we could to the angel and looked for any sorts of clues. We circled around and around looking high and low without seeing any sort of indication of trickery. I took her hands and gave gentle twists in various directions without results. I grabbed and palpitated every part of her torso and hoped Jenny wasn't getting jealous. We thumped and prodded the surfaces of the base but without knowing what solid or hollow bases sounded like, we couldn't tell one way or the other.

As the rain slackened, the fog was getting thicker and we were getting colder. I didn't know how long I could just stand there and stare at the old girl. Jenny continued to circle. On one of her revolutions, one of the angel's outreached hands snagged the umbrella. Jenny gave a squeak of surprise as she was brought up short. A first gentle tug didn't free the grasp of the angel. Jenny grabbed the handle with both hands and gave a more serious jerk without result. I thought her next series of short hard tugs would do the job of either dislodging the umbrella or breaking it. Instead, Jenny dropped to the ground and gave a howl of dismay. My first thought was that Auntie was pissed off over the disturbance and had reached up through the ground and grabbed her ankle. Jenny might have thought the same thing. I rushed around the statue to help her up and support her as she bent double and massaged her shin.

"Son of a bitch, something whacked me in the knee. What the hell?"

I noticed the angel wasn't exactly facing the front anymore and my first thought was we had broken something and we had better get right on out of there. Jenny's first thought was to find out what had clonked her. She fussed around in the underbrush around the base of the angel and gave out with an excited, "Yo, yo, look at this. Part of this thing has come apart! The whole angel rotated on the base."

I peered at where she indicated and, sure enough, one of the base's panels had popped open a few inches, just enough to clonk Jenny in the knee. I slipped my fingers into the crack and was able to drag the panel open enough to see the hollow behind. I could see something inside along with the carcasses of a hundred years of spiders. At least, I hoped there were only carcasses whose ghosts were keeping Auntie company.

I gingerly reached around the edge of the panel to see if I could drag the hidden parcel into the open. I couldn't. Repeated attempts to get the panel open farther proved fruitless so I resigned myself to reaching all the way into the recess and grabbing the parcel, which was wrapped in canvas or sailcloth. I could practically feel the critters crawling up my sleeve as I worked the thing back and forth trying to dislodge it from the floor of the cubbyhole to which it felt like it was glued.

Jenny waved at me with the umbrella, "Here, let me give it a try with this thing." She whapped it closed and edged me out of the way with the metal tip. Once in position she grabbed the tip with both hands and inserted the crooked handle into the hole and hooked it around the back of the parcel. A mighty tug managed to break the handle off the umbrella but more importantly, knock the parcel loose. It skidded to the front of the recess where it became lodged in the opening, slightly too wide to slip through. Jenny wound up on her ass on the wet ground.

I helped her onto her feet and she tried to brush off the worst of the debris. I was able to gain slightly more movement by working the door back and forth with vigor and purpose. Whomever had made the contraption in the first place could have put a little more effort into beveling the edges because after a couple of to's and fro's my hands were bleeding from the sharp corners. The rain turned the marble pink.

There was a lull in the action as I inspected my hands, Jenny grabbed the fabric of the covering and pulled again and this time the box scraped through the opening and plopped onto the ground. She peered into the recess to make sure we hadn't overlooked anything, but the only thing inside was the handle of the umbrella and a mass of cobwebs. She gave a jolt or two with her heel and the door swung closed and the angel faced forward again. I cradled my hands in my armpits.

Jenny brushed at the majority of the cobwebs that had accompanied the box and said, "So now we're officially grave robbers, maybe we should get the hell out of here and back to our happy place. Someplace where it might not be so wet and cold."

I heartily agreed, and as the grave robber with the most room under their slicker, Jenny grabbed the box and slipped it under cover.

We made our way back to the truck and if the caretaker happened to look out and happened to see us, he wouldn't have to wonder what we had found at the gravesite, only how Jenny had become so pregnant in such a short time.

Jenny offered to drive out of respect for my damaged palms but I declined, not ready for that particular brand of excitement just then.

We shed our slickers outside the truck, jumped inside and put the parcel behind the seats. Curiosity was overwhelmed by the need to get the heater on and get moving before Auntie's ghost came after us, even though I had left a blood sacrifice and substituted a valuable umbrella handle for whatever we had taken.

The rain continued to pour down, the black skies lowered overhead and we both were shivering in our soaked clothes. As I carefully drove back to the highway I wondered if the prize had been worth the game.

CHAPTER

THE rain had eased off a bit, but the howling wind made up for it. We crept along Skyline, around the lake and back up the Great Highway. In retrospect, perhaps not the smartest route as there was flooding and sand dunes blocking the road in many places. Most of the drivers stuck on the road acted like they had no idea what to do except sit there and drown. I decided to stretch our newly found powers of invisibility to see if they extended to unquestioning acceptance. I located the switch on the dash that activated the flashing yellow light on the roof and people edged this way and that until I could drive straight down the center of the road and reach the dune blocking our progress.

In reality it wasn't much of an obstacle and a four-wheeled drive vehicle could have navigated it easily. I noted several of the SUVs directly behind the blockage had that capability while we did not. To make up for our lack of hardware, I was counting on inertia, momentum and attitude. When we were fifty yards from the sand I prepared my co-pilot.

"Hang on!"

I floored the truck in second gear and plowed into the shifting abyss. Slewing back and forth, wheels churning and sand spraying everywhere we almost made it through. Our forward movement finally slowed and stopped. I put the truck in reverse and we were able to back up quite a ways in our own path. I floored it again and this time we managed to pop out the far side of the dune onto clean pavement. There was a chorus of horns to celebrate our victory and the large family haulers on the way home from church were able to follow our tracks through the mess and come out the other side. Within a short time they were all passing us apparently in a great hurry to arrive at the next obstacle. Jenny relaxed her grip on the Yikes handle over the door.

She said, "That was something, and not the daring path-finding part either. I'm astounded what a yellow light will make people believe."

"No kidding, eh. I wish I'd a thought of this years ago."

She gave me an incredulous look, "Implying you thought of it this time?"

"Well, at least I thought of turning it on, right?"

"Ha."

We made our way back to Geary without further drama. The parking lot at the Cliff House looked deserted. The waves were massive and churned everywhere at Kelly's Cove. I was glad to note no person, sane or insane, had ventured out into the maelstrom.

"So, about Jarno's papers, let's keep an eye out for a copy shop or something, OK?"

"Right-o, but if we don't pass one soon, how about we go home and check out the Angel's secret. And make out, if it comes to that."

"Sure, that would work for me."

It was only a few short blocks from the top of the hill leading away from the beach to our turn on 47th Ave. and mercifully, we didn't pass any copy establishments. Nothing looked amiss as we pulled into the driveway. Jenny's Toyota looked bedraggled, waterlogged and beat to death. We pulled our soaked slickers and the mystery box from the truck and ran to the front door. I fumbled the keys and had to retrieve them from the bottom step before we could get in out of the rain.

I had stupidly left the coffee pot on but turned the heat off. We cradled warm cups and huddled together while the furnace kicked in. I was torn between climbing back in bed with Jenny and a plate of cinnamon toast or tearing into the mystery package. Sadly, there was no contest: package first! At least I made the cinnamon toast before getting the box up onto the kitchen table. Jenny shivered but made no move to leave.

The parcel had been sewn into a covering of what looked to be waxed sailcloth. I sincerely hoped that precaution had been effective. I used a butcher knife to slit the most obvious seam up one side, over the top and down the other.

The box revealed certainly could have housed an accordion. The case had been elegantly covered in slick leather at one point, but time, damp and spiders had taken their toll and the outside of the case fell off in large flakes. There was a handle built into the top that folded flat into a recess. On either side of the handle were sturdy locks with sliding button releases. Those types of locks were fussy and difficult in the best of times and I was sure the rust and evident corrosion wouldn't make their operation easier.

Ever the careful tradesman I rummaged in the kitchen drawers till I found a can of 3-in-1 Oil. I placed a tidy drop on the surface and in the keyhole of each lock. I fidgeted with the dome shaped buttons for a few minutes and eventually they began so slide back and forth a bit. Jenny had absently consumed all of the coffee and most of the toast while watching all this.

Finally I reached the point where one of the locks released with a grinding pop. The other gave up soon after, and I eased the two halves of the case apart like a giant oyster.

With the halves of the case flat on the table, the item was further wrapped in a ragged velvet drape. All the signs pointed towards it being an accordion: size, shape, feel, smell, ultra super-sonic vibrations, everything. Jenny was poised with the final piece of toast halfway to her mouth, waiting for the revelation. I tenderly seized the uppermost fold of the drape and eased it off the box.

At last it was uncovered, most certainly C.L.Miller's accordion I had seen pictured in the Bohemian Club. There was mildew and corrosion on almost every surface. The straps were hardened and inflexible, and some of the pearl letters spelling his name had fallen out. The mermaids remained unspoiled and strangely erotic. I tentatively tried to unclasp one of the bellows locks and met with more corrosion and resistance. Another drop of the oil and a stealthy pry with a screwdriver popped it loose; its fellow on the bottom answered to the same treatment.

With the bellows loose and the accordion balanced on the table, I slipped my left hand under the hardened bass strap and gently let some wind in using the air button. The bellows creaked and groaned and popped ominously as I spread the instrument apart. I released the air button and allowed the instrument to close itself. I pushed one of the treble buttons, middle C, and was rewarded with an asthmatic mew. I tried again, this time forcing the pressure up and got a much more powerful but much shorter note.

Jenny observed, "So, that's it, eh? I guess I was sorta expecting a gold plated Lawrence Welk type of affair with all the bells and whistles. It looks pretty rough. Hey, at least it's not completely dead, right? I can feel the air escaping even way over here, though. Looks like lots of leaks."

"Lots of leaks for sure. I guess the glue the old guy was using wasn't guaranteed to survive outdoors for a hundred years. The joints of the instrument are fairly falling apart. Let's see if we can get her apart and look at the interior."

I pulled a pair of wire cutters from the tool drawer and gently latched onto the pins that held the bellows onto the accordion ends. Where an ordinary accordion's pins would sport a round metal head like a push-pin, these were fashioned like tiny faces. I carefully worked the jaws of the pliers underneath each one and, noting it's relative position on the instrument, worked it free. The ends came off cleanly and I marked the position of the bellows so I could reassemble it in the same way it came apart.

I hesitated to look inside for fear of living creatures, but none were there, the box being at least airtight enough to keep them out. I spread the pieces out on the table.

I heard the coffee grinder whirring but paid no attention. All of my focus was centered on the reed blocks of the instrument. Where regular blocks would be maple, birch or walnut, these were made out of rosewood or some dark tropical timber. A swinging metal plate held by a screw secured the reed blocks. I searched the tool drawer in vain for the right sized screwdriver and finally had to forage for one in the garage. I came up with one sad and abused example I figured might be up to the job. I gave the tip a few swipes with a file to give it at least some chance of gripping the slots in the screws and not jumping out.

By the time I returned to the kitchen, a fresh pot of coffee was brewed and a second plate of toast was waiting. I ignored these temptations until I had carefully loosened the screws and pulled the reed blocks out of the box.

Strangely enough, as I was wrangling the screws with a slightly too long screwdriver, the handle of the tool rubbed against the inside of the box and a shiny streak appeared in the dusky black. A little further rub-bing showed an additional shiny surface. I was perplexed but was so intrigued by the reed blocks that I moved on.

I washed the grime off my hands and sat down at the table with Jenny. I had a cup of coffee, a plate of cinnamon toast, I was holding hands with a pretty girl and had a blown up accordion, what bliss.

She said, "Well, at least it has plenty of parts. It looks a little more manageable now that it's apart. Fix one piece at a time. Right?"

"I guess. These reed blocks are pretty cool anyway. Look how each reed is dovetailed on the edges and slides into the mortises cut into the reed blocks perfectly. Usually they just sit on the surface and get wax slobbered all over them to hold them in place. Also the reed's tongues themselves are mounted in bases of silver instead of the usual zinc. That should give it some serious volume and tone. There's even tiny Chinese characters engraved on the reed bases, cool. The parts inside the box look like they're pretty well preserved; too bad it leaks like a sieve."

"As it turns out, I now have all of my tools cluttering up your liv-ing room. I'm sure I could dig out the necessary items to sort out the woodworking issues. There's even a workbench in the garage, if only it wasn't covered with greasy motorbike junk."

"Hmmm..., Yeah, I guess we could clear off a few square feet, spe-cial project and all."

Jenny declined to comment further about the state of the garage.

"Would there be any long adjustable clamps around? I'm pretty sure most of this stuff will have to come completely apart and be rebuilt to get it right, and you want it right, right?"

I had considered plugging the most heinous leaks with duct tape and wax just to see if I could get the thing going but that didn't sound like the most ideal path to go down just then.

"First class all the way for me."

Jenny smiled sweetly, "There's only a few joints here and they don't look that complicated so it won't take too long. So, about the clamps."

"I'm pretty sure my dad kept a few of them around, they'll prob-ably turn up when we excavate the workbench. I know they're out there somewhere."

"OK, we'll look. Say, Soren, that stuff I was going to tell you earlier, you know about the past and...."

The phone rang and I considered letting the machine pick it up based on the tenor of the last few calls, but I ignored my premonitions and answered anyway. The receiver was halfway to my ear and the caller was already ranting.

"Hello, hello, who is there? Who is there? Hello?"

I started off tentatively, "Hello? What can I do for you?"

"Is Vladimir, I am at shop and we are having much trouble here. A big mess of things is here. You should come now."

With that the connection was broken. I stared at the phone as if it could give me further clues. It couldn't.

"It looks as though I have to go down to the shop if I'm going to figure out what the hell Vladimir was just talking about. He said there was a big mess and I'm hoping he means an oil tank or something leaked out on the floor. He sounded a little more demented than usual, though. Do you want to come or hang here?"

"I'll wait here, I think I've gotten as wet as I need to already today. I'll scrounge through the garage for a while, I don't suppose I could do any damage out there no matter what."

I had various feelings about that, but I kept them to myself.

"I'll be back in a short while, I hope."

I leaned in and got a gratifyingly long and intense kiss. I decided I had better bolt fast if I was going to go at all.

The rain had eased off even more and the fog had crept in to replace it. I turned on the headlights pretending that would keep some dimwit from crashing into me if they weren't paying attention. And back across the city I went. Sunday parking was eerily available on Pacific. As I walked down the alley I could see unusual bits of lumber in the road. As I got closer I could see they were painted dark green, just like our front doors, I marveled. Not long after, the novelty wore off as I spied the gaping hole in what remained of our portal. It didn't take a detective to figure out an intruder had performed his stealthy entry with an axe.

I could see inside to where Vladimir was aimlessly kicking at a pile of stuff on the floor. I couldn't exactly make out what the pile might be so I decided to drop in and find out. As I pushed my way through the shattered entrance, Vladimir turned and shook his head, still bearing some remnants of his attack.

"Is big mess. Should close up and run now before we both get killed.

JOHN PEDERSEN

By customers if not maker of this mess."

"Yeah, no shit. Maybe whoever conked you on the head came back to finish the job and got mad you weren't here. You don't have any ideas about this, do you?"

"Ah, hmmm..., no, does not look like same people. Is not same style."

I looked around at the shop. Bikes had been toppled from the workbenches, boxes of parts had been haphazardly dumped on the floor, contents of toolbox drawers had been emptied onto the floor and a generous helping of smashed accordion parts topped the lot. Much of the loft's contents had been pitched over the edge. The worst of the actual damage looked like it was focused on my old Norton Mercury, which I had parked near the front doors. The original metal tank had been savaged with the same type of tool used to break in. It was caved in from every angle and the silver paint flaked off in shards and slivers. The upholstery of the seat had been slit with a knife and the taillight and headlight had been broken. The vandal had apparently tried to slit the clutch and throttle cables but had only succeeded in damaging the vinyl coverings, the inside being spring steel.

"This has a recognizable style to you? It looks like a maniac was in here looking for something and then went apeshit when they couldn't find it. Looking for something and couldn't find it, yeah."

As calm as I tried to remain, my anxiety over the violent scene in the shop and being separated from Jenny at the same time was getting the best of me. I though it might be wise to give Jenny a heads up on this new development. My old rotary phone had been whonked with the axe as well and the receiver had been broken in half. I picked up the pieces and was relieved to hear a dial tone, I duct taped the upper and lower pieces together and called out after thanking the Bell System of the '50's.

At home the phone rang until the machine picked up. I said, "Say, Jenny, I don't know if you are sitting there not picking up my phone or what, but from the condition of the shop I'd have to say your buddy has located us again. Possibly looking for those papers you were thinking of getting copied. Seeing as how he also knows where I live you might consider coming down here or finding a coffee shop or somewhere to hang out in for a while. I'll check back in a while. Bye."

Vladimir, for all his engineering expertise, didn't have the faintest idea where to start the clean up.

"Let's start by getting the tools off the floor and back into the boxes. That's something, right?"

It didn't appear as though the vandals had the energy to throw anything very far, so most of the tools were pretty near where they belonged. Vlad and I scrambled around on the floor picking up whatever we could find and stowing the big things away while dumping all of the little things into a large box to sort out later. It was actually astounding how much crud had accumulated in the bottoms of the toolbox drawers and in an offhand way, I though we might wind up far more organized than before.

An hour and a half later we were still standing in the midst of the jumble. It was like a giant puzzle.

I tried to call Jenny again to check in but the duct tape failed as I was dialing and the receiver dissolved into its elemental parts. I fished around in my pockets for my cell phone and deduced I had left it at home in my rush. An attempt was made to reassemble the smashed piece with questionable results.

"So, comrade, perhaps next we might get the machines up off the floor and back on the benches before we tackle the small stuff. OK?"

"Da, is good plan. Start with most valuable, no?"

I couldn't wait to see what Vladimir considered most valuable.

His first choice was to stand up the Alpha Romeo engine we had just completed. It had been toppled a few degrees off plumb and had come to rest against the wall. This was very fortunate for us because if it had actually fallen to the floor, it surely would have broken some very expensive bits clean off. No damage done, and it certainly was the most valuable item in the shop.

Various engines and bikes were turned upright and hefted back onto their stands. We made a casual assessment of their conditions as we went. Many "Oh My's and Good Gracious's" were spoken sarcastically.

My impression was there wasn't that much actual damage. A few dents and bent things, but nothing we couldn't repair in house. That I could see.

Several hours of heavy lifting and strenuous labor saw the majority of the stuff right side up again. I was anxious Vlad might be seriously overextending himself, but he waved off my inquiries.

Our next task was to somehow sort out the infinite array of nuts, bolts and parts littering the floor. We each wandered to a section of the shop and sat right down on the floor to begin sorting.

To the ordinary person a bolt is a bolt, but to us there exist scores of clues as to where a particular bolt might reside. Length, grade of strength, Metric, SAE, Whitworth, British Standard and degree of finish were all easily noted. Also the number of each type of bolt: if there were only three bolt holes in a part there wouldn't be four bolts lying around. Bolts on the insides of things aren't generally chromed. A grade eight bolt wouldn't be used to hold on a fender as it's overly strong.

Each manufacturer used to make their own fasteners, each had a distinct look, and long association with them had imprinted the look on our subconscious. Generic type bolts didn't matter so much and we often replaced them just as a safety precaution.

In a remarkably short time we had each sorted, by project, a high percentage of the rubble. We then switched piles and were able to further refine our efforts.

It was nearly ten o'clock by the time we sat on folding chairs in the middle of the shop and surveyed the results. The place looked almost normal and, in some respects, better than before. We had some fresh bodywork to do and some precise welding, but very few parts would have to be hunted down and bought. We were completely spent and filthy. From my seated position I looked around for a few planks we could use to nail the door closed and my gaze swept over the poor old Norton. Of course it could come back, but it certainly looked nasty at the moment. Big Red and the Norton in the same week, how much could a sentimental motorhead take? We located some ancient 2X10's in the rafters and wrestled them down. I took a portable drill and some long deck screws and after closing the doors as best we could, Vlad and I simply screwed the planks over the door. If somebody wanted to break in now, by God they'd better have a screwdriver. We agreed we shouldn't strive to open up until at least noon the following day. I thanked Vlad profusely for his help and we headed off to our respective baths and beds.

JOHN PEDERSEN

CHAPTER

I ROLLED back across town gliding through the intense fog that had come to visit. The streetlights on Geary glowed feebly illuminating little more than themselves. Neon lights on storefronts made islands of color and activity. Sound was deadened. The Outer Richmond was like a ghost town and for blocks I didn't see another soul. I pulled into the driveway and killed the motor. I just sat there for a few moments marshalling my energy for the walk to the front door. I was kind of relieved to see Jenny's car still lurking next to me proving she hadn't bolted during my absence.

The lights in the living room were off as well as those in the kitchen. Assuming Jenny had gotten tired and turned in, I ate some cold Spanish rice straight out of the pot and rinsed the spoon off when I was done. I noticed the dishes from the previous night and that morning had been washed.

The pieces of Miller's decrepit accordion sat on the kitchen table festooned with clamps and webbed strap devices. The table was covered with newspaper and junk mail. Jenny had found the clamps but wisely given up on the garage.

I enjoyed a long hot shower, which got most of the crud off of me. My strength was waning fast and as I went into my room and flopped onto the bed I was surprised to note that Jenny wasn't there. After a brief flash of panic I figured somehow she had used her feminine ESP to know I was totally spent and was bunking in the spare room just to save me from myself. I enjoyed the smell of her shampoo on the extra pillows. I considered peeking in on her just to check but was gone before I could act.

I had a deep sleep filled with dreams of mountains of nuts and bolts. I was relieved to wake up but had to deal with unfamiliar aches and pains. I didn't hear Jenny rustling around and was gratified she was comfortable enough to enjoy a nice sleep-in. I stepped out on the balcony to check the surf, and it was crap.

I dug up some pretty clean clothes and went down to the kitchen. Peeking into the spare room on my way by I saw Jenny was up, the room straightened and the bed made. I assumed she was in the bathroom. I made a pot of coffee and a couple of plates of poached eggs on toast and when she failed to show, I carried one of these and a giant cup of java up the stairs.

Entering the spare room with the grub, I was surprised to find no Jenny there. I felt a lurch in my guts. I went back down to the kitchen. The list of places she might be was severely limited and I had covered most of them. I looked into the living room and the garage without finding her. It looked like all of her tools and miscellaneous junk still graced the living room floor, though. I figured the breakfast would lose its charm rapidly so I ate all of the eggs, half of the toast and drank the coffee.

Searching again through the house, I failed to locate the pile of papers Jenny had liberated from Jarno's building. I glanced out the front window and saw her Toyota sitting in the driveway and I concluded at least she hadn't driven away. I didn't see any signs of a struggle, but it would have been hard to tell with the contents of her car and house spread all over the living room.

While I was mulling over the possibilities, I unclamped the accordion bits on the kitchen table and gathered up the newspapers Jenny had spread out to catch stray drips. Inspecting her work I was pleased with my own judgment not to have done the job myself. Even with the makeshift working space and limited tools her repairs were invisible and her joints perfect. Not a trace of duct tape to be seen.

I was pretty shocked to see every surface of the box's interior was faced with burnished silver. The wafer-thin plates were festooned with mystifying Chinese characters. I filed this information under "completely bizarre" and continued working. I thought a visit to Grandma Zhou might be required to decipher the intent of the plates.

JOHN PEDERSEN

By the time I made new weather stripping gaskets for the bellows ends and reinstalled the reed blocks, I was getting the creeps and made up my mind to treat her disappearance seriously. While subconsciously trying to come up with a plan I turned the bellows this way and that until I had the orientation right and then reattached the ends. I still needed to make a hand strap for the left hand but I thought I would have to let that wait for a while. I slid the accordion back into its musty case and got my stuff ready to go. I took another trip around the house to make sure I hadn't overlooked some cozy nook where someone might be tempted to sleep an entire night and be immune to the smells of coffee and break-fast. I didn't have any success.

I carefully locked the door feeling a bit like I was locking the barn after the horse had escaped and loaded my accordion and Miller's ac-cordion into the truck.

The drive across town took forever and the number of moronic and incompetent drivers seemed to be multiplying right in front of me. My anxiety levels were reaching my flat line point when I would become numb from overwhelming futility and switch to complete autopilot. At that point I would become a work zombie and remain unseeing and un-feeling. Someone could shoot me and I wouldn't know or care until I keeled over.

I made it all the way down O'Farrell and up Grant before the com-plete insanity of my fellow drivers woke me up a bit. I had to dodge and dive, hit the brakes and practically drive on the sidewalk to make my way to the shop.

It looked as though no burglar or urban terrorist had come equipped with a power screwdriver since the previous evening as the door still stood as Vlad and I had left it. I set the accordions where I could see them and attacked the multitude of high security deck screws with my cordless drill. After ten minutes I had nearly an entire box of screws in my shirt pocket and a nearly dead machine in my hand. The battery expired with a feeble click-click but I was able to wrench the last few inches of the final screw out by brute force.

The damage inside the shop looked no better or worse than the night before with the exception of the Norton which now wept oil from a deep dent in the oil tank. I did a slow walk-around of the benches to try to assess which bike had taken the worst abuse and needed to get priority help before it's owner showed up and became pissy.

At a casual glance I could see almost no real motor damage that couldn't be filled and repaired with an aluminum welding rod and a torch. There were plenty of dings and scrapes to tanks and fenders but almost all of those pieces were pre-body work anyway. Only one of the damaged bikes had already been completed and was almost ready to be picked up. Not anymore.

I decided to make a call to the police before Vladimir arrived and before any other distractions might make themselves known. I dialed the taped together phone survivor and got police headquarters.

"San Francisco Police, how may I help you?"

"Um, would this be the right number to report a missing person? That is to say, a possibly missing person?"

"You would have to talk to the missing persons department, I can connect you, one moment."

The line went blank for several minutes and I debated whether to hang up and try again or just wait. Eventually the line began to ring.

"Missing persons, Officer Donahue, how can I help you?"

"I'm worried about my girlfriend, I think she might have been abducted or gone missing."

"How long since she has been heard from?"

" I saw her last yesterday afternoon. She wasn't around this morning and as far as I can tell, she didn't leave a note or anything."

"It hasn't yet been 24 hours; we would consider this somewhat premature. I can take the information and make a report just in case an officer encounters her. What would make you think this person is missing and not just on a sleepover somewhere?"

"I'm not sure how to answer. We were pretty tight up until she just wasn't there, and she recently moved out or her apartment and didn't have anywhere else to go. Not only that, she was having trouble with her boss who is involved in some big scam. This guy was making a bunch of replica antique and pioneer style furniture and selling it as authentic stuff. One of his big customers was the State Parks Commission. He might have thought she was going to blow the whistle."

"Really, ya don't say. At the very least we should alert Antiques Roadshow."

There was a good deal of ineffectively covered up laughing, "Let's start from the top. Her name?"

I relayed everything I could think of from Jenny's past, which didn't amount to much after I was done. The officer on the phone sounded a little incredulous.

"So, Mr. Rauhe, you have only known this person five days, correct?"

"Well, yeah, if you look at it like that it does sound sorta sudden, but we were getting along really well."

"We have the information sir, and if we come across the lady, we'll suggest she call you; fair enough?"

I suddenly had the feeling my report was going straight into the paper shredder. I blurted out, "Not only that, but one of the guys she worked with got murdered down in the Tenderloin the other night. Could have been the big guy cleaning up loose ends or something."

"Murdered you say, when was this, sir?"

"Um…, we read about it in the Chronicle on Saturday morning, it must have been Friday night."

"Friday night, and you say this person whom might be missing is a woodworker?"

"Yeah, expert woodworker in fact."

"Sir, I think you need to come in and discuss this person with the homicide division. I'm pretty sure they would be very interested in talking with your friend, and therefore, you. Not to spread too much information around but the person who was killed on Friday night was murdered with a Swedish wood chisel. A technical college in Canada was found to be the major customer in North America for the brand. There might be a connection."

My heart sank to a new low. "Well, it couldn't have been her, she was with me pretty much all Friday night. A chisel you say, interesting."

"Nevertheless, I'm pretty sure Homicide would like a chat with your girlfriend. I'll relay this information to them and if they don't see you soon, I'm sure they will send someone around."

We disconnected. The chisel murder chilled my blood. I could just imagine Jenny's missing half-inch chisel protruding from some poor schmuck's chest.

I was glad I hadn't mentioned the fact that I didn't really have any idea where Jenny had been while I was in the Bohemian Club getting crocked.

While mulling over the implications of Jenny's disappearance and the connection between her tool and the dead man, I got Miller's accordion out of its nasty case and set it on one of the newly cleared benches. I got my Soprani out as well and set it adjacent. I unbuckled the shoulder strap from the Soprani and put it on the Miller. I was already terrified and anxious about all recent events, but now my unfaithfulness to my instrument made me feel like I was kicking a puppy.

The hand strap from the Soprani wouldn't fit the Miller so I had to get out some leather scraps and make a new one from scratch. My work wasn't particularly inspired but I figured if the box worked at all I could always make another later.

I sat in the back corner of the shop and strapped on the box. I opened and closed the bellows with the air button several times without making a sound except the creaking and wheezing of the stiff material. I finally let the button out at full stretch and was gratified to see how much the air tightness had improved. I gently tested the bass side chords: C, G, D, Bb, A, A minor, F # minor, B minor. I could practically smell the dust and debris making its way through the valves and reeds. The chords growled and buzzed at first but settled some with additional air pressure. Perhaps the instrument required a firm hand. I tested all the chords up and down the scale and found a few sticky buttons in the far reaches, places I rarely strayed. I felt lightheaded.

The pearl buttons of the treble scale felt strange and sticky under my fingertips, like shark-skin. The size and spacing was subtly different than that of the Soprani. I worked my fingers up and down without air, listening to the gentle clack of the keys. I finally sensed an urgency to get some noise out of the reeds and leaned into the first note. I played a long A, feeling the tone waver, settle and then build in volume and complexity. I played the note below, G, and could feel the tone do the same thing. When I played the A again the tone was immediate. I slowly worked my way up and down the entire keyboard noting where there were slight imperfections in tuning and buzzing valves. Well within the range of playable I thought, but the slowness and generally uninspired tone was kind of disappointing.

The first tune that came into my head was a slow air called "The Blackbird." It was all strange intervals and peculiar timing. I played it slowly and let my sadness and confusion over Jenny's disappearance occupy my thoughts as I was playing. Suddenly tears were running down my cheeks and the lights wavered. I thought I heard the rolling of thunder in the distance. The music swelled until the shop vibrated with funereal sorrow. Small tools and piles of random junk toppled over which I attributed to sloppy stacking the night before. As my thoughts and feeling cleared, the tone of the box had become a combination of pipe organ and choir. I thought my heart would break. I managed to stop squeezing the bellows and the notes faded. I realized I had my eyes open for quite a while but whatever I had been seeing was not the shop. It took a while for the real place to come into focus.

A few seconds later Vladimir came through the door swiveling his much less swaddled head left and right. "What was this thing, was like secret Russian force field which never worked? Was like waves of energy blocking door. Could not enter shop one minute ago. Not looking so bad in here today. What is wrong with yourself, pulled muscles, what? I have perfect remedy!"

I scrubbed the moisture from my face and shook my head. "Holy shit, what just happened to me? I was just playing a tune on the box here and suddenly it was like all life and hope was sucked out of existence. I could practically see the tune. I was living and breathing the emotions behind the notes, we were one. Wowser!"

Vladimir was less impressed by the moment. "Da, what to start on?"

I looked around the shop as if seeing it for the first time. I pointed to the bike, which had been nearly ready to be picked up. "Let's get this Harley apart, I think we can get away with painting only half the tank, as long as the paint shop has some left over from the first time around. Aside from that it looks like the damage to the bike is mostly the bolted on chrome crap, and I can go over to Dudley Perkins and just buy that stuff. I'll call the guy and stall him a couple of days, fine-tuning and all that nonsense. Let's check over the Alfa motor as well and make sure nothing is scratched or cracked, I'd hate to have that guy pissed off at me."

I tucked the accordion away and Vladimir and I made a slow tour of the shop making even more detailed notes about what damage would have to be repaired right away to get the decrepit bikes back to the sorry state they had arrived in. I quizzed Vladimir, "Say, are you off the coffee bean now? Usually you have a giant cup with you at this time of the morning. I was hoping you would bring one for me too."

"Nyet, nothing from usual place today. Is all smashed up inside and doors locked. Maybe had small fire. Nobody around there."

Panic seized my chest. "Listen Vladimir, I think the same bastards who smashed up the coffee place probably wrecked this place as well. They probably did it to get Big Chris to tell them where my shop is located and it looks like they did. They burned up my van at the house and I think they kidnapped Jenny too. They are the guys who probably came in here and knocked you on the head. I wouldn't blame you if you took off for home and didn't come back till I can sort this all out. I'm sorry you are involved in this mess."

Vladimir had an uncomfortable and shifty look about him and said, "Da, is probably them, not man with eye patch and blue coat."

"Eye patch and blue coat? Oh, right, now I remember your demented description. Hold on a second, though, if they could find you here and find my place in order to burn up Big Red, why would they have to smash up the coffee shop just to find us again? Something is slightly off here, no?"

Vladimir had moved away and was busily sifting through a large metal pan with long engine mounting studs in it, trying to find all the similar ones that might go to a single bike. I thought to quiz him further about the hinky timeline, but was derailed by the ringing phone.

I didn't have to answer to know who the caller was. I picked up the wobbly receiver and said, "Sean, I think I should have taken up the offer of the Fightin' Irish. Things are going to shit around here. This morning Jenny's missing, probably kidnapped by the fuckin' Finns, the Uncertain Grounds coffee joint got smashed up and maybe set on fire, and some assholes broke down the door of the shop here and knocked a bunch of shit over and made a general mess outta the place as well as royally fucking my Norton. I'm totally flipping here. Maybe you should take a mental health day and help me sort this all out, I'm sure old Heelan would understand."

"Yeah, he'd understand all right. He'd understand my friends are even more useless than I am. Hell, compared to you I might even look good. Nah, on second thought, forget it. Maybe later. Listen, I just called to make sure you're up for Virginia's tonight, seems like there is an attendance surge. Even Sloane said she was definitely going, and you know how she hates going up Potrero Hill."

"Sloan, is it? Incredible. Say, what's up with her lately? She was acting pretty funny at the Flower the other night and was dressed almost like a regular person, which for her means she looked homeless. I actually saw a smudge on her. Shocking!"

"Yeah, I don't know. She practically hit the roof when she saw Edain there. Speaking of which, a very satisfactory evening there. I'm still covered with contusions and bruises from that damn cast."

"I'm certainly thrilled for you, but the real question is how are we going to find Jenny and get her back? I think the Finn got into my place and abducted her while I was down at the shop cleaning up with Vlad. She had a whole bunch of incriminating invoices and shit like that, which disappeared with her. I'm tempted to get some boyos together and go over to Jackson and bust the place up. At least I'd feel like I was doing something."

"I don't suppose she was way smarter than all of your previous girlfriends and figured out really fast what a dork you are and just took off. Maybe she figured out all of her shit was just that and left it behind."

"Oh, thanks very much for the encouraging words pal. I'm not saying it couldn't have happened, but I don't think so this time."

"Whatever, we'll work this all out later. Connor1 and Connor2 are making the rounds of the job and I have to get looking busy. Let me know if you want to bust up them Finns on my lunch hour, otherwise, we'll talk at Virginia's."

Sean disconnected without further talk.

The history of Virginia's session was so lost in time most of the regular players didn't even know why they were there. Virginia was the mother of one of our regular gang, Molly, and she loved coming out to the pubs and bars to see us play. At one point she had become ill and Molly had convinced us we should head up to her mom's craftsman style house on Wisconsin high on Potrero Hill, to play a few tunes and cheer her up. We did so without expectations, but Virginia had set out such a splendid array of food and drink we played all night. She had such a great time when she invited us back we agreed to come again. The session grew little by little and soon the house was full of players, many of who brought their own contributions to the larder. After a quite a few years Virginia went into the hospital and on into a retirement community and the session followed her there. The fact that our Monday night sessions were the absolute highlight of the week for many of the residents was not lost on the players who felt truly appreciated for once.

After quite a while, Virginia declined and passed on but the session continued. We shifted over to Molly's house for a time, but eventually it was somehow moved back to the original location at Virginia's Potrero Hill place. At first it may have been a little disconcerting to the people who had rented the place but close inspection of their lease agreement revealed a "Monday Night" clause. There had been a certain amount of resistance at first, but soon it was clear they had come to enjoy and anticipate the musical evenings. The furniture was moved and arranged in session mode before we even got there. Also, Virginia's will provided a small trust to supply the food and drink so there was no out-of-pocket expense to anyone.

Vlad had abandoned the pile of engine studs and moved on to the Alpha Romeo engine, which he was inspecting with a magnifying glass. He completed his survey and gingerly turned the engine over with a long breaker bar and a socket attached to the crankshaft. Parts whirred and clicked with precision. He rendered his verdict with finality, "Is good, no damages. One scratch, file, sand, buff, is gone."

I had been busy stripping the abused bits off the old Knucklehead Harley Davidson and making a list of new shiny parts to buy. The phone rang again.

I answered the cobbled together receiver and heard Jenny's voice sounding strained, "Soren, Soren, are you there? Hello? Soren, Vladimir, anybody."

My answer was lost as the tape on the receiver failed and it fell to pieces ripping out wires as it crumbled. I tried frantically to rewire and reassemble some sort of jury rig contraption that might get a message across but failed.

I wailed in frustration and helplessness and tried to stomp the remaining pieces of the old phone into oblivion but succeeded only in hurting my foot.

CHAPTER

I WAS pretty certain Jenny's call had been a desperate plea for help and my inability to complete the call was tantamount to losing her. I was convinced Jarno had abducted her to keep the truth of his million-dollar scam hidden. If Sean had been available to help I probably would have stormed the iron gates of the Jackson address hoping to rescue her. As it was I had reservations about the talent available at that very moment. Vladimir was a bit skinny and vague-looking at the best of times and even more so with his shaved and patched dome. Monday morning was and is a notoriously bad time to get anything done by a motorcyclist. In my experience almost the entire range of bikers, from the weekend warriors to the hardened scooter tramps consider Monday an extension of the weekend. Some retail bike shops might be open, but all service-related shops are Tuesday through Saturday.

With that situation in mind I doubted whether I could round up a bunch of threatening-looking types to solidify my assault. Suddenly Leon Zhou and his collection of shimmering blades sprang into my mind. I tried to picture the impression he would make and decided it would certainly scare the crap out of me if I didn't know him.

I scratched around in the remaining debris of the back desk until I found his number. Without a working phone in the shop I was reduced to trying to get my notoriously unreliable cell phone to come to life. Eventually I got a signal by strolling around the block and holding it high up in the air. I rang his number.

Grandma Zhou snagged the call before it had even completed the first full ring. Amid a barrage of Chinese I simply kept repeating, "Leon, Leon, is that you?" Finally there was a shouted exchange and Leon himself came on the line.

"Hi, who's this? Anybody still there?"

"Leon, Soren Rauhe here, the guy interested in the old accordion. I wonder if I could come over and show you and your Grandmother what I've found. You might be able to shed light on some aspects of it. I might also have a big favor to ask."

"Fine, I don't have to leave for about forty minutes so right now would be good. Grandma's shows don't start for a while either, so she might even be interested this time."

I told Vladimir I had to skip out and would be back shortly. I cautioned him again against overextending himself. I doubted he heard me at all being mesmerized by the clicking and ticking of the Alpha's exposed valve train.

With the Norton out of commission I didn't think it particularly likely I could park the truck any closer than it already was to their address so decided to walk over. About halfway, the extra weight of the hardwood reed blocks and silver reed plates made themselves known, and my arms felt like they were being pulled out of their sockets. I felt a pang of pity for the poor clods who played the full-blown 120 bass concert accordions that weighed a ton.

I huffed my way up the stairs of their building resting at each landing. It felt like there were extra floors that hadn't been there before. I knocked on the door.

Leon answered wearing a sleeveless sweater, a bow tie and glasses. He looked far closer to the Studious Chinese student I had pictured before meeting him.

He invited me in and instantly went to make tea. Grandma Zhou sat in the living room as before, involved with the Chinese newspaper instead of the TV. She ignored me until Leon returned with the teapot and re-introduced us. She allowed me to clasp her hand and bow my head.

I relayed to Leon how Jenny and I had found Miller's journal and the drawings and how they had led us to the Chinese Cemetery in Colma. I told them how we finally located the marker at the site of his Great

Aunt's grave and managed to unlock the secret compartment by chance. Leon translated this all to Grandma and as I got to the secret compartment part I pulled the accordion out of its case. Both Grandma and Leon looked on with a certain amount of interest but didn't act inclined to exert any sort of claim or toss out allegations of grave robbery.

I set the accordion in my lap and pulled the pins with my trusty Leatherman tool. Handling the exposed ends carefully, I handed the lighter side to Grandma and pointed to the shining silver plates lining the walls. She put on a pair of thick reading glasses and peered into the innards. She reached out a tentative finger and gently touched the reeds her father had made. She shook her head and uttered a drawn out "Ohhhh."

After a few seconds of marshaling her thoughts she started a rapid-fire monologue directed at Leon accompanied by more head shaking and finger wagging. He listened impassively until there was a break in the flow and turning to me he said, "Grandma says the writing on the inside of the instrument is a blessing, like a prayer. But like a prayer in strong language, almost like a warning. Sort of like a spell, almost, telling the spirits in the metal to behave and not make trouble. Telling them to stay home and do their job, not to cause mischief. She says the metal sheets are the walls of their reed house, or even prison, but a nice one. She says you should not take these walls away, you might be sorry."

Grandma gave a slightly sinister sounding cackle at this point.

It was Leon's turn to shake his head. "I don't know if she's making this up or not. It doesn't really sound like her usual fairy tales about how great and mystical China is. You'll have to filter the story yourself."

Grandma turned to the TV with a smug look on her face and in two seconds was involved with one of her programs. Leon and I moved on to the kitchen.

"Say, Leon, I'm having issues with some guys over on Jackson and thought I might pay them a personal call to get some straight answers about their furniture business and where they think my girlfriend might be located. I doubt there would be any trouble at all, but I'd sorta like to have a fierce looking backup just to make sure it doesn't. I'd say you qualify pretty well. Any chance you could loose the bow tie and glasses and accompany me over there?

"Jeeze, I didn't know the accordion business got so rough. I wouldn't have any problem going with you, but I have to get to school-maybe tomorrow or Wednesday."

"Well... that might be too late, but if there still are issues up in the air by then, I'll give you a call. Thanks for the entertainment though, and thank Grandma for me, she's awfully cute and sweet."

"If you say so, see you later."

Leon let me out and I hauled the accordion back down the stairs and through the midday chaos of Chinatown.

I passed the truck on my way back to the shop and didn't see any signs of trouble. When I reentered the splintered doorway, Vladimir was nowhere to be seen. I set the accordion case near the back wall and scouted the place. No visible work had been completed in my absence but there wasn't additional damage either. I checked the door to the bathroom and saw indications of lengthy Russian occupation.

I finally allowed myself to succumb to the mounting panic surrounding Jenny's whereabouts. Since not finding her at the house, I had harbored deep hope I was merely being alarmist and maybe she had just popped out for an early dentist appointment and would come strolling in. That secret hope was fading with every passing minute. I never had a girlfriend abandon me without a scathing, personal and occasionally physically painful confrontation. For her to just not be there threw me into unfamiliar and terrifying territory. Without a single positive idea other than the most lowly and brutish need to pound somebody, I thought visiting the homicide division might give me a bit of focus and trust that the police were on the case and doing everything possible to find Jenny.

I shouted through the door to Vladimir I was heading to Vallejo and the police station. He should work till he didn't feel like it anymore and then close up and go home if I hadn't returned. He asked if I was going to talk to them about his assault and I assured him I would give them my full assistance in making sure his attacker was brought to justice. He came out with a slow "Da, good." The tone of his voice was hard to read after being filtered by the door, but I didn't waste any time trying to imagine what might have been going through his Slavic mind. I tried to plan ahead and think of any supplies or parts I could buy while I was out but gave up in disgust. All I could think of was finding Jenny Farrar with three "R"s.

I considered throwing some duct tape over the hole in the Norton's oil reservoir to see if I could get it started, bashed up as it was, as it would be so much easier to park. I decided against the thought as disrespectful and went off to get the truck.

I turned up Kearny, over Broadway and back down Montgomery in a big loop. By going such a way I thought I might slip down Gold Alley, behind Jarno's shop, and check out the situation there just in case I might be able to do a little solo pre-police action rescue work. As I cut across traffic to head down the alley, I thought briefly about the fact there were no driveways, pullouts, cut-throughs or any other way out of the alley except at the other end. I slowly cruised the length of the street noting how different everything looked sober and in the light.

When I spotted the dumpster where I had salvaged the Galleazzi stuff I also spotted the same large fellow Jenny had rapiered and knocked down the stairs. He was chucking a large box of stuff into the dumpster already overloaded with debris. As he stared at me through the window of the truck I hardly thought he would be able to recognize me but I was wrong. Without taking his eyes off me, he gently pushed the heavy dumpster straight across the alley. I had pegged him as a complete idiot to not realize I could just reverse down the alley in a big hurry. I was prepared to do just that till I noticed a white van had pulled into the alley after me. My first thought was, "Oh man, this guy is gonna be pissed off he's stuck here behind that dumpster and he's gonna start blowing the horn really soon." My second thought was, "This can't be good at all." The latter turned out to be the more accurate.

I wasted a few seconds trying to stare through the front window of the van to see who might be driving, seconds I should have spent locking the doors and praying. The lunk strolled around to my side of the Ford and wrenched open the door. I scanned the interior for a weapon of some sort, but failed to find anything at all. He seized me by the front of the jacket and plucked me out of the truck like I was a child. I was ready to put all of my considerable surfing years of upper body conditioning to use when he clocked me in the face with a fist the size of a Christmas ham. Much of my indignation deserted me in an instant and I was more of a third party observer as I was dragged into the building and dumped down the basement stairs. After arriving at the foot of the stairs I considered pulling myself together to check for broken parts but the brute clumped down directly after me and dragged me upright. A steel office chair was produced from among the crap in the center of the room and I was shoved onto it. My hands were tied behind me around the center post of the chair back with a handy piece of copper wire. I considered complaining this was extremely uncomfortable but didn't. I half expected to find Jenny roped to a similar chair down there but she was nowhere to be seen. The big guy acted like he was harboring a certain amount of resentment concerning his treatment a few days earlier as he hauled off and smacked the shit out of me without preamble or comment. The chair fell over along with its contents. The chair and I were jerked upright by my stylishly long hair.

Fortunately for myself, and my life expectancy, the brute didn't actually know anything about boxing or putting one's considerable weight behind a punch. It wasn't exactly a pillow fight, but if the monster had actually focused his power, I would have been dead after the first thunderclap of a blow. I had been in plenty of fights with guys half the size of this fellow and suffered much more painful shots.

I was knocked around for an indeterminate time during which my abuser learned not to knock over the chair with me in it because it took a lot of effort to pick us up. No questions were asked and no explanations or lies were tendered on my part.

After a certain amount of this treatment, a sharp command halted the latest punch in mid-flight. I couldn't identify the language or see the speaker. Slowly the big guy moved aside like the final stages of an eclipse revealing, who I took to be, Jarno. Certainly not the tall, fair-haired, lanky Finn I had imagined but rather a short, wiry-looking guy with hair as dark as my own. He wore steel-rimmed glasses perched on a long, narrow nose and a fierce scowl. He moved closer and regarded me with glacial blue eyes.

"So, you and your nosy friend have caused me very much trouble, no? Better she should have kept her nose from out of my business and just kept to her work, yes? Things might still have been all right with her. It is just as has been always said: women do not belong in the workplace. She will be surprised when she suffers the same fate as her friend, the traitor!"

The last statement gave me a small ray of hope even in my half-tenderized state, as I took it to mean she wasn't dead, at least not yet. I hoped I might last long enough to see her again.

JOHN PEDERSEN

"I doubt anyone will miss you before we have disappeared, certainly not your state department as they don't even know we are here stealing their money every day. Idiots!" With this he abruptly turned to the lunk and jerked his thumb dismissively in my direction. I did not take this as a good sign.

Throughout his talking I could hear comings and goings on the floor above. Suddenly there was a series of thumps and a crash that shook the frame of the building. I thought it was more than likely someone had tripped over the loose blocks of wood stacked on the stairs, as I had, but with more spectacular results. Jarno turned and quickly disappeared up the stairs.

My playmate cast around the cellar apparently searching for an implement to bash my head in more easily. He picked up, scrutinized and rejected various pieces as too fragile or light-weight. I knew from my own exploration of the cellar there was a pile of plumbing fixtures in one corner where almost every piece would be suitable for a casual murder.

I strained against the stranded wire securing my wrists and was rewarded with very little movement. To no avail, I tried to hop up and down in the chair in an effort to break something loose. I heard metallic rummaging in the corner behind me and knew the plumbing pile had been located. From the whooshing sounds coming from behind me I figured my time was very severely limited.

Just as I had steeled my cranium to accept a bash, Jarno poked his head down the stairs and shouted something in Finnish, which made the brute drop whatever iron implement he had found and lumber up the stairs.

I assumed there was no way I was going to be forgotten, and it was only a matter of time before the mess upstairs was cleaned up and I would be in the cross hairs again.

I found I could twist my torso in the chair and even though my shoulders threatened to pop out of their sockets, my fingers could touch the Leatherman tool in its belt sheath. Mercifully, the lunk didn't have an IQ to match his size or he would have removed the tool when he tied me up. Either that or he didn't think I would be alive long enough to use it.

Uncharacteristically for me, I realized if I dropped it I would probably not have enough time to knock myself over and then fish around on the floor for it so I tried to be very careful. I unsnapped the top of the sheath and found I could wiggle my fingers enough to work the tool up and out. To access the pliers and wire cutters I had to unfold the halves of the tool and flop them backwards to create the handles. At one time this would have been supremely easy but the action of the tool had been somewhat stiff since a practical joker had superglued the entire machine shut. I fumbled and dug in with my fingernails trying to pry it apart while my hands grew more numb every moment from the lack of circulation.

It felt like hours before I could get the tool open and the jaws clamped on the wire wrapped around my wrists. Even then, neither hand could reach both handles at the same time nor exert any pressure at all. My panic was mounting every moment as I could hear movement all over the floor above and expected to see someone come down the stairs any second.

In desperation I wedged the handles of the tool behind the central bar of the chair on the outside figuring I would take my only shot and tip over backwards and perhaps the floor would do the cutting. Or maybe I would knock myself out, and at the very least I wouldn't be conscious when I was murdered.

I tried to steady the pliers' handles as I prepared to take flight. I tipped forward as far as I dared for momentum and then pushed as hard as I could backward. I went over the top with a rush and cracked the shit out of my skull on the floor as I hit. As the pain in my head cleared it was instantly replaced by a pain in my back where the pointy ends of the pliers had stabbed me in the back. My hands were not free but I did feel a slight bit of slack where none existed before. Extensive kicking and scrambling to get my weight off my hands, arms and shoulders showed something in my restraints had changed. Either a loop of the wire had been cut or perhaps one of my numb hands had been taken clean off at the wrist, I couldn't tell which. Further frantic tugging and wrenching caused the wire to come undone slowly. Finally I was able to pull my hands free and roll away from the chair. The Leatherman clattered to the floor as it became dislodged from my back.

I figured my smartest move was to get the hell out of there and worry about the circulation in my hands later. I crept soundlessly up the stairs to find the door had been bolted. I crept soundlessly back down the stairs. There were no windows or other doors. I went to the cursed pile of plumbing debris and found the five-foot length of pipe, which had nearly been the instrument of my demise. At least I thought I would go down fighting. I looked around for a hiding place to increase my surprise advantage but saw little to give me hope. The scratching and shuffling around on the floor above sounded like it was moving generally in the direction of the basement stairs. I stood against the wall farthest from the foot of the stairs so at least my assassin would have to walk over or around the piles of junk to get at me. I prepared to make my last stand.

As I stood slowly swinging the pipe back and forth I felt a chill run down my spine. Premonition? Fear? Anxiety? Or a breeze coming from somewhere behind me? I turned to find the recently emptied section of shelving directly to my rear. I hadn't had much opportunity to study it last time I had been here as time was short and my flashlight was feeble. I still didn't have any surplus time but at least the light was on.

The shelves were ordinary pine but the back was plywood over the entire width and height of it and prevented one from seeing the bare brick of the wall. The right hand side of the shelf butted up against another unit, but the left side was tucked in behind a monstrous furnace. I stood directly before the shelves and held my hand with its slowly returning feeling out in front of me. By waving this way and that I finally realized there was a small amount of chill air leaking into the basement from behind the shelf.

Close inspection revealed the side rails of the shelf didn't actually touch the floor. I tried to wrench the unit away from the wall but only flexed it a bit. I reasoned there must be a catch and felt along the sides and top until I tripped a crude latch. I cleared a space on the floor in front of the shelf and with a bit of prying with the pipe of doom, I was able to swing it slightly away from the wall.

In the distant past I thought I might have heard stories of secret tunnels in San Francisco, originally used to Shanghai sailors and move contraband goods from the wharf area into the city. I hadn't given the tales much credence at the time and certainly had never run across one. I truly hoped this was an example and not just a drafty hole in the wall.

I heard the bolt being thrown on the cellar door and Jarno lashing out more emphatic instructions. I didn't have to speak Finnish to gather the intent. With no time to lose or explore the void I slipped in and pulled the shelf/door closed after me. I heard the latch click closed and hoped no one else had. Only after I had stood stock still in the dark for a few seconds did it occur to me I was effectively locked in. If I were ever to reenter the basement, someone would have to trip the latch again.

I heard the lunk come down the stairs and could just visualize him staring uncomprehendingly at the empty chair and the vacant basement. He thrashed around and called to the floor above. More feet pounded down the stairs and in the melee of shouting and crashing about I put out a hand almost invisible to me and moved a single step away from the door. I didn't fall into a hole or brush against skeletal remains I could identify. With one hand against the cold and clammy brick wall and the other clasping the pipe outstretched in front I took another step. I was not moving quite fast enough for my own taste and dreaded hearing some sharp-eyed Finn find the latch and discover me. I took two steps and the ground under my feet changed from concrete to uneven cobbles or brick. The air was dank and smelled earthy and dead despite the slight movement. It felt as though I was heading down a slope. The sides narrowed until there was just enough room for me to pass without going sideways. With a slight stoop the roof brushed my head. Step, cautious wave with the pipe, step, and wave…I went on. Any faint glimmer of light from the end of the tunnel was gone. I have no idea how long I walked or how far, all I was really concerned with was the fact I was walking instead of feeding the fishes of the bay with my head bashed in.

Occasionally my pipe would strike solid in front and the tunnel would take a turn or go off at an angle. If I had any sense of where I was at the start of the journey it was soon lost. I could hear rumbling overhead and assumed traffic or, God forbid, a streetcar was passing.

Eventually, my iron cane hit a surface with a hollow sound and I assumed my journey was at an end. For all I knew I had made a giant circle and wound up at the opposite wall of the same basement. I hoped not.

I reached out with my hands and explored the surface. Instead of plywood it was heavy, rough planks and a little force did nothing to budge it. Using my limited deductive powers I reasoned there had to be a release somewhere, a secret passage that locked from outside at both ends was just not safe, surely not up to code!

I got down on my knees and started feeling along the edges of the door. In my mind I was upsetting entire colonies of Black Widow and Brown Recluse spiders who were crawling up my sleeves to better gnaw at my vitals. The bottom edge reveled no secrets nor did the right side.

The top edge offered nothing in the way of escape but plenty in the way of dirt and other crap that rained down on my head. The left side was without handle as well, but I did find what felt like the mechanism for a lock much more complex than at the other end. I couldn't trip it with my fingers but congratulated myself for having a multipurpose tool right on my belt. Or back on the basement floor, as turned out to be the case.

There was not enough room to swing the pipe and a bout of pounding on the door failed to produce any results. I searched my pockets for any tool whatsoever and only came up with loose change and some lucky stones, which apparently weren't working. I dropped one of the stones as I was putting them back in my pocket and as I bent over to fish around on the floor for it. Just as I was picking it up I lost my balance and bonked my head on the center of the panel, which must have hit a button to release the catch because the next moment I was stuck in the partially open door.

I pushed as hard as I could and barely managed to squeeze through the gap. I had emerged in what looked like a storeroom packed with shelves and boxes filled with beauty products. A box or two of these had tumbled over and spilled a colorful selection of shampoos on the floor.

I pushed the door closed in case anyone was lucky enough to get into the tunnel at the other end and headed up the stairs. At the top of the stairs I was greeted by a couple of completely astonished women, one of whom was in the middle of a bikini wax and gave a shriek and jerked an entire pile of towels on top of herself to cover up.

As I walked through the rest of the salon I caught sight of myself in the mirrors and practically shrieked as well. Blood and dirt were caked roughly all over me and the left side of my face was black and blue from my recent pounding. The customers and staff cringed against the walls as I passed.

I strode out onto the sidewalk with as much dignity as I could muster, not very much, and looked up and down the street to get my bearings. I was astounded at where I had wound up.

JOHN PEDERSEN

CHAPTER

I GATHERED from the sun I was facing east and standing on Battery Street. The awning on the building I had just left informed me the salon was located at One Jackson Place, which houses quite a few other businesses as well. I thought it too bad I hadn't come out in the basement of a bar. That would have been more than useful.

I decided to skip the police visit for the time being and head back to the shop, the long way. Despite the emotional and physical toll of the last hour or so I was still only about four blocks from the shop. I added several blocks to the trip making sure I wouldn't run into any of my recent playmates. Nicely dressed business people avoided making eye contact or just crossed the street when they first spied me. I limped along rubbing my wrists and massaging my swelling face.

Coming up Pacific I peeked down the alley to make sure there was no ambush laid for me. All looked calm and clear. I approached the front door and saw Vladimir had cut down some of the long planks and screwed them to each side of the double doors allowing almost normal operation.

Thankfully his back was to me as I entered and made for the bathroom.

"Da, police let you go so soon? Police much more thorough in Soviet Union, sometimes need to talk for weeks, months. How to find out anything in one hour, not possible."

"I'm afraid I got sidetracked and missed visiting the authorities, maybe tomorrow. Any news here, any visitors?"

"Nyet, nothing, just work. Fix door, get new phone."

He gestured with a wrench in the direction of the wreckage of the old rotary phone, amid which a pink Princess phone proudly rested.

"Four US dollars at junk store next to new coffee place. Much closer than old place, more coffee faster, no?"

As if to prove its four-dollar worth, the phone started ringing at that moment. I answered in my business voice, "Dr. Revolution, what can we do for you?"

"Soren, Walter here, is everything OK down there? Are you OK?"

"Walter? I'm astounded you know this number, shocked in fact. And yes, things are OK at the moment, what brings you to ask, if I might be nosy?"

"I just had a call from the police who wanted to know why the Ford is parked with the keys in it in front of a hydrant down by Sidney Walton Park. They were running the registration number and found it was in my name. The officer on the stop is a friend of mine, and thought he'd better check with me before they towed it. Anything I should know about this situation?"

"Ah, yes, the truck, it was sort of borrowed by a fellow who might not be too clear on the rules of parking or truck borrowing. I'll get my ass right over there and claim it, if it's still there."

"Well, it might be, there were a couple of cops involved besides my friend, so I don't know. Take care of yourself, OK? And try not to completely lose the truck the first week."

"Thanks Walter, I'll try to keep that in mind."

I told Vladimir I had to take another walk to reclaim the truck and if I didn't return in twenty minutes or so he should call the police and tell them to look for me on Jackson Street. I also told him he might consider taking the rest of the day off, as the shit and the fan were about to meet. I told him I was serious and he should get the hell out of the alley before an army of angry Finns descended on his head. I wasn't sure if he heard me or not as he was preoccupied clicking the pieces of a transmission into gear and out, into gear and out.

I splashed a bit of water onto my face and put on a cleanish sweatshirt and picked up a two foot length of steel rod, just in case.

I hustled my beat-up self all the way up to Broadway thinking I could get lost in the swarm of people coming and going to the bars and strip clubs. Early afternoon on a Monday was a bit light on the crowds after I made the corner from Columbus and I was almost the only person walking east. However, I made my way over to and down Front without being recognized.

As I approached the park, I could see across the expanse of lawn to where the Ford was parked brazenly in front of a hydrant. There was a patrol car, a motorcycle cop and a tow truck clustered around it. The cop without the helmet was gesturing back and forth and acted like he was trying to slow things up. I skulked behind the statue of Sidney Walton himself trying to scout out any additional traps that might have been prepared for me. It occurred to me the last trap hadn't exactly been laid for me, I drove myself directly into it. I hoped the apparent lack of planning on the part of the Finns was consistent. I bolted from my hiding place as the tow truck maneuvered into position. I arrived on the scene waving my arms and making lame excuses.

"Hey, hey, hang on a second there, amigos. Let's not be hasty with the heavy machinery. My friend Walter just called to say you all found my stolen truck, and so you have. I'm obliged mightily. Perhaps I could just get the old feller out of your hair and not cause any more of an interruption in you busy schedules."

I don't think there has ever been an occasion where a San Francisco tow truck driver has driven away from a possible tow, especially with several guys with guns to back him. I had to try though.

All parties involved gave me a look that implied beat up space aliens had no justification to speak to them. I kept talking, "So, whadda ya think there, fellas, I should just grab 'er and go, OK? "

Finally one of the police officers deigned to speak to me, "Sir, I doubt seriously this vehicle is going anywhere except on the hook of this truck and subsequently to the Turk Street impound lot. Your license and registration please."

I turned over my driver's license and stammered out, " I just got the thing a coupla days ago from my friend WALTER, and the papers are still in the glove box, I think. Let's look there."

The towing process wasn't slowing down at all and I knew if the hook touched the bumper of the car, it was a done deal. The first cop said, " You don't need to say it again sir, I know you are Walter's neighbor and he sold you the truck recently, but that doesn't excuse willful disregard for parking laws."

"I already told ya it was stolen, right?"

"Do you have a police report for this?"

"Ah…well, not yet, it just happened. Not to mention they beat the shit out of me at the same time, I'm sure you can see that. In fact, I want to file a stolen truck and assault report right now!"

"You are free to make all the reports you want, sir, but they won't change the fact that this truck is going downtown soon. You can arrange to pay the fine and retrieve the vehicle at the impound lot." He practically flipped my driver's license back at me, unimpressed due to my lack of political connectedness.

The officer's hand was resting on the butt of his pistol and he didn't have the look of tolerating further nonsense. The tow truck was maneuvering into position and the hook was about four feet from the bumper. Inevitability loomed large. Suddenly the young motorcycle cop who was directing the truck driver held up his hand.

"Say, aren't you the old motor bike restoration guy over on Pacific? Dr. Restitution, or something like that?"

Glumly I answered, "Yeah, that would be me alright, but my name is Soren Rauhe, Revolution is just the name of the shop."

"Sure, sure, whatever. You fixed up a black 1947 Indian for my dad. Do you remember him? Jim Young was his name. I used to come in there with him to check up on it all the time. Man, it seemed like it took forever. Things are like that when you're a kid, eh? Yeah, we used to come in there and poke around and look at the shiny pieces and look inside the motors and you would explain to me what makes things work. I loved just being inside that place, it was the coolest shop I'd ever seen. I was just about 14 or 15 then. I think one of the most important days of my dad's life was the day we came to pick it up and you kicked it over for him and it just sat there in the alley idling. That was my first motorcycle ride and look where it got me."

He extended the hand holding up the tow truck driver to me to shake. The driver interpreted this as the signal to continue and started backing up again. The cop snapped his head around in annoyance, held up his hand to stop progress and after thinking about things for a moment, languidly flapped his hand as if to shoo the truck away. As the driver swarmed out of the truck to protest this gross irregularity the cop said to me, "Technically, I shouldn't do this, but pick your moment and get the fuck out of here, I'll take care of this guy."

The driver was waving his arms and getting louder and louder as the cop casually backed up a few feet at a time. I slipped over to the driver side and peeked in to find the keys were still in the ignition. I saw the first cop shake his head in disgust and then join the motorcycle cop in engaging the attention of the truck driver. Soon they were ten feet or so behind the Ford and I slid into the driver's seat. I fired it up, crammed it into gear and pulled out past the tow truck in as continuous and smooth an operation as I could. I could hear incredulous howls of protest from the tow truck driver.

As the scene receded in the mirror, I felt safe enough inside the truck to drive right up Pacific. I slowed a bit and peeked down the alley as I passed and was relieved not to see outright mayhem. I still thought it best for Vladimir and me to take the day off until I could confer with Sean, arrange some sort of protection network and figure out how to find Jenny. Either that or get in to talk with the police to get some sort of official involvement beyond towing my stolen vehicle.

Feeling relatively safe for the moment I continued west through the city. As I did, I began to really feel the effects of the abuse to which I had been subjected. In fact, I felt like shit. With no clear path in mind I just instinctively drove until I couldn't drive any further and wound up at the beach. I knew in my bones the tide was on the rise and a slight offshore breeze was creating nice peeling breakers in the five to six foot range, my conditions of choice. Suddenly I had the need to get wet as soon as possible. I thought an hour or so of salt-water immersion therapy might do me a world of good and help me formulate a plan to find and rescue Jenny. Not to mention I had a truck now and wouldn't have to carry my board down the hill wearing my wet suit like I had been doing since Big Red had been dead.

I turned the truck around and headed back to the house to get my stuff. I believed, despite the way the last few days had been going, there was no way a person could screw up a surfing session. I whipped into the driveway and parked next to Jenny's Toyota. I had a premonition and rushed into the house sensing there could be a message on the phone machine from her.

Sure enough the new message light was blinking as well as the light indicating the battery was low. Therefore the machine would accept no more messages, or play back the old ones either, it turned out. I frantically searched drawers and closets for a nine-volt battery without luck and finally robbed one out of the smoke detector in the kitchen, which I considered wildly over-sensitive anyway.

Always the ultimate mechanic, I removed the tiny cross head screw with the tip of a steak knife to get at the battery. I substituted the one with at least some life left in it for the old one, flipped the machine over and hit the Play button. With my heart in my throat I heard my own voice, "Say, Jenny, I don't know if you are sitting there not picking up my phone or what, but from the condition of the shop I'd have to say your buddy has located us again. Possibly looking for those papers you were thinking of getting copied. Seeing as how he also knows where I live you might consider coming down here or finding a coffee shop or somewhere like that to hang out for a while. I'll check back in a while. Bye."

I thought how fitting my attempted warning would be the message that killed the battery. I got up and gathered together random pieces of wetsuit stuff that hadn't gotten burned up in Big Red just to keep moving and not allow disappointment to overwhelm me. I threw the stuff into a laundry basket and filled a two gallon thermos with hot water in anticipation of climbing out of the frigid water in a couple of hours time.

I locked the front door and dumped the wetsuit and towels into the back of the truck and went around to the side of the house where my surfboard rack was located.

Over the years fashions and styles had changed quite a bit so there were several boards, each representing a phase of my surfing life: longboards, shortboards, big wave guns, and even belly-boards were represented. Each would work best for different conditions. However, I don't think conditions ever existed for fiberglass and foam boards that had been hacked up with a claw hammer, which is what my quiver had been reduced to. Even the oldest and most hidden boards had holes punched in them and jagged shards of fiberglass hanging loosely. My current favorite board, which had been shaped by Joe Leary's brother Jim had been drastically reshaped by the nail pulling end of the hammer which was still stuck in the redwood central stringer. I stared in shock at the wreckage and the enormous amount of repair work it represented. I reached out and with a certain amount of difficulty wrenched the hammer free. It was a 16 oz. framing hammer and the handle was taped up with friction tape. The head was sort of rusty except on the working ends, which looked like they saw use everyday. There were faint initials haphazardly carved onto the side of the handle near the head.

Squinting and tipping the tool in the light made me think they might have been an S and a T.

I went back out to the truck, dropped the offensive instrument on the floor of the passenger side and carted all of the surfing stuff back inside the house. I resigned myself to washing the beating and tunnel dirt off with plain old shower water, which was long and hot as opposed to the ocean's long and cold.

JOHN PEDERSEN

AFTER a decent dose of hot water therapy I climbed out of the
shower and wiped the mirror in order to survey the damage. With the
blood and dirt gone I was astounded at how much I looked like myself
considering the pounding I had taken. Ordinarily I'm not brave enough
to spend too much time staring at my visage in the mirror so I didn't
really have a concrete "before" image in my mind for comparison. I
surmised a large part of the damage must have been emotional and let
it go at that.

I dressed with the session at Virginia's in mind. I still had a couple
of hours before I picked up Sean, or he picked me up. Parking up on
Wisconsin was an issue so we always tried to car pool when we could.

In a fit of domesticity I lugged several baskets of laundry into the
garage and started the washing machine. Next I scanned the kitchen and
fridge for food and was astonished at the range of choices. I settled for
a mish-mash of a sandwich with smoked herring, pickles, onions and
pickled beets on thick, black rye bread. There were enough fish in the
can for several sandwiches so I ate them all. I pitied anyone who sat next
to me later in the evening.

With a few moments to spare and a load of weird food grumbling
in my stomach, I got out Miller's accordion to explore the sound a bit
more. Just to bask in my excess of riches, I brought out the Soprani as
well to do some comparisons.

With only one decent set of straps and two accordions, and having played the Miller last, I had to take the straps off it and put them back on the Soprani. I felt like a disloyal friend as I did. With that done I strapped on the Soprani and it settled in my lap like a favorite child. It snuggled up to me and I felt the familiarity of countless hours of playing. The tunes and my fingers were as one on the keyboard. Melodies escaped unbidden from the instrument, one after the other with no coherent thought process of my own. My fingers slipped and slid on the pearl buttons that had been worn to a glistening polish by my fingerprints. Almost all of my tunes were in the middle two octaves of the instrument and the buttons beyond that range felt rough and sticky by comparison.

I played for about fifteen minutes and had no recollection of what tunes I had played or why I had stopped. I sat for a moment almost afraid to try the Miller for fear it would fall so far short of the Soprani I would feel dissatisfied with it. I set the old box in its case and grabbed the Miller. It felt quite clunky by comparison. I stripped the straps off the Soprani and buckled into the Miller. The hassle of getting it ready to play further convinced me it wouldn't be able to meet my expectations. It felt different in my lap – heavier. The buttons felt different and rough, the spacing was different, and the bass notes were set up in a totally different system I would have to get used to. In short I was prepared to be disappointed.

The first few notes were weak and weedy. The Soprani took so little air to get the reeds going to their full potential, I was used to playing light; but such was not the way of the Miller. Ramping up the pressure and pushing the reeds produced better results. Unintentionally a slow air came to my fingers. Even without knowing the words the melody was heartbreaking. The flow of notes continued without interruption as the air transformed itself into a faster and more regular set dance. The set dance played itself out and a hornpipe took its place, slightly faster with a skipping lilt. Jigs – single, double and triple came sliding out of the box as my left hand found bass notes by instinct. Then reels came hard and fast, smoothly evolving from one to another. The room disappeared in my consciousness. I became the tunes with their repeats and hooks and turns. Electricity and energy snapped from my fingers and there was no limit to my perceived power. I felt as though I had the ability to split rock, part the waves, reverse time or almost anything at all. I wasn't quite clear how this might be accomplished by just playing tunes, but I knew I could do it. I had the impression the wind had changed direction and increased an awful lot as the house creaked and shuddered.

The jangling of the phone and a pounding on the front door abruptly interrupted my newly found sense of power. With a profound sense of loss and disappointment I seized control of the music, severed the thread and disentangled myself from the instrument. I grabbed the phone on my way to the front door.

I answered both at the same time and was not at all surprised to find Sean on the phone and the police at the door. The combination felt right and redolent. I stood aside and motioned for the authorities to enter as I said, " And....? What's it gonna be, me drive, you drive?"

"Best if you come get me, I'm having issues with the work truck. Seven? We don't want to get there too late or we'll have to sit over with the mouth breathers."

"Yeah, seven's good. See you then. Think of how we're gonna rescue Jenny." I disconnected. The uniformed police officer and the fellow in plain clothes were roaming around my living room looking at the various nooks and crannies with goofy stuff in them and at the stacks of Jenny's stuff on the floor.

The plainclothes cop sported double knit hound's-tooth slacks and a white belt. A slinky rayon shirt with an outlandishly loud pattern and oversized wings on the collar complimented the slacks. His sport coat did not compliment his slacks at all and his five-inch wide tie ended in the general area of his sternum. I was almost afraid the look down for fear the he wouldn't be wearing the absolutely necessary white loafers. He was.

All parties were introduced; I had Detective Michael Feldman and officer Froom in the house.

Detective Feldman spoke, "So, Mr. Rauhe, the impression down at homicide division was you were about to come in and share your knowledge of the circumstances surrounding the "chisel murder". As no one else has stepped up to offer help, and we have no leads otherwise, we thought we might as well drop by for a chat."

Directly to the point and for a change, the point was not Sean's whereabouts. I stalled for just a moment by inquiring if either of the city's finest wished to join me in a cup of coffee. They didn't but I went ahead and made a pot anyway while they continued to examine the contents of the living room. Finally the detective and I sat down at the kitchen table while the uniformed officer stood.

I led off, "I'm afraid what I know about your "chisel murder" is pretty limited. For me it's all connected to the disappearance of my girlfriend whom, I guess, technically isn't even a missing person yet. She worked for this guy Jarno down on Jackson who was scamming antiques buyers all over the place for piles of loot. I gather she was the only person in the shop who wasn't from Finland. The only guy who made any effort to get along with and stick up for her was the guy stabbed with the chisel. While we were getting her tools out of there she couldn't find one of her chisels, which was part of a set she got at technical college in Canada. I suppose there is a chance the one found in the dead guy was that one. The head Finn, Jarno, had seriously threatened her when she offered to blow the whistle on the operation and she may have purloined various invoices and business papers to bolster her position. She was with me pretty much all the time since last Wednesday and all day yesterday up until around six or seven o'clock. Somebody busted up my shop down on Pacific and when I got back from cleaning up I didn't see her and she might have been gone. She wasn't here this morning for sure and the stack of papers is gone as well. You can see all of her stuff is still here and that's her Toyota heap out in the driveway. I have no idea what might have caused Jarno or whoever to ace the guy downtown. His shop is located at 478 Jackson and he drives a big white panel van. You might not be able to tell, but I was doing a casual drive-by in the alley behind the place this morning and them guys dragged me out of my truck and tied me up in the basement. One of the big bastards beat the shit outta me while this Jarno asked questions about Jenny and stuff like that. I'm pretty sure they meant for me to never leave there alive but I managed to sneak out when they were preoccupied and got back here. Somebody burned up my van, wrecked up my shop and just mangled a bunch of my surfboards out back. As far as I know no one has a serious enough grudge against me to do all that except those guys. I think that's about the size of it."

The detective scratched his chin and looked thoughtful, the uniform looked uninterested. The moment stretched out and I found myself staring at the Miller accordion sitting on the coffee table and feeling uncomfortable having the police there, as though I had stolen it. Which I guess, technically, I had. Finally Feldman broke the silence, "Does it not seem to you, Mr. Rauhe, as though murder is a bit harsh treatment where a few antiques have been misrepresented and no other motive is readily apparent? A bit harsh, would you say? Severe?"

"Well, yeah, I guess you could say so. I mean, I don't really know what the hell is going on any more; the last week has been total pandemonium. It does sound a bit harsh on the surface, but who knows what them guys are up to over there. Maybe the furniture stuff is only the tip of the iceberg. Makes sense, right, something else going on which they are going to hide no matter what."

"And you, of course, would have no idea what that might be?"

"I never even heard of these guys until a couple of days ago. I wouldn't have a clue, believe me. The only reason I know as much as I do is because of the girl, Jenny, who is still missing by the way. No news there, I suppose."

"Mr. Rauhe, 24 hours have not yet elapsed since you last saw this young lady and it is entirely possible she has merely taken herself off for a day or so to think things over. Not uncommon at all, believe me."

"I don't know about that, we were pretty tight there. She didn't act like she was anxious to take off. I don't think I'll be able to wait around for a certain amount of time to go by just to start looking for her. I think she was snatched by them Finns and being held somewhere against her will. Whadda ya think of that?"

"Frankly I think it is highly unlikely. However, unofficially, I will give you the number of one of the head rangers of the Presidio national park, to whom the information about the alleged sale of the counterfeit antiques might be of interest. Possibly not, though, as from what you have told me the pieces sold to the park are known, ordered and delivered as reproductions. However, he is the inquisitive type and might be investigating the furniture shop." He scribbled a name on the back of his business card and handed it over. The name was Armando Quinterro. He continued, "We will, of course, continue the murder investigation and the connection of this fellow Jarno, and if any information comes to light concerning Ms. Farrar we will contact you. Depending on her wishes, that is."

"Right so, what in the hell should I be doing in the meantime except sitting on my thumbs? I might have failed to mention I'm very anxious about Jenny. Let's say them guys down there on Jackson are involved and have kidnapped her. It feels like every minute they have her she's getting closer to the sharp end of a chisel, if you know what I mean. If they don't have her, I can pretty surely bet they are looking damn hard and will continue to fuck with me and wreck my stuff until they grab me again, beat the crap out of me again, and then it's lights out!"

The detective gave a smirk and said, "Believe me, Mr. Rauhe, there is little you can do except get in the way and muddy the waters for the professionals. If I were you I'd arrange to stay somewhere else until we have this matter concluded. Stay out of sight if possible."

"Thanks for the advice Sherlock."

The interview was on the brink of deteriorating into name-calling and spitballs. The detective rose and with a stern look collected the uniformed officer, who was tinkering with some wind-up toys, and departed.

I packed up both accordions and debated which to take to the session. I threw caution to the wind and decided to take the Miller. I hit the fridge and drank a beer to steady my nerves. That didn't work so I chased it with a couple of shots of Jameson's Irish Whisky, which did the trick.

I locked up the house and tucked the box behind the driver's seat. I angled my way across town to get Sean. Straight back on Geary all the way to Webster where I turned right headed for the Lower Haight. I descended farther and farther into working class San Francisco until I turned left on Laussat Street.

Laussat was one block long and ran between Webster and Buchanan. It looked like a street of back doors and garages. The few entrances looked like afterthoughts. In a cramped space between two sets of quadruple garage doors was a dense wall of ivy vines with the barest interruption hinting at a passage. I knew beyond the foliage there was a small private yard with exotic plantings and even a fountain. Windowless walls on both sides added to the surreal air of the place.

After Sean had decided even my limited sense of order and structure was too much for him, he moved out and couch-surfed around for a couple of months until he lucked into the place on Laussat. An ancient carpenter named Carl Caldwell who also worked for Old Heelan owned the house. Mostly out of charity, apparently Sean had been covering for him and had taken up areas of slack in his work and attendance for years, and was finally invited to occupy space in the mostly empty house. The two got along perfectly, sharing a common standard and appreciation for chaos and entropy.

Sean's work truck was parked on the side of the narrow street. When I got close I could see the side windows had been smashed. Glass littered the hood and the surrounding area. Vandalism was common enough in the city, but I had an especially negative feeling about this. At least all four tires were present. I felt somewhat anxious about leaving my own truck unattended so I merely honked the horn several times to make my presence known. In time the novelty of a car horn in the city managed to alert the household, and finally Sean appeared carrying his battered guitar case and paper bag cleverly shaped like a fifth of whisky. He dumped the guitar into the back of the back of the truck and was opening the concealed weapon as he got into the cab. He took a long slug and handed it over.

"Lead on, MacDuff! Take 'er out Mr. Sulu! Let's get the fuck outta here."

I took what I considered a modest sip and started the motor.

"Looks like the neighborhood is going downhill, eh? Did you suddenly start having something worth stealing locked in the cab of the truck after all these years?"

"The only thing worth a shit in there was my tool belt and even that looked like hell. It's gone though, and as crappy and worn out as it was I don't have enough cash on me to replace it. Luckily I can use Carl's 'cause I don't think he's actually worn it in a couple of years. At least the bastards didn't take any of the power tools in the back: too heavy for them to cart around, I guess."

"I suppose that's the silver lining. Even though I would hope not, I suppose your truck customization might be connected with me, Jenny and the Finns somehow. I was just on my way out to Kelly's Cove and found my entire surfboard quiver in the same state as your windows. They were mangled and torn up "This Old House" style, with a claw hammer. That bastard there under your feet, in fact."

Sean shuffled and kicked around until he could bend over and grasp the offending instrument. He stared at it with amazement as he abused the open container law again.

"This boyo here, was it? I don't suppose you could return the rest of my tool belt while we're at it. I'm guessing you already had a good look at this feller and might have noticed the initials so laboriously carved into the handle. That is to say the initials of your best friend who might also be wondering what the hell is going on."

"Oh yeah, I saw something on the handle but couldn't make out exactly what it was. Your hammer, you say? Well, this certainly ties these dastardly events together, don't it. So, in light of us both being harassed by these damn pale-eyed devils, perhaps we should swing by their Jackson street lair on the way to Virginia's, just to see what might be up and visible in the way of evil plots against the Outer Richmond boys. Might get a glimpse of Jenny as well. "

"Despite the fact it's half a city away from our destination, I say let's go."

On the way I relayed the bizarre events of the last two days. After an endless series of questions and comments Sean finally agreed Jenny probably hadn't taken off just to get away from me. He also agreed Jarno and his gang probably had me, and those associated with me in their sights.

Having fallen for the "dumpster across the alley" trick once already I thought it would be best to head straight down Jackson and see if any activity could be seen from the street. Even though it was almost 7:00, there was a lot of particularly frustrating traffic on the streets. The light was red at the end of the block onto Sansome and our place in the pile up put us right out front of #478. I tried to scrunch down in my seat just in case there were any lookouts posted on the sidewalk. Sean had no such desire to remain inconspicuous and craned his neck to see out the driver's side window. When the view failed to prove interesting enough, he jumped out the passenger door and passed around behind the truck. He walked directly up the front door and tried the knob. I couldn't see what transpired next as the light changed and I had to move off and look for a parking spot further down the block. I had high hopes, but was forced to turn right on Sansome and loop the block. As I made the turn back onto Jackson from Montgomery, I could see Sean on the sidewalk in front of #478 waving his arms. I slowed to see what might happen but he broke off his negotiations and scooted across the street to the sidewalk on the other side. As I pulled up beside him he whipped open the door and hopped inside.

"Probably best to get moving now. I'm not sure my line of bullshit had that dude over there convinced."

I risked a glance over and saw my recent executioner-to-be staring slack-jawed at the truck and its inhabitants.

"Well, if them guys hadn't linked us together before, they sure do now. Welcome to the club. See anything interesting in there?"

"I didn't see your girlfriend tied up in the corner, if that's what you mean. I didn't see any furniture being made or big piles of cash either. They were mostly bustling around and dragging a bunch of shit down from the second floor. One guy was just standing there directing everybody else and that big lunk on the sidewalk was just too dumb to follow instructions fast enough. They acted pretty surprised to see me in there with my line about getting a table fixed. The head guy just nodded in my direction and the big guy started moving in on me. At least I didn't actually have to run down the street to get away."

"If you see them guys again you will have to run, and fast too."

I risked a glance in the rear view and saw the large fellow standing in the middle of the street shouting and pointing in our direction. At Sansome I thanked God for right turns on red and peeled out of there. On the way over to Potrero Hill I filled in a few more details of the accordion search and the events since, including the trashing of my shop and Vladimir's remarkable work ethic.

He stared out the window pensively until he blurted out, "Somethin' strange is goin' on here, dude."

"No, really? I'm glad you shared that with me. The question is what to do about it."

"Yeah, we'll have to keep our eyes peeled, eh?"

I refused to answer.

The normally stingy parking on Wisconsin only got worse on Monday nights and this night was no different. After cruising the length of the street twice without luck, I parked in the driveway of a house for sale that looked like it might have already been vacated.

We latched onto our musical junk and the, thankfully, mostly full bottle. The cacophony audible as we walked up the path hinted we had arrived a few moments tardy and music had already started to ferment. Had we the desire or energy I'm sure we could have identified the players by their styles from the sidewalk. Mostly we didn't care so we climbed the porch and in we went.

JOHN PEDERSEN

CHAPTER

ENTERING the front door of Virginia's house put a person directly in the middle of the maelstrom. Most of the chairs the hosts had put out were already occupied, and the players were shaking out the cobwebs with the first few tunes. Banjos, fiddles, mandolins, whistles, guitars and even the piano were being beaten without mercy. A lone concertina player hunkered in the corner pumping away without any audible effect. The wine glasses and beers scattered around were already half empty and there was a certain glazed look prevalent. There were no new faces and the most recognition we received was a glance and a nod.

We detoured through the kitchen to unpack our instruments and peruse the non-whisky alcoholic offerings. The table had perhaps fifteen or twenty opened bottles of wine on it; testimony to the fact our hosts didn't drink the remainders from each week, just re-corked them and brought them out the next time. The trick was to determine which bottle was newest, as the oldest might have been around for months and would certainly be crap. Of course, the good wine always got consumed first each week and even the remaining fresh wine was pretty crappy so there really wasn't too much difference. Our usual regime of whisky and beer always felt safest.

Several tunes came and went while we abused the food offerings and readied our hardware. As we threaded our way out the kitchen door past the chairs of players conveniently parked directly in the way, a couple of folks scooted right and left leaving two adjacent chairs vacant. It was a recognized session fact the music sounded stronger and better when Sean and I were seated next to each other. Also recognized was the fact that after a few drinks we were much less sarcastic to other players when we had each other to ridicule.

One could never be sure what style of music might be played during a night at Virginia's. Certainly there would be plenty of Irish music, but there could also be long stretches of Old Time Stringband tunes or sentimental 50's Rock and Roll ballads. The current waltz wound down and there was silence for a few seconds. A couple of folks got up to get refreshments or chat in the kitchen and the lull continued. As the last in, it would have been somewhat churlish to start dictating the tunes right away so Sean and I merely sat and waited. Finally the banjo player sitting next to the piano got tired of waiting and started singing some idiotic song about farmers and half pints and whanging out a marginally recognizable accompaniment. The words were almost lost across the din of the players but those that did make it to us were pretty funny. We added some tasteful clamor of our own to the tumult and any remaining lyrics were totally speculative.

After signaling the end of the song by kicking up his foot, the banjo player looked in my direction and raised an eyebrow implying a nice Irish tune might fit right in. Without another thought I started the most common of hornpipes, "The Wind That Shakes The Barley", relaxed in tempo and always charming. Within a few measures the entire herd was thundering away and having fun. Fortunately, those players with a tendency to speed up the tempo were perfectly balanced by those with a tendency to drag.

Sean sang a song, more tunes were played, jokes were made and everyone seemed to be having fun. Unexpectedly I saw Sloane's head peek out of the kitchen door and survey the scene.

At one time Sloane had been a regular at Virginia's and even occasionally sang one of her long and perhaps slightly overly dramatic songs. But since marrying her last husband, Gerald, we hadn't seen her so much.

She slyly motioned for either Sean or I to come into the kitchen. Since it was impossible to tell whom she was actually pointing to, we both went. She led us into the narrow area containing the stove and oven on one side and the kitchen sink on the other. There was just enough room for the three of us, friendly as we were. There was something slightly harried and disheveled about her which did not fit. Sean put his thoughts delicately into words, "Jesus, you look like shit, what the hell?"

Even though I was thinking almost the same thoughts and was not particularly noted for my tact, I might not have phrased the question quite that way. Sloane, however, didn't flinch. She leaned in to share a confidence and we leaned in to listen.

"I think somebody is stalking me!"

Sean and I leaned back and he said, "What's your point? I thought that was your natural state, being stalked by a whacko you wind up marrying sooner or later."

She gave him a withering stare, "Do not be an ass, I'm serious."

Sean looked unabashed. "Oh, come on Sloane, we've got serious problems here. Sam's girlfriend has gone missing and possibly kidnapped, he's been beat up and almost assassinated and somebody has smashed the shit out of my truck. Not to mention his entire rack of surfboards got mangled. Talk about stalking, eh?"

She leaned in again, "Someone has vandalized The Beast! Who but a completely demented maniac would bother that old thing? I'm getting heavy breathing calls on my phone. I have the feeling I'm being watched. Sometimes my skin crawls for no reason and I look around but can never see anything. I think little things in my house have been moved. I'm very distracted!"

I had to admit she looked pretty flustered. Her cautiously tended and pampered corona of impossibly red hair was pulled roughly back and secured with a rubber band. The makeup regime she adhered to with almost religious devotion had been abandoned or severely curtailed. Her normally porcelain skin was flushed and spotty and I thought I might have almost seen the hint of a zit. I'm sure by her standards she was a complete wreck.

I added my two cents, "The Beast, is it? Why would anybody mess with such a heap except for vandal practice? I can't imagine, but maybe the nasty types who have been screwing with Sean and me are lumping you in with us. If that's the case, you could actually be in danger. Maybe the three of us should group up till we can get this all figured out, safety in numbers and all that. You haven't actually seen anyone, have you? No large uncouth-looking lunks loitering around your place."

She gave me a steely look, "Other than you and your friends, I assume you mean. My neighborhood is not that kind of place. I may have spotted Gerald lurking around from time to time, but I have attributed that to simple post-separation anxiety. I'm sure we all agree he is quite harmless."

Gerald was Sloane's recently abandoned husband of several years. He had started his paranoid unhinging practically as soon as the cake was cut. Almost any type of contact with her former friends prompted bizarre sessions of accusatory whining. These grew to such proportions that she saw us less and less just to save herself the grief. He had actually accused both Sean and I of having romantic designs on Sloane during their marriage and trying to force them apart. That part, of course, was completely accurate but as always, unfulfilled. Fortunately for him he was not a particularly lumpy fellow, being more of the programmer type rather than the barroom scrapper and took his delusional toll on Sloane rather than either one of us. Even as devoted as she was, there was a certain point where nothing she did was good enough and she finally called it quits. We gathered Gerald had not taken the situation particularly well.

Sean said, "I'm not so sure about the harmless part. Once guys like him get their Porsche Turbo Carrera and their wide screen TV they usually get a big assed gun next. I can see old Gerald thinking the three of us being together in some twisted three-way and going completely postal. Actually, the three-way part sounds kind of cool."

Sloane drew back to deliver a punch to some undisclosed area of Sean but he threw up his hands, "Easy, easy there, just joking. I'm all bruised up and sore from Edain beating me to death with that friggin' cast of hers. I don't need any more contusions."

I returned to my idea, "So, what about grouping up so we can watch each other's backs?"

Sean grimaced, " No offense, brother, but I think I'd rather take my chances with Gerald and the Finns before moving back into your house, and I can already tell Miss Sloane isn't going for it either. You're too tidy for me and too sloppy for her. Sorry."

"Indeed, stalking and listening to heavy breathing sounds like a small price to pay for not being at your house. However, if you both would like to come over to ...."

We responded negatively in unison.

I said, "At least let us give you an escort home after the love fest here."

"Fine, whatever."

The music leaking into the kitchen was taking a bizarre path and getting slower and slower. Most of the confident players were grouped around the buffet like vultures and the guys left in the living room were playing tunes no one had ever heard before, possibly because they were just being written on Venus and being beamed directly in, and not necessarily together. Sean and I recognized the need for action and headed for the front lines.

I grabbed the Miller off my chair and slipped it on while Sean was fussing with further drinks. It definitely felt more familiar now and more business-like than the Soprani. The instant the moonbeam tunes ended I seized the last note of their set with my bass notes and drew it into a deep rumbling chordal progression. Switching between modal and minor with strange accidental notes thrown in to keep them guessing. I was just vamping to give myself time to think of something to play and to keep further interplanetary tunes from starting when a tune came unbidden to my fingers. I let it run its unexpected course and was more or less surprised at the directions it took. I kept the tempo in check just in case any of the tune-hounds cared to jump in. I closed my eyes and tried to picture what the tune could possibly be but failed to come up with anything. I played on with a feeling of loss and pain mixed with a positive joy. Not finding any takers, the tune sped up from a gentle hornpipe tempo and settled into a grinding, shrieking reel. What sounded like car alarms were going off up and down the street and the tune blended in seamlessly with the cacophony. My fingers fairly flew over the buttons and the bass notes were often not what I was expecting or hunting for, but always powerful and right sounding. The room spun around me and after an unknowable length of time I could actually feel the tune leaving me. The second it stopped I could not have restarted it for anything. I glanced around the circle. Some of the more sensitive players were white faced while others looked like they were on the verge of packing their instruments away. Sean sat beside me.

"What's with you, lame-o, are you crippled or what?" I said.

"I couldn't get in, the tune literally wouldn't let me. I tried but there was no way. I was walled out and it didn't really feel like a good idea to go over that particular wall. Where'd you get that box? Is it the grave-yard one? Pretty bitchin' wherever it came from, it's kind of intense, though."

"You're right there, I didn't know where I was for a while there. I can't place that tune, either, can you? It just sorta came to me."

"Yeah, no, I don't think it's one of the old tunes at all, maybe one of them modern ones or something. Probably some Lithuanian harmonica player wrote it. Pretty full of goofy notes, wasn't it? Or was it your own "variation?"

"I can't even think of where I might have heard it so how would I know?"

Without bothering to respond Sean started banging out a chord pro-gression, the rest of us were supposed to figure out what tune, if any, it belonged to and jump in with it. It was in jig time and in the key of E minor, so the field was wide open and the first person to get in picked the tune. That was me in this case and I kept playing "The Kid On the Mountain" even after several other players tried to muscle in with other tunes. The slip jig screamed out of the box, the notes coming crisp and clear, rolling and tumbling like superballs in a drainpipe. My fingers op-erated completely from muscle memory and were guided by the built up depth of repetition and instinct. I looked around the circle and saw the different faces of the players mirroring their concentration.

We flashed from tune to tune, sometimes without any pause at all. Players came and went. Some left quietly and others made a big show of abandoning their chairs, packing up and getting out the door while waving back at us like Queen Elizabeth. At a certain undefined point the re-mainder of the session just fell apart and the last few tunes were com-pletely uninspired. We packed our instruments and shifted the chairs, tables and couches back to where we thought they might belong. The hunt for random glasses and bottles went on for a while and Sloane and a few others shoveled debris off the table and washed up the collected glassware. The tenants had gone to bed already so the last of us just turned the lights off and let ourselves out.

Sloane said the Beast was not far away and Sean and I agreed we would follow her to her house in St. Francis Wood. She had resisted the temptation to move out of the Richmond District until Gerald had insisted and provided the means to do it. Their house was small and plain by the neighborhood standards but palatial and exotic by Richmond standards.

Sean and I sat in the truck until she rumbled past in the Buick and then pulled in behind her. We resigned ourselves to a scenic tour of the city according to Sloane's strange version of how to get from one place to another. Despite the fact we were sitting between two freeways which would transport a person across the city in a twinkling, I was pretty sure Sloane would choose to amble up Market and then all the way over Twin Peaks and onto Portola. At least the 11:30 traffic was sparse and we moved along at a reasonable pace. We had just made the left turn onto 19th St. when I noticed a large white van was mysteriously lurking in our wake.

"Uh Oh, I don't like the looks of this at all. I'm not sayin' there's not more than one white van in this city, but I think almost any one of them who wasn't following us wouldn't be poking along behind us poking along behind Sloane."

Sean craned his neck to peer out the back of the camper shell and after a good, long look announced, "Without sounding alarmed either I would have to report there is a fourth poker in line in the form of a black SUV. Of course we'll lead the whole damn parade right to Sloan's house at this rate. Maybe we should split off sudden like to see if we can alter the route. Go the opposite direction and all. I don't suppose you might have any kind of self-defense apparatus on board. Luckily I got my hammer right here, eh?

"Yeah, good plan, we'll hang back until Sloane gets a good lead on us then jink off in a different direction. If it's even possible to let that girl get ahead, dang!"

It had become clear Sloane intended to run west on 19th forever instead of traveling on Market or some other thoroughfare with fewer lights and more lanes. I was finally able to let her slip through the light on Mission while we got caught behind the light. I watched her taillights travel blithely up 19th.

"OK, I think this is it, hang on pardner."

I waited until a late night Muni bus was almost level with us on Mission then cranked the wheel and pulled out directly in front of it and started to haul ass up the street. The bus was immune to such shenanigans and didn't honk, change speed or even veer off course. I was rather hoping an alert police office might take offense at such rude behavior and get involved, but of course no such official was around. I wound the meager engine of the Ford up to the limit in every gear and eventually began to out pace the bus. Sean stared out the back intently and finally reported, "Looks like we got both of them on us, Sloan is in the clear. Now what?"

"Just enjoy the ride I guess. All we have to do is keep from crossing Sloane's tracks, you never know where the hell she's gonna turn up when she's behind the wheel. I wonder if they have Jenny in one of those cars and are trying to rub us all out at the same time. "

"Yeah, good thinking but kind of unlikely, I'd say."

I zigged and zagged up the street as though there was traffic to dodge, but there really wasn't much in that department. The van and the SUV had little trouble passing the bus and catching up with us. It looked as though they might be trying to maneuver themselves to get on either side of us so they could cause us harm but I pulled a left turn onto 14th and they had to single file it again.

I pushed the 2.3 liter agricultural truck motor as hard as I could and shot straight through the red light at Dolores and concentrated as fiercely as I could on the upcoming junction with Market. I timed my passage through on the tail of the yellow.

In retrospect I doubted guys who would murder someone with a woodworking tool would be fazed by a set of red lights, but I sort of hoped some sleepy driver might plow into the side of one or both of them. Of course, both vehicles shot straight through the intersection without slowing or encountering in any way the few customers at the light.

Sean was hanging onto the dashboard and the armrest for dear life. Between recoils from hitting potholes, where his head pounded the roof, he managed to shout out, "We have to get the hell off 14th, it dead-ends up there at the end. Castro! Try Castro."

With the tires howling I wheeled to the right at the next corner, cutting off the SUV, which was trying to come up on that side. Fashionably dressed couples of all possible combinations scattered out of the crosswalk and hurled insults at us. The motor screamed as I dropped the truck into a lower gear to try to keep the speed up on the insane hills.

I was leaning on the horn to warn further pedestrians, alert drivers and hopefully even the police, but with no apparent result. It finally gave a croak and died.

We rocketed over the humps and flats of Castro and blasted straight across Waller where the street turned into Divisadero and it felt like the tires were barely touching the ground.

Out of nowhere Sean said, "Hey, isn't that where Ed Gallagher, the fiddler, used to live? Wait, no, he was over on California. Who was it lived there? Pat O'Neill?"

I spared him a brief glance and got out, "Are you friggin' serious...?"

"Jesus, never mind. Wait, turn up Fell, now, do it!"

I cranked the wheel hard to the left and cut off the encroaching van forcing him to bounce and bash over the median. The gang of three sped up Fell and I idly wondered if Sean had a plan in mind or was just taking in the sights. My media born technique of weaving from side to side to discourage pursuit was much more effective on the narrower streets. The fact both of the vehicles chasing us were vastly more powerful and faster didn't give me much hope of out running them on the flats. We ran stop signs and lights with absolutely no interference from sparse traffic, pedestrians or police. Everyone took our procession, bombing right through the middle of the city, in stride.

We were getting near the end of the Golden Gate Park panhandle when Sean shouted out, "Here, take the left on Kezar and we can get right into the park, I'll bet we can lose the fuckers in there."

I had serious doubts but headed that direction anyway. I had to slow a bit at the complex intersection with Stanyan and thread my way around idiots already in the intersection who got in my way. I thought I heard one of our pursuers get clipped but couldn't give up any of my attention to finding out.

Golden Gate Park is pretty much the southern boundary of our neighborhood and Sean and I had spent an enormous amount of our youth exploring its hidden corners and convoluted by-ways. I certainly hoped our local insight would allow us to somehow shake off the guys behind us, who were more serious than ever.

I looped forward and back, I did circles and figure eights. I killed the lights and tried to hide behind bushes and stands of trees. Occasionally, it looked like there was only one set of lights behind us and once in a while I couldn't see any. But sooner or later we always had both of the bastards back on out tail.

Finally, Sean said, "Aw, screw it, head for the beach, maybe we can lose them down there."

Lacking any other plan, I did just that.

I casually noted as we flew down Fulton, the Arrow bar looked pretty dead for a Monday.

At the Great Highway, which runs along the beachfront, I had a choice to head north or south. Instinctively, I turned north towards Kelly's Cove just below the Cliff House Restaurant where we had spent countless hours in the water.

The long parking lot is parallel to the highway, and becoming kind of desperate, I squealed into the southern entrance. The van wasn't too far behind us, but the SUV kept going to the north entrance and came at us from the front.

"Pal, I fear we're screwed here", I said. "I think we're gonna have to abandon ship so get your life vest on. You could probably leave your hammer here."

There is a three-foot high concrete wall between the beach and the parking lot with openings to sets of stairs angling down to the seasonally changing level of sand. This being the winter, much of the sand was out under water forming the sand bars, which give the place such surfable waves. I pulled up as close to one of the cut-outs as I could, killed the lights and hit the brakes. I opened the driver's door and slithered straight out onto the pavement and scrabbled on hands and knees for the hole with Sean right behind me. We were barely clear of the truck when the van plowed into the back end shoving it forward. As we launched ourselves through the entrance to tumble and roll down the stairs multiple shots overcame the usual crashing of the waves. Flashlight beams started playing in the general area where we might have been.

We scrambled backwards and pressed our backs against the cement wall. Sean rasped out in a strangled whisper," What the fuck, dude? Flashlights and guns? We're totally shit-canned here. There's two cars fulla' them assholes and if they split up they can come at us from both sides."

The very instant the words came out of his mouth lights could be seen coming down the stairs on either side of us. I said, "Oh yeah, we're in it now. No problem getting' rid of our goddamn corpses, either, just drag 'em down to the surf line. I guess now would be the time to save them the trouble and make a break for it, eh?"

"Uh…yeah, I guess so, but these are new boots, I hate to lose them."

"I don't think these guys are chasing us for our boots, dipshit. If we survive we can come back for 'em later and if not, well at least we drowned like honorable surf rats and didn't just get shot like some Tenderloin pimps."

I had unlaced and kicked off my boots, stuffed my wallet deep inside and covered them mostly with sand while Sean did the same. We glanced at each other, pushed off from the wall at the same time and sprinted for the shore-break. The flashlights caught us and the firing followed. We ducked, covered our heads and bobbed up and down. I can't say if any bullets came close to us or not but at least I know none hit us.

The closer we got to the water the meaner the waves looked. With screams like the Outer Richmond Banshee we plowed straight into the water and almost got knocked on our asses by the first mountain of foam that crashed into us. We both dove deep to escape the roiling of the surf and surfaced in the space before the next wave. The lights blinked back and forth on the beach searching for us. I struggled out of my jacket and saw Sean's flannel shirt float up and drift away as well. The lights focused on us and the bright spark of firing could be seen right after. I grabbed Sean's head and pulled it close to be heard above the crash, "Get outside and go with the rip. Get out at Lincoln, if you live that long!"

I thought I heard Sean laugh at that and as we both turned and dove beneath the next Mt. Everest of salt water to try to fight our way beyond the breaking surf, I sincerely hoped it wouldn't be the last joke we would ever share.

JOHN PEDERSEN

OCEAN Beach in San Francisco is treacherous on its most benign days. Rogue sneaker waves come rolling in unhindered all the way from Japan, gathering strength, power and the element of surprise every foot of the way. They come growling up out of the offshore canyons and explode out of a placid shore break to drag fishermen off their rocky perches and unwary tourists off the beaches out to sea. Sean and I were born facing west, never turning our backs on the waves, always watching out for the set wave and the monster. Sometimes they could be taken and tamed, but sometimes they took you.

The roiling, boiling mish-mash of winter storm surf was a nightmare of undertow, rips, sand and debris lashing around. The idea for survival was to dive under the approaching waves and come up in the space before the next and swim like hell for the outside, where the waves weren't breaking so much. Which turns out to be drastically harder in practice than in theory.

The water temperature was probably around 53 or 54 degrees. I know this because that is almost always the temperature of the water at Ocean Beach, winter or summer. The water was actually several degrees warmer than the air, but still....

After the first dive I lost sight of Sean and had to concentrate on my timing. I was also regretting every piece of spare change and extra weight I carried.

The alcohol left over in my system from Virginia's might have lessened the initial shock of the water, but after a few trips to the bottom I didn't think it was much of an advantage. I will say at least I wasn't worried about jerks on the beach shooting at me anymore.

If I had been on a surfboard I'm pretty sure the existing conditions would have beat the living shit out of me and threw my exhausted and limp body back on the beach with casual distain. As a swimmer, however, things were vastly different. Progress was infinitely slower, but it was easier to not get flipped end-for-end by each wave. I didn't dare look behind me to check my progress for fear I would have been in exactly the same position as when I started and lose heart. I tried to relax and keep stroking with an even beat.

After what felt like an enormous amount of effort and time I found the waves were no longer breaking directly on top of my head but just lifting me up to what looked like the height of a three-storey building and rolling under me. I risked a short break and looked shoreward. I could still see lights playing back and forth on the beach but there were an awful lot of them. I gathered the Finns had called in reinforcements to deal with us. As I had suspected during the time I had been fighting my way outside the break, the rip had sucked me several hundred yards south. I could see myself traveling sideways pretty rapidly even as I was treading water.

I tried to re-focus my energy and started swimming south, still keeping an eye for any monster wave, which might break even further out than normal and send me and my feeble splashing to the bottom for good.

Swimming with the rip is like walking on a moving sidewalk at the airport; everything looks normal until you look over at the shore, which is rocketing past. Whenever the swell lifted me up I tried to identify where I might be but really couldn't see any landmarks from so low in the water. I could see the flashlight crowd was far to the north and had gathered together and were no longer pointing out to sea at all. I supposed it was safe enough to return to the beach, if only I could.

My instinct was to swim in close enough so I could body surf in on a small edition of the huge waves that were in the majority. The hard part of course, was being able to swim in against the undertow and not get crushed by a wave too soon. Instead of heading directly in I angled my trajectory so I could continue going with the rip obliquely. That worked out pretty well and it wasn't long before I was almost at the point where most of the waves were breaking.

With strength draining out of my body every second due to the cold, I rested for a few moments until a noticeably larger swell lifted me like a Ferris Wheel. Just after it passed under me I swam like a son of a bitch on its back trying to get as far in as I could before the next wave in line started to break.

I didn't get nearly as far as I had hoped. I could feel myself getting sucked down and out as the wave gathered strength. I really wasn't holding out much hope of being able to body surf this beast but I figured if I kicked like hell and made my body go rigid, even if I didn't make it any closer to the shore, at least my corpse would wash up at Ocean Beach and not somewhere far south like Pacifica.

As the wave formed and I was lifted up the face, I marveled at the view from this vantage before I was thrown off the lip like a bit of random spray. The drop looked like it had no end and I'm sure a scream of defiance – or pure terror – escaped me. I stuck one arm out in front, tucked the other close to my side and held my body as rigid as I could. As I started the slide down the face I reflected on the positive merits of simply getting shot.

I clattered over the bumps and lumps of the wave surface getting the sense knocked out of me. My speed felt like that of a headlong dive off the roof of a tall building. Every breath I tried to take was accompanied by a fire truck's worth of water. I could feel my clothes disintegrating around me. I tried to hold my direction at an angle to the face of the wave so I might just possibly reach a shoulder where the wave didn't break, but no such luck. I was still quite a ways from the trough when the wave top crashed over me and with what I assumed was my last breath for a while, my last thought was, "I am truly proper fucked now!"

The ride in the agitator cycle lived up to the advertised version. I assumed my limbs were wrenched from their sockets and torn off because I couldn't feel them anymore. I had no idea where up and down were located. My entire job in the universe was to hold my breath and stay somewhat conscious, which I tried to do with all my might.

Even if I had made the shoulder safely, I had no idea how I was going to get past the shore break. My current situation pretty well took care of that problem, as I was suddenly part of the shore break, grinding over the sand in a cacophony of foam and percussion.

At one point I found my head out of water for a few seconds and I gulped down a second breath before I was returned to the washing machine for the second spin cycle.

After an eternal repetition of these events I was finally slapped like a piece of meat onto the sand in only a foot of water. The breath was squeezed out of me by the following crash of water. I dug my fingers and toes into the sand to try to avoid getting sucked back out. As the wave receded, I was suddenly out of it. I tried without success to crawl up the incline of the beach. The next wave pushed me further up towards the dry sand and I had to dig in again to retain the movement.

Finally, grudgingly, the ocean let me go. I crawled a short ways onto the sand and flopped onto my back. I could feel water draining out of every orifice. The cold air hit me and I knew I had to get going before I froze to death. A quick survey revealed my clothes had not accompanied me out of Davy Jones's locker. I fervently hoped I might get arrested for indecent exposure, and very soon.

Without lights of any kind on the beach it was impossible to look around for signs of Sean. As I considered myself by far the stronger swimmer and waterman I didn't hold out much hope he could have survived the combined ordeals of getting out and getting back in. I supposed if the wracking chills beginning to assault me didn't actually finish me off I would have to call the Coast Guard and report him missing and have them mount a search for his remains.

In my addled and waterlogged state I wasn't coming up with many options on how to get somewhere safe and get some clothes on me. Even as flexible as they are, I doubted whether the residents would approve of strolling around the Sunset or Richmond Districts completely nude.

I finally managed to lever myself up off the sand and became even colder yet when the wind hit me. I started running as steadily as I could figuring to cross the Great Highway and find out where the hell I was. My feet had no feeling as I woodenly pounded across the sand towards the nearest opening on the sea wall. Looking to the North I couldn't see any groups of flashlights or any other sign of our pursuers.

After what felt like ages I made the wall and huddled in the lee of it for a few seconds to catch my breath. I hoped I hadn't over shot my mark by too far. I had told Sean to try to get out of the water at Lincoln, and I now regretted not trying to keep closer touch with him. The part of my heart not fighting for my life was filled with sadness to have lost both my new love and my best friend on the same day.

I steeled my resolve and pushed off from the wall and climbed the stairs. I was a little startled to see the Beach House Chalet Restaurant, which was situated almost at the end of Fulton. Apparently, I had struggled out of the surf a bit prematurely having covered just a bit more than half the distance to Lincoln. There wasn't any traffic on the highway so I crossed straight over. I thought it was a pity the hour was so late and the Chalet was closed, as my entrance would have given them something to talk about for quite a while.

I headed up the jogging path fronting the highway with a stumbling, leaden trot. I had only floated with the rip about four and a half blocks, so I thought it was pretty likely I could make it to my house without collapsing. Many clumping steps later I crossed Cabrillo and wondered idly if the Wise surf shop had any Goodwill boxes of old clothes out on the sidewalk. I seriously doubted so.

A few cars sped by on the highway without bothering to notice the naked guy or slow in any way. By the time I reached Balboa my breath was rasping and choking and stars were spinning around in my head. A short ways up Balboa I had to stop and regard the challenge of the long flight of steps that went straight up the hill through the woods to connect with Sutro Heights, literally a block from my house.

I put my foot on the bottom step and tried to push up with all my might. I just barely made it to step two. I repeated the process but had no idea where the strength would come from to reach the top. I blanked my mind against the despair I was feeling and moved as if in slow motion, ever upward, bit-by-bit. My slowness allowed whatever small amount of heat I had generated during my jog to evaporate quickly and before I was half way to the top I was shaking uncontrollably. I felt lucky my feet were numb because I was pretty sure I would have had serious pain as I plowed through piles of trash and broken glass. The wind screeched around me and threatened to knock me down.

After several centuries of struggle and blankness I emerged out of the woods onto 48th only a few hundred feet from my house. No light shown in the windows of any of my neighbors in either direction.

THE SHAKING REEDS

257

I shuffled up the sidewalk like a wraith till I gained my driveway. The sight of Jenny's car re-awoke my anguish at failing to find her or protect Sean. Somehow I managed to get up the steps and was brought up short by the realization I might be locked out and have to wake up Walter and Anna to help me get in.

Strangely enough the front door was not locked, the heat was blowing and the lights were on in the kitchen. With a searing blast of hope and joy I realized I could hear the shower running. I did the best running I could up the stairs and was completely overwhelmed by the need to see Jenny at the first possible moment.

I threw open the door and forged my way through the steam and slid back the shower cur-tain.

Sean stared out at me and said," Dude, wait your turn!"

CHAPTER

THE disappointment of not finding Jenny in the shower was tempered with relief at finding Sean alive. I wrapped myself in a towel and sat on the commode until he emerged looking as though he had just taken a dip in the neighborhood wading pool. He gave me a curious look as I forced myself up off the seat and into the pre-heated shower.

The hot water that poured over my frozen carcass felt like it was boiling. I resisted the urge to scream, and I noted the sand and pebbles washing out of my hair, ears, nose and other assorted crevasses and collecting on the floor of the tub. It looked like a fair-sized beach's worth.

After a while I was either starting to warm up or the hot water was about to run out. I gave up and got out showing at least some color other than blue or gray. I dressed in sweat pants and sweatshirt and got fuzzy slippers on my feet. I was completely exhausted to the point of dizziness, but I thought I had better check on Sean, whom I could hear clattering around in the kitchen.

He had a big cast iron skillet on the stove with all manner of vegetables and meats frying up. There were eggs ready to be added and the teakettle whistled merrily. Bread had been sliced for toasting and a large lump of butter was sitting on the counter ready to be added to anything that looked dry.

Sean noticed the specter of myself standing there and started talking, "Man, you were so right about getting out at Lincoln. I was gettin' kinda' chilly out there in the rip and I almost came in at Fulton, around the Chalet, but I didn't 'cause you said get out at Lincoln. And you were so right on 'cause there was a hole there big enough to hold Candlestick Park and the tide was coming in and everything. I just headed for shore and paddled in like nobody's business. I walked right out and up the beach. As soon as I hit the highway some concerned citizen saw me leaking water all over the place and gave me a ride right to your door. Cool, huh? My wallet fell out somewhere though; I'm kinda' pissed at that. Where the hell did you get to, by the way, and what happened to all your clothes? You look sorta' like crap, you know."

"Um, yeah, I might have headed in a bit prematurely and might not have found that hole and might have also gotten massively worked. Some mermaid must have taken my duds 'cause they weren't on me when I was dumped on the sand. Jesus Christ what a fuckin' day! First I get the shit beat out of me by some random monster and then get the big waterboard treatment. What are we cookin' there? Let's eat it, done or not."

Sean dumped the eggs into the mess already in the skillet and kept a keen eye on it as it all set up. The bread went down in the toaster, the tea was poured and a mysterious bottle of rum was found to bolster its effectiveness. The cat-shaped clock on the kitchen wall said 2:45.

Once the first round of toast was clunked onto the table and the contents of the pan were halved and dumped onto plates all conversation stopped. I saw the crusted remains inside my carefully babied cast iron skillet. For a second I almost cared until I remembered that, against all odds I had skated around the edges of doom twice in one day. Then it didn't sound all that tragic.

For a relatively skinny and wiry guy Sean wolfed down an impressive amount of food in a very short time. It was like magic watching him eat. Soon, he had cleaned his side of the table and was further reducing and fortifying his tea with more rum. Finally he said, "So did ya see all the flashy lights and shit in the beach lot when you went by? It looked like the carnival was in town, fer Crissake. I can only assume it had something to do with your pals there, maybe some old parking tickets catching up with them."

I swallowed a mouthful and washed it down with tea before I replied, "I didn't see a dang thing when I went by. I was frozen, naked, exhausted and still afraid some assholes with guns were looking for me. I wasn't looking at the pretty lights. I wonder if perhaps our little caravan through the city interrupted some drowsy cop's personal donut time and he got pissed off. Maybe they rounded up the whole lot and took 'em to jail before deporting 'em. That would be good, as unlikely as it sounds. Probably it was the street sweeper or something like that. Well done on the eats amigo, but I think the time has come to recharge. I vote we get up in a couple of hours and go see what happened to the truck and the instruments. I'd go now but I don't think I can move a goddamn inch. I don't want you to feel uncomfortable amid all this tidiness so I think we'll just leave these dishes till later."

I could see the consciousness draining out of Sean as I was speaking and hoped he would be able to make it to his customary berth on the couch in the living room and drag a blanket over himself before passing out. Getting up the stairs to the spare room was out of the question for him. I pushed up from the table and made the supreme effort to pull myself up the stairs to collapse onto the bed. I was afraid the seawater that continued to leak out of my sinuses and ears would keep me awake but I needn't have worried; I was out instantly.

After what felt like a few seconds there was a pounding on the door and a shaking of my body. Sean was yelling a message at me so laden with curse words it was completely unintelligible. I managed to slow him down a bit and got him to repeat in English.

"I said there are a couple of friggin' cops who came in and made themselves comfortable in your living room. One of 'em asked me to make him goddamn tea. They'd like to have a chat with your highness, if you don't mind."

Sean departed and I tried to fight my way out of my coma. I had never felt the level of pain in every joint I experienced then. I had been beat up plenty by the ocean in my day but never to the extent of the previous evening. As I forced myself to sit up I could see the pillow was damp and there was sand in the bed having leaked from unknown spots. I tried to flex a bit and was rewarded with searing bolts of agony. I shuffled to the bathroom and ate a handful of Advil and stared at myself in the mirror. Pretty lumpy was my assessment. There was clearly nothing positive to be done about my appearance so I settled on brushing the seaweed out of my teeth and getting dressed.

I shuffled down the stairs holding tight to the handrail for fear my reluctant muscles would completely give way. I found Sean, Detective Feldman and Officer Froom sitting around the kitchen table sipping tea and noshing away on toasted English Muffins and marmalade. Sean looked antsy and very uncomfortable in the presence of police officers despite being innocent of anything, as far as I knew. A strange sickly light oozed though the windows. Feldman looked up, "Ah, Mr. Rauhe, good morning to you. A lovely Tuesday it might be if it doesn't storm, which it certainly will. We just thought we would drop by and report the various comings and goings concerning the case we discussed yesterday. I'm sure Mr. Tierney here would excuse us."

Sean bolted from the room and headed up the stairs. Feldman watched him go as though it would only be a matter of time before they would meet again under different circumstances. He shifted his gaze back to me.

"After we chatted yesterday, I took the liberty of phoning Mr. Quintero at the Presidio, assuming, if you called him at all it would be at some distant time in the future. He exhibited a very keen interest in the allegations you were leveling against Mr. Viljanen, and was not completely unaware of certain irregularities in his dealings with the State of California as well. The possible connection to the murder of the fellow in the Tenderloin spurred a collaborative effort during which we hoped to interview Mr. Viljanen. It seems though, the entire work force of 478 Jackson was recently on the move and a decision was made to tag along for a few blocks to see what might develop. Obviously their eventual destination was the Potrero Hill residence where you and Mr. Tierney were located. Eventually the Jackson Street fellows set off in pursuit of a certain Ford Ranger truck, which had almost been towed earlier in the day: perhaps you know the one. In any case, the departure of all concerned took our officers somewhat by surprise and they fell rather behind during the greater part of the chase, which ended at Ocean Beach. When they did arrive however, the driver of the truck and his passenger had disappeared. The truck was found and several musical instruments inside were recovered and taken into protective custody. Quite a few of the occupants of the vehicles from Jackson were asked to accompany the officers to the station for interviews, during which it was revealed many of them were residing in San Francisco with expired visitor visas. They have been remanded to the Immigration officials. Mr. Viljanen was not among the crowd firing illegal weapons in the direction of Japan. The registered owner of the Ford has been contacted and he directed us back to this address, which of course, we already have visited. It was feared perhaps you and Mr. Tierney had suffered negatively at the hands of the illegal fellows during the chase through the city or somehow at Ocean Beach, but we see now that was not the case. None the worse for wear, apparently."

"In view of these recent developments it would now be very fortunate to find Ms. Farrar and her alleged documents in order to tie certain elements of this case together. Hence our visit, besides taking the opportunity to make sure you two lads had not been reduced to the status of the Tenderloin chisel fellow. Any chance you might have heard from her since we last spoke? Further ideas where she might be, any thing like that?"

"Are you kidding? You're the cops for Christ's sake! I just saw you yesterday afternoon and all I've done is play a few tunes and rampage all over the city trying unsuccessfully to attract the notice of the police. Sean and me had to swim out into the surf last night just to get away from those dudes with the guns, and that almost finished us off for sure. You must know we've only been here a few hours."

Feldman looked around at the scatter of dishes and nodded. "Quite so, we just thought we'd try a long shot and drop by. However, if you do have any contact with her, you will let us know, right?"

"You guys are a riot, you know that? I already told you I think Viljanen has her and her papers. If you get off your asses and find him you'd probably find her. Dipshits!"

My tone and volume might have gone a bit testy by this time and Officer Froom looked distractedly off into space as if expecting some sort of harsh return of my salvo. He got up to re-inspect the junk in my living room and get out of the line of fire.

Feldman passed on the opportunity to lash out and merely nodded again. "Indeed, well, if you do hear from her you will let us know, right? If you have the opportunity, you might also drop by the Richmond Police Station to relieve them of the responsibility of looking after your instruments. That would be at 461 6th, just in case you might have forgotten where it is, which I doubt. The Ford Ranger remains at Ocean Beach."

Feldman collected Officer Froom who had become involved in a book about classic motorcycles, with pictures! They left and Sean returned to the kitchen.

"Jaaysus, what a pair of clowns them two were, eh. 'If you happen to solve this case, could you ring us up, and bring in some treats and coffee as well?' Christ! No wonder this town used to run better on straight corruption and sin. Speaking of which, if the head guy is still on the loose, maybe it's time we armed up. I don't think it would be too much of an imposition on some of the militant boyos to supply us with the odd Uzi or whatever."

I gave him a long, sad stare. "Sean, sonny, best friend in the world, brother in all but blood, you do realize I'd much rather face a room full of thirsty Finns wearing a suit made of vodka bottles than have a friend such as yourself guarding my back with a firearm. Right? I mean, really."

"Ah, point taken, we don't actually have the best record with the guns, do we?"

"Not even. The question is what to do right now."

"Right now we have to get our asses back to the beach to get the truck and see if our boots are still down there. I gotta' get to work and I can't go barefoot. I might get a sliver and hurt my tootsies. I don't think our midnight swim is enough of an excuse to get a day off from Old Heelan."

"Yeah, the truck, right, lets get going."

I forced myself off the kitchen chair and back up the stairs to don working attire. By the time I returned to the living room Sean had rustled up clothes from a secret cache he must have left somewhere in the house and an old pair of flip-flops.

We shuffled out into a blindingly clear day and I was careful to lock the door, just in case there was anything anybody might want inside I might not want to give up. We went back down 48th and onto the path through the park that led to the steps to Balboa. As we clomped down the endless stairs Sean kept up a continual rant about something or other, which I couldn't really hear at all. From the heights, the ocean looked benign and inviting; a far cry from the murderous beast it had been a few hours earlier.

We hiked down Balboa and crossed the Great Highway to the beach parking lot. Sure enough, the Ford was sitting almost where we had abandoned it but was now surrounded by the vehicles of the early surfers. The back bumper was knocked out of level with the rest of the body but other than that things looked fine. The doors were unlocked and the keys were on the floor. I thought it might have been a rather cavalier way to handle the situation on the part of the police, but also reasoned that it worked out pretty well for us. We went down the stairs to the beach and came across a homeless-looking guy just unearthing Sean's boots. I did some dead reckoning and started poking around in the sand looking for my own footwear while Sean tried to reason his shoes out of the guy. When that failed, threats followed, followed immediately by an offer to buy his shoes back. A deal was struck and he said, "Soren, thanks to you I don't have any cash on me, give this guy five bucks."

I felt around in my pockets and remembered that my wallet was buried with my boots. Based on where Sean and the bum were standing, I scraped around in the sand until I ran across my own footwear. I dumped the sand out and my wallet followed. The bum's eyes widened and I could see he was cursing his luck for having found the wrong pair of boots first. I dug out a five-dollar bill and handed it over. He departed with a grumble. Sean dumped the sand out as well and whacked his boots against the wall several times to knock out the remainder.

He said, "I gotta get moving, pal. I'm working up in Pacific Heights today and showing up with my shitty old truck all bashed in is gonna be bad enough without being late on top of it all."

We returned to the truck noting the spent brass on the ground, any one of which could have been the end of either of us. It started without fuss and because time was tight we decided the instruments would have to remain comfortable at the Police station until the afternoon. We could pick them up on the way to the session at the Arrow bar that evening. I tried to scoot along without delay, but without flagrantly breaking any traffic laws. I was sure all the Peace Officers who were non-existent the previous night were waiting to tag us for something or other.

Eventually we made it all the way down Haight and turned off towards Sean's house. He said, "You don't mind if I reclaim my hammer do you? I'd hate to have to borrow one from Hector, the foreman, again. It makes me look bad."

"No, by all means, be my guest. I'm sure you'll get so many extra points for showing up with your very own hammer. We'll talk later."

He hopped out as I pulled up alongside his decrepit looking truck. I continued in the same direction deciding even though it was wicked early and I didn't want to set any sort of precedent at the shop, I might as well attempt to get some work done while considering how I was going to find Jenny on my own.

I rolled through the early-riser traffic down to North Beach and found a parking spot quite near the shop on Pacific. I hobbled up to Columbus and got a vast jug of coffee at a place I didn't particularly like. The brew was always bitter and the half and half was almost solid. I skipped the ancient pastry offerings, as I was still pretty full of Sean's late-night snack.

I didn't expect Vladimir to be there when I finally staggered down the alley but I could see the doors were not locked from the outside. I peered inside through the smallest gap I could create and saw nothing but dark. I definitely considered getting a permanent night light. I slipped inside as stealthily as I could and waited in the dark long enough to find I couldn't see shit. I could hear very disturbing noises coming from the back of the shop that sounded like someone strangling a goat. I crept along the bench side of the wall in the direction of the main light switch hoping not to knock over any large chunks of machinery on the way. Stifling a gasp of pain as I stumbled over what I assumed was the Alfa motor I patted down the wall till I found the switch.

I flipped the lever and scrabbled on the bench to find a large tool to defend myself with if it became necessary. Instead of a scene of devastation and carnage I found Vladimir struggling to cover his nakedness. In this case he was trying to cover himself with a tall, non-wife like, ash-blond woman of remarkable proportions.

CHAPTER

I STARED in stunned confusion as Vlad and the woman fished around for clothing of any sort. I was frankly amazed and admiring of the woman's super hero physique. I mean, I had been with some pretty girls and even some outright hot ones, but none of them boasted the combination of toned muscles and generous curves this girl did. She didn't act particularly self-conscious or flustered to have had her tryst with Vladimir interrupted.

Vladimir, on the other hand, was rattling on and on in Russian and pointing this way and that, not always with his fingers. The woman apparently understood his ranting and responded with one-word answers in Russian as well. After a few moments of frenzied activity she understood I belonged there and relaxed a bit. She deliberately selected, and donned, various slinky items of underclothing and tight apparel.

I finally gained control of my motor skills and turned away to continue on toward the rear of the shop. Vladimir had calmed down considerably.

"Is very early for the beach bums to be arriving at work, no? Also, is for me as well but with bad beck, is impossible to sleep. Is lucky I can get appointment for house call from therapist so early. Feeling much better now."

I had to turn again to gape in astonishment at this explanation. Vlad gestured with an up-turned palm at the woman, "Soren might have back trouble sometime and have to call, this is Triinu Rebane, back pain specialist."

She gave me a look that sent a bolt of electricity up my spine. After a few seconds she leaned in and gave Vladimir a long searing kiss, which I assumed was reserved for Gold Card carrying customers, and sashayed out with an action no less a marvel than any of the machines in the shop.

"If wife asks is best if, umm…."

"Indeed! If you can find a cup you would be willing to drink out of, you can split this execrable excuse for coffee. Let's figure out some shit to do."

With absolutely no idea of how to track down Jenny or her evil boss I was resigned to follow my own advise.

I looked at the board and mentally figured all of the facets of each entry there. Date due, date promised, amount of work left to do, parts to get, parts on hand, damage done during recent vandalism, and amount of cash due upon completion, especially the latter. I decided to return to the old Enfield, which hadn't suffered too much from the shake up. With a great show of concentration and focus, Vladimir started fussing with the very Alfa engine that had lately claimed my shin flesh. I sincerely hoped he was nearly done with it.

I checked the wreckage of the old Tape/CD player and was gratified to see at least the lights came on when the power button was pushed. I thought even though the tape machine was inoperable, the CD player might still work. I selected a calming CD of Irish tunes by a Portland band called "Bridgetown" and shoved it in. A warbling, static howl filled the shop, and by the time I could slap the volume knob down, Vladimir had dropped a box of peripheral Alfa parts and I had spilled a good portion of my tarry coffee. The screech certainly hadn't helped the state of my flayed nerves. I returned to the bench, determined to complete some job or other and make some dough.

I was engrossed in the innards of the old engine, measuring carefully and writing down calculations when I heard the front door creak a bit. I didn't bother to look up until I sensed someone standing close to me. I felt the malice even before he started speaking. I looked up to see a pistol of some large bore type waved menacingly in my direction, and I immediately reassessed my position on gun control.

"I think you have fucked with me for the last time. I require your underhanded and bitchy friend to return that which was taken from my office and then the pair of you will be sorry you have ever decided to annoy my business. Why this has come so I cannot tell, but if you want the hassle, you have gotten it. My property, now!"

The micrometer and pencil I held felt pretty ineffective as weapons and they slowly slipped from my fingers as I backed up from the bench. I held my hands up in front of me in my best western "put your hands up" manner. Jarno followed along. He looked a lot more stressed than he had been when he was having his goon beat the crap out of me, and it didn't look good on him. Strangely enough, the fact that he didn't seem to know where Jenny was buoyed my spirits somewhat.

Vladimir had adopted a furtive pose and seemed like he might be getting ready to do something dramatic. At that moment, I sincerely hoped his real job might have been secret agent posing as humble engineer to infiltrate an international old motorbike smuggling scheme, but from his transparent and clumsy actions I truly doubted such was the case.

Jarno had not failed to notice his ferrety movements and deflected his aim just long enough to fire a deafening round in his direction. A squeak of alarm escaped Vladimir as the bullet buried itself in the wall over the bench and caused a cascade of tools and parts.

I wondered how I would be able to convince Jarno I couldn't supply him with any of the items he mentioned. My strategy was to just start babbling, "So, yeah, listen, I think we may have gotten off on the wrong foot here. I'm pretty sure you have seen Jenny since I have, I mean, you can't deny you guys had her, right? And she had the papers, so, I don't know how she got away, especially with all that shit, but I can't help you there, pal. No matter how you cut it, I haven't seen or heard from her since you guys were pounding me in your damn basement yesterday. Or since you assholes chased me and Sean into the water last night. She's not here, and if you can't figure that out you're as dim as that clod she speared with the screwdriver."

The stream of words faltered and stopped coming out when it appeared they were having no visible calming effect on the pistol wielder. Possibly even making the situation worse. Vladimir was standing stock-still after his chastening.

Suddenly, the formerly dead CD player started groaning and chattering. The effect on Jarno was unnerving and I flinched as I thought further rounds might be coming my way. It looked like Jarno was suddenly convinced of my inability to help his cause and might just end our part of the conflict permanently. I prepared myself to make a desperate dive behind a customer's historic vehicle and hope for the best.

Jarno's pistol wavered between Vladimir's and my direction, and finally settled on Vlad's. Shots were fired in rapid succession but I didn't see the result as I was already diving for temporary cover behind the iron bulk of an old Harley Davidson. I scrambled along the floor in hopes of prolonging Jarno's inevitable search for me.

I could hear Vladimir screaming and the clatter of tools being hurled. I had a terrible feeling the poor bastard had escaped the communists and traveled all this way just to meet his end by merely being associated with me and being in the wrong place at the wrong time. The fact that I wasn't being shot at told me Jarno was going to deal with the tool hurler first. Another pistol shot rang out and the shooting stopped along with the tool cascade. Glass from one of the overhead lights rained down, then silence.

After a few extremely tense moments, an unfamiliar voice started a sharp harangue and yet more tools were in the air. I tentatively poked my head around the Harley to identify the new participant if I could. There was a dark-haired woman, stocky and dressed in a blue smock, standing over a cowering Vladimir brandishing the same exhaust nut wrench that had probably brained him before. With her free hand she was picking random tools off the bench and chunking them in Vlad's direction in order to add emphasis to her monologue. After a short reflection I assumed we might be in the presence of Mrs. Rostropovitch who, as far as I could gather, had been a doctor before fleeing to the US with Vladimir. Now she found employment as a vet's assistant.

Further investigation showed Jarno lying on the floor suffering from a nasty clout on the melon very, very reminiscent of Vladimir's injury. The pistol was nowhere to be seen. I figured it was safe to come out of hiding, as long as I was prepared to dodge the odd wrench or hammer.

As soon as she spotted me, the tirade changed from Russian to English and a long string of questions were directed at me without letup. I was suddenly nostalgic for the bucolic moment when we were merely being shot at. Amid the onslaught I managed to identify the words "Estonian whore" and "fake injury". Staying out all-night and drinking Slivovitz figured in as well.

In a flash of insight, Vladimir's previous injury and vague, changing, description of his attacker made sense. I thought there was a strong chance Mrs. R. might have encountered the very physical therapist lately in the shop while charging up the hill from the bus stop. I hoped not. The fact that Jarno might shoot her husband before she had a chance to belittle and berate him had earned him a smash in the head. I assumed, by that point Vladimir would have far preferred the quick finality of a bullet. At least no tool items were being directed at me. Perhaps she had run out of handy candidates. Vladimir crawled to a safer spot during the lull. I didn't see any obvious leaky holes in him other than some scrapes and scratches on his face, perhaps from shrapnel. Jarno moaned on the floor.

With no answers available, or even required, I turned my back on Mrs. R. and went to the back of the shop to dial 911 on the pink Princess. My conversation with the dispatcher sounded very familiar. I mentioned Detective Feldman and officer Froom in passing and an ambulance and police were promised directly.

The tirade from Vlad's wife had not noticeably eased but at least he was temporarily safe from injury due to Snap-On tools. I went to his side and crouched down to better view his condi-tion. He grasped my shirtfront, pulled me close and whispered in my ear.

"Soren, as my brother, you must help me now. The wife is very upset and believes I have been with the therapist. You must help her become calm or this will not end well, believe me."

I nodded to indicate I did indeed believe him. I rose and tried placating gestures towards Mrs. R. - very similar to those recently used to placate Jarno. I believe they had much the same effect. She did taper off on the vocalization but started looking around on the floor, I assumed for the pistol. I knew that was an undesirable combination, so I started looking myself. I spotted it under one of the lift benches but she saw me looking and darted in that direction first. Being smaller, lower to the ground and infinitely quicker than me, she had an easy time being the winner in that race. I idly wondered who would merit the first slug, Vladimir, the drunken cheater of a husband, or myself, the hapless, witless bystander. From the looks of the situation, the witness was going to be the first to go.

The scream of police and ambulance sirens became suddenly and powerfully obvious. I think early conditioning to drop things when sirens went off took over in Vlad's wife as she instantly released her grip on the gun and darted out the door, head down and hands in pockets. Vladimir struggled to his knees and grabbed a paper towel to mop the blood oozing from a series of tiny facial punctures. I looked around the area to locate the source of the flying debris and spotted a nasty chunk torn out of the side of the aluminum cylinder fins of the poor old Norton. Better than having a dead assistant but still, was there no end to the indignities my faithful steed needed to endure.

Suddenly the alley was filled with blinking lights and crackling radios. Paramedics were the first to arrive and toolboxes filled with lifesaving articles were lugged in and spread around the shop. Jarno's head was examined and emergency procedures were initiated. One of the medics was of the same team that had treated Vladimir only a few days before. He did a double take when he saw the condition of the fellow on the floor and also the remainder of Vlad's head dressing. He said to me, "What the hell, is this some kind of occupational hazard or something?" He jerked his thumb over his shoulder, "Looks like you finally got some police participation, if that's what you wanted."

Officer Froom and Detective Feldman entered the shop and gave a slow look around. Feldman said to me, "I see a certain stylistic similarity between your living space and your working environment. How symmetrical."

I was amazed, given the circumstances, this was what he chose to comment on. He continued, "Ah, I see we have the larger part of Mr. Viljanen here, somewhat subdued. Your work or...?" He waited for me to fill in the gaps while I glanced around the shop and finally at Vlad, who twitched and looked away while subtly shaking his head.

"Damn straight it was me." I grabbed the exhaust nut wrench and waved it around to confuse any fingerprints, just in case anybody ever cared to check. I snatched the pistol off the floor and was careful to twist the grip back and forth in my fist before handing it over to Officer Froom who looked completely uncomfortable while I held the gun. "Here's the goddamn cannon he was trying to kill us with. Nearly finished off old Vlad there, thank God he only blasted the shit out of the Norton instead. Still got Vlad with a bunch of British aluminum even so. Highest quality metal, of course."

For some reason, it looked like Detective Feldman suspected every word that had ever come out of my mouth. Doubt clouded his features, but then I could see him let all that go in view of the tidy resolution lying on the floor in front of him.

"After seeing you this morning, Mr. Quintero's office and ours collaborated on an investigation of Mr. Viljanen's place of business, and many interesting aspects of his endeavors were uncovered, not the least of which was the fraudulent sale and billing of antiques to the state. Antique reproduction was hardly the most ambitious of his schemes, however. In light of his inevitable prosecution, it has become even more desirable we find Ms. Farrar and have a look at her cache of records."

He offhandedly waved at the still unconscious Jarno as the paramedics were wheeling him out, "We will, of course, interview Mr. Viljanan when and if he regains consciousness, as well as the rest of his associates. He didn't happen to mention anything to you just now concerning her whereabouts, did he?"

"Feldman, for crying out loud, you're killing me. If I had any ideas about where Jenny might be, I'd be on the way there myself. As far as I can tell, the SFPD isn't really being very aggressive in this case, considering all the shit that's been going on. So, in a nutshell, if I find her I'll let you know, OK?

"Hmmm…, fine for now, but I must inform you there is a possibility Mr. Viljanen has a wider sphere of influence than we had previously estimated and he may have additional associates who may resent his incarceration and might be inclined to, how to say it, mete out retaliatory action."

"What in the Holy Hell are you talking about? I don't even know the guy or what he was involved with, so I can't even begin to know where you're going with this. Let's just leave it here, OK? Let me know if you find Jenny, or Jarno wakes up and tells you where she is or what he did with her. I'll do the same, but don't hold your breath."

Officer Froom took a sort of statement from Vlad and I gave what I hoped was a close version of the same to Feldman. They acted more or less satisfied and took the exhaust nut wrench and Jarno's pistol and departed. We were left to clean up the mess on the floor again. During this gruesome labor, I puzzled over in my mind how I could possibly track Jenny, either where she had gone or where she had come from. I supposed, given the opportunity, I could riffle through her stuff and see if I could find any clues. She did say she had grown up in Brooklyn and I guessed I might start there somehow. Technical college in Canada, I was sure there were many and not so easy to track down.

After the floor was relatively clean again and Vladimir and I had regained a small portion of our wits, we dug in and worked seriously for the remainder of the morning. Vlad tried to make calls home on the Pink Princess periodically but didn't have much success. I managed to get the bulk work done on a simple job that had not suffered too much in the last couple of days. I put in a small amount of gas and wheeled it out into the alley and was gratified when it started on the first kick. A small amount of tinkering had it idling nicely and running smooth. The job hadn't involved any cosmetic work so I duct-taped the plate from the Norton on the unregistered bike, put on a helmet and rode it around the block, keeping a keen eye out for the police. Everything ran pretty smooth, so I made up a bill and called the owner to hit the bank and come get it.

Vladimir was working like a maniac-perhaps to prove he was not a complete sleaze dog. An engine was taking shape under his hands in record time.

By mid afternoon the watery beating and the regular beating of the previous day were starting to take their toll on me. With Jarno and his crew of Finnish clods safely locked or on their way back to Finland, I thought it was probably safe enough to leave Vladimir in charge. He would have to worry about the threat from his wife and girlfriend on his own. I gave him random instructions about various items and headed home to catch a nap and ransack Jenny's belongings for clues before the Tuesday night session at the Arrow.

THE early afternoon trip across the city was smooth and with-out hassle. Every wing-nut who generally managed to get in front of me somehow wound up just a car or two behind. To save myself later trouble, I dropped in at the police station on 6th and wrangled with the desk sergeant for a while. Eventually, with much ID flashing and naming of Detectives and such, I was allowed to reclaim The Miller and Sean's guitar. Neither looked much worse for wear. I resisted the temptation to drop in at the Plough and Stars on Clement for an afternoon picker-upper and headed to the outer Richmond.

I was parking at home in record time. Jenny's old Toyota still lurked forlornly in the driveway and I took a casual peek inside to see if anything shouted out its "clueness". Casual inspection indicated the car had been pretty well emptied. I didn't see any letters or misplaced driver's licenses sitting on the floor. I guessed I break in and go through the glove box and under the seats for the hidden treasure.

Fortunately, part of the training in the Outer Richmond/Outside Lands Active Youth Corps had to do with breaking into parked cars without do-ing noticeable damage. I considered myself a talented amateur in such activities.

I unlocked the front door of the house and carefully entered the living room, just in case there might have been random and overlooked Finns intent on wrecking more of my stuff. No one was to be lurking there. I checked the answering machine on my way by and noticed I had failed to plug in the line to the phone after having installed the battery pirated from the smoke detector. Not only did I have the possibility of being consumed in flames unaware, but also wouldn't even know who had been trying to call me while it was happening. I sighed and continued on to the garage to find a car-jacking implement. I opened the garage door to afford better access to the toolbox.

Jenny's car was so old it still had door lock buttons with handy knobs on top of the doors. I took a piece of rebar tie wire and built a loop on the end. I wiggled it through the perished and cracked weather sealing around the window and popped up the lock. Elapsed time was 40 seconds. I thought I must be losing my touch from lack of practice. I remembered the unlockable wing window on the passenger's side after I had already broken in.

The glove box, like all glove boxes, was not locked. Dragging its contents out onto the seat was interesting but less than informative. A pile of receipts for old repairs, tire changes and things like that. The ones that did have her name on them didn't have any address to go with them. Some were from Canadian Tire in Toronto but were pretty ancient. I also found a flashlight, tire pressure gauge, random Milky Way wrappers and a few crusty packages of stale crackers. I gave up and shoved everything back and forced the door shut.

Under the seat investigation turned up almost exactly the same crap, which might be found underneath any seat: empty water bottles, pencils, used tissues and a strangely shaped thing that looked like a baby's teething toy. I found nothing with a name or an address.

A quick scan of the back seat didn't turn up anything worthwhile either. I supposed anything of value was in the pile in my living room.

I reflected I should get some parts and do a thorough tune-up on the car so Jenny would be able to drive it when she returned, and I firmly believed she would. I knew somehow I would be able to find her and save her. I also believed she was not at that moment floating towards China with a chisel in her heart.

I relocked the car as well as possible and went back inside to continue my sleuthing. She had been gone almost 48 hours and in surveying the pile there didn't look to be any personal items missing she would have taken with her. Clothes, tools, bags of blankets and linens all were present.

I focused my investigation on a small, locked suitcase. I got out my pliers and pieces of wire and went to work. Fifteen minutes later I was rewarded with a solid pop as one lock gave up. The other side didn't resist nearly as long and gave up almost instantly.

As I had guessed, the suitcase was crammed with the details of Jenny's life. Letters to her parents in Brooklyn, papers of attendance and graduation from various schools and the technical college in Canada, cards and notes to and from various people. I found a phone number pretty easily on her parent's old-fashioned engraved stationary. The date on the letter was almost six years earlier and the tone sounded pretty stiff citing difficult choices and lasting consequences.

I thought there was nothing to lose by calling the number, so I did and found it had been disconnected--kind of a dead end there.

Another letter with a letterhead from a law firm in Houston filled with terminology I couldn't make out. By the end I gathered there was a will involved and in order to participate Jenny had to fulfill certain conditions. I was taken aback when I saw the signature on the letter had Jenny's surname. I concluded it was probably not coincidence, perhaps a brother. A quick call to the law firm allowed me to leave my number with the assurance Mr. Farrar was not available but would call me back at his earliest convenience to discuss his sister's whereabouts.

Amid the general clutter I managed to find yet another letter from a different brother who was living in San Luis Obispo and stated everything was fine and going along well. There were no details and no phone number.

I found piles of kid drawings, which must have come from a niece or nephew.

I was losing steam fast and debated calling Feldman to relay the moved parents and the two brother connections. I decided to have a nice little nap and call later, if I could remember.

I did call Sean and left a message on his phone to the effect that I had reclaimed his guitar from the Richmond Police Station, and how they wanted to talk to him very badly concerning a large amount of illegal material they found in the case. I said I would fill him in completely at the Arrow that night.

I looked in the kitchen for something easy to eat but found only the pile of crusty pans and dishes from earlier in the morning. I settled for a shot of the rum sitting on the table and headed to the couch for a bit of shut-eye.

No sooner had I drawn the handy blanket over myself and closed my eyes but the phone rang. It turned out to be Sloane, who told me she had spoken with the Russian madman at my shop and found out I had gone home. She wondered if I was in any shape to attend the session at the Arrow that evening as we had things to discuss. It all sounded sort of mysterious and she was unwilling to give out any hints as to the nature of her anxiety. I promised her we would have a nice chat later on.

I had returned to the couch and pulled the comforter over myself once again when Sean called.

"So I assume the whole business about the illegal material was just you jerking my chain, right? 'Cause if they really had found anything, I'm assuming they would just come down here, based on your accurate directions, beat me up and arrest me. Also, if there were any illegal material in my case, it would be very well concealed and not likely to be found by any casual cop rooting around. Not to mention there would be elements of illegal search involved. Right?"

"Sean, calm down, I'm sure if the Richmond district cops had any interest in picking you up they wouldn't have to stoop to snooping through your guitar case; they probably have a file full of shit on you they are holding just for insurance. You can either pick it up here before the Arrow or I'll bring it with me."

"Better if you bring it. Edain just called me and there might be a little pre-session action on my part; it's hard to tell with that girl, though. I'll see you there regular time. If I don't show up, have my gravestone say I died for love, or of love, whichever."

"Fine, later then."

I hung up and resumed couching. This time I managed to drift into a fitful daze in which I dreamt Jenny had returned and joy filled me to the brim, overflowing. When I saw her we achieved a psychic bond that locked us together forever. As soon as she started talking she explained where she had been and how she had been thinking of me the entire time, missing me terribly. I said the same to her. She then went on to tell me how circumstances were such that she was already committed to someone and would have to leave me for good. The statement felt terribly

278   JOHN PEDERSEN

definite and final. My heart broke without chance of redemption.

I awoke with a start and terrible sadness. All I could do for a while was lay unmoving as tears leaked from my eyes to puddle in my ears. After quite a while, I made the decision to get up and face the fact nothing was known and nothing had been decided. If I had any positive traits at all, the ability to think positively was at the top of the list and I tried to push myself in that direction. Despite the conscious effort, a heaviness and an aura of grief clung to me. I debated skipping out on the Arrow session but realized I didn't have the option: I had to at least deliver Sean's guitar.

I glanced out the kitchen window and was alarmed at the complete blackness of the western horizon. The formerly decent weather was about to take a change for the worse. I debated making some sort of dinner but decided to indulge myself in fish and chips or some other fried comfort food at the Arrow, with a good few pints I was certain.

It was still pretty early for me to arrive but I knew from habit Sean would be there directly after work and at least we could play darts or something until the rest of the players arrived. Or focus on drinking pints.

I again tried to shake off the negative feelings haunting me, but couldn't help feeling like some calamity was right around the corner.

The Arrow wasn't too far away and on pleasant evenings I had been known to walk over. But with the extra burden of the guitar and the first raindrops starting to bounce off the Ford, I didn't consider the option.

Just as I closed the door, the phone rang and I scrambled to manage the instruments and get back inside; too late, of course. I grabbed the receiver just as the now-operational answering machine kicked in and was greeted with a scream of feedback that made me reel and drop the instrument. By the time I had retrieved it off the floor, whoever had been calling was long gone.

In the few seconds it took to get out, lock the front door, and grab the instruments the rain had picked up, accompanied by serious gusts of screechy wind. I jammed them into the cab with me and had to idle the engine for a few minutes before the defroster could clear the sudden fog inside the windshield. I carefully backed out of the drive and headed for The Arrow hoping a change in scenery and some company would cheer me up. The trees across 48th were rolling and lashing in the wind. Driving in the truck made me concerned about getting blown off the road, and then when the wind got worse, about getting blown completely over. I knew it was not likely or even possible, but it sure felt like I could get flipped. I also knew the nasty weather would keep all but the most faithful and fanatic players away from the session: the cloud's silver lining.

I made my way down the Great Highway carefully and slowly while marveling at the fierce attack of the storm front. The other drivers on the road were unimpressed as they flew by me at about one and a half times the speed limit. Sheets of water flew up and over me. I was glad I only had a few blocks to go before turning up Fulton. I zigged and zagged around a bit so I could get pointed in the right direction to park on the same side of the street as the bar and not have to slog the stuff across four lanes of unaware drivers. I didn't think I would be exactly "welcome" parking in the Norton's usual spot on the sidewalk.

I found a spot barely longer than the truck a few doors away from the Arrow and managed to squeeze in - with only the most innocent and gentle bumps on either end. I pulled the instruments out and didn't bother to lock up, because with Sean's hammer gone there wasn't anything at all to steal. I scampered up the sidewalk to the protection of the awning advertising the bar to any neighborhood residents who might have been ignorant of its existence. The rain sluiced off the domed top and splattered off the sidewalk. I thought to myself, despite all the trouble and grief of the last week, how comforting it was to go into a cozy pub and play some Irish tunes on a wet night.

No other players had arrived and I was able to clunk my case down on my usual chair in the corner without kicking anybody out. I set Sean's guitar case in his spot and headed to the bar to greet the lovely and comely bartenders.

Joanne and Meghan always acted so genuinely glad to see a person it made one feel pretty special. The fact that they greeted every drink buyer pretty much the same made me admire them for their universal treatment. Meghan had promised to meet us at the beach for a dawn surfing lesson for years but hadn't yet managed to actually set a date.

As primary players, but not the principal players responsible for keeping order in the session, Sean and I (and a very few others) enjoyed the privilege of drinking for free without getting paid. We generally made up for the savings by leaving large tips for the ladies.

280   JOHN PEDERSEN

Luckily, I was in the mood for a shot and a pint of Guinness because both were waiting for me when I got to the bar. The shot was gone in an instant and the first pint followed quickly. Their offspring lasted a little longer. By the time the third in the series had arrived in front of me, I was developing a comfortable glow and managed to glance around.

Several of the more timid players had arrived and were sitting at tables near the session area pretending they might have something to do there besides wait for one of us old timers to start a tune, which, generally being teetotalers, they didn't. I watched Sean stagger in, accompanied by a soggy blast of wind. He wore a Mexican serape and a wide cowboy hat, both streaming water. Further pints and shots hit the bar in anticipation of his arrival.

"Holy crap, I'm glad we don't have to go swimming tonight, we wouldn't know which way was dry land, eh?"

He swept off his hat and cape and sprayed the surrounding patrons with a healthy dose of precipitation. There were ignored mutterings on the part of the serious, early evening drinkers. Sean hung his garb near the extinct fireplace, perhaps in the hope that for the first time in twenty years it would be lit despite its condemnation as the number one fire hazard in the Outer Richmond district.

"I rather thought you might be a bit later, date with Edain and all."

"I'm lucky I escaped at all. Everything started out all hot and heavy with her clunking the shit outta' me with that cast of hers, and then she started goin' off about bein' chased by the FBI or somebody like that. Somethin' about diamonds, shootings, buildings falling on her and crap I couldn't make out at all. She did mention stupid fiddlers though, so she couldn't have been all nuts. Anyway, she wanted me to pack up all my shit and go to New Zealand or someplace like that with her. Or take her there because she doesn't have hardly any cash left. Once she found out I didn't have much in that direction either, things cooled off pretty fast and she practically kicked me out of my own place, so here I am."

"That's more than I found out from her, she was pretty closed off about the past to me."

"With good reason, I suppose, being a lunatic and all."

There was hardly a pause between words as he consumed the first shot and pint and looked expectantly towards Joanne in hope of replacements.

"Perfect weather for a bit of the old Skideredee. I think we should get a few tunes out before that lot there starts weeping in frustration or the place fills up with snotty youths playing stuff we don't know and probably couldn't play if we did."

"Right, off we go."

We grabbed our fresh drinks and headed in the direction of the circle of chairs.

I had gone about half the length of the bar when Sloane powered through the door followed by a thoroughly soaked and dejected Gerald. I had to look twice to make sure she wasn't actually dragging him along by the ear. He did not look happy to be there. Sloane had clearly taken control of her appearance and kicked it up a notch since the previous evening. Her hair, complexion and outfit were all perfect and she looked untouched by the howling gale outside. Gerald was not so lucky and water dripped from all parts of his body.

"So, there you two are! I think Gerald has something he would like to say to you. Don't you Gerald?"

Sean was the first to react, "Hey there, Gerry, long time no see, eh?"

Gerald flinched. His eyes scanned the floor as if there were a speech written there. He started mumbling and couldn't be heard at all over the growing din of the pub. Sloane's voice cracked out and hit him like a whip.

"Gerald, speak up, I don't think the lads here can understand you!"

His head slumped even lower into the protection of his shoulders.

"Ahem, I said, I may have been responsible for a certain amount of vandalism towards you two which may have been somewhat misguided. If so, I'm sorry."

Before we could speak Sloane jumped in, "Oh really Gerald, and what sort of vandalism might you have perpetrated upon the boys, and why?"

He shrunk even smaller, "Ummm, I burned up the van, smashed the windows out of the truck and hammered on those surfboards because I though you were in love with Sloane and I couldn't stand it. Sorry."

Sloane had adopted a fierce expression and seemed to be about to say further nasty things but Gerald continued.

"I'd hate to have to deal with the police about this and I'm prepared to compensate you for any damages or inconvenience, physical, mental or otherwise.

Sean looked stunned by this revelation. For the most part, I assumed, because none of us had ever thought Gerald capable of any kind of decisive action, much less burning and smashing the vehicles of known unstable musician types.

He said, "Well, Gerald, you have been a bad boy. Soren and I will have to think about how we want to handle this. I mean, we wouldn't want a deranged and unhinged maniac roaming the streets, would we?"

I know he was just fooling around and he would jump at the opportunity to have someone pay for his new windows and possibly even a bit more. I myself wasn't sure how I felt about the sudden news. I thought if Gerald was responsible for all those things, the Finn's had far less to answer to than I had previously thought. However, there were still a myriad of issues unexplained and I couldn't say I was much less confused.

Sloane's posture had softened considerably since we had been standing there and seemed to be warming back up to Gerald after his confession. It was decided they would get some drinks and enjoy, or endure in Gerald's case, some tunes while we thought about the proper course of action.

Sean and I sat down in the circle and there was a scramble among the early arrivers to claim seats as well. The actual boss of the session, who was paid a meager sum to make sure at least some sort of music happened on Tuesday nights, parked his fiddle-playing self directly next to me. I sighed and accepted this because he was a nice guy and an old friend, but had the supremely annoying habit of never accepting the fact that sometimes he just flat out did not know a tune. If faced with a melody he was unfamiliar with he would just noodle around in what he perceived as the right key hoping there would be divine intervention and the notes would just fall out of their own accord. They rarely did.

I unboxed the Miller accordion and slipped the straps over my shoulders. Because they were the old straps from the Soprani, at least something felt familiar. Once again, the cold pearl buttons felt sticky and coarse. I hit the air button and flexed the bellows in and out a few times to loosen them up and played a long "A" note for the string players to tune to. After a short interval the fiddler turned that note into an actual tune in the key of A. The session started.

I could see Gerald and Sloane sitting in a booth off to the side. She holding onto the stern look and him pleading his case. From where I was I couldn't tell if his whining was having any effect.

Every now and then a blast of wind would rattle the front windows and make the entire building creak, audible even over the pounding tunes.

We finished a blistering set of reels about forty-five minutes into the cacophony and in the following silence, a few random notes escaped the accordion, and then a few more. Bass chords came up out of nowhere. I didn't recognize the tune seeping out and I closed my eyes trying to visualize what might happen next. Suddenly the grief and sense of emptiness I had been feeling since Jenny had disappeared swept over me with a rush. I tried with all my might to think of something I could do to find her or bring her back, but failed miserably to come up with anything, which made me feel worse. In my mind I could picture her clearly and felt the tune shift gears as her image came to mind. Subconsciously, I thought I could feel the howling wind ease up and the sheeting rain lessen its intensity. No one was playing along.

I opened my eyes to see what might be the problem and found the entire circle of players sitting woodenly, loosely grasping their instruments. I looked farther into the crowd and, as if by magic, saw Jenny standing at the bar. I thought for a moment I had merely conjured her image in my mind, but as I continued to stare and play she shook the rain off the jacket she was wearing and looked right at me.

My heart fairly skipped a beat and the tune changed underneath my fingers. The room became visibly brighter. I thought I could see her smile. My entire outlook changed in an instant. Sadly, it changed again radically in the next instant.

As I played and watched, a tall handsome guy carrying a young child approached Jenny and instead of ignoring him to focus on me and run into my arms, Jenny's face absolutely glowed. She embraced the two of them tightly and I could feel an impenetrable circle of love there.

They looked like a family. I assumed they were. In a flash of insight I now assumed Jenny had resolved the lurking issues she had been trying to tell me about, reconciled with her loved ones and had come to get her stuff. I couldn't imagine why they had come to the Arrow to parade their family unit instead of humiliating me in private. My emotions boiled within me.

I closed my eyes so as not to have to look further on what I had lost and would not regain. The tune that had been oozing out of my accordion now changed again dramatically. Darkness had crept in, and an intensity that was putting even me on edge.

I could vaguely hear Sean telling me to knock it off and lighten up. I was powerless to do so. My fingers slid and pounded the buttons and I pushed the old box to the limit. At least, what I considered the limit. Pain, rage, heartbreak, betrayal were all being realized in the screeching reel I was finding. The souls of the individual reeds howling out their grief inside their silver prison. I was part of a rampaging mob. In a flash I could clearly picture the swordsmith at his anvil creating the steel, Grandma Zhou's beautiful aunt and Miller swooning in her presence. I could feel his love for her and his unbearable sorrow after the earthquake when he found she had been killed. His abandonment of all hope crushed my heart.

I was dimly aware the storm had ratcheted up in intensity as well. Rain was absolutely pounding the windows behind the band and the wind was screaming outside in sympathy with my emotions.

Suddenly with a terrible, thunderous crash the windows exploded inward showering the session guys with glass and water. The feeble old excuse for a roof started peeling away allowing the elements direct access to the patrons. As if to finish the job, the ground started shaking in a manner familiar to all native San Franciscans. We were born anticipating "The next Big One." It may have arrived.

The players in the circle started scattering and heading for doorways, as we were always told to do. I doubted the validity of that advice in this case as all of the doorways had had goofy decoration stuff hanging over them. Notably swords, iron spikes, axes and old circular saw blades. Not my idea of earthquake safety.

Deprived of the marginal stiffness of the roof and front windows the poor old shack started twisting and undulating alarmingly. Most of the bar patrons were jammed up near the front door trying to push their way out into the street. I didn't think that was particularly safe either, but it had to be better than inside. Without knowing how I got there, I found myself at the rear end of the mob trying to exit. I looked around and saw the blown-out window directly behind where I had been sitting and Sean's ass disappearing out of it. Purely in the interest of traffic flow, I decided to follow his example. As I was re-crossing the tiny stage area I dimly notice the Miller lying on its side near the wall. I debated grabbing it on my way by but the debris falling from the rafters was giving me serious concerns about getting the hell out.

I took the precaution of knocking out a few deadly looking daggers of glass still stuck in the window frame that hadn't slowed Sean down one bit, the skinny bastard. I squeezed through with the briefest of scrapes and with a quick look back inside to see if anyone too stupid or dazed to bail out remained in the session circle, I jogged across the sidewalk and across the street to the relative safety of the park verge. It looked like the rest of the crowd shared the same idea, as everyone I could think of was there staring though the rain at the rapidly deteriorating condition of the bar. The screaming of the wind had either tapered way off or was just not as bad as we had thought.

There was a hubbub of talk from the natives who refused to discuss the severity or duration of the tremblor but instead marveled at the shifting sand underneath the road, the bar and all the structures between them and the beach.

I became aware of a single voice rising above the others.

"Jenny, Jenny are you out here? Jenny, are you here?"

I identified the shouter and made my way to the side of Jenny's husband, still carrying the child. As soon as he spotted me he frantically grabbed my shoulder.

"Soren? Are you Soren, you must be. My sister pointed you out, but I can't find her now. She went to the ladies room just as the place started to fall apart and I haven't seen her since. She might still be in there. Oh my God, she'll be crushed!"

I scanned the crowd but failed to see her. The "My Sister" part eventually penetrated my brain and my feelings of jubilation and joy were tempered with equal parts of complete, flaming idiocy. My next actions were less a product of decision than ones of necessity.

I ran back across the street dodging the sinkholes and pits which had opened up, and ducked back under the half-collapsed marquee. Staring through the door I couldn't see Jenny sitting at the bar enjoying free drinks or filling her backpack with bottles of whisky. To guys like Sean and me such actions in the face of an earthquake would not have been out of the question, but apparently Jenny was made of more sophisticated stock.

Beams were falling and pipes were rupturing, not the least of which were the feeds to the beer taps. Brew was spraying out over the remains of the bar and covering the floor with a layer of slimy foam.

With more than a little apprehension, I kicked the stuck door open and headed for the gloomy depths of the bar where the restrooms were situated. The area, gloomy at the best of times, like a sunny Sunday afternoon, was now positively black. My first few steps put me in contact with the morass of booze as I fell flat on my face almost immediately. Literally swimming in beer. A roof rafter directly overhead popped loose and fell in my direction but luckily hit the bar before it could crush me. I scrambled towards the back with renewed enthusiasm. The empty kegs lining the walls, which previously had provided overflow seating, had all been knocked over and were rolling around with abandon.

I finally fought my way through the clanging aluminum obstacle course to the black pit of a hallway that led to the restrooms, men's on the left, women's on the right. I struggled to my feet lest I look foolish crawling on my knees as I burst in to save my love. The beer was much shallower there so I was able to retain my footing.

The door to the ladies room was either locked or obstructed so I had to use one of the handy kegs to batter the wood to pieces. When I finally got inside, the jumbled stall dividers made everything very hard to make out. I couldn't figure out exactly where a person might go missing in such a small area. I got down on my knees again and peered through the darkness trying to find some semblance of human form.

It was her blond hair that finally allowed me to identify where she was. All I could see was her facedown form with the hair floating on the surface of the water, which continued to spew out of the ruptured plumbing. It looked as though she had been pinned down under a beam and a stall divider. At first glance it certainly looked as though I was too late to save her.

Drawing on an entire lifetime of last-second salvations and miraculous escapes perpetrated by the entertainment industry, I started frantically dragging pieces of rubble off of her body and tossing them heroically aside. At last I arrived at the ultimate test in the form of the hand-adzed black oak beam that had her pinned across the shoulders. I gauged the size of it as roughly eight by eight, meaning the piece in front of me could weigh six or seven hundred pounds. I seized it in the middle and figured if the lift didn't kill me, she would be saved.

As it turned out, the beam immediately broke in the middle revealing its foam core. The entire ersatz beam of fifteen feet couldn't have weighed ten pounds. I tossed it aside and dove to Jenny's side. I scooped her up and rolled her face up out of the pooled water. I knew in my heart this was a perfect time for mouth-to-mouth resuscitation and was about to give it a go when she coughed, spit out an entire mouthful of fluid and shouted, "Holy Shit, where am I? If this is hell, it's a lot wetter than I thought it'd be. I think I'm blind or it's pitch black in here." She continued to sputter and hack up spouts of water.

"Jenny, listen, its Soren. We're stuck in the bathroom at the Arrow. I know its cozy in here but we really should get moving. Are you OK or should I carry you out? Either way you'll have to wiggle out from under that metal thing there so I can grab you."

"Soren? Well it's about time! I can get up. Just give me a hand here. You're pretty slippery pal, hold tighter."

I latched onto her wrist and pulled her free of the junk on the floor with as much delicacy as I could muster. From the sounds coming in from the bar, the rest of the building was continuing to succumb to entropic forces.

Jenny was able to stand up on her own but with the sloshing tide of beer between us and the street I doubted whether that would last long.

I held her hand and led her out into the chaos. The empty kegs had settled down but I still managed to clonk my shin on a hidden one. The way to the front door was a tangle of beams, tables and chairs, and toppled booths.

"Ah, crap, it looks like we crawl from here anyway."

We dove to the floor and started scrambling under and around the obstructions and through the foam. I resisted the temptation to open my mouth and gulp down a few pints-worth on our way through a geyser of an eruption.

We had almost made the front door when a nasty shiver in the building knocked the bar's signature quiver of arrows off of its perch over the entrance and spilled them between us. I could hear the multiple thunks as they buried their hunting tipped broad-heads into the wooden floor.

I had once asked the owner of the bar why he had hunting arrows with the deadly tips up there (instead of more benign target arrows) and he had replied they would come in handy when the zombies came out of the park. I had to agree.

We scooted out the door and onto the sidewalk clinging to each other as we struggled to our feet. The crowd across the street cheered and Jenny's brother and the child met us in the middle of the street. Jenny hugged them and then wrapped herself around me.

JOHN PEDERSEN

CHAPTER

WHEN she finally released me a fraction she said, "Christ Almighty you've been hard to get a hold of for the last couple of days. I finally found out where you were going to be from that Russian nut down at your shop. What's the deal, anyway?"

"I've been hard to find? How about you with the disappearing act? I've been frantic since Monday morning. I was afraid maybe you thought better of dealing with a guy who would fall in love so easily and completely. Simple minded, as it were."

"Disappearing act my ass, how about the long heartfelt note I left on your kitchen table right under the accordion. I knew you'd see it there. I didn't leave out any details I can remember. I even left my brother's phone number, but no call. Not to mention I tried to call your house and your shop every day but got zilch. Is there bad service everywhere up here or just to you?"

"All I remember under the accordion was a pile of newspapers and... Crap! I guess I gathered all that stuff up together and threw it out. I suppose I can go back and read it now though, it's still in the recycling bin. As far as the phone situation, I guess I've been going through a patch of bad luck, ineptitude and clumsiness in that department. I did almost get a call from you yesterday but the instrument itself fell apart in my hand. It was just one of the victims of an all-over trashing your ex-boss's clods performed on my shop. I thought they were the ones who beat the crap out of Vladimir, but recent information concerning Vlad and an Estonian massage artist rather points to Mrs. Vlad as the culprit there. I also thought the Finns were responsible for burning up Big Red and trashing my entire quiver of surfboards but I guess Sloan's ex, or maybe not ex, husband was over-reacting to jealous fantasies."

Under the circumstances, I thought enough information had been exchanged. Without further easing our embrace I changed directions. "So without waiting for me to dig through the trash to read your note, perhaps you could fill me in on the high points so I don't die of suspense."

At this she finally stepped back and held me at arms length. She stared into my eyes as well as the dark, the rain and the crowd surrounding us would allow. "Well, shit, it was hard enough to write the note and now I have to give it to you in person? OK, here's the unsentimental gist of it. What I've been trying to get around to telling you these last few days is I'm not exactly alone in the world."

She looked around and motioned her brother and the child over. Sean was lurking nearby and took that as his clue to move in as well.

"Soren, this is Ray and Tanya. Tanya has been staying with my brother down in San Luis Obispo while I've been slaving away up here trying to get a foothold. I have been going down as often as I could, which hasn't been nearly enough. After my car wouldn't start on Sunday I took a cab to the bus station, as explained in the note."

Ray looked to be in his mid forties and the little girl about five.

"Anyway, believe it or not, when we met I thought I had found the most amazing partner on the planet and I think you felt the same way. I couldn't wait any longer for you two to meet. If this freaks you out or gives you heart palpitations, we can stay the night and then move on, if I can get the dang Toyota started."

"Absolutely not! I couldn't be more thrilled. I wouldn't let you go even if you traveled around with a mime troop or a banjo band, or worse. There's plenty of room and I can clean the place up--really, I can."

"For cryin' out loud, slow down buddy. I was just talking about a few days or so. I doubt if I'm ready to sign a long-term contract yet. I mean, early indicators are pretty positive, but really, I hardly know you at all. We'll have to see just how close to the ideal motorbike-surfer-accordion guy you can be. We'll just go day by day for the moment, OK?"

The little girl, Tanya reached out in my direction as though to touch me. Instead she pointed to my back. I became aware of a burning ache there and craned my head around but was unable to see anything. Sean said, "Oh, man, what the hell, are there Indians around here?"

The connection failed to reach me until Jenny said, "Oh no, Soren, there's an arrow sticking out of you. Stand still."

Twisting both ways still didn't allow me to see the offending shaft. Sean leaned in to view the wound more closely and said, "Ah, I don't think it's stuck in very far. Hey, what's that over there?"

As everybody except me turned to look he flashed out his hand and jerked the arrow free. I stifled a scream and thought I had reason to be glad the head hadn't been really stuck in, if that's what a shallow penetration felt like. I reached my arm around but was unable to clap my hand over the hole. Sean held the zombie-killer arrow up in triumph.

The storm appeared to have spent its fury and settled down to an annoying drizzle. The wind had died off almost completely. The ground had completely stopped any sort of movement. The only indication of the pandemonium of a few minutes before was the cockeyed and collapsed hulk of the pub and some sink holes in the street.

Surprisingly little damage, structural or otherwise, was evident anywhere but right at the bar and the street between it and us. Some sand might have shifted down along the highway but that might have been due to only the wind and storm.

There were still spraying pipes and random clunks and bumps from inside the bar, so the general consensus was as soon as the authorities arrived we would abandon the place and rendezvous at my house. We didn't have long to wait as interested citizens recently in the bar had used their cell phones to alert some agency with sirens and flashing lights. They swarmed down the street and in an instant they had the street cordoned off and crews were busily doing all sorts of things. News vans were not far behind. From the looks of it all, I didn't think there was any way they were going to let us in to sift through the rubble to recover what might be left of our instruments. We turned away and drifted over to the truck. Jenny said she would accompany her brother and Tanya to my house. I was almost reluctant to let her out of my sight but reasoned I had better learn to trust fate to deliver her to my door, as I doubted whether she was the type to appreciate or tolerate smothering. Sean allowed as how he would force Sloane and Gerald to give him a ride over there and would certainly manage to stop somewhere for additional fortifications.

The Arrow crowd of regulars accepted the end of the action and dispersed, either to other drinking establishments, homes or possibly midnight masses to give thanks for escaping alive. I climbed into the truck and for a moment just sat watching the emergency crews clambering around the periphery of the poor old Arrow. I started up and drove the short way homewards.

At the house I was relieved to see Jenny, Ray and Tanya parked in the driveway and unloading stuff from a large looking Land Rover SUV. I parked in the street and seized an armload of whatever was handed me and staggered up the stairs. With one hand I fished out my keys and unlocked the door. When I entered the living room I tried to look at it from a new family home perspective. Quite a bit of my stuff was easily identifiable as way too goofy for anybody but myself to appreciate. I figured spaces would be cleared and junk moved around soon enough; I didn't have to worry about it just then.

Jenny, Ray and Tanya came in and I could see Ray looking the place over and smiling at some of the knick-knacks festooning the shelves and walls. Not everything was lost on him. Jenny went directly to the kitchen and found enough remaining bread to make a peanut butter and jelly sandwich for Tanya. I quickly scooted in there as well and started drawing water to clean up the dishes from that morning.

Tanya looked pretty pooped so Jenny took her upstairs to get her situated in the spare room, which wasn't spare any longer. While she was occupied, Sean, Sloane and Gerald arrived with a grocery bag of snacks and drinkables. Introductions were made again all around.

When Jenny came back downstairs we all sat at the kitchen table and I relayed, with Sean and Sloane's invaluable help, the bizarre events of the last couple of days. Jenny said I didn't look too bad considering, and wished she could have seen me running up the Great Highway naked. I went over to the paper-recycling can and dug for a moment before finding the long note Jenny had written me crumpled up with the newspapers. A quick read certainly would have been much more informative two days before. I sat back down at the table and admitted to her I had sort of ransacked her belongings and car searching for clues to her whereabouts. I told her I had called a lawyer with her last name but didn't think he had called back yet.

She said Ray was a lawyer as well and they had spoken with the other brother that morning. They were confused about the reasons for my search with all the information Jenny had laid out in the note, which I had thrown away. They figured their arrival would pretty much clear up the mystery.

Sean was pouring out Jameson and beers all around and after the harrowing evening up to that point, nobody was going to refuse. Jenny said having gone through her papers I might be somewhat confused about a few things. For instance, the letter from the Houston brother about the conditions of her parents will. Even though they were still among the living they wanted the contents of their will known. She said they were not particularly thrilled she had gotten pregnant during a very short-lived affair with a yoga instructor nor that she continued to remain unmarried. They loved Tanya and treated her as grandparents should, but were adamant sooner or later Jenny should be married, and until such time she had no stake in their estate. I thought to myself in view of my level of infatuation, there probably wouldn't be a problem for much longer. How the family of lawyers was going to take to an accordion playing, surfer-motorbike mechanic would have to be seen. One day at a time.

By the time we had sorted out our activities of the last few days, the bottle of Jameson was dangerously low and the beer was gone completely. Gerald, who hadn't uttered a word all evening, said he would be driving Sean back to the lower Haight on the way to dropping Sloane off at her/his house. From their snuggly behavior since the bar's collapse, I doubted he would be leaving there too soon. Ray admired the couch and said the ride up from San Luis had taken its toll on him as well. For myself, I was barely functioning but could not have been happier. Jenny was back and alive, she had a sweet little girl I was looking forward to getting to know, and her brother didn't seem to hate me completely, which I found positive.

I was pretty sure Sean had not seen the last of Edain but couldn't imagine where that whole relationship was headed. Perhaps he would indeed find a way to scoot off with her to New Zealand and start a new career there. Sloane's history with men was too predictable to count on any surprises there after Gerald had confessed his sins against us. After all our years as friends, her taste in men was certain to continue in the same vein as it always had, effectively removing anyone we would like from being a candidate.

Sloane, Sean and Gerald left and Ray was provided with the makings of a comfortable couch nest. Jenny and I headed upstairs and after making sure Tanya was fast asleep, headed into the bathroom to save water by showering the dried beer off together.

I'd like to report we had wild, passionate, reunion sex that night but in reality, it didn't happen. We were both too exhausted to contemplate anything more than blissful embraces.

The next day we all went out for breakfast and Ray said he would hang around for a while in order to drive Jenny wherever she needed to go. They needed to find a kindergarten and get Tanya registered and things like that. They looked to have things completely in hand so I decided to head down to the shop to create some income.

As soon as I strolled down the alley I saw a notice tacked up on the doors of the shop. It took me several readings to finally get the drift. In short, the city had decided my alley was no longer going to be a public thoroughfare; instead it was going to be converted into the driveway for the apartment building at the end, and gated at Pacific. I was flabbergasted and completely dismayed. Just when I really needed to focus on making a living and sharpening up my business skills, I was to be kicked to the curb, and not even my own curb.

There was a phone number on the notice so after unlocking the doors, turning on the lights and carefully scouting around for anything out of the ordinary, whatever that could possibly have been, I called it. I explained the situation to the person I had gotten connected to and they said a certain Mr. Yee was on his way over to talk to me. All I could do was wait.

While I waited, I marveled at the number of jobs that had been crossed off the list on the wall, indicating Vladimir had been a work-demon the previous day. I gathered he was still trying to impress upon me what a sleazy skank he was not. Unfortunately, I don't think I was the person who needed impressing.

I made several calls to the owners of completed jobs and got promises to pick up and pay.

When Mr. Yee did arrive I was astounded to find he was the same Asian fellow whom we had noticed several times lurking around in the alley, sometimes with his camera. In the daylight he didn't look very mysterious at all especially accompanied by a briefcase full of paperwork proving the city had every right to turn the alley into a private gated driveway, having come to some sort of agreement with the owners of the building at the end.

Before I could even work up a good head of self-righteous indignation and rage, Mr. Yee allowed as how in the circumstances, the city was prepared to help me move into another building and was furthermore prepared to pay the difference in rent for a certain term, perhaps several years.

An uncharacteristic flash of clear thinking allowed me to blurt out I knew of a recently vacated building over on Jackson that would do fine. Mr. Yee said he would investigate and if he could, he would set up the deal.

I could already envision the new shop, the showroom, and the woodworking shop on the second floor where Jenny could ply her trade. I wondered how the neighbors on Jackson would take to the monthly visits by the Roadoilers. I guessed they would get used to them.

A few days later Sean and I and a few of the other session guys were grouped outside the remains of the Arrow. We were being schooled by the head of the city's Historical Architectural Something-or-Other team about what we could touch and what we couldn't once we were escorted inside the propped up shell of the bar. Clearly there was some significance attached to the building and there was to be no looting, treasure hunting or memento taking. We all agreed to the conditions laid down and as a unit assured her we were interested only in those items belonging to us.

We were escorted in one at a time. Sean went first and returned shortly with his guitar looking waterlogged and dingy, but not too much different than when it went in. A few others had their chances and returned with different instruments in varying states of shabbiness. Eventually I was escorted in the front door and around and under the scaffolding holding up the wreckage where it had come to rest. I directed the Architectural Historian to the area where I had last seen the Miller against the wall. Sadly, of all the instruments I had seen come out the door, the poor old accordion was the least recognizable. Some framing part or other had landed directly on top of the box and had crushed it beyond recognition. There was a serious discussion with the Historic Society before I was allowed to shift the chunk of lumber, a real piece this time, and start collecting the mangled bits. I took off my coat and piled as many of the pieces as I could into it. The front face with the pearl mermaids was almost intact and loads of the pearl buttons had survived. The reed blocks had been blown apart and the reeds and their silver plates had been scattered all over the danged place. I scooped them up as quickly as I could but left behind an infinite assortment of toothpick-sized bits along with the hopelessly destroyed bass mechanism. Shards of the silver that had lined the inside of the box were still attached to the pieces, the largest of which was about the size of a post card. My archeological guide appeared to be getting restive, so I decided to abandon the search for all the tiny scraps. The old Soprani straps still had life in them and I felt a little better as I snagged them out of the wreckage.

As I left the bar I showed results of my feeble salvage attempt to the remaining musicians outside. Sean's comment was a succinct, "Well, that's fucked!" I thought there was a general lack of sadness and understanding over the loss of a historic instrument. Sean and I headed over to my house to have a memorial for the departed accordion.

Once there, with a suitable parting glass on hand I spread the pieces out on the kitchen table. Jenny and Tanya stared at the wreckage somberly. Despite my best intentions at cleaning up and organizing the living room, I could feel another shrine about to take shape. I casually started counting the reed plates and organizing them according to size and position in the instrument. I had a thought if I had somehow managed to rescue the full set, I could always install them into another, lesser box because, after all, the reeds were the heart and the magic of the instrument.

The array on the table didn't hold the attention of Jenny, Tanya and Sean for too long and they each drifted off. Sean was constantly looking for something to eat and he and Tanya scouted the offerings in the fridge. Jenny was sorting and moving stuff around in the living room. I poked around in there looking for a shelf full of random junk I could replace with a display of the remainder of Miller's legacy when I became aware of a low humming. Almost like a wind chime the tones drifted apart and came back together in different forms. I couldn't imagine where the sound was coming from and I checked the radio and TV and found they were off. Jenny stopped scattering her belongings around and tilted her

JOHN PEDERSEN

head to listen as well. I walked around noting when the sound got louder and softer and finally narrowed the source of the ethereal tones as the kitchen. When I stepped through from the living room Sean and Tanya were standing by the open refrigerator door but the snacks were forgotten. They both were staring at the table where the reeds lay.

I was astonished to see they were gently vibrating without benefit of any air passing through them, and the wood of the table was amplifying the sound. I reached out and spaced the reeds out evenly around the perimeter of the table leaving much more space between them and slowly, reluctantly the humming stopped.

Tanya said practically the first words I had heard out of her, it sounded like "Shénshèng de gou shi". Sean and I looked uncomprehendingly at her.

The need for the accordion's silver lining with the Chinese inscriptions came into a much shaper focus for me and before I did anything else I thought I might have to visit Grandma Zhou again to see if she could help me get a handle on controlling the behavior of these willful minded creations of her father.

In a completely disapproving tone of voice Jenny said, "She said, 'Holy shit', in Chinese."

And then, "I think I might possibly have a few more explanations due at this point."

I was pretty confused about what exactly was going on there, but one thought that was clear to me was perhaps I would wait until I moved someplace less prone to earthquakes before I contemplated using Miller's reeds again.

END

JOHN PEDERSEN

About John Pedersen

JOHN PEDERSEN was born and raised on the Hudson River near Albany in historic Upstate New York. His grandfather was a fiddler and banjo player who, along with numerous other musical relatives, steered him down the path of folk music. He spent several years in Toronto doing stringed instrument repairs and winning the affection of his wife, Judy.

In the mid 70's they moved to San Anselmo, California, in Marin County, where they went to work at *Amazing Grace* music store, eventually bought it and continue to operate it.

John's abilities as a Master Luthier have earned him a wide following among players from all over the country.

He is an avid motorcycle enthusiast and has owned and rebuilt many bikes, as well as being a founding member of the *Roadoilers Vintage Motorcycle Club*.

John's surfing reputation was made on large boards and small waves and his accordion-playing career is rightfully non-existent.

He performs with his band, handily also called *The Roadoilers*, with whom he plays old time banjo and fiddle.

John is thrilled that his friends and family have given him enough story material to write novels. He is also the author of the novel, *"Scroll and Curl."*

JOHN PEDERSEN